THUMBELINA CAME TO LIVE WITH THE FIELD-MOUSE.

CHILDHOOD'S FAVORITES AND FAIRY STORIES

HAMILTON WRIGHT MABIE
EDWARD EVERETT HALE
WILLIAM BYRON FORBUSH
Editors

JENNIE ELLIS BURDICK
Assistant Editor

Volume  One

NEW YORK
THE UNIVERSITY SOCIETY
INCORPORATED
1921

THE UNIVERSITY SOCIETY INC
USI
FOUNDED 1897

EDITORS

HAMILTON WRIGHT MABIE, L.H.D., LL.D.
EDWARD EVERETT HALE, D.D., LL.D.
WILLIAM BYRON FORBUSH, Ph.D., Litt.D.

ASSISTANT EDITOR
JENNIE ELLIS BURDICK

Partial List of Authors and Editors Represented in The Young Folks Treasury by Selections from Their Writings:

WOODROW WILSON, Twenty-eighth President of the United States.
THEODORE ROOSEVELT, Twenty-sixth President of the United States.
HENRY VAN DYKE, poet, essayist, and diplomatist.
LYMAN ABBOTT, editor of "The Outlook."
RUDYARD KIPLING, poet and story-teller.
General SIR R. S. BADEN-POWELL, founder of the Boy Scouts.
BECKLES WILLSON, author of "The Romance of Canada."
IDA PRENTICE WHITCOMB, author of "Young People's Story of Art."
ELLEN VELVIN, writer of animal stories.
MARY MACGREGOR, author of "King Arthur's Knights," etc.
RALPH HENRY BARBOUR, author of boys' stories.
T. GILBERT PEARSON, executive secretary, National Association of Audubon Societies.
JOSEPH JACOBS, authority upon folklore.
THEODORE WOOD, writer on natural history.
ERNEST THOMPSON SETON, writer of stories about natural history and founder of the Woodcraft League.
AMY STEEDMAN, writer on biography.

PARTIAL LIST OF EDITORS AND CONTRIBUTORS

Everett T. Tomlinson, author of boys' stories.
Ralph D. Paine, author of boys' stories.
A. Frederick Collins, author of boys' books.
Don C. Bliss, educator.
Bliss Carman, poet and essayist.
Sir James Matthew Barrie, novelist.
William Canton, story-teller.
Hermann Hagedorn, poet.
Elbridge S. Brooks, writer of boys' stories.
Alfred G. Gardiner, editor of "The London News."
Franklin K. Lane, United States Secretary of the Interior.
Joel Chandler Harris, creator of "Uncle Remus."
Ernest Ingersoll, naturalist.
William L. Finley, State biologist, Oregon.
Charles G. D. Roberts, writer of animal stories.
E. Nesbit, novelist and poet.
Archibald Williams, author of "How It Is Done," etc.
Ira Remsen, former president of Johns Hopkins University.
Gifford Pinchot, professor of forestry, Yale University.
Gustave Kobbé, writer of biographies.
Jacob A. Riis, philanthropist and author.
Emily Huntington Miller, story-writer and poet.
John Lang, writer of children's books.
Jeanie Lang, writer of children's books.
John H. Clifford, editor and writer.
Herbert T. Wade, editor and writer on physics.
Charles R. Gibson, writer on electricity.
Lilian Gask, writer on natural history.
Blanche Marchesi, opera singer and teacher.
John Finnemore, traveler and writer of boys' stories.
Alexander Graham Bell, inventor of the telephone.
James Whitcomb Riley, poet.
Charles H. Caffin, author of "A Guide to Pictures."
James Cardinal Gibbons.
Andrew F. Currier, M.D., popular medical writer.
Helen Keller, the blind and deaf writer.
Oliver Herford, humorist and illustrator.

GENERAL INTRODUCTION

BOOKS are as much a part of the furnishing of a house as tables and chairs, and in the making of a home they belong, not with the luxuries but with the necessities. A bookless house is not a home; for a home affords food and shelter for the mind as well as for the body. It is as great an offence against a child to starve his mind as to starve his body, and there is as much danger of reducing his vitality and putting him at a disadvantage in his lifework in the one as in the other form of deprivation. There was a time when it was felt that shelter, clothing, food and physical oversight comprised the whole duty of a charitable institution to dependent children; to-day no community would permit such an institution to exist unless it provided school privileges. An acute sense of responsibility toward children is one of the prime characteristics of American society, shown in the vast expenditures for public education in all forms, in the increasing attention paid to light, ventilation, and safety in school buildings, in the opening of play grounds in large cities, in physical supervision of children in schools, and the agitation against the employment of children in factories, and in other and less obvious ways.

Children are helpless to protect themselves and secure what they need for health of body and mind; they are exceedingly impressionable; and the future is always in their hands. The first and most imperative duty of parents is to give their children the best attainable preparation for life, no matter at what sacrifice to themselves. There are hosts of fathers and mothers who recognize this obligation but do not know how to discharge it; who are eager to give their children the most wholesome conditions, but do not know how to secure them; who are especially anxious that their children should start early and start right on that highway of education which is the open road to honorable success. There are many homes in which books would find abundant room if the heads of the families knew what books to buy, or had the means to put into the hands of the growing child the reading matter it needs in the successive periods of its growth.

This condition of eagerness to give the best, and of ignorance of how or where to find the best is the justification for the publication of this set of books. The attempt has been made in a series of twelve volumes to bring together in convenient form the fairy stories, myths, and legends which have fed the children of many generations in the years when the imagination is awakening and craving stimulus and material to work upon;—that age of myth-making which is a prelude to the more scientific uses of the mind and of immense importance in an intensely practical age;—a group of tales of standard quality and an interest and value which have placed them among the permanent possessions of English literature; a careful selection of stories of animal life; a natural history, familiar in style and thoroughly trustworthy in fact; an account of those travels and adventures which have opened up the earth and made its resources available, and which constitute one of the most heroic chapters in the history of the long struggle of men to possess the earth and make it a home for the highest kind of civilization; a record of heroism taken from the annals of the patriots and of those brave men who, in all ages, ranks of society and occupations, have dared to face great dangers in the path of duty and science, with special attention to that everyday heroism in which the age is specially rich and of which so many good people are grossly ignorant; a survey of scientific achievement, with reports of recent discoveries in knowledge and adaptation of knowledge to human need; a group of biographies of the men and women—mostly Americans—who are the most stimulating companions for boys and girls; a volume on the Fine Arts dealing with music, painting, sculpture, architecture, in a way to instruct young readers and making accessible a large number of those songs which appeal in the best way to children in schools and homes; a collection of the best poetry for the youngest and oldest readers, chosen not only for excellence from the standpoint of art, but deep and abiding human interest; and a volume devoted to the occupations and resources of the home, addressed to parents no less than to children, with practical suggestions about books and reading, games and amusements, exercise and health, and those kindred topics which have to do with making the home wholesome and attractive.

These twelve volumes aim, in brief, to make the home the most inspiring school and the most attractive place for pleasure, and to bring the best the world has to offer of adventure, heroism, achievement and beauty within its four walls.

Special attention has been given to the youngest children whose interests are often neglected because they are thought to be too immature to receive serious impressions from what is read to them. Psychology is beginning to make us understand that no greater mistake can be made in the education of children than underrating the importance of the years when the soil receives the seed most quickly. For education of the deepest sort—the planting of those formative ideas which give final direction and quality to the intellectual life—there is no period so important as the years between three and six, and none so fruitful. To put in the seed at that time is, as a rule, to decide the kind of harvest the child will reap later; whether he shall be a shrewd, keen, clever, ambitious man, with a hard, mechanical mind, bent on getting the best of the world; or a generous, fruitful, open-minded man, intent on living the fullest life in mind and heart. No apology is offered for giving large space to myths, legends, fairy stories, tales of all sorts, and to poetry; for in these expressions of the creative mind is to be found the material on which the imagination has fed in every age and which is, for the most part, conspicuously absent from our educational programmes.

America has at present greater facility in producing "smart" men than in producing able men; the alert, quick-witted, money-maker abounds, but the men who live with ideas, who care for the principles of things, and who make life rich in resource and interest are comparatively few. America needs poetry more than it needs industrial training; though the two ought never to be separated. The time to awaken the imagination, which is the creative faculty, is early childhood; and the most accessible material for this education is the literature which the race created in its childhood. The creative man, whether in the arts or in practical affairs, in poetry, in engineering or in business, is always the man of imagination.

In this library for young people the attempt has been made not only to give the child what it needs but in the form which is most easily understood. For this reason some well-known stories have been retold in simpler English than their classic forms present. This is especially true of many tales for any young children reprinted by special arrangement from recent English sources. In some cases, where the substance has seemed of more importance to the child than the form, simpler words and forms of expression have been substituted for more complex or abstract phrases, and passages of minor importance have been condensed or omitted.

The aim in making the selections in this set of books has been to interest the child and give it what it needs for normal growth; the material has been taken from many sources old and new; much of the reading matter presented has been familiar in one form or another, to generations of children; much has appeared for the first time within the last ten years; a considerable part has been prepared especially for the Treasury and a large part has been selected from the best writing in the various fields.

It is the hope of the Editor that this "Treasury" or "Library" will justify its title by its real and fundamental service to children and parents alike.

HAMILTON W. MABIE

INTRODUCTION

SINCE this series of books is intended for all young people from one to one hundred, it opens with about eighty of the old MOTHER GOOSE RHYMES. Nothing better was ever invented to tell to little folks who are young enough for lullabies. Their rhythm, their humor, and their pith will always cause us to prize them as the Babies' Classics.

Next come a score of the most famous NURSERY TALES, the kind that children cry for and love to hear fifty times over. And since, just as soon as little folks like stories they love to hear them in rhyme, here are forty CHILDREN'S FAVORITE POEMS.

What would young life be without "Puss in Boots" and "Little Red Riding Hood" and "The Sleeping Beauty"? Our TREASURY would indeed be poor without them, so these FAVORITE STORIES come next, yoked with some OLD-FASHIONED POEMS in story-form, as "The Night before Christmas," "The Wonderful World," and "Little Orphant Annie." All who love pets and animals have always liked FABLES, so here are the noted parables of Æsop, and the lesser-known but even more jolly tales from East Indian sources.

The fairy-tale age is supposed to come from four to nine, but the editors are sure it lasts much longer than that. However this may be, the better half of our first volume is given up to FAIRY TALES AND LAUGHTER STORIES from all over the world.

It ends with TALES FOR TINY TOTS, the kind that mother reads beside the fire at bedtime, some of them old, like the "Little Red Hen" and "Peter Rabbit," and some of them newer, like "The Greedy Brownie" and "The Birthday Honors of the Fairy Queen."

WILLIAM BYRON FORBUSH.

CONTENTS

NURSERY RHYMES

NURSERY TALES

CHILDREN'S FAVORITE POEMS

CHILDREN'S FAVORITE STORIES

OLD-FASHIONED POEMS

FABLES

Fables from Æsop

Fables of India

Adapted by P. V. Ramaswami Raju

FAIRY TALES AND LAUGHTER STORIES

Scandinavian Stories

German Stories

East Indian Stories

American Indian Stories

Arabian Stories

Chinese Stories

Russian Stories

Tales for Tiny Tots

Fanciful Stories

ILLUSTRATIONS

(Many of the illustrations in this volume are reproduced by special permission of E. P. Dutton & Company, owners of the American rights.)

CHILDHOOD'S FAVORITES

AND

FAIRY STORIES

NURSERY RHYMES

HUSH-A-BYE, baby, on the tree-top,
When the wind blows the cradle will rock;
When the bough breaks the cradle will fall,
Down will come baby, bough, cradle, and all.

☙ ☙ ☙

Rock-a-bye, baby, thy cradle is green;
Father 's a nobleman, mother 's a Queen;
Betty 's a lady, and wears a gold ring;
And Johnny 's a drummer, and drums for the King.

☙ ☙ ☙

Bye, baby bunting,
Daddy 's gone a-hunting,
To get a little rabbit-skin,
To wrap his baby bunting in.

☙ ☙ ☙

Hush thee, my babby,
Lie still with thy daddy,
Thy mammy has gone to the mill,
To grind thee some wheat
To make thee some meat,
And so, my dear babby, lie still.

Sleep, baby, sleep!
Thy father watches the sheep;
Thy mother is shaking the dream-land tree,
And down falls a little dream on thee:
Sleep, baby, sleep!

Sleep, baby, sleep.
The large stars are the sheep,
The wee stars are the lambs, I guess,
The fair moon is the shepherdess:
Sleep, baby, sleep!

☙ ☙ ☙

This little pig went to market;
This little pig stayed at home;
This little pig had roast beef;
This little pig had none;
This little pig said, "Wee, wee!
I can't find my way home."

☙ ☙ ☙

Brow bender,
Eye peeper,
Nose smeller,
Mouth eater,
Chin chopper.
Knock at the door—peep in,
Lift up the latch—walk in.

Eye winker,
Tom Tinker,
Nose smeller,
Mouth eater,
Chin chopper.
Chin chopper.

Old Mother Goose, when
  She wanted to wander,
Would ride through the air
  On a very fine gander.

Mother Goose had a house,
  'T was built in a wood,
Where an owl at the door
  For sentinel stood.

She had a son Jack,
  A plain-looking lad;
He was not very good,
  Nor yet very bad.

She sent him to market,
  A live goose he bought:
"Here! mother," says he,
  "It will not go for nought."

Jack's goose and her gander
  Grew very fond;
They'd both eat together,
  Or swim in one pond.

Jack found one morning,
  As I have been told,
His goose had laid him
  An egg of pure gold.

Jack rode to his mother,
  The news for to tell.
She called him a good boy,
  And said it was well.

Goosey, goosey, gander,
  Where shall I wander?
Upstairs, downstairs,
  And in my lady's chamber.
There I met an old man
  Who would not say his prayers;
I took him by the left leg,
  And threw him downstairs.

☙ ☙ ☙

I'll tell you a story
About Mary Morey,
  And now my story's begun.
  I'll tell you another
About her brother,
  And now my story's done.

☙ ☙ ☙

Three wise men of Gotham,
Went to sea in a bowl;
If the bowl had been stronger,
My song had been longer.

☙ ☙ ☙

There was a crooked man,
  And he went a crooked mile,
He found a crooked sixpence
  Upon a crooked stile:
He bought a crooked cat,
  That caught a crooked mouse—
And they all lived together
  In a little crooked house.

☙ ☙ ☙

There was a man in our town,
  And he was wondrous wise,
He jumped into a bramble bush,
  And scratched out both his eyes;

But when he saw his eyes were out,
With all his might and main,
He jumped into another bush,
And scratched 'em in again.

☙ ☙ ☙

Hey! diddle diddle,
The cat and the fiddle,
The cow jumped over the moon;
The little dog laughed
To see such sport,
While the dish ran away with the spoon.

☙ ☙ ☙

Hickory, dickory, dock,
The mouse ran up the clock;
The clock struck one,
The mouse ran down,
Hickory, dickory, dock.

☙ ☙ ☙

There was an old woman who lived in a shoe,
She had so many children she didn't know what to do;
She gave them some broth without any bread,
She whipped them all soundly and put them to bed.

☙ ☙ ☙

Little Miss Muffet
Sat on a tuffet,
Eating her curds and whey;
There came a great spider,
And sat down beside her,
And frightened Miss Muffet away.

If all the seas were one sea,
What a *great* sea that would be!
And if all the trees were one tree,
What a *great* tree that would be!
And if all the axes were one axe,
What a *great* axe that would be!
And if all the men were one man,
What a *great* man he would be!
And if the *great* man took the *great* axe,
And cut down the *great* tree,
And let it fall into the *great* sea,
What a splish splash *that* would be!

☙ ☙ ☙

There was an old man,
And he had a calf,
  And that's half;
He took him out of the stall,
And tied him to the wall,
  And that's all.

☙ ☙ ☙

The man in the wilderness asked me,
How many strawberries grew in the sea?
I answered him as I thought good,
As many as red herrings grew in the wood.

☙ ☙ ☙

If all the world were apple-pie,
  And all the sea were ink,
And all the trees were bread and cheese,
  What should we have for drink?

☙ ☙ ☙

I saw a ship a-sailing,
A-sailing on the sea;
And it was full of pretty things
For baby and for me.

There were sweetmeats in the cabin,
And apples in the hold;
The sails were made of silk,
And the masts were made of gold.

The four-and-twenty sailors
That stood between the decks,
Were four-and-twenty white mice,
With chains about their necks.

The captain was a duck,
With a packet on his back;
And when the ship began to move,
The captain cried, "Quack, quack!"

❧ ❧ ❧

My dear, do you know,
How a long time ago,
Two poor little children,
Whose names I don't know,
Were stolen away on a fine summer's day,
And left in a wood, as I've heard people say.

And when it was night,
So sad was their plight!
The sun it went down,
And the moon gave no light!
They sobbed and they sighed, and they bitterly cried,
And the poor little things, they lay down and died.

And when they were dead,
The robins so red,
Brought strawberry-leaves
And over them spread;
And all the day long,
They sung them this song:
"Poor babes in the wood! Poor babes in the wood!
Oh don't you remember the babes in the wood?"

The Queen of Hearts, she made some tarts
  All on a summer's day;
The Knave of Hearts, he stole the tarts,
  And took them clean away.

The King of Hearts called for the tarts,
  And beat the Knave full sore;
The Knave of Hearts brought back the tarts,
  And vowed he'd steal no more.

☙ ☙ ☙

I had a little husband,
  No bigger than my thumb;
I put him in a pint-pot,
  And there I bade him drum.

I bought a little horse,
  That galloped up and down;
I bridled him, and saddled him,
  And sent him out of town.

I gave him little garters,
  To garter up his hose,
And a little handkerchief,
  To wipe his little nose.

☙ ☙ ☙

Sing a song of sixpence,
  A pocket full of rye;
Four-and-twenty blackbirds
  Baked in a pie;

When the pie was opened
  The birds began to sing;
Was not that a dainty dish
  To set before the King?

The King was in his counting-house,
  Counting out his money;
The Queen was in the parlor,
  Eating bread and honey;

The maid was in the garden
  Hanging out the clothes;
When up came a blackbird,
  And nipped off her nose.

⁂

Little Bo-peep, she lost her sheep,
  And can't tell where to find them;
Leave them alone, and they'll come home,
  And bring their tails behind them.

Little Bo-peep fell fast asleep,
  And dreamed she heard them bleating;
When she awoke she found it a joke,
  For they still were all fleeting.

Then up she took her little crook,
  Determined for to find them;
She found them indeed, but it made her heart bleed,
  For they'd left their tails behind them!

It happened one day, as Bo-peep did stray,
  Unto a meadow hard by—
There she espied their tails side by side,
  All hung on a tree to dry.

She heaved a sigh, and wiped her eye,
  And over the hillocks she raced;
And tried what she could, as a shepherdess should,
  That each tail should be properly placed.

What are little boys made of, made of?
What are little boys made of?
Snips and snails, and puppy-dogs' tails;
And that's what little boys are made of, made of.

What are little girls made of, made of?
What are little girls made of?
Sugar and spice, and all that's nice;
And that's what little girls are made of, made of.

☙ ☙ ☙

A farmer went trotting
  Upon his gray mare;
Bumpety, bumpety, bump!
With his daughter behind him,
  So rosy and fair;
Lumpety, lumpety, lump!

A raven cried "Croak";
  And they all tumbled down;
Bumpety, bumpety, bump!
The mare broke her knees,
  And the farmer his crown;
Lumpety, lumpety, lump.

The mischievous raven
  Flew laughing away;
Bumpety, bumpety, bump!
And vowed he would serve them
  The same the next day;
Bumpety, bumpety, bump!

☙ ☙ ☙

This is the way the ladies ride—
Saddle-a-side, saddle-a-side!

This is the way the gentlemen ride—
Sitting astride, sitting astride!

This is the way the grandmothers ride—
Bundled and tied, bundled and tied!

This is the way the babykins ride—
Snuggled inside, snuggled inside!

❧ ❧ ❧

WHAT DOES LITTLE BIRDIE SAY?

What does little birdie say,
In her nest at peep of day?
  "Let me fly," says little birdie,
"Mother, let me fly away."

Birdie, rest a little longer,
Till the little wings are stronger.
So she rests a little longer,
  Then she flies away.

What does little baby say,
In her bed at peep of day?
  Baby says, like little birdie,
"Let me rise and fly away."

Baby, sleep a little longer,
Till the little limbs are stronger.
If she sleeps a little longer,
  Baby, too, shall fly away.

Alfred, Lord Tennyson

❧ ❧ ❧

GOOD NIGHT

Little baby, lay your head
On your pretty cradle-bed;

Shut your eye-peeps, now the day
And the light are gone away;
All the clothes are tucked in tight;
Little baby dear, good night.

Yes, my darling, well I know
How the bitter wind doth blow;
And the winter's snow and rain
Patter on the window-pane:
But they cannot come in here,
To my little baby dear;

For the window shutteth fast,
Till the stormy night is past;
And the curtains warm are spread
Round about her cradle-bed:
So till morning shineth bright,
Little baby dear, good night.

Jane Taylor

❧ ❧ ❧

SWEET AND LOW

Sweet and low, sweet and low,
  Wind of the western sea,
Low, low, breathe and blow,
  Wind of the western sea!
Over the rolling waters go,
Come from the dying moon, and blow,
  Blow him again to me:
While my little one, while my pretty one, sleeps.

Sleep and rest, sleep and rest,
  Father will come to thee soon;
Rest, rest, on mother's breast,
  Father will come to thee soon;

Father will come to his babe in the nest,
Silver sails all out of the west
Under the silver moon:
Sleep, my little one, sleep, my pretty one, sleep.

ALFRED, LORD TENNYSON

❧ ❧ ❧

BABY-LAND

Which is the way to Baby-Land?
Any one can tell;
Up one flight,
To your right;
Please to ring the bell.

What can you see in Baby-Land?
Little folks in white,
Downy heads,
Cradle-beds,
Faces pure and bright.

What do they do in Baby-Land?
Dream and wake and play,
Laugh and crow,
Shout and grow,
Jolly times have they.

What do they say in Baby-Land?
Why, the oddest things;
Might as well
Try to tell
What a birdie sings.

Who is the Queen of Baby-Land?
Mother kind and sweet;
And her love,
Born above,
Guides the little feet.

GEORGE COOPER

Old Mother Hubbard, she went to the
cupboard,
To get her poor dog a bone.
When she got there, the cupboard was
bare,
And so the poor dog had none.

She went to the baker's to buy him some
bread,
But when she came back the poor dog
was dead.

She went to the undertaker's to buy him
a coffin,
And when she came back the dog was
laughing.

She went to the draper's to buy him some
linen,
And when she came back the good dog
was spinning.

She went to the hosier's to buy him some
hose,
And when she came back he was dressed
in his clothes.

The dame made a curtsy, the dog made
a bow,
The dame said "your servant," the dog
said "Bow-wow."

She went to the hatter's to buy him a
hat,
And when she came back he was feeding
the cat.

OLD MOTHER HUBBARD.

She went to the tailor's to buy him a
coat,
And when she came back he was riding
the goat.

She went to the barber's to buy him a
wig,
And when she came back he was dancing
a jig.

She went to the butcher's to get him some
tripe,
And when she came back he was smoking
a pipe.

She went to the fish-shop to buy him some
fish,
And when she came back he was washing
the dish.

She went to the tavern for white wine and
red,
And when she came back the dog stood
on his head.

☙ ☙ ☙

As I was going to St. Ives
I met a man with seven wives;
Every wife had seven sacks,
Every sack had seven cats,
Every cat had seven kits.
Kits, cats, sacks, and wives,
How many were going to St. Ives?

☙ ☙ ☙

POLLY

Brown eyes, straight nose;
Dirt pies, rumpled clothes.

Torn books, spoilt toys:
Arch looks, unlike a boy's;

Little rages, obvious arts;
(Three her age is), cakes, tarts:

Falling down off chairs;
Breaking crown down stairs;

Catching flies on the pane;
Deep sighs—cause not plain;

Bribing you with kisses
For a few farthing blisses.

Wide-a-wake; as you hear,
"Mercy's sake, quiet, dear!"

New shoes, new frock;
Vague views of what's o'clock

When it's time to go to bed,
And scorn sublime for what is said.

Folded hands, saying prayers,
Understands not nor cares—

Thinks it odd, smiles away;
Yet may God hear her pray!

Bed gown white, kiss Dolly;
Good night!—that's Polly,

Fast asleep, as you see,
Heaven keep my girl for me!

WILLIAM BRIGHTY RANDS

CRADLE HYMN

Hush, my dear, lie still and slumber;
  Holy angels guard thy bed;
Heavenly blessings without number
  Gently falling on thy head.

Sleep, my babe, thy food and raiment,
  House and home, thy friends provide;
All without thy care, or payment,
  All thy wants are well supplied.

How much better thou'rt attended
  Than the Son of God could be,
When from heaven He descended,
  And became a child like thee!

Soft and easy is thy cradle;
  Coarse and hard thy Saviour lay,
When His birthplace was a stable,
  And His softest bed was hay.

See the kindly shepherds round him,
  Telling wonders from the sky!
When they sought Him, there they found Him,
  With his Virgin-Mother by.

See the lovely babe a-dressing;
  Lovely infant, how He smiled!
When He wept, the mother's blessing
  Soothed and hushed the holy child.

Lo, He slumbers in His manger,
  Where the honest oxen fed;
—Peace, my darling! here's no danger!
  Here's no ox a-near thy bed!

Mayst thou live to know and fear Him,
Trust and love Him all thy days;
Then go dwell forever near Him,
See His face, and sing His praise!

I could give thee thousand kisses,
Hoping what I most desire;
Not a mother's fondest wishes
Can to greater joys aspire.

Isaac Watts

I LIKE LITTLE PUSSY

I like little Pussy,
Her coat is so warm;
And if I don't hurt her
She'll do me no harm.
So I'll not pull her tail,
Nor drive her away,
But Pussy and I
Very gently will play;
She shall sit by my side,
And I'll give her some food;
And she'll love me because
I am gentle and good.

I'll pat little Pussy,
And then she will purr,
And thus show her thanks
For my kindness to her;
I'll not pinch her ears,
Nor tread on her paw,
Lest I should provoke her
To use her sharp claw;

I never will vex her,
  Nor make her displeased,
For Pussy can't bear
  To be worried or teased.

JANE TAYLOR

☙ ☙ ☙

THE GRAVEL PATH

  Baby mustn't frown,
  When she tumbles down;
If the wind should change—Ah me,
What a face her face would be!

  Rub away the dirt,
  Say she wasn't hurt;
What a world 'twould be—O my,
If all who fell began to cry!

LAURENCE ALMA TADEMA

☙ ☙ ☙

Little Robin Redbreast sat upon a tree,
Up went pussy-cat, and down went he;
Down came pussy-cat, and away Robin ran;
Said little Robin Redbreast, "Catch me if you can."

Little Robin Redbreast jumped upon a wall,
Pussy-cat jumped after him, and almost got a fall;
Little Robin chirped and sang, and what did pussy say?
Pussy-cat said naught but "Mew," and Robin flew away.

☙ ☙ ☙

SLEEP, MY TREASURE

  Sleep, sleep, my treasure,
  The long day's pleasure
Has tired the birds, to their nests they creep;
  The garden still is
  Alight with lilies,
But all the daisies are fast asleep.

Sleep, sleep, my darling,
Dawn wakes the starling,
The sparrow stirs when he sees day break;
But all the meadow
Is wrapped in shadow,
And you must sleep till the daisies wake!

E. Nesbit

❧ ❧ ❧

LULLABY OF AN INFANT CHIEF

Oh, hush thee, my babie, thy sire was a knight,
Thy mother a lady, both lovely and bright;
The woods and the glens from the tower which we see.
They all are belonging, dear babie, to thee.

Oh, fear not the bugle, though loudly it blows,
It calls but the warders that guard thy repose;
Their bows would be bended, their blades would be red,
Ere the step of a foeman draws near to thy bed.

Oh, hush thee, my babie, the time will soon come,
When thy sleep shall be broken by trumpet and drum;
Then hush thee, my darling, take rest while you may,
For strife comes with manhood, and waking with day.

Sir Walter Scott

❧ ❧ ❧

THE ORPHAN'S SONG

I had a little bird,
I took it from the nest;
I prest it and blest it,
And nurst it in my breast.

I set it on the ground,
Danced round and round,
And sang about it so cheerly,
  With "Hey, my little bird,
  And ho! my little bird,
And oh! but I love thee dearly!"

I make a little feast
  Of food soft and sweet,
I hold it in my breast,
  And coax it to eat;

I pit, and I pat,
I call this and that,
And I sing about so cheerly,
  With "Hey, my little bird,
  And ho! my little bird,
And oh! but I love thee dearly!"

Sydney Dobell

☙ ☙ ☙

THE DEATH AND BURIAL OF COCK ROBIN

Who killed Cock Robin?
  "I," said the Sparrow,
  "With my bow and arrow,
I killed Cock Robin."

Who saw him die?
  "I," said the Fly,
  "With my little eye,
I saw him die."

Who caught his blood?
  "I," said the Fish,
  "With my little dish,
I caught his blood."

Who'll make his shroud?
"I," said the Beetle,
"With my thread and needle,
I'll make his shroud"

Who'll bear the torch?
"I," said the Linnet,
"I'll come in a minute,
I'll bear the torch."

Who'll be the clerk?
"I," said the Lark,
"I'll say Amen in the dark;
I'll be the clerk."

Who'll dig his grave?
"I," said the Owl,
"With my spade and trowel,
I'll dig his grave."

Who'll be the parson?
"I," said the Rook,
"With my little book,
I'll be the parson."

Who'll be chief mourner?
"I," said the Dove,
"I mourn for my love;
I'll be chief mourner."

Who'll sing his dirge?
"I," said the Thrush,
"As I sing in a bush,
I'll sing his dirge."

❧ ❧ ❧

DO YOU KNOW HOW MANY STARS?

Do you know how many stars
There are shining in the skies?

THE DEATH OF COCK-ROBIN.

Do you know how many clouds
Ev'ry day go floating by?
God in heaven has counted all,
He would miss one should it fall.

Do you know how many children
Go to little beds at night,
And without a care or sorrow,
Wake up in the morning light?
God in heaven each name can tell,
Loves you, too, and loves you well.

☙ ☙ ☙

WHERE DO ALL THE DAISIES GO?

Where do all the daisies go?
    I know, I know!
Underneath the snow they creep,
Nod their little heads and sleep,
In the springtime out they peep;
    That is where they go!

Where do all the birdies go?
    I know, I know!
Far away from winter snow
To the fair, warm South they go;
There they stay till daisies blow,
    That is where they go!

Where do all the babies go?
    I know, I know!
In the glancing firelight warm,
Safely sheltered from all harm,
Soft they lie on mother's arm,
    That is where they go!

Unknown

Cock crows in the morn,
To tell us to rise,
And he who lies late
Will never be wise.
For early to bed,
And early to rise,
Is the way to be healthy
And wealthy and wise.

☘ ☘ ☘

THE HOUSE THAT JACK BUILT

This is the house that Jack built.

This is the malt
That lay in the house that Jack built.

This is the rat
That ate the malt
That lay in the house that Jack built.

This is the cat,
That killed the rat,
That ate the malt
That lay in the house that Jack built.

This is the dog,
That worried the cat,
That killed the rat,
That ate the malt
That lay in the house that Jack built.

This is the cow with the crumpled horn,
That tossed the dog,
That worried the cat,
That killed the rat,
That ate the malt
That lay in the house that Jack built.

This is the maiden all forlorn,
That milked the cow with the crumpled horn,
That tossed the dog,
That worried the cat,
That killed the rat,
That ate the malt
That lay in the house that Jack built.

This is the man all tattered and torn,
That kissed the maiden all forlorn,
That milked the cow with the crumpled horn,
That tossed the dog,
That worried the cat,
That killed the rat,
That ate the malt
That lay in the house that Jack built.

This is the priest all shaven and shorn,
That married the man all tattered and torn,
That kissed the maiden all forlorn,
That milked the cow with the crumpled horn,
That tossed the dog,
That worried the cat,
That killed the rat,
That ate the malt
That lay in the house that Jack built.

This is the cock that crowed in the morn,
That waked the priest all shaven and shorn,
That married the man all tattered and torn,
That kissed the maiden all forlorn,
That milked the cow with the crumpled horn,
That tossed the dog,
That worried the cat,
That killed the rat,
That ate the malt
That lay in the house that Jack built.

This is the farmer sowing his corn,
That kept the cock that crowed in the morn,
That waked the priest all shaven and shorn,
That married the man all tattered and torn,
That kissed the maiden all forlorn,
That milked the cow with the crumpled horn,
That tossed the dog,
That worried the cat,
That killed the rat,
That ate the malt
That lay in the house that Jack built.

☙ ☙ ☙

TREE ON THE HILL

On yonder hill there stands a tree;
Tree on the hill, and the hill stood still.

And on the tree there was a branch;
Branch on the tree, tree on the hill, and the hill
stood still.

And on the branch there was a nest;
Nest on the branch, branch on the tree, tree on
the hill, and the hill stood still.

And in the nest there was an egg;
Egg in the nest, nest on the branch, branch on
the tree, tree on the hill, and the hill stood
still.

And in the egg there was a bird;
Bird in the egg, egg in the nest, nest on the
branch, branch on the tree, tree on the hill,
and the hill stood still.

And on the bird there was a feather;
Feather on the bird, bird in the egg, egg in the nest, nest on the branch, branch on the tree, tree on the hill, and the hill stood still.

☙ ☙ ☙

A LITTLE BOY'S POCKET

Do you know what's in my pottet?
Such a lot of treasures in it!
Listen now while I bedin it:
Such a lot of sings it holds,
And everysin dats in my pottet,
And when, and where, and how I dot it.
First of all, here's in my pottet
A beauty shell, I pit'd it up:
And here's the handle of a tup
That somebody has broked at tea;
The shell's a hole in it, you see:
Nobody knows dat I dot it,
I teep it safe here in my pottet.
And here's my ball too in my pottet,
And here's my pennies, one, two, free,
That Aunty Mary dave to me,
To-morrow day I'll buy a spade,
When I'm out walking with the maid;
I tant put that in here my pottet!
But I can use it when I've dot it.
Here's some more sings in my pottet,
Here's my lead, and here's my string;
And once I had an iron ring,
But through a hole it lost one day,
And this is what I always say—
A hole's the worst sing in a pottet,
Be sure and mend it when you've dot it.

UNKNOWN

NURSERY TALES

THE THREE BEARS

LITTLE Goldilocks was a pretty girl who lived once upon a time in a far-off country.

One day she was sitting on the hearthrug playing with her two kittens, and you would have thought she was as happy as a queen, and quite contented to stay where she was instead of wanting to run about the world meddling with other people's property. But it happened that she was rather a mischievous little maid, and could not resist teasing her pets, so one of them scratched her, and then she would play with them no longer.

She got up and trotted away into the wood behind her mother's house, and it was such a warm, pleasant day that she wandered on and on until she came into a part of the wood where she had never been before.

Now, in this wood there lived a family of three Bears. The first was a GREAT BIG BEAR, the second was a MIDDLING-SIZED BEAR, and the third was a LITTLE TEENY TINY BEAR, and they all lived together in a funny little house, and very happy they were.

Goldilocks stopped when she came to the Bears' house, and began to wonder who lived there.

"I'll just look in and see," she said, and so she did; but there was no one there, for the Bears had all gone out for a morning walk, whilst the soup they were going to have for dinner cooled upon the table.

Goldilocks was rather hungry after her walk, and the soup smelt so good that she began to wish the people of the house would come home and invite her to have some. But although she looked everywhere, under the table and into the cupboards, she could find no one, and at last she could resist no longer, but made up her mind to take just a little sip to see how the soup tasted. The soup had been put into three bowls—a Great Big Bowl for the Great Big Bear, a Middling-sized Bowl for the Middling-sized Bear, and a Teeny Tiny Bowl for the Teeny Tiny Bear; beside each bowl lay a spoon, and Goldilocks took one and helped herself to a spoonful of soup from the Great Big Bowl.

Ugh! how it burnt her mouth; it was so hot with pepper that she did not like it at all; still, she was very hungry, so she thought she would try again.

This time she took a sip of the Middling-sized Bear's soup, but she liked that no better, for it was too salt. But when she tasted the Teeny Tiny Bear's soup it was just as she liked it; so she ate it up every drop, without thinking twice about it.

When she had finished her dinner she noticed three chairs standing by the wall. One was a Great Big Chair, and she climbed upon that and sat down. Oh, dear! how hard it was! She was sure she could not sit there for long, so she climbed up on the next, which was only a Middling-sized Chair, but that was too soft for her taste; so she went on to the last, which was a Teeny Tiny Chair and suited her exactly.

It was so comfortable that she sat on and on until, if you'll believe it, she actually sat the bottom out. Then, of course, she was comfortable no longer, so she got up and began to wonder what she should do next.

There was a staircase in the Bears' house, and Goldilocks thought she would go up it and see where it led to. So up she went, and when she reached the top she laughed outright, for the Bears' bedroom was the funniest she had ever seen. In the middle of the room stood a Great Big Bed, on one side of it there was a Middling-sized Bed, and on the other side there was a Teeny Tiny Bed.

Goldilocks was sleepy, so she thought she would lie down and have a little nap. First she got upon the Great Big Bed, but it was just as hard as the Great Big Chair had been; so she jumped off and tried the Middling-sized Bed, but it was so soft that she sank right down into the feather cushions and was nearly smothered.

"I will try the Teeny Tiny Bed," she said, and so she did, and it was so comfortable that she soon fell fast asleep.

Whilst she lay there, dreaming of all sorts of pleasant things, the three Bears came home from their walk very hungry and quite ready for their dinners.

But, oh! dear me! how cross the Great Big Bear looked when he saw his spoon had been used and thrown under the table.

"WHO HAS BEEN TASTING MY SOUP?"

he cried, in a Great Big Voice.

"AND WHO HAS BEEN TASTING MINE?" cried the Middling-sized Bear, in a Middling-sized Voice.

"BUT WHO HAS BEEN TASTING MINE AND TASTED IT ALL UP?"

cried the poor little Teeny Tiny Bear in a Teeny Tiny Voice, with the tears running down his Teeny Tiny Face.

When the Great Big Bear went to sit down in his Great Big Chair, he cried out in his Great Big Voice:

"WHO HAS BEEN SITTING ON MY CHAIR?"

And the Middling-sized Bear cried, in a Middling-sized Voice:

"WHO HAS BEEN SITTING ON MY CHAIR?"

But the Teeny Tiny Bear cried out in a Teeny Tiny Voice of anger:

"WHO HAS BEEN SITTING ON MY CHAIR, AND SAT THE BOTTOM OUT?"

By this time the Bears were sure that someone had been in their house quite lately; so they looked about to see if someone were not there still.

There was certainly no one downstairs, so they went up the staircase to their bedroom.

As soon as the Great Big Bear looked at his bed, he cried out, in his Great Big Voice:

"WHO HAS BEEN LYING ON MY BED?"

And the Middling-sized Bear, seeing that the coverlet was all rumpled, cried out, in a Middling-sized Voice:

"WHO HAS BEEN LYING ON MY BED?"

"WHO HAS BEEN TASTING MY SOUP?"

But the Teeny Tiny Bear cried out, in a Teeny Tiny Voice of astonishment:

"WHO HAS BEEN LYING ON MY BED AND LIES THERE STILL?"

Now, when the Great Big Bear began to speak, Goldilocks dreamt that there was a bee buzzing in the room, and when the Middling-sized Bear began to speak, she dreamt that it was flying out of the window; but when the Teeny Tiny Bear began to speak, she dreamt that the bee had come back and stung her on the ear, and up she jumped. Oh! how frightened she was when she saw the three Bears standing beside her.

She hopped out of bed and in a second was out through the open window. Never stopping to wonder if the fall had hurt her, she got up and ran and ran and ran until she could go no farther, always thinking that the Bears were close behind her. And when at length she fell down in a heap on the ground, because she was too tired to run any more, it was her own mother who picked her up, because in her fright she had run straight home without knowing it.

☘ ☘ ☘

CINDERELLA

ONCE upon a time there lived a noble gentleman who had one dear little daughter. Poor child! her own kind mother was dead, and her father, who loved her very dearly, was afraid that his little girl was sometimes lonely. So he married a grand lady who had two daughters of her own, and who, he thought, would be kind and good to his little one. But no sooner did the stepmother enter her new home than she began to show her true character. Her stepdaughter was so much prettier and sweeter than her own children, that she was jealous of her, and gave her all the hard work of the house to do, whilst the two proud sisters spent their time at pleasant parties and entertainments.

The only pleasure the poor child had was to spend her evenings sitting in the chimney-corner, resting her weary limbs, and for this reason her sisters mockingly nicknamed her "Cinderella." The sisters' fine clothes made Cinderella feel very shabby; but, in her little torn frock and ragged shoes, she was a thousand times more lovely than they.

Now, it chanced that the King's son gave a grand ball, to which he invited all the lords and ladies in the country, and, amongst the rest, Cinderella's two sisters were asked. How pleased and excited they were when the invitation arrived! For days they could talk of nothing but the clothes they should wear and the grand folk they hoped to meet.

When at last the great day arrived, Cinderella was kept running about from early till late, decking the sisters, and dressing their hair.

"Don't you wish you were going to the ball?" said one of them.

"Indeed I do," sighed the poor little maid. The sisters burst out laughing. "A pretty spectacle *you* would be," they said rudely. "Go back to your cinders—they are fit company for rags." Then, stepping carefully into their carriage so that they might not crush their fine clothes, they drove away to the ball.

Cinderella went back to her chimney-corner, and tried not to feel envious, but the tears *would* gather in the pretty eyes, and trickle down the sorrowful little face.

"What are you crying for, child?" cried a silvery voice.

Cinderella started, and raised her eyes. Who could it be? Then in a moment she knew—it was her fairy Godmother!

"I do so want——" began Cinderella; then her sobs stopped her.

"To go to the ball," finished the Godmother. Cinderella nodded. "Well, leave off crying—be a good girl, and you shall go. Run quickly into the garden, and bring the largest pumpkin you can find."

Cinderella could not imagine how a pumpkin could help her to go to the ball, but her only thought was to obey her Godmother. In a few moments she was back again, with a splendid pumpkin. Her Godmother scooped out the inside—one touch of the wand, and the pumpkin was a golden coach, lined with white satin.

"Now, godchild, quick—the mouse-trap from the pantry!"

"Here it is, Godmother," said Cinderella breathlessly.

One by one six fat sleek mice passed through the trap door. As each appeared, a touch of the wand transformed it into a cream-colored horse, fit for a queen.

"Now, Cinderella, can you find a coachman?"

"There is a large gray rat in the rat-trap—would he do, Godmother?"

"Run and fetch him, child, and then I can judge." So Cinderella ran to fetch the rat, and her Godmother said he was just made for a coachman; and I think you would have agreed with her had you seen him a moment later, with his powdered wig and silk stockings.

Six lizards from behind the pumpkin-frame became six footmen in splendid liveries—you would have thought they had been footmen all their lives. Cinderella was so excited that she could scarcely speak.

"Oh! Godmother," she cried, "it is all so lovely!" Then suddenly she thought of her shabby frock. "There is my white muslin," she said wistfully, "if—do you think——"

But before Cinderella could realize what was happening, her Godmother's wand tapped her lightly on the shoulder, and in place of the shabby frock, there was a gleam of satin, silver, and pearls.

Ah! who can describe a robe made by the fairies? It was white as snow, and as dazzling; round the hem hung a fringe of diamonds, sparkling like dew-drops in the sunshine. The lace about the throat and arms could only have been spun by fairy spiders. Surely it was a dream! Cinderella put her daintily-gloved hand to her throat, and softly touched the pearls that encircled her neck.

"Come, child," said the Godmother, "or you will be late."

As Cinderella moved, the firelight shone upon her dainty shoes.

"They are of diamonds," she said.

"No," answered her Godmother, smiling; "they are better than that—they are of glass, made by the fairies. And now, child, go, and enjoy yourself to your heart's content. Only remember, if you stay at the palace one instant after midnight, your coach and servants will vanish, and you will be the little gray Cinderella once more!"

A few moments later, the coach dashed into the royal courtyard, the door was flung open, and Cinderella alighted. As she walked slowly up the richly-carpeted staircase, there was a murmur of admiration, and the King's son hastened to meet her. "Never," said he to himself, "have I seen anyone so lovely!" He led her into the ball-room, where the King, who was much taken with her sweet face and pretty, modest manners, whispered to the Queen that she must surely be a foreign Princess.

The evening passed away in a dream of delight, Cinderella dancing with no one but the handsome young Prince, and being waited on by his own hands at supper-time. The two sisters could not recognize their ragged little sister in the beautiful and graceful lady to whom the Prince paid so much attention, and felt quite pleased and flattered when she addressed a few words to them.

Presently a clock chimed the three quarters past eleven, and, remembering her Godmother's warning, Cinderella at once took leave of the Prince, and, jumping into her coach, was driven rapidly home. Here she found her Godmother waiting to hear all about the ball. "It was *lovely,*" said Cinderella; "and oh! Godmother, there is to be another to-morrow night, and I *should* so much like to go to it!"

"Then you shall," replied the kind fairy, and, kissing her godchild tenderly, she vanished. When the sisters returned from the ball, they found a sleepy little maiden sitting in the chimney-corner, waiting for them.

"How late you are!" cried Cinderella, yawning. "Are you not very tired?"

"Not in the least," they answered, and then they told her what a delightful ball it had been, and how the loveliest Princess in the world had been there, and had spoken to them, and admired their pretty dresses.

"Who was she?" asked Cinderella slyly.

"That we cannot say," answered the sisters. "She would

IT WAS HER FAIRY GODMOTHER!

not tell her name, though the Prince begged her to do so on bended knee."

"Dear sister," said Cinderella, "I, too, should like to see the beautiful Princess. Will you not lend me your old yellow gown, that I may go to the ball to-morrow with you?"

"What!" cried her sister angrily; "lend one of my dresses to a little cinder-maid? Don't talk nonsense, child!"

The next night, the sisters were more particular than ever about their attire, but at last they were dressed, and as soon as their carriage had driven away, the Godmother appeared. Once more she touched her godchild with her wand, and in a moment she was arrayed in a beautiful dress that seemed as though it had been woven of moon-beams and sunshine, so radiantly did it gleam and shimmer. She put her arms round her Godmother's neck and kissed and thanked her. "Good-bye, childie; enjoy yourself, but whatever you do, remember to leave the ball before the clock strikes twelve," the Godmother said, and Cinderella promised.

But the hours flew by so happily and so swiftly that Cinderella forgot her promise, until she happened to look at a clock and saw that it was on the stroke of twelve. With a cry of alarm she fled from the room, dropping, in her haste, one of the little glass slippers; but, with the sound of the clock strokes in her ears, she dared not wait to pick it up. The Prince hurried after her in alarm, but when he reached the entrance hall, the beautiful Princess had vanished, and there was no one to be seen but a forlorn little beggar-maid creeping away into the darkness.

Poor little Cinderella!—she hurried home through the dark streets, weary, and overwhelmed with shame.

The fire was out when she reached her home, and there was no Godmother waiting to receive her; but she sat down in the chimney-corner to wait her sisters' return. When they came in they could speak of nothing but the wonderful things that had happened at the ball.

The beautiful Princess had been there again, they said, but had disappeared just as the clock struck twelve, and though the Prince had searched everywhere for her, he had been unable to find her. "He was quite beside himself with grief," said the elder sister, "for there is no doubt he hoped to make her his bride."

Cinderella listened in silence to all they had to say, and, slipping her hand into her pocket, felt that the one remaining glass slipper was safe, for it was the only thing of all her grand apparel that remained to her.

On the following morning there was a great noise of trumpets and drums, and a procession passed through the town, at the head of which rode the King's son. Behind him came a herald, bearing a velvet cushion, upon which rested a little glass slipper. The herald blew a blast upon the trumpet, and then read a proclamation saying that the King's son would wed any lady in the land who could fit the slipper upon her foot, if she could produce another to match it.

Of course, the sisters tried to squeeze their feet into the slipper, but it was of no use—they were much too large. Then Cinderella shyly begged that she might try. How the sisters laughed with scorn when the Prince knelt to fit the slipper on the cinder-maid's foot; but what was their surprise when it slipped on with the greatest ease, and the next moment Cinderella produced the other from her pocket. Once more she stood in the slippers, and once more the sisters saw before them the lovely Princess who was to be the Prince's bride. For at the touch of the magic shoes, the little gray frock disappeared for ever, and in place of it she wore the beautiful robe the fairy Godmother had given to her.

The sisters hung their heads with sorrow and vexation; but kind little Cinderella put her arms round their necks, kissed them, and forgave them for all their unkindness, so that they could not help but love her.

The Prince could not bear to part from his little love again, so he carried her back to the palace in his grand coach, and they were married that very day. Cinderella's stepsisters were present at the feast, but in the place of honor sat the fairy Godmother.

So the poor little cinder-maid married the Prince, and in time they came to be King and Queen, and lived happily ever after.

THE THREE BROTHERS

THERE was once a man who had three sons, but no fortune except the house he lived in. Now, each of them wanted to have the house after his death; but their father was just as fond of one as of the other, and did not know how to treat them all fairly. He did not want to sell the house, because it had belonged to his forefathers, or he might have divided the money between them.

At last an idea came into his head, and he said to his sons: "Go out into the world, and each learn a trade, and when you come home, the one who makes best use of his handicraft shall have the house."

The sons were quite content with this plan, and the eldest decided to be a farrier, the second a barber, and the third a fencing master. They fixed a time when they would all meet at home again, and then they set off.

It so happened that they each found a clever master with whom they learned their business thoroughly. The farrier shod the King's horses, and he thought, "I shall certainly be the one to have the house."

The barber shaved nobody but grand gentlemen, so he thought it would fall to him.

The fencing master got many blows, but he set his teeth, and would not let himself be put out, because he thought, "If I am afraid of a blow, I shall never get the house."

Now, when the given time had passed, they all went home together to their father; but they did not know how to get a good opportunity of showing off their powers, and sat down to discuss the matter.

Suddenly a hare came running over the field.

"Ah!" cried the barber, "she comes just in the nick of time."

He took up his bowl and his soap, and got his lather by the time the hare came quite close, then he soaped her and shaved her as she raced along, without giving her a cut or missing a single hair. His father, astonished, said: "If the others don't look out, the house will be yours."

Before long a gentleman came along in his carriage at full gallop.

"Now, father, you shall see what I can do," said the farrier, and he ran after the carriage and tore the four shoes off the horse as he galloped along, then, without stopping a second, shod him with new ones.

"You are a fine fellow, indeed," said his father. "You know your business as well as your brother. I don't know which I shall give the house to at this rate."

Then the third one said: "Let me have a chance, too, father."

As it was beginning to rain, he drew his sword and swirled it round and round his head, so that not a drop fell on him. Even when the rain grew heavier, so heavy that it seemed as if it were being poured from the sky out of buckets, he swung the sword faster and faster, and remained as dry as if he had been under a roof.

His father was amazed, and said: "You have done the best; the house is yours."

Both the other brothers were quite satisfied with this decision, and as they were all so devoted to one another, they lived together in the house, and carried on their trades, by which they made plenty of money, since they were so perfect in them.

They lived happily together to a good old age, and when one fell ill and died, the others grieved so much over him that they pined away and soon after departed this life.

Then, as they had been so fond of one another, they were all buried in one grave.

☙ ☙ ☙

THE WREN AND THE BEAR

ONE summer's day the bear and the wolf were walking in the forest, and the bear heard a bird singing very sweetly, and said: "Brother Wolf, what kind of bird is that which is singing so delightfully?"

"That is the King of the birds, before whom we must do reverence," replied the wolf; but it was only the wren.

"If that be so," said the bear, "I should like to see his royal palace; come, lead me to it." "That cannot be as you like," replied the wolf. "You must wait till the Queen returns." Soon afterward the Queen arrived with some food in her bill, and the King, too, to feed their young ones, and the bear would have gone off to see them, but the wolf, pulling his ear, said: "No, you must wait till the Queen and the King are both off again."

So, after observing well the situation of the nest, the two tramped off, but the bear had no rest, for he wished still to see the royal palace, and after a short delay he set off to it again. He found the King and Queen absent, and, peeping into the nest, he saw five or six young birds lying in it. "Is this the royal palace?" exclaimed the bear; "this miserable place! You are no King's children, but wretched young vagabonds." "No, no, that we are not!" burst out the little wrens together in a great passion, for to them this speech was addressed. "No, no, we are born of honorable parents, and you, Mr. Bear, shall make your words good!" At this speech the bear and the wolf were much frightened, and ran back to their holes; but the little wrens kept up an unceasing clamor till their parents' return. As soon as they came back with food in their mouths the little birds began, "We will none of us touch a fly's leg, but will starve rather, until you decide whether we are fine and handsome children or not, for the bear has been here and insulted us!"

"Be quiet," replied the King, "and that shall soon be settled." And thereupon he flew with his Queen to the residence of the bear, and called to him from the entrance, "Old grumbler, why have you insulted my children? That shall cost you dear, for we will decide the matter by a pitched battle."

War having thus been declared against the bear, all the four-footed beasts were summoned: the ox, the ass, the cow, the goat, the stag, and every animal on the face of the earth. The wren, on the other hand, summoned every flying thing; not only the birds, great and small, but also the gnat, the hornet, the bee, and the flies.

When the time arrived for the commencement of the war,

the wren King sent out spies to see who was appointed commander-in-chief of the enemy. The gnat was the most cunning of all the army, and he, therefore, buzzed away into the forest where the enemy was encamped, and alighted on a leaf of the tree beneath which the watchword was given out. There stood the bear and called the fox to him, and said: "You are the most crafty of animals, so you must be general, and lead us on." "Well," said the fox, "but what sign shall we appoint?" Nobody answered. Then the fox said: "I have a fine long bushy tail, which looks like a red feather at a distance; if I hold this tail straight up, all is going well and you must march after me; but if I suffer it to hang down, run away as fast as you can." As soon as the gnat heard all this she flew home and told the wren King everything to a hair.

When the day arrived for the battle to begin, the four-footed beasts all came running along to the field, shaking the earth with their roaring and bellowing. The wren King also came with his army, whirring and buzzing and humming enough to terrify any one out of his senses. Then the wren King sent the hornet forward to settle upon the fox's tail and sting it with all his power. As soon as the fox felt the first sting he drew up his hind leg with the pain, still carrying, however, his tail as high in the air as before; at the second sting he was obliged to drop it a little bit; but at the third he could no longer bear the pain, but was forced to drop his tail between his legs. As soon as the other beasts saw this, they thought all was lost, and began to run each one to his own hole; so the birds won the battle without difficulty.

When all was over the wren King and his Queen flew home to their children, and cried out: "Rejoice! rejoice! we have won the battle; now eat and drink as much as you please."

The young wrens, however, said: "Still we will not eat till the bear has come to our nest and begged pardon, and admitted that we are fine and handsome children."

So the wren King flew back to the cave of the bear, and called out, "Old grumbler, you must come to the nest and beg pardon of my children for calling them wretched young brats, else your ribs shall be crushed in your body!"

In great terror the bear crept out and begged pardon; and afterward the young wrens, being now made happy in their minds, settled down to eating and drinking, and I am afraid they were over-excited and kept up their merriment far too late.

❧ ❧ ❧

CHICKEN-LICKEN

AS Chicken-licken was going one day to the wood, whack! an acorn fell from a tree on to his head.

"Gracious goodness me!" said Chicken-licken, "the sky must have fallen; I must go and tell the King."

So Chicken-licken turned back, and met Hen-len.

"Well, Hen-len, where are you going?" said he.

"I'm going to the wood," said she.

"Oh, Hen-len, don't go!" said he, "for as I was going the sky fell on to my head, and I'm going to tell the King."

So Hen-len turned back with Chicken-licken, and met Cock-lock.

"I'm going to the wood," said he.

Then Hen-len said: "Oh Cock-lock, don't go, for I was going, and I met Chicken-licken, and Chicken-licken had been at the wood, and the sky had fallen on to his head, and we are going to tell the King."

So Cock-lock turned back, and they met Duck-luck.

"Well, Duck-luck, where are you going?"

And Duck-luck said: "I'm going to the wood."

Then Cock-lock said: "Oh! Duck-luck, don't go, for I was going, and I met Hen-len, and Hen-len met Chicken-licken, and Chicken-licken had been at the wood, and the sky had fallen on to his head, and we are going to tell the King."

So Duck-luck turned back, and met Drake-lake.

"Well, Drake-lake, where are you going?"

And Drake-lake said: "I'm going to the wood."

Then Duck-luck said: "Oh! Drake-lake, don't go, for I was going, and I met Cock-lock, and Cock-lock met Hen-len, and Hen-len met Chicken-licken, and Chicken-licken had been at the wood, and the sky had fallen on to his head, and we are going to tell the King."

So Drake-lake turned back, and met Goose-loose.

"Well, Goose-loose, where are you going?"

And Goose-loose said: "I'm going to the wood."

Then Drake-lake said: "Oh, Goose-loose, don't go, for I was going, and I met Duck-luck, and Duck-luck met Cock-lock, and Cock-lock met Hen-len, and Hen-len met Chicken-licken, and Chicken-licken had been at the wood, and the sky had fallen on to his head, and we are going to tell the King."

So Goose-loose turned back, and met Gander-lander.

"Well, Gander-lander, where are you going?"

And Gander-lander said: "I'm going to the wood."

Then Goose-loose said: "Oh! Gander-lander, don't go, for I was going, and I met Drake-lake, and Drake-lake met Duck-luck, and Duck-luck met Cock-lock, and Cock-lock met Hen-len, and Hen-len met Chicken-licken, and Chicken-licken had been at the wood, and the sky had fallen on to his head, and we are going to tell the King."

So Gander-lander turned back, and met Turkey-lurkey.

"Well, Turkey-lurkey, where are you going?"

And Turkey-lurkey said: "I'm going to the wood."

Then Gander-lander said: "Oh! Turkey-lurkey, don't go, for I was going, and I met Goose-loose, and Goose-loose met Drake-lake, and Drake-lake met Duck-luck, and Duck-luck met Cock-lock, and Cock-lock met Hen-len, and Hen-len met Chicken-licken, and Chicken-licken had been at the wood, and the sky had fallen on to his head, and we are going to tell the King."

So Turkey-lurkey turned back, and walked with Gander-lander, Goose-loose, Drake-lake, Duck-luck, Cock-lock, Hen-len, and Chicken-licken.

And as they were going along, they met Fox-lox. And Fox-lox said:

"Where are you going?"

And they said: "Chicken-licken went to the wood, and the sky fell on to his head, and we are going to tell the King."

And Fox-lox said: "Come along with me, and I will show you the way."

But Fox-lox took them into the fox's hole, and he and his young ones soon ate up poor Chicken-licken, Hen-len, Cock-lock, Duck-luck, Drake-lake, Goose-loose, Gander-lander, and Turkey-lurkey; and they never saw the King to tell him that the sky had fallen.

☙ ☙ ☙

THE FOX AND THE CAT

IT happened once that the cat met Mr. Fox in the wood, and because she thought he was clever and experienced in all the ways of the world, she addressed him in a friendly manner.

"Good-morning, dear Mr. Fox! how are you, and how do you get along in these hard times?"

The fox, full of pride, looked at the cat from head to foot for some time, hardly knowing whether he would deign to answer or not. At last he said:

"Oh, you poor whisker-wiper, you silly piebald, you starveling mouse-hunter! what has come into your head? How dare you ask me how I am getting on? What sort of education have you had? How many arts are you master of?"

"Only one," said the cat meekly.

"And what might that one be?" asked the fox.

"When the dogs run after me, I can jump into a tree and save myself?"

"Is that all?" said the fox. "I am master of a hundred arts, and I have a sackful of cunning tricks in addition. But I pity you. Come with me, and I will teach you how to escape from the dogs."

Just then a huntsman came along with four hounds. The cat sprang trembling into a tree, and crept stealthily up to the topmost branch, where she was entirely hidden by twigs and leaves.

"Open your sack, Mr. Fox! open your sack!" cried the cat, but the dogs had gripped him, and held him fast.

"Oh, Mr. Fox!" cried the cat, "you with your hundred arts, and your sackful of tricks, are held fast, while I, with my one, am safe. Had you been able to creep up here, you would not have lost you life."

❧ ❧ ❧

THE RATS AND THEIR SON-IN-LAW

THERE once lived in Japan a rat and his wife, folk of noble race, who had one beautiful daughter. They were exceedingly proud of her charms, and dreamed, as parents will, of the grand marriage she was sure to make in time. Proud of his pure rodent blood, the father saw no son-in-law more to be desired than a young rat of ancient lineage, whose attentions to his daughter were very marked. This match, however, brilliant as it was, seemed not to the mother's taste. Like many people who think themselves made out of special clay, she had a very poor opinion of her own kind, and was ambitious for an alliance with the highest circles. To the stars! was her motto, she always said, and really, when one has a daughter of incomparable beauty, one may well hope for an equally incomparable son-in-law.

"Address yourself to the sun at once, then," cried the impatient father one day; "there is nothing above him, surely."

"Quite so; I had already thought of it," she answered, "and since you, too, are in sympathy with the idea, we will make our call to-morrow."

So, on the following morning the proud father and the

haughty mother-rat went together to present their lovely daughter to the orb of day.

"Lord Sun," said the mother, "let me present our only daughter, who is so beautiful that there is nothing like her in the whole world. Naturally we desire a son-in-law as wonderful as she, and, as you see, we have come to you first of all."

"Really," said the sun, "I am extremely flattered by your proposal, but you do me too much honor; there is some one greater than I; it is the cloud. Look, if you do not believe." . . . And at that moment the cloud arrived, and with one waft of his folds extinguished the sun with all his golden rays.

"Very well; let us speak to the cloud, then," said the mother-rat, not in the least disconcerted.

"Immensely honored, I am sure," replied the cloud in his turn, "but you are again mistaken; there is some one greater than I; it is the wind. You shall see."

At the same moment along came the wind, and with one blow swept the cloud out of sight, after which, overturning father, mother, and daughter, he tumbled with them, pell-mell, at the foot of an old wall.

"Quick, quick," cried the mother-rat, struggling to her feet, "and let us repeat our compliments to the wind."

"You'd better address yourself to the wall," growled the wind roughly. You see very well he is greater than I, for he stops me and makes me draw back."

No sooner had she heard these words than mother-rat faced about and presented her daughter to the wall. Ah, but now the fair rat-maiden imitated the wind; she drew back also. He whom she really adored in her heart of hearts was the fascinating young rat who had paid his court to her so well. However, to please her mother, she had consented to wed the Sun, in spite of his blinding rays, or the cloud, in spite of his sulky look, even the wind, in spite of his brusque manner; but an old, broken wall! . . . No! death would be better a thousand times.

Fortunately the wall excused himself, like all the rest. "Certainly," he said, "I can stop the wind, who can sweep away the cloud, who can cover up the Sun, but there is some one greater than I: it is the rat, who can pass through my body, and can even, if he chooses, reduce me to powder with his teeth. Believe me, you need seek no better son-in-law; greater than the rat, there is nothing in the world."

"Do you hear that, wife, do you hear it?" cried father-rat in triumph. "Didn't I always say so?"

"Quite true! you always did," returned the mother-rat in wonder, and suddenly glowed with pride in her ancient name and lineage.

So they all three went home, very happy and contented, and on the morrow the lovely rat-maiden married her faithful rat-lover.

☙ ☙ ☙

THE MOUSE AND THE SAUSAGE

ONCE upon a time a little mouse and a little sausage, who loved each other like sisters, decided to live together, and made their arrangements in such a way that every day one would go to walk in the fields, or make purchases in town, while the other remained at home to keep the house.

One day, when the little sausage had prepared cabbage for dinner, the little mouse, who had come back from town with a fine appetite, enjoyed it so greatly that she exclaimed: "How delicious the cabbage is to-day, my dear!"

"Ah!" answered the little sausage, "that is because I popped myself into the pot while it was cooking."

On the next day, as it was her turn to prepare the meals, the little mouse said to herself: "Now I will do as much for my friend as she did for me; we will have lentils for dinner, and I will jump into the pot while they are boiling," and she let the action follow the word, without reflecting that a simple sausage can do some things which are out of the reach of even the wisest mouse.

When the sausage came home, she found the house lonely and silent. She called again and again, "My little mouse! Mouse of my heart!" but no one answered. Then she went to look at the lentils boiling on the stove, and, alas! found within the pot her good little friend, who had perished at the post of duty.

Poor mousie, with the best intentions in the world, had stayed too long at her cookery, and when she desired to climb out of the pot, had no longer the strength to do so.

And the poor sausage could never be consoled! That is why to-day, when you put one in the pan or on the gridiron, you will hear her weep and sigh, "M-my p-poor m-mouse! Ah, m-my p-poor m-mouse!"

☙ ☙ ☙

JOHNNY AND THE GOLDEN GOOSE

THERE was once a man who had three sons. Johnny, the youngest, was always looked upon as the simpleton of the family, and had very little consideration or kindness shown him.

It happened one day that the eldest son was going out into the wood to cut fuel; and before he started, his mother gave him a slice of rich plum-cake and a flask of wine, so that he might not suffer from hunger or thirst.

Just as he reached the wood, he met a queer old man, dressed in gray, who wished him "Good day," and begged for a piece of the young man's cake and a drink of wine.

But the greedy youth replied: "If I were to give you cake and wine, I should not have enough left for myself; so be off with you, and leave me in peace."

Then he pushed the little man rudely on one side and went his way. He soon came to a likely-looking tree, and began to hew it down, but he made a false stroke, and instead of striking the tree he buried his axe in his own arm, and was obliged to hurry home as fast as he could to have the wound dressed.

And this was what came of offending the little gray man!

The following day the second son set out to the wood, and his mother treated him just as she had done her eldest son—gave him a slice of cake and a flask of wine, in case he should feel hungry. The little gray man met him at the entrance to the wood, and begged for a share of his food, but the young man answered:

"The more I give to you, the less I have for myself. Be off with you."

Then he left the little gray man standing in the road, and went on his way. But it was not long before he, too, was punished; for the first stroke he aimed at a tree glanced aside and wounded his leg, so that he was obliged to be carried home.

Then said the Simpleton: "Father, let me go to the wood for once. *I* will bring you home plenty of fuel."

"Nonsense," answered the father. "Both your brothers have got into trouble, and it is not likely that I am going to trust you."

But Johnny would not give up the idea, and worried his father, till at last he said:

"Very well, my son, have your own way. You shall learn by experience that I know better than you."

There was no rich cake for the simpleton of the family. His mother just gave him a little loaf of dough and a bottle of sour beer.

No sooner did he reach the wood than the little gray man appeared.

"Give me a piece of your cake and a drink of your wine?" said he.

But the young man told him he had only a dough loaf and a bottle of sour beer.

"Still," said he, "you are welcome to a share of the food, such as it is."

So the two sat down together; but when Johnny took his humble fare from his pocket, what was his surprise to find it changed into the most delicious cake and wine. Then the young man and his guest made a hearty meal, and when it was ended the little gray man said:

"Because you have such a kind heart, and have willingly shared your food with me, I am going to reward you. Yonder stands an old tree: hew it down, and deep in the heart of the roots you will find something."

The old man then nodded kindly, and disappeared in a moment.

Johnny at once did as he had been told, and as soon as the tree fell he saw, sitting in the midst of the roots, a goose with feathers of purest gold. He lifted it carefully out, and carried it with him to the inn, where he meant to spend the night.

Now, the landlord had three daughters, and no sooner did they see the goose than they wanted to know what curious kind of bird it might be, for never before had they seen a fowl of any kind with feathers of pure gold. The eldest made up her mind to wait for a good opportunity and then pluck a feather for herself. So as soon as Johnny went out of the room she put out her hand and seized the wing of the goose, but what was her horror to find that she could not unclasp her fingers again, nor even move her hand from the golden goose!

Very soon the second sister came creeping into the room, meaning also to steal a feather; but no sooner did she touch her sister than she, too, was unable to draw her hand away.

Lastly came the third, anxious to secure a feather before the goose's master returned.

"Go away! go away!" screamed her two sisters, but she could not understand why she should not help herself as well as the others.

So she paid no heed to their cries, but came toward them and stretched out her hand to the goose.

In doing so she touched her second sister, and then, alas! she too, was held fast.

They pulled and tugged with might and main, but it was all of no use; they could not get away, and there they had to remain the whole night.

The next morning Johnny tucked the goose under his arm,

and went on his way, never troubling himself about the three girls hanging on behind.

Then what a dance he led them: over hedges and ditches, highways and byways! Wherever he led they were bound to follow. Half way across a sunny meadow, they met the parson, who was terribly shocked to see the three girls running after a young man.

"For shame!" he cried angrily, and seized the youngest by the hand to drag her away.

But no sooner did he touch her than the poor parson was made fast too, and had to run behind the girls, whether he would or no.

They had scarcely gone half a dozen paces before they met the sexton, who stared with astonishment to see his master running at the heels of the three girls.

"Hi! stop, your reverence," he cried. "You will be late for the christening."

He seized the parson's sleeve as he ran past him, but the poor sexton had to join the procession too.

So now there were five of them, and just as they turned a corner the parson saw two peasants, and called to them to set him and his sexton free.

They threw down their spades at once and tried to do so, but they too, stuck fast, and so Johnny had a fine string of seven folk hanging on to the wing of his golden goose.

On and on they ran, until at length they came into the country of a powerful King.

This King had an only daughter, who all her life had been so sad that no one had ever been able to make her laugh. So the King made a decree that the man who could bring a smile to his daughter's face should have her for his bride.

When Johnny heard what the King had promised, he at once made his way into the Princess's presence, and when she saw the goose, with the seven queer-looking companions hanging on behind, she burst into such a hearty fit of laughter that it was thought she would never be able to stop again.

Of course, the Simpleton claimed her as his bride, but the King did not fancy him for a son-in-law, so he made all sorts of excuses.

"You shall have her," said he, "if you can first bring me a man who can drink up a whole cellarful of wine."

Johnny at once remembered the little gray man, and, feeling sure that he would help him, he set out for the wood where he had first met him.

When he reached the stump of the old tree which he had himself hewn down, he noticed a man sitting beside it, with a face as gloomy as a rainy day.

Johnny asked politely what ailed him, and the man answered:

"I suffer from a thirst I cannot quench. Cold water disagrees with me, and though I have, it is true, emptied a barrel of wine, it was no more to me than a single drop of water upon a hot stone."

You can think how pleased Johnny was to hear these words. He took the man to the King's cellar, where he seated himself before the huge barrels, and drank and drank till, at the end of the day, not a drop of wine was left.

Then Johnny claimed his bride, but the King could not make up his mind to give his daughter to "a ne'er-do-weel" who went by such a name as "Simpleton."

So he made fresh excuses, and said that he would not give her up until the young man had found someone who could eat up a mountain of bread in a single day.

So the young man had no choice but to set out once more for the wood.

And again he found a man sitting beside the stump of the tree. He was very sad and hungry-looking, and sat tightening the belt round his waist.

"I have eaten a whole ovenful of bread," he said sadly, "but when one is as hungry as I am, such a meal only serves to make one more hungry still. I am so empty that if I did not tighten my belt I should die of hunger."

"You are the man for me!" said Johnny. "Follow me, and I will give you a meal that will satisfy even your hunger."

He led the man into the courtyard of the King's palace, where all the meal in the kingdom had been collected together and mixed into an enormous mountain of bread.

The man from the wood placed himself in front of it and began to eat, and before the day was over the mountain of bread had vanished.

A third time the Simpleton demanded his bride, but again the King found an excuse.

"First bring me a ship that can sail both on land and sea, and then you shall wed the Princess," he said.

Johnny went straightway to the wood, where he met the little gray man with whom he had once shared his food.

"Good day," he said, nodding his wise little head. "So you've come to visit me again, eh? It was I, you know, who drank the wine and ate the bread for you, and now I will finish by giving you the wonderful ship which is to sail on either land or sea. All this I do for you because you were kind and good to me."

Then he gave him the ship, and when the King saw it he could find no further excuse.

So he gave the young man his daughter, and the pair were married that very day.

When the old King died, the Simpleton became King in his stead, and he and his wife lived happily ever after.

❧ ❧ ❧

TITTY MOUSE AND TATTY MOUSE

TITTY Mouse and Tatty Mouse both lived in a house,
Titty Mouse went a-leasing and Tatty Mouse went a-leasing,
So they both went a-leasing.
Titty Mouse leased an ear of corn, and Tatty Mouse leased an ear of corn,
So they both leased an ear of corn.
Titty Mouse made a pudding, and Tatty Mouse made a pudding,
So they both made a pudding.
And Tatty Mouse put her pudding into the pot to boil,

But when Titty went to put hers in, the pot tumbled over, and scalded her to death.

Then Tatty sat down and wept, and a three-legged stool said: "Tatty, why do you weep?" "Titty's dead," said Tatty, "and so I weep." "Then," said the stool, "I'll hop." So the stool hopped.

Then a broom in the corner of the room said: "Stool, why do you hop?" "Oh!" said the stool, "Titty's dead, and Tatty weeps, and so I hop." "Then," said the broom, "I'll sweep." So the broom began to sweep.

"Then," said the door, "Broom, why do you sweep?" "Oh!" said the broom, "Titty's dead, and Tatty weeps, and the stool hops, and so I sweep." "Then," said the door, "I'll jar." So the door jarred.

"Then," said the window, "Door, why do you jar?" "Oh!" said the door, "Titty's dead, and Tatty weeps, and the stool hops, and the broom sweeps, and so I jar."

"Then," said the window, "I'll creak." So the window creaked. Now there was an old form outside the house, and when the window creaked, the form said: "Window, why do you creak?" "Oh!" said the window, "Titty's dead, and Tatty weeps, and the stool hops, and the broom sweeps, the door jars, and so I creak."

"Then," said the old form, "I'll run round the house." Then the old form ran round the house. Now there was a fine large walnut-tree growing by the cottage, and the tree said to the form: "Form, why do you run round the house?" "Oh!" said the form, "Titty's dead, and Tatty weeps, and the stool hops, and the broom sweeps, the door jars, and the window creaks, and so I run round the house."

"Then," said the walnut-tree, "I'll shed my leaves." So the walnut-tree shed all its beautiful green leaves. Now there was a little bird perched on one of the boughs of the tree, and when all the leaves fell, it said: "Walnut-tree, why do you shed your leaves?" "Oh!" said the tree, "Titty's dead, and Tatty weeps, the stool hops, and the broom sweeps, the door jars, and the window creaks, the old form runs round the house, and so I shed my leaves."

"Then," said the little bird, "I'll moult all my feathers." So he moulted all his pretty feathers. Now there was a little girl walking below, carrying a jug of milk for her brothers' and sisters' supper, and when she saw the poor little bird moult all its feathers, she said: "Little bird, why do you moult all your feathers?" "Oh!" said the little bird, "Titty's dead, and Tatty weeps, the stool hops, and the broom sweeps, the door jars, and the window creaks, the old form runs round the house, the walnut-tree sheds its leaves, and so I moult all my feathers."

"Then," said the little girl, "I'll spill the milk." So she dropped the pitcher and spilt the milk. Now there was an old man just by on the top of a ladder thatching a rick, and when he saw the little girl spill the milk, he said: "Little girl, what do you mean by spilling the milk? Your little brothers and sisters must go without their supper." Then said the little girl: "Titty's dead, and Tatty weeps, the stool hops, and the broom sweeps, the door jars, and the window creaks, the old form runs round the house, the walnut-tree sheds all its leaves, the little bird moults all its feathers, and so I spill the milk."

"Oh!" said the old man, "then I'll tumble off the ladder and break my neck." So he tumbled off the ladder and broke his neck; and when the old man broke his neck, the great walnut-tree fell down with a crash, and upset the old form and house, and the house falling knocked the window out, and the window knocked the door down, and the door upset the broom, and the broom upset the stool, and poor little Tatty Mouse was buried beneath the ruins.

☙ ☙ ☙

TEENY TINY

THERE was once upon a time a teeny-tiny woman who lived in a teeny-tiny house in a teeny-tiny village. Now, one day this teeny-tiny woman put on her teeny-tiny bonnet, and went out of her teeny-tiny house to take a teeny-tiny walk. And when this teeny-tiny woman had gone a teeny-tiny way, she came to a teeny-tiny gate; so the teeny-tiny woman opened the teeny-tiny gate, and went into a teeny-tiny churchyard. And when this teeny-tiny woman had got into the teeny-tiny churchyard, she saw a teeny-tiny bone on a teeny-tiny grave, and the teeny-tiny woman said to her teeny-tiny self: "This teeny-tiny bone will make me some teeny-tiny soup for my teeny-tiny supper." So the teeny-tiny woman put the teeny-tiny bone into her teeny-tiny pocket, and went home to her teeny-tiny house.

Now, when the teeny-tiny woman got home to her teeny-tiny house, she was a teeny-tiny tired; so she went up her teeny-tiny stairs to her teeny-tiny bed, and put the teeny-tiny bone into a teeny-tiny cupboard. And when this teeny-tiny woman had been to sleep a teeny-tiny time, she was awakened by a teeny-tiny voice from the teeny-tiny cupboard, which said—

"GIVE ME MY BONE!"

And this teeny-tiny woman was a teeny-tiny frightened, so she hid her teeny-tiny head under the teeny-tiny clothes, and went to sleep again. And when she had been asleep again a teeny-tiny time, the teeny-tiny voice cried out from the teeny-tiny cupboard a teeny-tiny louder—

"GIVE ME MY BONE!"

This made the teeny-tiny woman a teeny-tiny more frightened, so she hid her teeny-tiny head a teeny-tiny farther under the teeny-tiny clothes. And when the teeny-tiny woman had been asleep again a teeny-tiny time, the teeny-tiny voice from the teeny-tiny cupboard said again a teeny-tiny louder—

"GIVE ME MY BONE!"

At this the teeny-tiny woman was a teeny-tiny bit more frightened; but she put her teeny-tiny head out of the teeny-tiny clothes, and said in her loudest teeny-tiny voice—

"TAKE IT!!"

THE SPIDER AND THE FLEA

A SPIDER and a Flea dwelt together in one house, and brewed their beer in an egg-shell. One day, when the Spider was stirring it up, she fell in and scalded herself. Thereupon the Flea began to scream. And then the door asked: "Why are you screaming, Flea?"

"Because little Spider has scalded herself in the beer-tub," replied she.

Thereupon the door began to creak as if it were in pain; and a broom, which stood in the corner, asked, "What are you creaking for, door?"

"May I not creak?" it replied:

"The little Spider's scalt herself,
And the Flea weeps."

So the broom began to sweep industriously, and presently a little cart came by, and asked the reason. "May I not sweep?" replied the broom:

"The little Spider's scalt herself,
And the Flea weeps;
The little door creaks with the pain,"—

Thereupon the little cart said: "So will I run," and began to run very fast, past a heap of ashes, which cried out: "Why do you run, little cart?"

"Because," replied the cart:

"The little Spider's scalt herself,
And the Flea weeps;
The little door creaks with the pain,
And the broom sweeps."

"Then," said the ashes, "I will burn furiously." Now, next the ashes there grew a tree, which asked: "Little heap, why do you burn?"

"Because," was the reply:

"The little Spider's scalt herself,
And the Flea weeps;
The little door creaks with the pain,
And the broom sweeps;
The little cart runs on so fast,"—

Thereupon the tree cried, "I will shake myself!" and went on shaking till all its leaves fell off.

A little girl passing by with a water-pitcher saw it shaking, and asked: "Why do you shake yourself, little tree?"

"Why may I not?" said the tree:

"The little Spider's scalt herself,
And the Flea weeps;
The little door creaks with the pain,
And the broom sweeps;
The little cart runs on so fast,
And the ashes burn."

Then the maiden said: "If so, I will break my pitcher;" and she threw it down and broke it.

At this the streamlet, from which she drew the water, asked: "Why do you break your pitcher, my little girl?"

"Why may I not?" she replied; for

"The little Spider's scalt herself,
And the Flea weeps;
The little door creaks with the pain,
And the broom sweeps;
The little cart runs on so fast,
And the ashes burn;
The little tree shakes down its leaves—
Now it is my turn!"

"Ah, then," said the streamlet, "now must I begin to flow." And it flowed and flowed along, in a great stream, which kept getting bigger and bigger, until at last it swallowed up the little girl, the little tree, the ashes, the cart, the broom, the door, the Flea, and, last of all, the Spider, all together.

☘ ☘ ☘

THE LITTLE SHEPHERD BOY

ONCE upon a time there was a little shepherd boy who was famed far and wide for the wise answers which he gave to all questions. Now the King of the country heard of this lad, but he would not believe what was said about him, so the boy was ordered to come to court. When he arrived the King said to him: "If you can give me answers to each of the three questions which I will now put to you, I will bring you up as my own child, and you shall live here with me in my palace."

"What are these three questions?" asked the boy.

"The first is: How many drops of water are there in the sea?"

"My lord King," replied the shepherd boy, "let all the waters be stopped up on the earth, so that not one drop shall run into the sea before I count it, and then I will tell you how many drops there are in the sea!"

"The second question," said the King, "is: How many stars are there in the sky?"

"Give me a large sheet of paper," said the boy; and then he made in it with a pin so many minute holes that they were far too numerous to see or to count, and dazzled the eyes of whomsoever looked at them. This done, he said: "So many stars are there in the sky as there are holes in this paper; now count them. But nobody was able. Thereupon the King said: "The third question is: How many seconds are there in eternity?"

"In Lower Pomerania is situated the adamantine mountain, one mile in height, one mile in breadth, and one mile deep; and thither comes a bird once in every thousand years which rubs its beak against the hill, and, when the whole shall be rubbed away, then will the first second of eternity be gone by."

"You have answered the three questions like a sage," said the King, "and from henceforward you shall live with me in my palace, and I will treat you as my own child."

☙ ☙ ☙

THE THREE SPINNERS

ONCE upon a time there was a lazy maiden who would not spin, and, let her mother say what she would, she could not make her do it. At last, the mother, in a fit of impatience, gave her a blow which made the girl cry out loudly.

At that very instant, the Queen drove by, and, hearing the screams, she stopped the carriage, came into the house, and asked the mother why she beat her daughter in such a way that people in passing could hear the cries.

Then the mother felt ashamed that her daughter's laziness should be known, so she said: "Oh, your Majesty, I cannot take her away from her spinning: she spins from morning till night, and I am so poor that I cannot afford to buy the flax."

"There is nothing I like better than to hear the sound of spinning," the Queen replied, "and nothing pleases me more than the whirl of spinning-wheels. Let me take your daughter home with me to the castle; I have flax enough, and she may spin there to her heart's content."

The mother rejoiced greatly in her heart, and the Queen took the maiden home with her. When they arrived in the castle, she led her up into three rooms, which were piled from top to bottom with the finest flax.

"Now spin me this flax," said the Queen, "and when thou has spun it all, thou shalt have my eldest son for a husband. Although thou art poor, yet I do not despise thee on that account, for thy untiring industry is dowry enough."

The maiden was filled with inward terror, for she could not have spun the flax had she sat there day and night until she was three hundred years old! When she was left alone, she began to weep, and thus she sat for three days without stirring a finger.

On the third day the Queen came, and when she saw that nothing was as yet spun, she wondered over it, but the maiden excused herself by saying that she could not begin in consequence of the great sorrow she felt in being separated from her mother.

This satisfied the Queen, who, on leaving her, said: "Thou must begin to work for me to-morrow."

But when the maiden was once more alone, she did not know what to do, or how to help herself, and in her distress she went to the window and looked out. She saw three women passing by, the first of whom had a great broad foot, the second such a large under-lip that it hung down to her chin, and the third an enormous thumb.

They stopped under the window, and, looking up, asked the maiden what was the matter.

When she had told them of her trouble, they immediately offered her their help, and said:

"Wilt thou invite us to the wedding, and not be ashamed of us, but call us thy aunts, and let us sit at thy table? If thou wilt, we will spin all the flax, and do it in a very short time."

"With all my heart," answered the girl, "only come in, and begin at once."

Then she admitted the three strange women, and, making a clear space in the first room, they sat themselves down and began spinning.

One drew the thread and trod the wheel, the other moistened the thread, the third pressed it and beat it on the table, and every time she did so, a pile of thread fell on the ground spun in the finest way.

The maiden concealed the three spinners from the Queen, but showed her the heaps of spun yarn whenever she came, and received no end of praise for it.

When the first room was empty, the second was commenced, and when that was finished, the third was begun, and very soon cleared.

Then the three spinners took their leave, saying to the maiden:

"Forget not what thou hast promised us; it will make thy fortune."

When the girl showed the Queen the empty rooms and the great piles of thread, the wedding was announced. The bridegroom rejoiced that he had won so clever and industrious a wife, and he praised her exceedingly.

"I have three aunts," said the maiden, "and as they have done me many kindnesses, I could not forget them in my good fortune; permit me to invite them to our wedding and allow them to sit with me at table."

So the Queen and the bridegroom consented.

When the feast commenced, the three old women entered, clothed in the greatest splendor, and the bride said—

"Welcome, my dear aunts!"

"Alas!" exclaimed the bridegroom, "how is it you have such ugly relations?" and going up to the one with a broad foot, he asked:

"Why have you such a broad foot?"

"From threading, from threading," she answered.

Then he went to the second, and asked:

"Why have you such an overhanging lip?"

"From moistening the thread," she replied, "from moistening the thread."

Then he asked the third:

"Why have you such a big thumb?"

"From pressing the thread," answered she.

Then the Prince became frightened, and said:

"Then shall my lovely bride never more turn a spinning wheel, as long as she lives!"

Thus was the maiden freed from the hated flax-spinning.

☙ ☙ ☙

THE CAT AND THE MOUSE IN PARTNERSHIP

A CAT having made the acquaintance of a mouse, told her so much of the great love and affection that he had for her, that the mouse at last consented to live in the same house with him, and to have their domestic affairs in common. "But we must provide for the winter," said the cat, "or we shall be starved; you, little mouse, cannot go everywhere looking for food, or you will meet with an accident."

This advice was followed, and a pot was brought with some grease in it. However, when they had got it, they could not imagine where it should be put; but at last, after a long consideration, the cat said: "I know no better place to put it than in the church, for there no one dares to steal anything; we will set it beneath the organ, and not touch it till we really want it."

So the pot was put away in safety; but not long afterward the cat began to wish for it again, so he spoke to the mouse and said: "I have to tell you that I am asked by my aunt to stand godfather to a little son, white with brown marks, whom she has just brought into the world, and so I must go to the christening. Let me go out to-day, and do you stop at home and keep house."

"Certainly," answered the mouse; "pray, go; and if you eat anything nice, think of me; I would also willingly drink a little of the sweet red christening-wine."

But, alas! it was all a story; for the cat had no aunt, and had not been asked to stand godfather to any one. He went straight to the church, crept up to the grease-pot, and licked it till he had eaten off the top; then he took a walk on the roofs of the houses in the town, thinking over his situation, and now and then stretching himself in the sun and stroking his whiskers as often as he thought of his meal. When it was evening he went home again, and the mouse said: "So you have come at last; what a charming day you must have had!"

"Yes," answered the cat; "it went off very well!"

"What have you named the kitten?" asked the mouse.

"*Top-off*," said the cat very quickly.

"*Top-off!*" replied the mouse; "that is a curious and remarkable name; is it common in your family?"

"What does that matter?" said the cat; "it is not worse than Crumb-stealer, as your children are called."

Not long afterward the cat felt the same longing as before, and said to the mouse: "You must oblige me by taking care of the house once more by yourself; I am again asked to stand godfather, and, since the youngster has a white ring round his neck, I cannot get off the invitation." So the good little mouse consented, and the cat crept away behind the wall to the church again, and ate half the contents of the grease-pot. "Nothing tastes better than what one eats by one's self," said he, quite contented with his day's work; and when he came home the mouse asked how this child was named.

"*Half-out*," answered the cat.

"*Half-out!* What do you mean? I never heard such a name before in my life; I will wager anything it is not in the calendar," but the cat replied nothing.

Pussy's mouth soon began to water again at the recollection of the feasting. "All good things come in threes," said he to the mouse. "I am again required to be godfather; this child is quite black, and has little white claws, but not a single white hair on his body; such a thing only happens once in two years, so pray excuse me this time."

"*Top-off! Half-out!*" answered the mouse; "those are such curious names, they make me a bit suspicious."

"Ah!" replied the cat, "there you sit in your gray coat and long tail, thinking nonsense. That comes of never going out."

The mouse busied herself during the cat's absence in putting the house in order, but meanwhile greedy puss licked the grease-pot clean out. "When it is all done one will rest in peace," thought he to himself, and as soon as night came he went home fat and tired. The mouse, however, again asked what name the third child had received. "It will not please you any better," answered the cat, "for he is called *All-out.*"

"*All-out!*" exclaimed the mouse; "well, that is certainly the most curious name by far. I have never yet seen it in print. *All-out!* What can that mean?" and, shaking her head, she rolled herself up and went to sleep.

After that nobody else asked the cat to stand godfather; but the winter had arrived, and nothing more was to be picked up out of doors; so the mouse bethought herself of their store of provision, and said, "Come, friend cat, we will go to our grease-pot which we laid by; it will taste well now."

"Yes, indeed," replied the cat; "it will taste as well as if you stroked your tongue against the window."

So they set out on their journey, and when they arrived at the church the pot stood in its old place—but it was empty! "Ah," said the mouse, "I see what has happened; now I know you are indeed a faithful friend. You have eaten the whole as you stood godfather; first *Top-off*, then *Half-out*, then—"

"Will you be quiet?" cried the cat. "Not a word, or I'll eat you." But the poor mouse had "*All-out*" at her tongue's end, and had scarcely uttered it when the cat made a spring, seized her in his mouth, and swallowed her.

This happens every day in the world.

THE SWEET SOUP

ONCE on a time there was a poor but very good little girl, who lived alone with her mother, and when my story begins, they had nothing in the house to eat. So the child went out into the forest, and there she met an old woman, who already knew her distress, and who presented her with a pot which had the following power. If one said to it, "Boil, little pot!" it would cook sweet soup; and when one said: "Stop, little pot!" it would immediately cease to boil. The little girl took the pot home to her mother, and now their poverty and distresses were at an end, for they could have sweet broth as often as they pleased.

One day, however, the little girl went out, and in her absence the mother said: "Boil, little pot!" So it began to cook, and she soon ate all she wished; but when the poor woman wanted to have the pot stop, she found she did not know the word. Away, therefore, the pot boiled, and very quickly was over the edge; and as it boiled and boiled the kitchen presently became full, then the house, and the next house, and soon the whole street. It seemed likely to satisfy all the world, for, though there was the greatest necessity to do so, nobody knew how to stop it. At last, when only a very small cottage of all the village was left unfilled with soup, the child returned and said at once: "Stop, little pot!"

Immediately it ceased to boil; but whoever wishes to enter the village now must eat his way through the soup! ! !

☘ ☘ ☘

THE STRAW THE COAL AND THE BEAN

ALL alone, in a quiet little village, lived a poor old woman. One day she had a dish of beans which she wanted to cook for dinner, so she made a fire on the hearth, and in order that it should burn up quickly she lighted it with a handful of straw.

She hung the pot over the fire, and poured in the beans; but one fell on to the floor without her noticing it, and rolled away beside a piece of straw. Soon afterwards a live coal flew out of the fire and joined their company. Then the straw began to speak.

"Dear friends," said he, "whence come you?"

"I was fortunate enough to spring out of the fire," answered the coal. "Had I not exerted myself to get out when I did, I should most certainly have been burnt to ashes."

"I have also just managed to save my skin," said the bean. "Had the old woman succeeded in putting me into the pot, I should have been stewed without mercy, just as my comrades are being served now."

"My fate might have been no better," the straw told them. "The old woman burnt sixty of my brothers at once, but fortunately I was able to slip through her fingers."

"What shall we do now?" said the coal.

"Well," answered the bean, "my opinion is that, as we have all been so fortunate as to escape death, we should leave this place before any new misfortune overtakes us. Let us all three become traveling companions and set out upon a journey to some unknown country."

This suggestion pleased both the straw and the coal, so away they all went at once. Before long they came to a brook, and as there was no bridge across it they did not know how to get to the other side; but the straw had a good idea: "I will lay myself over the water, and you can walk across me as though I were a bridge," he said. So he stretched himself from one bank to the other, and the coal, who was of a hasty disposition, at once tripped gaily on to the newly-built bridge. Half way across she hesitated, and began to feel afraid of the rushing water beneath her. She dared go no farther, but neither would she return; but she stood there so long that the straw caught fire, broke in two, and fell into the stream. Of course, the coal was bound to follow. No sooner did she touch the water than —hiss, zish! out she went, and never glowed again.

The bean, who was a careful fellow, had stayed on the bank, to watch how the coal got across, before trusting himself to such a slender bridge. But when he saw what very queer figures his friends cut, he could not help laughing. He laughed and laughed till he could not stop, and at length he split his side.

It would have gone badly with him then, had not a tailor happened to pass by. He was a kind-hearted fellow, and at once took out his needle and thread and began to repair the mischief.

The bean thanked him politely, for he knew that the tailor had saved his life, but unfortunately he had used black thread, and from that time till to-day every bean has a little black stitch in its side.

WHY THE BEAR HAS A STUMPY TAIL

ONE winter's day the bear met the fox, who came slinking along with a string of fish he had stolen.

"Hi! stop a minute! Where did you get those from?" demanded the bear.

"Oh, my Lord Bruin, I've been out fishing and caught them," said the fox.

So the bear had a mind to learn to fish, too, and bade the fox tell him how he was to set about it.

"Oh, it is quite easy," answered the fox, "and soon learned. You've only got to go upon the ice, and cut a hole and stick your tail down through it, and hold it there as long as you can. You're not to mind if it smarts a little; that's when the fish bite. The longer you hold it there, the more fish you'll get; and then all at once out with it, with a cross pull side ways and a strong pull, too."

Well, the bear did as the fox said, and though he felt very cold, and his tail smarted very much, he kept it a long, long time down in the hole, till at last it was frozen in, though of course he did not know that. Then he pulled it out with a strong pull, and it snapped short off, and that's why Bruin goes about with a stumpy tail to this day!

☙ ☙ ☙

THE THREE LITTLE PIGS

ONCE upon a time, when pigs could talk and no one had ever heard of bacon, there lived an old piggy mother with her three little sons.

They had a very pleasant home in the middle of an oak forest, and were all just as happy as the day was long, until one sad year the acorn crop failed; then, indeed, poor Mrs. Piggy-wiggy often had hard work to make both ends meet.

One day she called her sons to her, and, with tears in her eyes, told them that she must send them out into the wide world to seek their fortune.

She kissed them all round, and the three little pigs set out upon their travels, each taking a different road, and carrying a bundle slung on a stick across his shoulder.

The first little pig had not gone far before he met a man carrying a bundle of straw; so he said to him: "Please, man, give me that straw to build me a house?" The man was very good-natured, so he gave him the bundle of straw, and the little pig built a pretty little house with it.

No sooner was it finished, and the little pig thinking of going to bed, than a wolf came along, knocked at the door, and said: "Little pig, little pig, let me come in."

But the little pig laughed softly, and answered: "No, no, by the hair of my chinny-chin-chin."

Then said the wolf sternly: "I will *make* you let me in; for I'll huff, and I'll puff, and I'll blow your house in!"

So he huffed and he puffed, and he blew his house in, because, you see, it was only of straw and too light; and when he had blown the house in, he ate up the little pig, and did not leave so much as the tip of his tail.

The second little pig also met a man, and *he* was carrying a bundle of furze; so piggy said politely: "Please, kind man, will you give me that furze to build me a house?"

The man agreed, and piggy set to work to build himself a snug little house before the night came on. It was scarcely finished when the wolf came along, and said: "Little pig, little pig, let me come in."

"No, no, by the hair of my chinny-chin-chin," answered the second little pig.

"Then I'll huff, and I'll puff, and I'll blow your house in!" said the wolf. So he huffed and he puffed, and he puffed, and he huffed, and at last he blew the house in, and gobbled the little pig up in a trice.

Now, the third little pig met a man with a load of bricks and mortar, and he said: "Please, man, will you give me those bricks to build a house with?"

So the man gave him the bricks and mortar, and a little trowel as well, and the little pig built himself a nice strong little house. As soon as it was finished the wolf came to call, just as he had done to the other little pigs, and said: "Little pig, little pig, let me in!"

But the little pig answered: "No, no, by the hair of my chinny-chin-chin."

"Then," said the wolf, "I'll huff, and I'll puff, and I'll blow your house in."

Well, he huffed, and he puffed, and he puffed, and he huffed, and he huffed, and he puffed; but he could *not* get the house down. At last he had no breath left to huff and puff with, so he sat down outside the little pig's house and thought for awhile.

Presently he called out: "Little pig, I know where there is a nice field of turnips."

"Where?" said the little pig.

"Behind the farmer's house, three fields away, and if you will be ready to-morrow morning I will call for you, and we will go together and get some breakfast."

"Very well," said the little pig; "I will be sure to be ready. What time do you mean to start?"

"At six o'clock," replied the wolf.

Well, the wise little pig got up at five, scampered away to the field, and brought home a fine load of turnips before the wolf came. At six o'clock the wolf came to the little pig's house and said: "Little pig, are you ready?"

"Ready!" cried the little pig. "Why, I have been to the field and come back long ago, and now I am busy boiling a potful of turnips for breakfast."

The wolf was very angry indeed; but he made up his mind to catch the little pig somehow or other; so he told him that he knew where there was a nice apple-tree.

"Where?" said the little pig.

"Round the hill in the squire's orchard," the wolf said. "So if you will promise to play me no tricks, I will come for you to-morrow morning at five o'clock, and we will go there together and get some rosy-cheeked apples."

The next morning piggy got up at four o'clock and was off and away long before the wolf came.

But the orchard was a long way off, and besides, he had the tree to climb, which is a difficult matter for a little pig, so that before the sack he had brought with him was quite filled he saw the wolf coming towards him.

He was dreadfully frightened, but he thought it better to put a good face on the matter, so when the wolf said: "Little pig, why are you here before me? Are they nice apples?" he replied at once: "Yes, very; I will throw down one for you to taste." So he picked an apple and threw it so far that whilst the wolf was running to fetch it he had time to jump down and scamper away home.

The next day the wolf came again, and told the little pig that there was going to be a fair in the town that afternoon, and asked him if he would go with him.

"Oh! yes," said the pig, "I will go with pleasure. What time will you be ready to start?"

"At half-past three," said the wolf.

Of course, the little pig started long before the time, went to the fair, and bought a fine large butter-churn, and was trotting away with it on his back when he saw the wolf coming.

He did not know what to do, so he crept into the churn to hide, and by so doing started it rolling.

Down the hill it went, rolling over and over, with the little pig squeaking inside.

The wolf could not think what the strange thing rolling down the hill could be; so he turned tail and ran away home in a fright without ever going to the fair at all. He went to the little pig's house to tell him how frightened he had been by a large round thing which came rolling past him down the hill.

"Ha! ha!" laughed the little pig; "so I frightened you, eh? I had been to the fair and bought a butter-churn; when I saw you I got inside it and rolled down the hill."

This made the wolf so angry that he declared that he *would* eat up the little pig, and that nothing should save him, for he would jump down the chimney.

But the clever little pig hung a pot full of water over the hearth and then made a blazing fire, and just as the wolf was coming down the chimney he took off the cover and in fell the wolf. In a second the little pig had popped the lid on again.

Then he boiled the wolf, and ate him for supper, and after that he lived quietly and comfortably all his days, and was never troubled by a wolf again.

CHILDREN'S FAVORITE POEMS

THE THREE CHILDREN

Three children sliding on the ice
  Upon a summer's day,
As it fell out they all fell in,
  The rest they ran away.

Now, had these children been at home,
  Or sliding on dry ground,
Ten thousand pounds to one penny
  They had not all been drowned.

You parents all that children have,
  And you too that have none,
If you would have them safe abroad
  Pray keep them safe at home.

ANONYMOUS

❧ ❧ ❧

THE OWL AND THE PUSSY-CAT

I

The Owl and the Pussy-cat went to sea
  In a beautiful pea-green boat:
They took some honey, and plenty of money
  Wrapped up in a five-pound note.

The Owl looked up to the stars above,
And sang to a small guitar,
"Oh lovely Pussy, O Pussy, my love,
What a beautiful Pussy you are,
You are,
You are!
What a beautiful Pussy you are!"

II

Pussy said to the Owl, "You elegant fowl,
How charmingly sweet you sing!
Oh! let us be married; too long we have tarried:
But what shall we do for a ring?"
They sailed away, for a year and a day,
To the land where the bong-tree grows;
And there in a wood a Piggy-wig stood,
With a ring at the end of his nose,
His nose,
His nose,
With a ring at the end of his nose.

III

"Dear Pig, are you willing to sell for one shilling
Your ring?" Said the Piggy, "I will."
So they took it away, and were married next day
By the turkey who lives on the hill.
They dined on mince and slices of quince,
Which they ate with a runcible spoon;
And hand in hand, on the edge of the sand,
They danced by the light of the moon,
The moon,
The moon,
They danced by the light of the moon.

Edward Lear

KINDNESS TO ANIMALS

Little children, never give
Pain to things that feel and live:
Let the gentle robin come
For the crumbs you save at home,—
As his meat you throw along
He'll repay you with a song;
Never hurt the timid hare
Peeping from her green grass lair,
Let her come and sport and play
On the lawn at close of day;
The little lark goes soaring high
To the bright windows of the sky,
Singing as if 'twere always spring,
And fluttering on an untired wing,—
Oh! let him sing his happy song,
Nor do these gentle creatures wrong.

UNKNOWN

❧ ❧ ❧

HOW DOTH THE LITTLE BUSY BEE

How doth the little busy bee
  Improve each shining hour,
And gather honey all the day
  From every opening flow'r!

How skilfully she builds her cell!
  How neat she spreads the wax!
And labors hard to store it well
  With the sweet food she makes.

In works of labor or of skill,
  I would be busy too;
For Satan finds some mischief still
  For idle hands to do.

In books, or work, or healthful play,
  Let my first years be past,
That I may give for ev'ry day
  Some good account at last.

ISAAC WATTS

☙ ☙ ☙

SUPPOSE!

Suppose, my little lady,
  Your doll should break her head,
Could you make it whole by crying
  Till your eyes and nose are red?
And wouldn't it be pleasanter
  To treat it as a joke,
And say you're glad 't was Dolly's,
  And not your head that broke?

Suppose you're dressed for walking,
  And the rain comes pouring down,
Will it clear off any sooner
  Because you scold and frown?
And wouldn't it be nicer
  For you to smile than pout,
And so make sunshine in the house
  When there is none without?

Suppose your task, my little man,
  Is very hard to get,
Will it make it any easier
  For you to sit and fret?
And would n't it be wiser
  Than waiting, like a dunce,
To go to work in earnest
  And learn the thing at once?

Suppose that some boys have a horse,
  And some a coach and pair,
Will it tire you less while walking
  To say, "It is n't fair?"
And would n't it be nobler
  To keep your temper sweet,
And in your heart be thankful
  You can walk upon your feet?

And suppose the world don't please you,
  Nor the way some people do,
Do you think the whole creation
  Will be altered just for you?
And is n't it, my boy or girl,
  The wisest, bravest plan,
Whatever comes, or does n't come,
  To do the best you can?

PHŒBE CARY

❧ ❧ ❧

TWINKLE, TWINKLE

Twinkle, twinkle, little star;
How I wonder what you are!
Up above the world so high,
Like a diamond in the sky.

When the glorious sun is set,
When the grass with dew is wet,
Then you show your little light,
Twinkle, twinkle, all the night.

When the blazing sun is gone,
When he nothing shines upon,
Then you show your little light,
Twinkle, twinkle, all the night.

In the dark-blue sky you keep,
And often through my curtains peep;
For you never shut your eye
Till the sun is in the sky.

As your bright and tiny spark
Lights the traveler in the dark,
Though I know not what you are,
Twinkle, twinkle, little star!

ANONYMOUS

PRETTY COW

Thank you, pretty cow, that made
Pleasant milk to soak my bread,
Every day and every night,
Warm, and fresh, and sweet, and white.

Do not chew the hemlock rank,
Growing on the weedy bank;
But the yellow cowslips eat,
That will make it very sweet.

Where the purple violet grows,
Where the bubbling water flows,
Where the grass is fresh and fine,
Pretty cow, go there and dine.

JANE TAYLOR

THE THREE LITTLE KITTENS

(A CAT'S TALE, WITH ADDITIONS)

Three little kittens lost their mittens;
And they began to cry,
O mother dear,
We very much fear
That we have lost our mittens.

Lost your mittens!
You naughty kittens!
Then you shall have no pie.
Mee-ow, mee-ow, mee-ow.
No, you shall have no pie.
Mee-ow, mee-ow, mee-ow.

The three little kittens found their mittens,
And they began to cry,
O mother dear,
See here, see here;
See, we have found our mittens.

Put on your mittens,
You silly kittens,
And you may have some pie.
Purr-r, purr-r, purr-r,
O let us have the pie.
Purr-r, purr-r, purr-r.

The three little kittens put on their mittens,
And soon ate up the pie;
O mother dear,
We greatly fear
That we have soiled our mittens.

Soiled your mittens!
You naughty kittens!
Then they began to sigh,
Mee-ow, mee-ow, mee-ow,
Then they began to sigh.
Mee-ow, mee-ow, mee-ow.

The three little kittens washed their mittens,
And hung them out to dry;
O mother dear,
Do not you hear,
That we have washed our mittens?

Washed your mittens!
O, you're good kittens.
But I smell a rat close by;
  Hush! hush! mee-ow, mee-ow.
We smell a rat close by,
  Mee-ow, mee-ow, mee-ow.

ELIZA LEE FOLLEN

☙ ☙ ☙

THE LAND OF COUNTERPANE

When I was sick and lay a-bed,
I had two pillows at my head,
And all my toys beside me lay
To keep me happy all the day.

And sometimes for an hour or so
I watched my leaden soldiers go,
With different uniforms and drills,
Among the bed-clothes, through the hills;

And sometimes sent my ships in fleets
All up and down among the sheets;
Or brought my trees and houses out,
And planted cities all about.

I was the giant great and still
That sits upon the pillow-hill,
And sees before him, dale and plain,
The pleasant land of counterpane.

ROBERT LOUIS STEVENSON

☙ ☙ ☙

THERE WAS A LITTLE GIRL

There was a little girl,
And she had a little curl
  Right in the middle of her forehead.
When she was good
She was very, very good,
  And when she was bad she was horrid.

I WAS THE GIANT GREAT AND STILL
THAT SITS UPON THE PILLOW-HILL.

One day she went upstairs,
When her parents, unawares,
  In the kitchen were occupied with meals,
And she stood upon her head
In her little trundle-bed,
  And then began hooraying with her heels.

Her mother heard the noise,
And she thought it was the boys
  A-playing at a combat in the attic;
But when she climbed the stair,
And found Jemima there,
  She took and she did spank her most emphatic.

HENRY WADSWORTH LONGFELLOW

☙ ☙ ☙

THE BOY WHO NEVER TOLD A LIE

Once there was a little boy,
  With curly hair and pleasant eye—
A boy who always told the truth,
  And never, never told a lie.

And when he trotted off to school,
  The children all about would cry,
"There goes the curly-headed boy—
  The boy that never tells a lie."

And everybody loved him so,
  Because he always told the truth,
That every day, as he grew up,
  'Twas said, "There goes the honest youth."

And when the people that stood near
  Would turn to ask the reason why,
The answer would be always this:
  "Because he never tells a lie."

FOREIGN CHILDREN

Little Indian, Sioux or Crow,
Little frosty Eskimo,
Little Turk or Japanee,
O! don't you wish that you were me?

You have seen the scarlet trees
And the lions over seas;
You have eaten ostrich eggs,
And turned the turtles off their legs.

Such a life is very fine,
But it's not so nice as mine:
You must often, as you trod,
Have wearied *not* to be abroad.

You have curious things to eat,
I am fed on proper meat;
You must dwell beyond the foam,
But I am safe and live at home.
Little Indian, Sioux or Crow,
Little frosty Eskimo,
Little Turk or Japanee,
O! don't you wish that you were me?

ROBERT LOUIS STEVENSON

THE UNSEEN PLAYMATE

When children are playing alone on the green,
In comes the playmate that never was seen.
When children are happy and lonely and good,
The Friend of the Children comes out of the wood.

Nobody heard him and nobody saw,
His is a picture you never could draw,
But he's sure to be present, abroad or at home,
When children are happy, and playing alone.

He lies in the laurels, he runs on the grass,
He sings when you tinkle the musical glass;
Whene'er you are happy and cannot tell why,
The Friend of the Children is sure to be by!

He loves to be little, he hates to be big,
'T is he that inhabits the caves that you dig;
'T is he when you play with your soldiers of tin
That sides with the Frenchmen and never can win.

'T is he when at night you go off to your bed,
Bids you go to your sleep and not trouble your head;
For wherever they're lying, in cupboard or shelf,
'T is he will take care of your playthings himself!

ROBERT LOUIS STEVENSON

❧ ❧ ❧

I SAW THREE SHIPS

I saw three ships come sailing in,
  On Christmas day, on Christmas day;
I saw three ships come sailing in,
  On Christmas day in the morning.

. . . .

Pray whither sailed those ships all three
  On Christmas day, on Christmas day?
Pray whither sailed those ships all three
  On Christmas day in the morning?

Oh, they sailed into Bethlehem
  On Christmas day, on Christmas day:
Oh, they sailed into Bethlehem
  On Christmas day in the morning.

And all the bells on earth shall ring
  On Christmas day, on Christmas day;
And all the bells on earth shall ring
  On Christmas day in the morning.

And all the angels in heaven shall sing
  On Christmas day, on Christmas day;
And all the angels in heaven shall sing
  On Christmas day in the morning.

And all the souls on earth shall sing
  On Christmas day, on Christmas day;
And all the souls on earth shall sing
  On Christmas day in the morning.

Old Carol

☘ ☘ ☘

A WAS AN ANT

A was an ant
  Who seldom stood still,
And who made a nice house
  In the side of a hill.
a
Nice little ant!

B was a book
  With a binding of blue,
And pictures and stories
  For me and for you.
b
Nice little book!

C was a cat
Who ran after a rat;
But his courage did fail
When she seized on his tail.
c
Crafty old cat!

D was a duck
With spots on his back,
Who lived in the water,
And always said 'Quack!"
d
Dear little duck!

E was an elephant,
Stately and wise:
He had tusks and a trunk,
And two queer little eyes.
e
Oh, what funny small eyes!

F was a fish
Who was caught in a net;
But he got out again,
And is quite alive yet.
f
Lively young fish!

G was a goat
Who was spotted with brown:
When he did not lie still
He walked up and down.
g
Good little goat!

H was a hat
  Which was all on one side;
Its crown was too high,
  And its brim was too wide.
h
Oh, what a hat!

I was some ice
So white and so nice,
But which nobody tasted;
And so it was wasted.
i
All that good ice!

J was a jackdaw
  Who hopped up and down
In the principal street
  Of a neighboring town.
j
All through the town!

K was a kite
Which flew out of sight,
  Above houses so high,
  Quite into the sky.
k
Fly away, kite!

L was a light
Which burned all the night,
  And lighted the gloom
  Of a very dark room.
l
Useful nice light!

M was a mill
Which stood on a hill,
And turned round and round
With a loud hummy sound.
m
Useful old mill!

N was a net
Which was thrown in the sea
To catch fish for dinner
For you and for me.
n
Nice little net!

O was an orange
So yellow and round:
When it fell off the tree,
It fell down to the ground.
o
Down to the ground!

P was a pig,
Who was not very big;
But his tail was too curly,
And that made him surly.
p
Cross little pig!

Q was a quail
With a very short tail;
And he fed upon corn
In the evening and morn.
q
Quaint little quail!

R was a rabbit,
Who had a bad habit
  Of eating the flowers
  In gardens and bowers.
r
Naughty fat rabbit!

S was the sugar-tongs,
  Nippity-nee,
To take up the sugar
  To put in our tea.
s
Nippity-nee!

T was a tortoise,
  All yellow and black:
He walked slowly away,
  And he never came back.
t
Torty never came back!

U was an urn
  All polished and bright,
And full of hot water
  At noon and at night.
u
Useful old urn!

V was a villa
  Which stood on a hill,
By the side of a river,
  And close to a mill.
v
Nice little villa!

W was a whale
With a very long tail,
Whose movements were frantic
Across the Atlantic.
w
Monstrous old whale!

X was King Xerxes,
Who, more than all Turks is,
Renowned for his fashion
Of fury and passion.
x
Angry old Xerxes!

Y was a yew,
Which flourished and grew
By a quiet abode
Near the side of a road.
y
Dark little yew!

Z was some zinc,
So shiny and bright,
Which caused you to wink
In the sun's merry light.
z
Beautiful zinc!

EDWARD LEAR

☙ ☙ ☙

THE TABLE AND THE CHAIR

I

Said the Table to the Chair,
"You can hardly be aware
How I suffer from the heat
And from chilblains on my feet.

If we took a little walk,
We might have a little talk;
Pray let us take the air,"
Said the Table to the Chair.

II

Said the Chair unto the Table,
"Now, you *know* we are not able:
How foolishly you talk,
When you know we *cannot* walk!"
Said the Table with a sigh,
"It can do no harm to try.
I've as many legs as you:
Why can't we walk on two?"

III

So they both went slowly down,
And walked about the town
With a cheerful bumpy sound
As they toddled round and round;
And everybody cried,
As they hastened to their side,
"See! the Table and the Chair
Have come out to take the air!"

IV

But in going down an alley,
To a castle in a valley,
They completely lost their way,
And wandered all the day;
Till, to see them safely back,
They paid a Ducky-quack,
And a Beetle, and a Mouse,
Who took them to their house.

V

Then they whispered to each other,
"O delightful little brother,
What a lovely walk we've taken!
Let us dine on beans and bacon."
So the Ducky and the leetle
Browny-Mousy and the Beetle
Dined, and danced upon their heads
Till they toddled to their beds.

EDWARD LEAR

☘ ☘ ☘

PRECOCIOUS PIGGY

Where are you going to, you little pig?
"I'm leaving my Mother, I'm growing so big!"
So big, young pig,
So young, so big!
What, leaving your Mother, you foolish young pig?

Where are you going to, you little pig?
"I've got a new spade, and I'm going to dig!"
To dig, little pig!
A little pig dig!
Well, I never saw a pig with a spade that could dig!

Where are you going to, you little pig?
"Why, I'm going to have a nice ride in a gig!"
In a gig, little pig!
What, a pig in a gig!
Well, I never yet saw a pig ride in a gig!

Where are you going to, you little pig?
"Well, I'm going to the Queen's Head to have a nice swig!"
A swig, little pig!
A pig have a swig!
What, a pig at the Queen's Head having a swig!

Where are you going to, you little pig?
"Why, I'm going to the Ball to dance a fine jig!"
A jig, little pig!
A pig dance a jig!
Well, I never before saw a pig dance a jig!

Where are you going to, you little pig?
"I'm going to the fair to run a fine rig!"
A rig, little pig!
A pig run a rig!
Well, I never before saw a pig run a rig!

Where are you going to, you little pig?
"I'm going to the Barber's to buy me a wig!"
A wig, little pig!
A pig in a wig!
Why, whoever before saw a pig in a wig!

. . . .

Thomas Hood

❧ ❧ ❧

A BOY'S SONG

Where the pools are bright and deep,
Where the gray trout lies asleep,
Up the river and o'er the lea,
That's the way for Billy and me.

Where the blackbird sings the latest,
Where the hawthorn blooms the sweetest,
Where the nestlings chirp and flee,
That's the way for Billy and me.

Where the mowers mow the cleanest,
Where the hay lies thick and greenest,
There to trace the homeward bee,
That's the way for Billy and me.

Where the hazel bank is steepest,
Where the shadow falls the deepest,
Where the clustering nuts fall free,
That's the way for Billy and me.

Why the boys should drive away
Little sweet maidens from the play,
Or love to banter and fight so well,
That's the thing I never could tell.

But this I know, I love to play,
Through the meadow, among the hay;
Up the water and o'er the lea,
That's the way for Billy and me.

JAMES HOGG

☙ ☙ ☙

BUTTERCUPS AND DAISIES

Buttercups and daisies,
  Oh, the pretty flowers;
Coming ere the spring time,
  To tell of sunny hours.
While the trees are leafless,
  While the fields are bare,
Buttercups and daisies
  Spring up here and there.

Ere the snowdrop peepeth,
  Ere the crocus bold,
Ere the early primrose
  Opes its paly gold,
Somewhere on the sunny bank
  Buttercups are bright;
Somewhere 'mong the frozen grass
  Peeps the daisy white.

Little hardy flowers,
  Like to children poor,
Playing in their sturdy health
  By their mother's door,
Purple with the north wind,
  Yet alert and bold;
Fearing not, and caring not,
  Though they be a-cold!

What to them is winter!
  What are stormy showers!
Buttercups and daisies
  Are these human flowers!
He who gave them hardships
  And a life of care,
Gave them likewise hardy strength
  And patient hearts to bear.

MARY HOWITT

❧ ❧ ❧

THE VIOLET

Down in a green and shady bed
  A modest violet grew;
Its stalk was bent, it hung its head,
  As if to hide from view.

And yet it was a lovely flower,
  Its color bright and fair;
It might have graced a rosy bower
  Instead of hiding there.

Yet there it was content to bloom,
  In modest tints arrayed;
And there diffused its sweet perfume
  Within the silent shade.

Then let me to the valley go,
  This pretty flower to see,
That I may also learn to grow
  In sweet humility.

JANE TAYLOR

☙ ☙ ☙

IF EVER I SEE

If ever I see,
On bush or tree,
Young birds in their pretty nest,
I must not in play,
Steal the birds away,
To grieve their mother's breast.

My mother, I know,
Would sorrow so,
Should I be stolen away;
So I'll speak to the birds
In my softest words,
Nor hurt them in my play.

And when they can fly
In the bright blue sky,
They'll warble a song to me;
And then if I'm sad
It will make me glad
To think they are happy and free.

LYDIA MARIA CHILD

☙ ☙ ☙

THE LITTLE LAND

When at home alone I sit
And am very tired of it,
I have just to shut my eyes
To go sailing through the skies—

To go sailing far away
To the pleasant Land of Play;
To the fairy land afar
Where the Little People are;
Where the clover-tops are trees,
And the rain-pools are the seas,
And the leaves like little ships
Sail about on tiny trips;
And above the daisy tree
    Through the grasses,
High o'erhead the Bumble Bee
    Hums and passes.
In that forest to and fro
I can wander, I can go;
See the spider and the fly,
And the ants go marching by
Carrying parcels with their feet
Down the green and grassy street.
I can in the sorrel sit
Where the ladybird alit.
I can climb the jointed grass;
    And on high
See the greater swallows pass
    In the sky,
And the round sun rolling by
Heeding no such thing as I.

Through the forest I can pass
Till, as in a looking-glass,
Humming fly and daisy tree
And my tiny self I see,
Painted very clear and neat
On the rain-pool at my feet.
Should a leaflet come to land
Drifting near to where I stand,
Straight I'll board that tiny boat
Round the rain-pool sea to float.

Little thoughtful creatures sit
On the grassy coasts of it;
Little things with lovely eyes
See me sailing with surprise.
Some are clad in armor green—
(These have sure to battle been!)
Some are pied with ev'ry hue,
Black and crimson, gold and blue;
Some have wings and swift are gone;—
But they all look kindly on.

When my eyes I once again
Open and see all things plain;
High bare walls, great bare floor;
Great big knobs on drawer and door;
Great big people perched on chairs,
Stitching tucks and mending tears,
Each a hill that I could climb,
And talking nonsense all the time—
O dear me,
That I could be
A sailor on the rain-pool sea,
A climber in the clover-tree,
And just come back, a sleepy-head,
Late at night to go to bed.

Robert Louis Stevenson

☙ ☙ ☙

A LOBSTER QUADRILLE

"Will you walk a little faster?" said a whiting to a snail,
"There's a porpoise close behind us, and he's treading on my tail.
See how eagerly the lobsters and the turtles all advance!
They are waiting on the shingle—will you come and join the dance?

Will you, won't you, will you, won't you, will
you join the dance?
Will you, won't you, will you, won't you, won't
you join the dance?

"You can really have no notion how delightful it will be
When they take us up and throw us, with the
lobsters, out to sea!"
But the snail replied, "Too far, too far!" and
gave a look askance—
Said he thanked the whiting kindly, but he
would not join the dance.
Would not, could not, would not, could not,
would not join the dance,
Would not, could not, would not, could not,
could not join the dance.

"What matters it how far we go?" his scaly
friend replied,
"There is another shore, you know, upon the
other side.
The further off from England the nearer is to
France—
Then turn not pale, beloved snail, but come and
join the dance.
Will you, won't you, will you, won't you, will
you join the dance?
Will you, won't you, will you, won't you, won't
you join the dance?"

LEWIS CARROLL

❧ ❧ ❧

WHERE GO THE BOATS?

Dark brown is the river,
Golden is the sand.
It flows along forever
With trees on either hand.

Green leaves a-floating,
  Castles of the foam,
Boats of mine a-boating—
  Where will all come home?

On goes the river
  And out past the mill,
Away down the valley,
  Away down the hill.

Away down the river,
  A hundred miles or more,
Other little children
  Shall bring my boats ashore.

ROBERT LOUIS STEVENSON

❧ ❧ ❧

THE WIND AND THE MOON

Said the Wind to the Moon, "I will blow you out;
    You stare
    In the air
    Like a ghost in a chair,
Always looking what I am about—
I hate to be watched; I'll blow you out."

The Wind blew hard, and out went the Moon.
    So, deep
    On a heap
    Of clouds to sleep,
Down lay the Wind, and slumbered soon,
Muttering low, "I've done for that Moon."

He turned in his bed; she was there again!
    On high
    In the sky,
    With her one ghost eye,
The Moon shone white and alive and plain.
Said the Wind, "I will blow you out again."

The Wind blew hard, and the Moon grew dim.
"With my sledge,
And my wedge,
I have knocked off her edge!
If only I blow right fierce and grim,
The creature will soon be dimmer than dim."

He blew and he blew, and she thinned to a thread.
"One puff
More's enough
To blow her to snuff!
One good puff more where the last was bred,
And glimmer, glimmer, glum will go the thread."

He blew a great blast, and the thread was gone.
In the air
Nowhere
Was a moonbeam bare;
Far off and harmless the shy stars shone—
Sure and certain the Moon was gone!

The Wind he took to his revels once more;
On down,
In town,
Like a merry-mad clown,
He leaped and hallooed with whistle and roar—
"What's that?" The glimmering thread once more!

He flew in a rage—he danced and blew;
But in vain
Was the pain
Of his bursting brain;
For still the broader the Moon-scrap grew,
The broader he swelled his big cheeks and blew.

Slowly she grew—till she filled the night,
And shone
On her throne
In the sky alone,
A matchless, wonderful silvery light,
Radiant and lovely, the queen of the night.

Said the Wind: "What a marvel of power am I!
With my breath,
Good faith!
I blew her to death—
First blew her away right out of the sky—
Then blew her in; what strength have I!"

But the Moon she knew nothing about the affair;
For high
In the sky,
With her one white eye,
Motionless, miles above the air,
She had never heard the great Wind blare.

George Macdonald

WHERE ARE YOU GOING, MY PRETTY MAID?

"Where are you going, my pretty maid?"
"I am going a-milking, sir," she said.
"May I go with you, my pretty maid?"
"You're kindly welcome, sir," she said.
"What is your father, my pretty maid?"
"My father's a farmer, sir," she said.
"What is your fortune, my pretty maid?"
"My face is my fortune, sir," she said.
"Then I won't marry you, my pretty maid."
"Nobody asked you, sir," she said.

Anonymous

THE LOST DOLL

I once had a sweet little doll, dears,
  The prettiest doll in the world;
Her cheeks were so red and white, dears,
  And her hair was so charmingly curled.
But I lost my poor little doll, dears,
  As I played on the heath one day;
And I cried for her more than a week, dears,
  But I never could find where she lay.

I found my poor little doll, dears,
  As I played on the heath one day;
Folks say she is terribly changed, dears,
  For her paint is all washed away,
And her arms trodden off by the cows, dears,
  And her hair not the least bit curled;
Yet for old sake's sake, she is still, dears,
  The prettiest doll in the world.

Charles Kingsley

✣ ✣ ✣

FOREIGN LANDS

Up into the cherry tree
Who should climb but little me?
I held the trunk with both my hands
And looked abroad on foreign lands.

I saw the next-door garden lie,
Adorned with flowers, before my eye,
And many pleasant faces more
That I had never seen before.

I found my poor little doll dears
As I played on the heath one day

I saw the dimpling river pass
And be the sky's blue looking-glass;
The dusty roads go up and down
With people tramping in to town.

If I could find a higher tree
Farther and farther I should see,
To where the grown-up river slips
Into the sea among the ships,

To where the roads on either hand
Lead onward into fairy land,
Where all the children dine at five,
And all the playthings come alive.

ROBERT LOUIS STEVENSON

❧ ❧ ❧

BED IN SUMMER

In winter I get up at night
And dress by yellow candle-light.
In summer, quite the other way,
I have to go to bed by day.

I have to go to bed and see
The birds still hopping on the tree,
Or hear the grown-up people's feet
Still going past me in the street.

And does it not seem hard to you,
When all the sky is clear and blue,
And I should like so much to play,
To have to go to bed by day?

ROBERT LOUIS STEVENSON

TRY AGAIN

'Tis a lesson you should heed,
Try, try, try again;
If at first you don't succeed,
Try, try, try again.

Once or twice though you should fail,
Try again;
If you would at last prevail,
Try again.
If we strive, 'tis no disgrace
Though we may not win the race;
What should you do in that case?
Try again.

If you find your task is hard,
Try again;
Time will bring you your reward,
Try again.
All that other folks can do,
With your patience should not you?
Only keep this rule in view—
Try again.

ANONYMOUS

☙ ☙ ☙

A GOOD PLAY

We built a ship upon the stairs
All made of the back-bedroom chairs,
And filled it full of sofa pillows
To go a-sailing on the billows.

We took a saw and several nails,
And water in the nursery pails;
And Tom said, "Let us also take
An apple and a slice of cake;"—
Which was enough for Tom and me
To go a-sailing on, till tea.

We sailed along for days and days,
And had the very best of plays;
But Tom fell out and hurt his knee,
So there was no one left but me.

Robert Louis Stevenson

☙ ☙ ☙

GOOD NIGHT AND GOOD MORNING

A fair little girl sat under a tree
Sewing as long as her eyes could see;
Then smoothed her work and folded it right,
And said, "Dear work, good night, good night!"

Such a number of rooks came over her head,
Crying, "Caw, caw!" on their way to bed,
She said, as she watched their curious flight,
"Little black things, good night, good night!"

The horses neighed, and the oxen lowed,
The sheep's "Bleat! bleat!" came over the road;
All seeming to say, with a quiet delight,
"Good little girl, good night, good night!"

She did not say to the sun, "Good night!"
Though she saw him there like a ball of light;
For she knew he had God's time to keep
All over the world and never could sleep.

The tall pink foxglove bowed his head;
The violets courtesied, and went to bed;
And good little Lucy tied up her hair,
And said, on her knees, her favorite prayer.

And, while on her pillow she softly lay,
She knew nothing more till again it was day;
And all things said to the beautiful sun,
"Good morning, good morning! our work is
begun."

RICHARD MONCKTON MILNES
(LORD HOUGHTON)

☙ ☙ ☙

THE WIND

I saw you toss the kites on high
And blow the birds about the sky;
And all around I heard you pass,
Like ladies' skirts across the grass—
O wind, a-blowing all day long,
O wind, that sings so loud a song!

I saw the different things you did,
But always you yourself you hid.
I felt you push, I heard you call,
I could not see yourself at all—
O wind, a-blowing all day long,
O wind, that sings so loud a song!

O you that are so strong and cold,
O blower, are you young or old?
Are you a beast of field and tree,
Or just a stronger child than me?
O wind, a-blowing all day long,
O wind, that sings so loud a song!

ROBERT LOUIS STEVENSON

A fair little girl sat under a tree,
Sewing as long as her eyes could see.

THE SPIDER AND THE FLY

"Will you walk into my parlor?" said the spider to the fly;
"'Tis the prettiest little parlor that ever you did spy.
The way into my parlor is up a winding stair,
And I have many curious things to show when you are there."
"Oh no, no," said the little fly; "to ask me is in vain,
For who goes up your winding stair can ne'er come down
again."

"I'm sure you must be weary, dear, with soaring up so high.
Will you rest upon my little bed?" said the spider to the fly.
"There are pretty curtains drawn around; the sheets are fine
and thin,
And if you like to rest a while, I'll snugly tuck you in!"
"Oh no, no," said the little fly, "for I've often heard it said,
They never, never wake again who sleep upon your bed!"

Said the cunning spider to the fly: "Dear friend, what can
I do
To prove the warm affection I've always felt for you?
I have within my pantry good store of all that's nice;
I'm sure you're very welcome—will you please to take a
slice?"
"Oh no, no," said the little fly; "kind sir, that cannot be:
I've heard what's in your pantry, and I do not wish to see!"

"Sweet creature!" said the spider, "you're witty and you're
wise;
How handsome are your gauzy wings; how brilliant are your
eyes!
I have a little looking-glass upon my parlor shelf;
If you'll step in one moment, dear, you shall behold your-
self."
"I thank you, gentle sir," she said, "for what you're pleased
to say,
And, bidding you good morning now, I'll call another day."

The spider turned him round about, and went into his den,
For well he knew the silly fly would soon come back again:
So he wove a subtle web in a little corner sly,
And set his table ready to dine upon the fly;
Then came out to his door again, and merrily did sing:
"Come hither, hither, pretty fly, with pearl and silver wing;
Your robes are green and purple; there's a crest upon your head;
Your eyes are like the diamond bright, but mine are dull as lead!"

Alas, alas! how very soon this silly little fly,
Hearing his wily, flattering words, came slowly flitting by;
With buzzing wings she hung aloft, then near and nearer drew,
Thinking only of her brilliant eyes and green and purple hue,
Thinking only of her crested head. Poor, foolish thing! at last
Up jumped the cunning spider, and fiercely held her fast;
He dragged her up his winding stair, into the dismal den—
Within his little parlor—but she ne'er came out again!

And now, dear little children, who may this story read,
To idle, silly, flattering words I pray you ne'er give heed;
Unto an evil counselor close heart and ear and eye,
And take a lesson from this tale of the spider and the fly.

Mary Howitt

❧ ❧ ❧

LET DOGS DELIGHT TO BARK AND BITE

Let dogs delight to bark and bite,
For God hath made them so;
Let bears and lions growl and fight,
For 'tis their nature to;

But, children, you should never let
  Your angry passions rise:
Your little hands were never made
  To tear each other's eyes.

Let love through all your actions run,
  And all your words be mild;
Live like the blessèd Virgin's Son,—
  That sweet and lovely child.

His soul was gentle as a lamb;
  And as his stature grew,
He grew in favor both with man
  And God his father, too.

Now, Lord of all, he reigns above;
  And from his heavenly throne,
He sees what children dwell in love,
  And marks them for his own.

Isaac Watts

CHILD'S EVENING HYMN

Now the day is over,
  Night is drawing nigh,
Shadows of the evening
  Steal across the sky.

Now the darkness gathers,
  Stars begin to peep,
Birds and beasts and flowers
  Soon will be asleep.

Jesu, give the weary
  Calm and sweet repose;
With thy tenderest blessing
  May our eyelids close.

Grant to little children
  Visions bright of thee;
Guard the sailors tossing
  On the deep blue sea.

Comfort every sufferer
  Watching late in pain;
Those who plan some evil
  From their sin restrain.

Through the long night-watches
  May thine angels spread
Their white wings above me,
  Watching round my bed.

When the morning wakens,
  Then may I arise
Pure and fresh and sinless
  In thy holy eyes.

Glory to the Father,
  Glory to the Son,
And to thee, blessed Spirit,
  Whilst all ages run. AMEN.

SABINE BARING-GOULD

CHILDREN'S FAVORITE STORIES

HANSEL AND GRETEL

MANY years ago, a woodcutter and his wife, with their two children, Hansel and Gretel, lived upon the outskirts of a dense wood. They were very poor, so that when a famine fell upon the land, and bread became dear, they could no longer afford to buy sufficient food for the whole family.

One night, as the poor man lay tossing on his hard bed, he cried aloud in his grief and anguish:

"Alas! what will become of us? How can I feed my hungry little ones when we have no food for ourselves?"

"Listen to me, good-man," answered his wife, who was stepmother to the children. "As it is no longer possible for us to keep our children, we will take them into the wood with us to-morrow, light a fire for them, and give each a piece of bread and leave them. They will not easily find their way back, and so we shall be rid of the burden of them."

But the father said: "No, no! I could not find it in my heart to leave my darlings to perish. The wild beasts would tear them limb from limb."

"Then," answered the wife, "we must all four die of hunger." She gave her husband no peace until he promised to do as she wished, and at last, very unwillingly, he consented.

Now, the two children had been too hungry to go to sleep that night, and so it happened that they overheard all that their parents were saying. Gretel wept bitterly, but brave little Hansel did his best to comfort her. "Don't be afraid," he said; "I will take care of you."

As soon as his father and stepmother were asleep, he slipped on his coat, and, opening the door softly, went out into the garden. The moon was shining brightly, and by its light he could see the little white pebbles that lay scattered in front of the house, shining like little pieces of silver. He stooped and filled his pockets as full as he could, and then went back to Gretel, and once more bidding her be comforted, for God would be sure to watch over them, he jumped into bed, and they both fell fast asleep.

Early in the morning, before the sun had risen, the stepmother came and wakened the children. "Rise, little lie-a-beds," she said, "and come with us into the wood to gather fuel."

She gave them each a piece of bread for their dinner, and told them to be sure not to eat it too soon, for they would get nothing more.

Gretel carried the bread in her pinafore, because Hansel had his pockets full, and then they all set out upon their way to the wood.

As they trudged along, the father noticed that his little son kept turning back to look at the house. "Take care, my boy," he said, "or you will slip. What are you looking at so earnestly?"

"I am watching my kitten, father: she is sitting on the roof to bid me good-by."

"Silly little lad, that is not your cat," said the stepmother; "it is only the morning sun shining on the chimney."

But Hansel had not been watching his cat at all; he had stayed behind to drop the pebbles upon the path.

When they reached the thickest part of the forest, the father bade the children gather wood, that he might kindle a fire for them, so that they might rest beside it and warm themselves whilst he and his wife were cutting the fuel. So they gathered a pile of brushwood and twigs, and as soon as it was well alight, the parents left them, promising to return as soon as they had finished their work.

Hansel and Gretel sat down by the fire, and when midday came they ate their bread and sat listening to the strokes of their father's axe, thinking all the time that he was near to them. But what they heard was only a dry branch which the man had bound to a tree, so that the wind swung it hither and thither, and the noise it made deceived the children. At last the poor, tired, little eyelids closed, and, side by side, brother and sister fell asleep.

When they awoke, the night was very dark, and Gretel was frightened, and began to cry. Hansel put his arms around her and whispered. "Wait, dearie, till the moon rises; we shall soon find our way home then."

As soon as the bright moon rose, Hansel took his little sister by the hand, and all night long they followed the track of the little white pebbles, until at daybreak they came to their father's house.

They knocked at the door, and no sooner did the stepmother open it than she began to scold them for having stayed out so long in the wood; but the father greeted them kindly, for he had grieved sorely for his little ones.

In a short time they were as badly off as ever, and one night they again heard their mother trying to persuade her husband to take them out into the wood and lose them. "There is nothing left in the house but half a loaf of bread," she said; "for our own sakes it is better to get rid of the children; but this time we will lead them farther away, so that they will not be able to find their way home."

But the man would not agree. "Better to divide our last morsel with them," he said, "and then die together."

His wife would not listen to what he said, but scolded him for his want of thought for her; and at last the poor man gave way a second time, just as he had done at first.

But the children had overheard all that was said, and as soon as the mother and father were asleep, Hansel stole down to the door, meaning to go and collect pebbles as he had done before; but the door was locked and bolted, and he could not get out. "Never mind, Gretel," he said consolingly, "the good God will surely help us."

Early in the morning the woman wakened the children, and, giving them a small piece of bread, bade them follow her and their father into the wood. As they went, Hansel crumbled his morsel of bread in his pocket and strewed the crumbs upon the path.

"Come, Hansel," said the father, "don't loiter so, sonny What can you see to stare at so often?"

"My little dove, father. It is sitting on the housetop, bidding me good-by."

"Nonsense," said the woman, "it is not your dove; it is only the rising sun shining upon the chimney."

Hansel did not answer, but he went on strewing his crumbs carefully until the last morsel of bread was gone.

Deeper and deeper into the wood they went, where the children had never been before. There a great fire was kindled, and the mother said: "Stay here, children, whilst your father and I go to cut wood. If you are tired you may sleep a while, and we will fetch you when it is time to go home."

When dinner-time came, Gretel divided her piece of bread with Hansel, because he had scattered all his share upon the road; and then they went to sleep. The evening shadows fell, but still no one came to fetch the poor children, and it was not until midnight that they awakened.

Hansel put his arms round his sister and told her not to fear, for when the moon rose they would easily be able to see the crumbs, and so find their way home again.

So when the moon rose they set out upon their way; but alas! there were no crumbs to be seen, for the little birds that lived in the green wood were as hungry as the children, and had eaten them all up.

"We will find the way somehow," cried cheerful little Hansel; but though they traveled all night long, and the next day too, they could not find it. Poor little mites, how tired and hungry they were, for they had nothing to eat but the berries that grew by the roadside!

When at length the weary little feet could go no farther, the children lay down beneath a tree and slept.

On the third day they were still as far away as ever, and it seemed to them that the longer they walked the deeper they got into the wood, and they began to be afraid that they would die of cold and hunger.

But presently, when the midday sun was shining brightly, they noticed a little snow-white bird singing so sweetly that they could not help but stay to listen. When the birdie's song was ended, he spread his wings and flew away.

The children followed him until they reached a little house, on the roof of which he perched. Then the children saw with surprise that the strange little house was built entirely of bread, roofed with cakes, and with windows of barley sugar.

"See, Gretel," cried Hansel joyfully, "there is food for us in plenty. I will take a piece of the roof, and you shall have one of the windows."

He stretched out his hand to help himself, and Gretel had already begun to nibble one of the window-panes, when suddenly they heard a voice call from within:—

"Nibbly, nibbly, mouse!
Who's nibbling at my house?"

The children answered quickly:—

"'Tis my Lady Wind that blows,
As round about the house she goes."

And then they went on eating as though nothing had happened for the cake of which the roof was made just suited Hansel's taste, whilst the barley-sugar window-panes were better than any sweetmeat Gretel had ever tasted before.

All at once the door of the cottage flew wide open, and out came an old, old woman, leaning upon a crutch. The children were so frightened that they dropped their food and clung to each other.

The old woman nodded her head to them, and said: "Who brought you here, my pets? Come inside, come inside; no one will hurt you."

She took their hands and led them into the house, and set before them all kinds of delicious foods, milk, sugared pancakes, apples, and nuts. When they had finished their meal she showed them two cosy little white beds, and as Hansel and Gretel lay snugly tucked up in them, they thought to themselves that surely they had now found the most delightful place in the whole wide world.

But the old woman had only pretended to be friendly and kind, for she was really a wicked old witch, who was always lying in wait to catch little children, indeed, she had built the little house of bread and cakes especially to entice them in. Whenever anyone came into her power, she cooked and ate him, and thought what a fine feast she had had.

Witches have red eyes and cannot see far, but they have keen scent, like animals, and can tell at once when a human being is near to them.

As soon as Hansel and Gretel came into her neighborhood she laughed to herself and said mockingly: "Ha, ha! they are mine already; they will not easily escape me."

Early in the morning, before the children were awake, she stood beside them and admired their rosy cheeks and soft round limbs.

"What nice tit-bits for me," murmured she. Then, seizing Hansel by the hand, she led him to a little stable, and, in spite of his cries and screams, shut him up and left him. Then she shook Gretel until she was awake, and bade her get up at once and carry food and drink to her brother, and it must be of the best too, for she wished to fatten him.

"When he is nice and plump, I shall eat him," said the cruel old witch. Gretel wept bitterly, but it was quite in vain, for she was obliged to do the witch's bidding; and every day she cooked the choicest food for her brother, while she herself lived upon nothing but oyster-shells.

Day by day the old woman visited the stable and called to Hansel to put his finger through the window bars, that she might see if he were getting fat; but the little fellow held out a bone instead, and as her eyes were dim with age, she mistook the bone for the boy's finger, and thought how thin and lean he was. When a whole month had passed without Hansel becoming the least bit fatter, the old witch lost patience and declared she would wait no longer. "Hurry, Gretel," she said to the little girl, "fill the pot with water, for to-morrow, be he lean or fat, Hansel shall be cooked for my dinner."

The tears chased each other down Gretel's cheeks as she carried in the water, and she sobbed aloud in her grief. "Dear God," she cried, "we have no one to help us but Thou. Alas! if only the wild beasts in the wood had devoured us, at least we should have died together."

HANSEL AND GRETEL.

"Cease your chattering," cried the old witch angrily. "It will not help you, so you may as well be still."

The next morning poor Gretel was forced to light the fire and hang the great pot of water over it, and then the witch said: "First we will bake. I have kneaded the dough, and heated the oven; you shall creep inside it to see if it is hot enough to bake the bread."

But Gretel guessed that the old witch meant to shut the door upon her and roast her, so she pretended that she did not know how to get in.

"Silly goose," said the witch. "The door is wide enough, to be sure. Why, even I could get inside it." As she spoke, she popped her head into the oven. In a moment Gretel sprang towards her, pushed her inside, shut the iron door, and shot the bolt. Oh! how she squealed and shrieked, but Gretel ran off as fast as she could, and so there was an end of the cruel old witch.

Quick as thought, Gretel ran to her brother. "We are saved, Hansel," she cried, opening the door of the stable, "the wicked old witch is dead."

Hansel flew from his prison as a bird from its cage, and the two happy little children kissed each other and jumped for joy. No longer afraid of the old witch, they entered the house, hand in hand, and then they saw that in every corner of the room were boxes of pearls and diamonds, and all kinds of precious gems.

"Ah!" said Hansel merrily, "these are better than pebbles, Gretel," and he stuffed his pockets with the jewels, whilst Gretel filled her pinafore. "Now," said Hansel, "we will leave the witch's wood behind us as fast as we can."

So off they ran, and never stopped until they came to a lake, upon which swam a large white duck.

"How can we cross," said Hansel, "for there is no bridge anywhere?"

"And no ship either," Gretel answered; "but we will ask the pretty white duck to carry us over." So they cried aloud:—

"Little duck, little duck,
With wings so white,
Carry us over
The waters bright."

The duck came at once, and, taking Hansel upon her back, carried him over to the other side, and then did the same for Gretel. They went merrily on their way, and very soon they found themselves in a part of the wood they knew quite well.

When they saw the roof of their father's house in the distance they began to run, and, breathless with haste, half laughing and half crying, they rushed into the cottage and flung themselves into their father's arms.

Oh! how pleased he was to see them once again, for he had not known a happy hour since he had left them alone in the wood. Gretel shook out her pinafore, and Hansel emptied his pockets, and the floor of the little room was quite covered with glittering precious stones.

So now their troubles were at an end, for the cruel stepmother was dead, and Hansel and Gretel and their father lived together happily ever after.

My story is ended, and see, there runs a little mouse, and the first who catches him shall have a fur cap made from his skin.

❧ ❧ ❧

THE FAIR CATHERINE AND PIF-PAF POLTRIE

GOOD day, Father Hollenthe. How do you do?" "Very well, I thank you, Pif-paf Poltrie." "May I marry your daughter?" "Oh, yes! if the mother Malcho (*Milk-Cow*), the brother Hohenstolz (*High and Mighty*), the sister Kâsetraut (*Cheese-maker*), and the fair Catherine are willing, it may be so."

"Where is, then, the mother Malcho?"

"In the stable, milking the cow."

"Good day, mother Malcho. How do you do?" "Very well, I thank you, Pif-paf Poltrie." "May I marry your daughter?" "Oh, yes! if the father Hollenthe, the brother Hohenstolz, the sister Kâsetraut, and the fair Catherine are willing, it may be so."

"Where is, then, the brother Hohenstolz?"

"In the yard, chopping up the wood."

"Good day, brother Hohenstolz. How are you?" "Very well, I thank you, Pif-paf Poltrie." "May I marry your sister?" "Oh, yes! if the father Hollenthe, the mother Malcho, the sister Kâsetraut, and the fair Catherine are willing, it may be so.

"Where is, then, the sister Kâsetraut?"

"In the garden, cutting the cabbages."

"Good day, sister Kâsetraut. How do you do?" "Very well, I thank you, Pif-paf Poltrie." "May I marry your sister?" "Oh, yes! if the father Hollenthe, the mother Malcho the brother Hohenstolz, and the fair Catherine are willing, it may be so."

"Where is, then, the fair Catherine?"

"In her chamber, counting out her pennies."

"Good day, fair Catherine. How do you do?" "Very well, I thank you, Pif-paf Poltrie." "Will you be my bride?" "Oh, yes! if the father Hollenthe, the mother Malcho, the brother Hohenstolz, and the sister Kâsetraut are willing, so am I."

"How much money have you, fair Catherine?"

"Fourteen pennies in bare money, two and a half farthings owing to me, half a pound of dried apples, a handful of prunes, and a handful of roots; and don't you call that a capital dowry? Pif-paf Poltrie, what trade are you? Are you a tailor?"

"Better than that."

"A shoemaker?"

"Better still!"

"A plowman?"

"Better still!"

"A joiner?"

"Better still!"

"A smith?"

"Better still!"

"A miller?"

"Better still!"

"Perhaps a broom-binder?"

"Yes, so I am; now, is not that a pretty trade?"

THE WOLF AND THE FOX

A WOLF, once upon a time, caught a fox. It happened one day that they were both going through the forest, and the wolf said to his companion: "Get me some food, or I will eat you up."

The fox replied: "I know a farmyard where there are a couple of young lambs, which, if you wish, we will fetch."

This proposal pleased the wolf, so they went, and the fox, stealing first one of the lambs, brought it to the wolf, and then ran away. The wolf devoured it quickly, but was not contented, and went to fetch the other lamb by himself, but he did it so awkwardly that he aroused the attention of the mother, who began to cry and bleat loudly, so that the peasants ran up. There they found the wolf, and beat him so unmercifully that he ran, howling and limping, to the fox, and said: "You have led me to a nice place, for, when I went to fetch the other lamb, the peasants came and beat me terribly!"

"Why are you such a glutton, then?" asked the fox.

The next day they went again into the fields, and the covetous wolf said to the fox: "Get me something to eat now, or I will devour you!"

The fox said he knew a country house where the cook was going that evening to make some pancakes, and thither they went. When they arrived, the fox sneaked and crept around round the house, until he at last discovered where the dish was standing, out of which he stole six pancakes, and took them to the wolf, saying, "There is something for you to eat!" and then ran away. The wolf dispatched these in a minute or two, and, wishing to taste some more, he went and seized the dish, but took it away so hurriedly that it broke in pieces. The noise of its fall brought out the woman, who, as soon as she saw the wolf, called her people, who, hastening up, beat him with such a good will that he ran home to the fox, howling, with two lame legs! "What a horrid place you have drawn me into now," cried he; "the peasants have caught me, and dressed my skin finely!"

"Why, then, are you such a glutton?" said the fox.

When they went out again the third day, the wolf limping along with weariness, he said to the fox: "Get me something to eat now, or I will devour you!"

The fox said he knew a man who had just killed a pig, and salted the meat down in a cask in his cellar, and that they could get at it. The wolf replied that he would go with him on condition that he helped him if he could not escape. "Oh, of course I will, on mine own account!" said the fox, and showed him the tricks and ways by which they could get into the cellar. When they went in there was meat in abundance, and the wolf was enraptured at the sight. The fox, too, had a taste, but kept looking round while eating, and ran frequently to the hole by which they had entered, to see if his body would slip through it easily. Presently the wolf asked: "Why are you running about so, you fox, jumping in and out?" "I want to see if any one is coming," replied the fox cunningly; "but mind you do not eat too much!"

The wolf said he would not leave till the cask was quite empty; and meanwhile the peasant, who had heard the noise made by the fox, entered the cellar. The fox, as soon as he saw him, made a spring, and was through the hole in a jiffy; and the wolf tried to follow his example, but he had eaten so much that his body was too big for the opening, and he stuck fast. Then came the peasant with a cudgel, and beat him sorely; but the fox leaped away into the forest, very glad to get rid of the old glutton.

☘ ☘ ☘

DISCREET HANS

HANS'S mother asked: "Whither are you going, Hans?" "To Grethel's," replied he. "Behave well, Hans." "I will take care; good-by, mother." "Good-by, Hans."

Hans came to Grethel. "Good day," said he. "Good

day," replied Grethel, "what treasure do you bring to-day?" "I bring nothing. Have you anything to give?" Grethel presented Hans with a needle. "Good-by," said he. "Good-by, Hans." Hans took the needle, stuck it in a load of hay, and walked home behind the wagon.

"Good evening, mother." "Good evening, Hans. Where have you been?" "To Grethel's." "And what have you given her?" "Nothing; she has given me something." "What has Grethel given you?" "A needle," said Hans. "And where have you put it?" "In the load of hay." "Then you have behaved stupidly, Hans; you should put needles on your coat-sleeve." "To behave better, do nothing at all," thought Hans.

"Whither are you going, Hans?" "To Grethel's, mother." "Behave well, Hans." "I will take care; good-by, mother." "Good-by, Hans."

Hans came to Grethel. "Good day," said he. "Good day, Hans. What treasure do you bring?" "I bring nothing. Have you anything to give?" Grethel gave Hans a knife. "Good-by, Grethel." "Good-by, Hans." Hans took the knife, put it in his sleeve, and went home.

"Good evening, mother." "Good evening, Hans. Where have you been?" "To Grethel's." "And what did you take to her?" "I took nothing; she has given to me." "And what did she give you?" "A knife," said Hans. "And where have you put it?" "In my sleeve." "Then you have behaved foolishly again, Hans; you should put knives in your pocket." "To behave better, do nothing at all," thought Hans.

"Whither are you going, Hans?" "To Grethel's, mother." "Behave well, Hans." "I will take care; good-by, mother." "Good-by, Hans."

Hans came to Grethel. "Good day, Grethel." "Good day, Hans. What treasure do you bring?" "I bring nothing. Have you anything to give?" Grethel gave Hans a young goat. "Good-by, Grethel." "Good-by, Hans." Hans took the goat, tied its legs, and put it in his pocket.

Just as he reached home it was suffocated. "Good evening, mother." "Good evening, Hans. Where have you been?"

"To Grethel's." "And what did you take to her?" "I took nothing; she gave to me." "And what did Grethel give you?" "A goat." "Where did you put it, Hans?" "In my pocket." "There you acted stupidly, Hans; you should have tied the goat with a rope." "To behave better, do nothing," thought Hans.

"Whither away, Hans?" "To Grethel's, mother." "Behave well, Hans." "I'll take care; good-by, mother." "Good-by, Hans."

Hans came to Grethel. "Good day," said he. "Good day, Hans. What treasure do you bring?" "I bring nothing. Have you anything to give?" Grethel gave Hans a piece of bacon. "Good-by, Grethel." "Good-by, Hans." Hans took the bacon, tied it with a rope, and swung it to and fro so that the dogs came and ate it up. When he reached home he held the rope in his hand, but there was nothing on it.

"Good evening, mother," said he. "Good evening, Hans. Where have you been?" "To Grethel's, mother." "What did you take there?" "I took nothing; she gave to me." "And what did Grethel give you?" "A piece of bacon," said Hans. "And where have you put it?" "I tied it with a rope, swung it about, and the dogs came and ate it up." "There you acted stupidly, Hans; you should have carried the bacon on your head." "To behave better, do nothing," thought Hans.

"Whither away, Hans?" "To Grethel's, mother." "Behave well, Hans." "I'll take care; good-by, mother." "Good-by, Hans."

Hans came to Grethel. "Good day," said he. "Good day, Hans. What treasure do you bring?" "I bring nothing. Have you anything to give?" Grethel gave Hans a calf. "Good-by," said Hans. "Good-by." Hans took the calf, set it on his head, and the calf scratched his face.

"Good evening, mother." "Good evening, Hans. Where have you been?" "To Grethel's." "What did you take her?" "I took nothing; she gave to me." "And what did Grethel give you?" "A calf," said Hans. "And what did you do with it?" "I set it on my head, and it kicked my face." "Then you acted stupidly, Hans; you should have led the calf home, and put it in the stall." "To behave better, do nothing," thought Hans.

"Whither away, Hans?" "To Grethel's, mother." "Behave well, Hans." "I'll take care; good-by, mother." "Good by, Hans."

Hans came to Grethel. "Good day," said he. "Good day, Hans. What treasure do you bring?" "I bring nothing. Have you anything to give?" Grethel said: "I will go with you, Hans." Hans tied a rope round Grethel, led her home, put her in the stall, and made the rope fast; and then he went to his mother.

"Good evening, mother." "Good evening, Hans. Where have you been?" "To Grethel's." "What did you take her?" "I took nothing." "What did Grethel give you?" "She gave nothing; she came with me." "And where have you left her, then?" "I tied her with a rope, put her in the stall, and threw in some grass." "Then you acted stupidly, Hans; you should have looked at her with friendly eyes." "To behave better, do nothing," thought Hans; and then he went into the stall, and made sheep's eyes at Grethel.

And after that Grethel became Hans's wife.

☙ ☙ ☙

PUSS IN BOOTS

ONCE upon a time there was a miller, who was so poor that at his death he had nothing to leave to his three children but his mill, his ass, and his cat. The eldest son took the mill, and the second the ass, so there was nothing left for poor Jack but to take Puss.

Jack could not help thinking that he had been treated shabbily. "My brothers will be able to earn an honest livelihood," he sighed, "but as for me, though Puss may feed himself by catching mice, I shall certainly die of hunger."

The cat, who had overheard his young master, jumped upon

DO·NOT·GRIEVE·DEAR·MASTER

his shoulder, and, rubbing himself gently against his cheek, began to speak. "Dear master," said he, "do not grieve. I am not as useless as you think me, and will undertake to make your fortune for you, if only you will buy me a pair of boots, and give me that old bag."

Now, Jack had very little money to spare, but, knowing Puss to be a faithful old friend, he made up his mind to trust him, and so spent all he possessed upon a smart pair of boots made of buff-colored leather. They fitted perfectly, so Puss put them on, took the old bag which his master gave him, and trotted off to a neighboring warren in which he knew there was a great number of rabbits.

Having put some bran and fresh parsley into the bag, he laid it upon the ground, hid himself, and waited. Presently two foolish little rabbits, sniffing the food, ran straight into the bag, when the clever cat drew the strings and caught them.

Then, slinging the bag over his shoulder, he hastened off to the palace, where he asked to speak to the King. Having been shown into the royal presence, he bowed and said:

"Sire, my Lord the Marquis of Carabas has commanded me to present these rabbits to your Majesty, with his respects."

The monarch having desired his thanks to be given to the Marquis (who, as you will guess, was really our poor Jack), then ordered his head cook to dress the rabbits for dinner, and he and his daughter partook of them with great enjoyment.

Day by day Puss brought home stores of good food, so that he and his master lived in plenty, and besides that, he did not fail to keep the King and his courtiers well supplied with game.

Sometimes he would lay a brace of partridges at the royal feet, sometimes a fine large hare, but whatever it was, it always came with the same message: "From my Lord the Marquis of Carabas"; so that everyone at Court was talking of this strange nobleman, whom no one had ever seen, but who sent such generous presents to his Majesty.

At length Puss decided that it was time for his master to be introduced at Court. So one day he persuaded him to go and bathe in a river near, having heard that the King would soon pass that way.

Jack stood shivering up to his neck in water, wondering what was to happen next, when suddenly the King's carriage appeared in sight. At once Puss began to call out as loudly as he could:

"Help, help! My Lord the Marquis of Carabas is drowning!"

The King put his head out of the carriage window and, recognizing the cat, ordered his attendants to go to the assistance of the Marquis. While Jack was being taken out of the water, Puss ran to the King and told him that some robbers had run off with his master's clothes whilst he was bathing, the truth of the matter being that the cunning cat had hidden them under a stone.

On hearing this story the King instantly despatched one of his grooms to fetch a handsome suit of purple and gold from the royal wardrobe, and arrayed in this, Jack, who was a fine, handsome fellow, looked so well that no one for a moment supposed but that he was some noble foreign lord.

The King and his daughter were so pleased with his appearance that they invited him into their carriage. At first Jack hesitated, for he felt a little shy about sitting next to a Princess, but she smiled at him so sweetly, and was so kind and gentle, that he soon forgot his fears and fell in love with her there and then.

As soon as Puss had seen his master seated in the royal carriage, he whispered directions to the coachman, and then ran on ahead as fast as he could trot, until he came to a field of corn, where the reapers were busy.

"Reapers," said he fiercely, "the King will shortly pass this way. If he should ask you to whom this field belongs, remember that you say, 'To the Marquis of Carabas.' If you dare to disobey me, I will have you all chopped up as fine as mincemeat." The reapers were so afraid the cat would keep his word that they promised to obey. Puss then ran on and told all the other laborers whom he met to give the same answer, threatening them with terrible punishments if they disobeyed.

Now, the King was in a very good humor, for the day was fine, and he found the Marquis a very pleasant companion, so he told the coachman to drive slowly, in order that he might admire the beautiful country. "What a fine field of wheat!" he said presently. "To whom does it belong?" Then the men answered as they had been told: "To our Lord the Marquis of Carabas." Next they met a herd of cattle, and again to the King's question, "To whom do they belong?" they were told, "To the Marquis of Carabas." And it was the same with everything they passed.

The Marquis listened with the greatest astonishment, and thought what a very wonderful cat his dear Puss was; and the King was delighted to find that his new friend was as wealthy as he was charming.

Meanwhile Puss, who was well in advance of the Royal party, had arrived at a stately castle, which belonged to a cruel Ogre, the richest ever known, for all the lands the King had admired so much belonged to him. Puss knocked at the door and asked to see the Ogre, who received him quite civilly, for he had never seen a cat in boots before, and the sight amused him.

So he and Puss were soon chatting away together.

The Ogre, who was very conceited, began to boast of what clever tricks he could play, and Puss sat and listened, with a smile on his face.

"I once heard, great Ogre," he said at last, "that you possessed the power of changing yourself into any kind of animal you chose—a lion or an elephant, for instance."

"Well, so I can," replied the Ogre.

"Dear me! how much I should like to see you do it now," said Puss sweetly.

The Ogre was only too pleased to find a chance of showing how very clever he was, so he promised to transform himself into any animal Puss might mention.

"Oh! I will leave the choice to you," said the cat politely.

Immediately there appeared where the Ogre had been seated, an enormous lion, roaring, and lashing with its tail, and looking as though it meant to gobble the cat up in a trice.

Puss was really very much frightened, and, jumping out of the window, managed to scramble on to the roof, though he could scarcely hold on to the tiles on account of his high-heeled boots.

There he sat, refusing to come down, until the Ogre changed himself into his natural form, and laughingly called to him that he would not hurt him.

Then Puss ventured back into the room, and began to compliment the Ogre on his cleverness.

"Of course, it was all very wonderful," he said, "but it would be more wonderful still if you, who are so great and fierce, could transform yourself into some timid little creature, such as a mouse. That, I suppose, would be quite impossible?"

"Not at all," said the vain Ogre; "one is quite as easy to me as the other, as I will show you." And in a moment a little brown mouse was frisking about all over the floor, whilst the Ogre had vanished.

"Now or never," said Puss, and with a spring he seized the mouse and gobbled it up as fast as he could.

At the same moment all the gentlemen and ladies whom the wicked Ogre had held in his castle under a spell, became disenchanted. They were so grateful to their deliverer that they would have done anything to please him, and readily agreed to enter into the service of the Marquis of Carabas when Puss asked them to do so.

So now the cat had a splendid castle, which he knew to be full of heaped-up treasures, at his command, and ordering a magnificent feast to be prepared, he took up his station at the castle gates to welcome his master and the royal party.

As soon as the castle appeared in sight, the King enquired whose it was, "For," said he, "I have never seen a finer."

Then Puss, bowing low, threw open the castle gates, and cried:

"May it please your Majesty to alight and enter the home of the most noble the Marquis of Carabas."

Full of surprise, the King turned to the Marquis. "Is this splendid castle indeed yours?" he asked. "Not even our own palace is more beautiful, and doubtless it is as splendid within as without."

Puss then helped his Majesty to alight, and conducted him into the castle, where a group of noble gentlemen and fair ladies were waiting to receive them. Jack, or the Marquis as he was now called, gave his hand to the young Princess, and led her to the banquet. Long and merrily they feasted, and when at length the guests rose to depart, the King embraced the Marquis, and called him his dear son; and the Princess blushed so charmingly and looked so shy and sweet, that Jack ventured to lay his heart and fortune at her feet.

And so the miller's son married the King's daughter, and there were great rejoicings throughout the land.

On the evening of the wedding-day a great ball was given, to which princes and noblemen from far and near were invited. Puss opened the ball, wearing for the occasion a pair of boots made of the finest leather, with gold tassels and scarlet heels. I only wish you could have seen him.

When the old King died, the Princess and her husband reigned in his stead, and their most honored and faithful friend at Court was Puss himself, for his master never forgot to whom he owed all his good fortune. He lived upon the daintiest meat and most delicious cream, and was petted and made much of all the days of his life, and never again ran after mice and rats, except for exercise and amusement.

☙ ☙ ☙

THE ELVES AND THE SHOEMAKER

THERE was once a shoemaker who, through no fault of his own, had become so poor that at last he had only leather enough left for one pair of shoes. At evening he cut out the shoes which he intended to begin upon the next morning, and since he had a good conscience, he lay down quietly, said his prayers, and fell asleep.

In the morning when he had prayed, as usual, and was preparing to sit down to work, he found the pair of shoes standing finished on his table. He was amazed, and could not understand it in the least.

He took the shoes in his hand to examine them more closely. They were so neatly sewn that not a stitch was out of place, and were as good as the work of a master-hand.

Soon after a purchaser came in, and as he was much pleased with the shoes, he paid more than the ordinary price for them, so that the shoemaker was able to buy leather for two pairs with the money.

He cut them out in the evening, and next day, with fresh courage was about to go to work; but he had no need to, for when he got up, the shoes were finished, and buyers were not lacking. These gave him so much money that he was able to buy leather for four pairs of shoes.

Early next morning he found the four pairs finished, and so it went on; what he cut out at evening was finished in the morning, so that he was soon again in comfortable circumstances, and became a well-to-do man.

Now it happened one evening, not long before Christmas, when he had cut out shoes as usual, that he said to his wife: "How would it be if we were to sit up to-night to see who it is that lends us such a helping hand?"

The wife agreed, lighted a candle, and they hid themselves in the corner of the room behind the clothes which were hanging there.

At midnight came two little naked men, who sat down at the shoemaker's table, took up the cut-out work, and began with their tiny fingers to stitch, sew, and hammer so neatly and quickly, that the shoemaker could not believe his eyes. They did not stop till everything was quite finished, and stood complete on the table; then they ran swiftly away.

The next day the wife said: "The little men have made us rich, and we ought to show our gratitude. They run about with nothing on, and must freeze with cold. Now I will make them little shirts, coats, waistcoats, and hose, and will even knit them stout stockings, and you shall make them each a pair of shoes."

The husband agreed, and at evening, when they had everything ready, they laid out the presents on the table, and hid themselves to see how the little men would behave.

At midnight they came skipping in, and were about to set to

work; but, instead of the leather ready cut out, they found the charming little clothes.

At first they were surprised, then excessively delighted. With the greatest speed they put on and smoothed down the pretty clothes, singing:

"Now we're dressed so fine and neat,
Why cobble more for others' feet?"

Then they hopped and danced about, and leaped over chairs and tables and out at the door. Henceforward, they came back no more, but the shoemaker fared well as long as he lived, and had good luck in all his undertakings.

❧ ❧ ❧

HANS IN LUCK

HANS had served his master seven long years; so he said to him: "Master, my time is out, and my wish is to return home to my mother: give me, if you please, my reward."

The master answered: "Thou hast truly and faithfully served me; as the service was, so shall the reward be." And he gave Hans a piece of gold as big as his head.

Hans pulled out his handkerchief, wrapped up the lump of gold in it, and, throwing it over his shoulder, made his way home. As he went on his way, always putting one foot before the other, he met a man galloping briskly along on a fine horse.

"Ah!" said Hans, quite aloud, "what a capital thing it is to ride! There you sit as comfortably as in a chair, kicking against no stones, saving your shoe-leather, and getting to your journey's end almost without knowing it!"

The horseman, who heard this, pulled up and cried, "Hullo, Hans why do you trudge on foot?"

"Because I must," answered he; "for I have this big lump to carry home. It is real gold, you know; but, all the same, I can scarcely hold up my head, it weighs so terribly on my shoulders."

"I'll tell you what," said the horseman: "we'll just exchange. I'll give you my horse and you give me your lump of gold."

"With all my heart!" said Hans. "But I warn you, you'll have a job to carry it."

The horseman dismounted, took the gold, and helped Hans up; and, giving the bridle into his hand, said: "If you want him to go at full speed, you must cluck with your tongue and cry 'C'ck! c'ck!'"

Hans was heartily delighted, as he sat on his horse and rode gaily along.

After a while he fancied he would like to go faster, so he began to cluck with his tongue and cry "C'ck! c'ck!" The horse broke into a smart trot, and before Hans was aware he was thrown off—splash!—into a ditch which divided the highway from the fields, and there he lay. The horse, too, would have run away had it not been stopped by a peasant, as he came along the road, driving his cow before him.

Hans pulled himself together and got upon his legs again. He felt very downcast, and said to the peasant: "It's a poor joke, that riding, especially when one lights upon such a brute as this, which kicks and throws one off so that one comes near to breaking one's neck. You don't catch me on his back again. Now, there's more sense in a cow like yours, behind which you can walk in peace and quietness, besides having your butter, milk, and cheese every morning for certain. What would I not give for such a cow!"

"Well," said the peasant, "if it would give you so much pleasure, I will exchange my cow for your horse."

Hans gladly consented, and the peasant flung himself on the horse and rode quickly off.

Hans drove the cow peacefully along, thinking: "What a lucky fellow I am! I have just to get a bit of bread (and that isn't a difficult matter) and then, as often as I like, I can eat my butter and cheese with it. If I am thirsty, I just milk my cow and drink. What more could I desire?"

When he came to an inn, he made a stop, and in his great joy ate all the food he had with him right up, both dinner and supper.

With his two last farthings, he bought himself half a glass of beer. Then he drove his cow towards his mother's village.

As the morning went on, the more oppressive the heat became, and Hans found himself in a field some three miles long.

Then he felt so hot that his tongue was parched with thirst. "This is soon cured," thought Hans. "I have only to milk my cow, drink, and refresh myself."

He tied the cow to a withered tree, and as he had no pitcher he placed his leathern cap underneath her; but in spite of all his trouble not a drop of milk could be got.

And he went to work so clumsily that the impatient brute gave him such a kick with her hind leg that he was knocked over and quite dazed, and for a long time did not know where he was.

Luckily a butcher came by just then, wheeling a young pig in a barrow.

"What kind of joke is this?" cried he, helping our friend Hans to rise.

Hans told him what had happened. The butcher passed him his bottle and said:

"There, drink and revive yourself. That cow will never give any milk; she is an old animal and, at the best, is only fit for the plow or the butcher."

"Oho!" said Hans, running his fingers through his hair. "Who would have thought it? It is all right indeed when you can slaughter such a beast in your own house. But I don't think much of cow's flesh; it is not tender enough. Now, if one had a young pig! That would taste far different, to say nothing of the sausages!"

"Listen, Hans," said the butcher. "For your sake, I will exchange, and let you have my pig for your cow."

"May Heaven reward your friendship!" said Hans, and at once gave him the cow.

The man untied the pig from the wheelbarrow, and gave the rope with which it was bound into Hans's hand.

Hans marched on, thinking: "What a lucky fellow I am. As soon as anything goes wrong, something turns up and all's right again."

Just then, up came a youth, carrying a fine white goose under his arm. They were friends, and Hans began to talk about his luck and how he always came off best in his exchanges. The youth told him he was taking the goose to a christening feast.

"Just hold it," he continued, seizing it by the wings, "and feel how heavy it is: yet it was only fattened for eight weeks. It will be a rich morsel when roasted."

"Yes," said Hans, weighing it with his hand, "it is certainly heavy, but my pig is by no means to be despised."

Meanwhile the lad was looking thoughtfully around, shaking his head. "Listen," he said, "I don't think it's all right about your pig. In the village I have just come through, one has lately been stolen from the magistrate's own sty. I fear it is the one you have. They have sent people out, and it would be a bad business if they found you with the pig. The least they would do would be to throw you into jail."

Our friend Hans was downcast. "Alas," he cried, "help me in my need! You know your way here better than I. Take my pig then, and give me your goose."

"I shall be running great risks," said the youth, "but at least I will prevent your getting into trouble."

He took the rope in his hand and drove the pig quickly away down a by-path, and Hans went on relieved of his sorrow, towards home, with the goose under his arm.

"What a lucky fellow I am!" he said to himself. "First, I shall have a good roast; then there is the quantity of dripping that will fall out, which will keep me in bread-and-dripping for a quarter of a year; and lastly, the splendid white feathers, with which I will have my pillow stuffed; then I shall fall asleep without rocking. How glad my mother will be!"

When he was at length come to the village, there stood in the street a scissors-grinder with his truck. His wheel hummed, and he sang the while:

"My wheel I turn, and the scissors I grind,
And my cloak hangs flowing free in the wind."

Hans remained standing, and watched him; at length he spoke to him, and said:

"You must be doing well since you are so merry over your grinding."

"Yes," said the scissors-grinder; "the work has gold at the bottom of it. A proper scissors-grinder is the sort of man who, whenever he puts his hand in his pocket, finds money there. But where have you bought that fine goose?"

"I did not buy it, but exchanged it for my pig."

"And the pig?"

"I obtained him for a cow."

"And the cow?"

"I had her for a horse."

"And the horse?"

"For him I gave a lump of gold as big as my head."

"And the gold?"

"Why, that was my reward for seven years of service."

"You have certainly done well for yourself each time," said the scissors-grinder. "If you could only hear money rattling in your pocket every time you got up, your fortune would be made."

"How shall I set about it?" said Hans.

"You must become a grinder, like me. All you want is a grindstone: the rest comes of itself. I have one which is a little damaged indeed, but for which I would ask nothing more than your goose; would that suit you?"

"How can you ask me?" answered Hans. "I shall be the luckiest fellow on earth. If I have money as often as I feel in my pocket, what else shall I have to care about?" And he handed over the goose, and took the grindstone in receipt.

"Now," said the grinder, lifting up an ordinary heavy field-stone, which lay beside him. "There you have a capital stone, which will be just the thing to hammer your old nails straight upon. Take it and lift it up carefully."

Hans raised the stone and marched on with a joyful heart, his eyes shining with pleasure.

"I must have been born lucky," he cried out. "All that I desire comes to me, as to a Sunday-child."

Meanwhile, having been on his legs since daybreak, he began to feel tired; besides which, he was tormented by hunger, for he had eaten up all his provision in his joy over the exchange of the cow.

At length he could only proceed with great trouble and must

needs stop every minute; the stones, too, crushed him terribly. Then he could not conceal the thought: "How nice it would be now to have nothing to carry!"

Like a snail he crept up to a well, wishing to rest himself and enjoy a refreshing drink.

In order not to spoil the stones in setting them down, he laid them carefully on the ground one beside the other, and bent himself down to drink, but by an accident he gave them a little push, and both stones went splashing down.

Hans, when he saw them sinking in the depths of the well, jumped up with joy, kneeled down and thanked God, with tears in his eyes, that He had shown him this grace and, without troubling him to think what to do with them, had relieved him of the heavy stones which would have been such a hindrance to him.

"There is no man under the sun," he cried out, "so lucky as I."

With a bright heart and free from all care, he sprang upon his way, until he was home at his mother's.

☙ ☙ ☙

MASTER OF ALL MASTERS

A GIRL once went to the fair to hire herself for a servant. At last a funny-looking old gentleman engaged her, and took her home to his house. When she got there, he told her that he had something to teach her, for that in his house he had his own names for things.

He said to her: "What will you call me?"

"Master or mister, or whatever you please, sir," says she.

He said: "You must call me 'Master of all Masters.' And what would you call this?" pointing to his bed.

"Bed or couch, or whatever you please, sir."

"No, that's my 'barnacle.' And what do you call these?" said he, pointing to his pantaloons.

"Breeches or trousers, or whatever you please, sir."

"You must call them 'squibs and crackers.' And what would you call her?" pointing to the cat.

"Cat or kit, or whatever you please, sir."

"You must call her 'white-faced simminy.' And this, now," showing the fire, "what would you call this?"

"Fire or flame, or whatever you please, sir."

"You must call it 'hot cockalorum.' And what, this?" he went on, pointing to the water.

"Water or wet, or whatever you please, sir."

"No, 'pondalorum' is its name. And what do you call all this?" asked he, as he pointed to the house.

"House or cottage, or whatever you please, sir."

"You must call it 'high topper mountain.'"

That very night the servant woke her master up in a fright and said: "Master of all Masters, get out of your barnacle and put on your squibs and crackers. For white-faced simminy has got [illegible]park of hot cockalorum on its tail, and unless you get some po[illegible] high topper mountain will be all on hot cockalorum." [illegible]. That's all.

❧ ❧ ❧

BELLING THE CAT

ONCE upon a time the mice sat in council and talked of how they might outwit their enemy, the Cat. But good advice was scarce, and in vain the president called upon all the most experienced mice present to find a way.

At last a very young mouse held up two fingers and asked to be allowed to speak, and as soon as he could get permission he said:

"I've been thinking for a long time why the Cat is such a dangerous enemy. Now, it's not so much because of her quickness, though people make so much fuss about that. If we could only *notice* her in time, I've no doubt we're nimble enough to jump into our holes before she could do us any harm. It's in her velvet paws, there's where she hides her cruel claws till she gets us in her clutches—that's where her power lies. With those paws she can tread so lightly that we can't hear her coming. And so, while *we* are still dancing heedlessly about the place, she creeps close up, and before we know where we are she pounces down on us and has us in her clutches. Well, then, it's my opinion we ought to hang a bell round her neck to warn us of her coming while there's yet time."

Every one applauded this proposal, and the council decided that it should be carried out.

Now the question to be settled was, who should undertake to fasten the bell round the Cat's neck?

The president declared that no one could be better fitted for the task than he who had given such excellent advice.

But at that the young mouse became quite confused and stammered an excuse. He was too young for the deed, he said. He didn't know the Cat well enough. His grandf[illegible]ho knew her better, would be more suited to the job.

But the grandfather declared that just because [illegible]w the Cat very well he would take good care not to attempt [illegible]uch a task.

And the long and the short of it was that no other mouse would undertake the duty; and so this clever proposal was never carried out, and the Cat remained mistress of the situation.

❧ ❧ ❧

LITTLE RED RIDING-HOOD

IN a great wide forest, full of beautiful trees, and green glades, and thorny thickets, there lived a long time ago a wood-cutter and his wife, who had only one child, a little girl. She was so pretty, and so good, that the sun seemed to shine more brightly when its light fell upon her rosy little face, and the birds would seem to sing more sweetly when she was passing by.

Her real name was Maisie; but the neighbors round about

LITTLE
RED
RIDING
HOOD

all called her "Little Red Riding-Hood," because of a scarlet riding-hood and cloak that her kind old grandmother had made for her, and which she nearly always wore.

She was a happy, merry little child, with a smile and a gentle word for everybody, and so you may easily believe that everybody loved her, and was glad to catch a glimpse of her golden curls and her scarlet cloak as she tripped along, singing, under the green boughs.

Now, this, let me tell you before I forget, was at the time when all the birds and beasts, or very nearly all, could speak just as well as you or I; and nobody was surprised to hear them talk, as I suppose one would be nowadays.

Well, as I was saying, Little Red Riding-Hood lived with her parents in a little white cottage with a green door and a thatched roof, and red and white roses climbing all over the walls, and even putting their pretty heads in at the latticed windows, to peep at the child who was so like them.

It was on a bright spring morning early in May, when little Red Riding-Hood had just finished putting away the breakfast-cups, that her mother came bustling in from the dairy.

"Here's a to-do," she said. "Farmer Hodge has this very minute told me that he hears your Grannie isn't quite well, and I can't leave the cheese-making this morning for love or money! Do you go, my dear, and find out how she is—and—stay—take her this little pot of sweet fresh butter, and these two new-laid eggs, and these nice tasty little pasties. Maybe they'll tempt her to eat a bit. Here's your basket, and don't be too long away, honey."

So little Red Riding-Hood pulled her hood over her curls, and set off down the sunny green slope, with her basket in her hand, at a brisk pace. But as she got deeper into the forest, she walked more slowly. Everything was so beautiful; the great trees waved their huge arms over her, the birds were calling to one another from the thorns all white with blossom, and the child began singing as she went, she could not have told why, but I think it was because the beautiful world made her feel glad.

The path wound along through the trees, and, as it grew wider after turning a corner, Red Riding-Hood saw that she was likely to have company on her walk; for, where two cross-paths divided, there sat a big gray Wolf licking his long paws, and looking sharply about him. And "Good morning, Red Riding-Hood," said he.

"Good morning, Mr. Wolf," she answered.

"And where may you be going, sweet lass?" said the Wolf, as he walked beside her.

"Oh, Grannie isn't very well, and mother cannot leave the cheese-making this morning, and so I'm taking her some little dainties in my basket, and I am to see how she is, and tell mother when I get back," said the child, with a smile.

"And," said the Wolf, "where does your good Grannie live, little lady?"

"Through the copse, and down the hollow, and over the bridge, and three meadows after the mill."

"Does she indeed?" cried he. "Why, then, I do believe she is a very dear old friend of mine, whom I have not seen for years and years. Now, I'll tell you what we'll do, you and I: I will go by this way, and you shall take that, and whoever gets there first shall be the winner of the game."

So the Wolf trotted off one way, and Red Riding-Hood went the other; and I am sorry to say that she lingered and loitered more than she ought to have done on the road.

Well, what with one thing and another, the sun was right up in the very mid-most middle of the sky when she crossed the last meadow from the mill and came in sight of her grandmother's cottage, and the big lilac-bushes that grew by the garden gate.

"Oh! dear, how I must have lingered!" said the child, when she saw how high the sun had climbed since she set out on her journey; and, pattering up the garden-path, she tapped at the cottage door.

"Who's there?" said a very gruff kind of voice from inside.

"It's only I, Grannie dear, your little Red Riding-Hood with some goodies for you in my basket," answered the child.

"Then pull the bobbin," cried the voice, "and the latch will go up."

"What a dreadful cold poor Grannie must have, to be sure, to make her so hoarse," thought the child. Then she pulled the

RED RIDING-HOOD AND THE WOLF.

bobbin, and the latch went up, and Red Riding-Hood pushed open the door, and stepped inside the cottage.

It seemed very dark in there after the bright sunlight outside, and all Red Riding-Hood could see was that the window-curtains and the bed-curtains were still drawn, and her grandmother seemed to be lying in bed with the bed-clothes pulled almost over her head, and her great white-frilled nightcap nearly hiding her face.

Now, you and I have guessed by this time, although poor Red Riding-Hood never even thought of such a thing, that it was not her Grannie at all, but the wicked Wolf, who had hurried to the cottage and put on Grannie's nightcap and popped into her bed, to pretend that he was Grannie herself.

And where was Grannie all this time, you will say? Well, we shall see presently.

"Come and sit down beside my bed, dearie," wheezed the Wolf, "and let us have a little chat." Then the Wolf stretched out his large hairy paws and began to unfasten the basket.

"Oh!" said Red Riding-Hood, "what great arms you have, Grannie!"

"All the better to hug you with," said the Wolf.

"And what great rough ears you have, Grannie!"

"All the better to hear you with, my little dear."

"And your eyes, Grannie; what great yellow eyes you have!"

"All the better to see you with, my pet," grinned the Wolf.

"And oh! oh! Grannie," cried the child, in a sad fright, "what great sharp teeth you have!"

"All the better to eat you with!" growled the Wolf, springing up suddenly at Red Riding-Hood. But just at that very moment the door flew open, and two tall wood-cutters rushed in with their heavy axes, and killed the wicked Wolf in far less time than it takes me to tell you about it.

"But where is Grannie?" asked Little Red Riding-Hood, when she had thanked the brave wood-cutters. "Oh! where can poor Grannie be? Can the cruel Wolf have eaten her up?"

And she began to cry and sob bitterly—when, who should walk in but Grannie herself, as large as life, and as hearty as ever, with her marketing-basket on her arm! For it was another old dame in the village who was not very well, and Grannie had been down to visit her and give her some of her own famous herb-tea.

So everything turned out right in the end, and all lived happily ever after; but I promise you that little Red Riding-Hood never made friends with a Wolf again!

❧ ❧ ❧

THE NAIL

A TRADESMAN had once transacted a good day's business at a fair, disposed of all his goods, and filled his purse with gold and silver. He prepared afterward to return, in order to reach home by the evening, so he strapped his portmanteau, with the money in it, upon his horse's back, and rode off. At noon he halted in a small town, and as he was about to set out again, the stable-boy who brought his horse said to him: "Sir, a nail is wanting in the shoe on the left hind foot of your animal."

"Let it be wanting," replied the tradesman; "I am in a hurry and the iron will doubtless hold the six hours I have yet to travel."

Late in the afternoon he had to dismount again, and feed his horse, and at this place also the boy came and told him that a nail was wanting in one of the shoes, and asked him whether he should take the horse to a farrier. "No, no, let it be!" replied the master; "it will last out the couple of hours that I have now to travel; I am in haste." So saying he rode off; but his horse soon began to limp, and from limping it came to stumbling, and presently the beast fell down and broke its leg. Thereupon the tradesman had to leave his unfortunate horse lying on the road, to unbuckle the portmanteau, and to walk home with it upon his shoulder, where he arrived at last late at night.

"And all this misfortune," said he to himself, "is owing to the want of a nail. More haste, the less speed!"

JACK AND THE BEANSTALK

ONCE upon a time there lived a poor widow who had an only son named Jack. She was very poor, for times had been hard, and Jack was too young to work. Almost all the furniture of the little cottage had been sold to buy bread, until at last there was nothing left worth selling. Only the good cow, Milky White, remained, and she gave milk every morning, which they took to market and sold. But one sad day Milky White gave no milk, and then things looked bad indeed.

"Never mind, mother," said Jack. "We must sell Milky White. Trust me to make a good bargain," and away he went to the market.

For some time he went along very sadly, but after a little he quite recovered his spirits. "I may as well ride as walk," said he; so instead of leading the cow by the halter, he jumped on her back, and so he went whistling along until he met a butcher.

"Good morning," said the butcher.

"Good morning, sir," answered Jack.

"Where are you going?" said the butcher.

"I am going to market to sell the cow."

"It's lucky I met you," said the butcher. "You may save yourself the trouble of going so far."

With this, he put his hand in his pocket, and pulled out five curious-looking beans. "What do you call these?" he said.

"Beans," said Jack.

"Yes," said he, "beans, but they're the most wonderful beans that ever were known. If you plant them overnight, by the next morning they'll grow up and reach the sky. But to save you the trouble of going all the way to market, I don't mind exchanging them for that cow of yours."

"Done!" cried Jack, who was so delighted with the bargain that he ran all the way home to tell his mother how lucky he had been.

But oh! how disappointed the poor widow was.

"Off to bed with you!" she cried; and she was so angry that she threw the beans out of the window into the garden. So poor

Jack went to bed without any supper, and cried himself to sleep.

When he woke up the next morning, the room was almost dark; and Jack jumped out of bed and ran to the window to see what was the matter. The sun was shining brightly outside, but from the ground right up beside his window there was growing a great beanstalk, which stretched up and up as far as he could see, into the sky.

"I'll just see where it leads to," thought Jack, and with that he stepped out of the window on to the beanstalk, and began to climb upwards. He climbed up and up, till after a time his mother's cottage looked a mere speck below, but at last the stalk ended, and he found himself in a new and beautiful country. A little way off there was a great castle, with a broad road leading straight up to the front gate. But what most surprised Jack was to find a beautiful maiden suddenly standing beside him.

"Good morning, ma'am," said he, very politely.

"Good morning, Jack," said she; and Jack was more surprised than ever, for he could not imagine how she had learned his name. But he soon found that she knew a great deal more about him than his name; for she told him how, when he was quite a little baby, his father, a gallant knight, had been slain by the giant who lived in yonder castle, and how his mother, in order to save Jack, had been obliged to promise never to tell the secret.

"All that the giant has is yours," she said, and then disappeared quite as suddenly as she came.

"She must be a fairy," thought Jack.

As he drew near to the castle, he saw the giant's wife standing at the door.

"If you please, ma'am," said he, "would you kindly give me some breakfast? I have had nothing to eat since yesterday."

Now, the giant's wife, although very big and very ugly, had a kind heart, so she said: "Very well, little man, come in; but you must be quick about it, for if my husband, the giant, finds you here, he will eat you up, bones and all."

So in Jack went, and the giant's wife gave him a good breakfast, but before he had half finished it there came a terrible knock at the front door, which seemed to shake even the thick walls of the castle.

"Dearie me, that is my husband!" said the giantess, in a terrible fright; "we must hide you somehow," and she lifted Jack up and popped him into the empty kettle.

No sooner had the giant's wife opened the door than her husband roared out:

> "Fee, fi, fo, fum,
> I smell the blood of an Englishman;
> Be he alive, or be he dead,
> I'll grind his bones to make my bread!"

It's a boy, I'm sure it is," he continued. "Where is he? I'll have him for my breakfast."

"Nonsense!" said his wife; "you must be mistaken. It's the ox's hide you smell." So he sat down, and ate up the greater part of the ox. When he had finished he said: "Wife, bring me my money-bags." So his wife brought him two full bags of gold, and the giant began to count his money. But he was so sleepy that his head soon began to nod, and then he began to snore, like the rumbling of thunder. Then Jack crept out, snatched up the two bags, and though the giant's dog barked loudly, he made his way down the beanstalk back to the cottage before the giant awoke.

Jack and his mother were now quite rich; but it occurred to him one day that he would like to see how matters were going on at the giant's castle. So while his mother was away at market, he climbed up, and up, and up, and up, until he got to the top of the beanstalk again.

The giantess was standing at the door, just as before, but she did not know Jack, who, of course, was more finely dressed than on his first visit. "If you please, ma'am," said he, "will you give me some breakfast?"

"Run away," said she, "or my husband the giant will eat you up, bones and all. The last boy who came here stole two bags of gold—off with you!" But the giantess had a kind heart, and after a time she allowed Jack to come into the kitchen, where she set before him enough breakfast to last him a week. Scarcely had he begun to eat than there was a great rumbling like an earthquake, and the giantess had only time to bundle Jack into the oven when in came the giant. No sooner was he inside the room than he roared:

"Fee, fi, fo, fum,
I smell the blood of an Englishman;
Be he alive, or be he dead,
I'll grind his bones to make my bread!"

But his wife told him he was mistaken, and after breakfasting off a roasted bullock, just as if it were a lark, he called out: "Wife, bring the little brown hen!" The giantess went out and brought in a little brown hen, which she placed on the table.

"Lay!" said the giant; and the hen at once laid a golden egg. "Lay!" said the giant a second time; and she laid another golden egg. "Lay!" said the giant a third time; and she laid a third golden egg.

"That will do for to-day," said he, and stretched himself out to go to sleep. As soon as he began to snore, Jack crept out of the oven, went on tiptoe to the table, and, snatching up the little brown hen, made a dash for the door. Then the hen began to cackle, and the giant began to wake up; but before he was quite awake, Jack had escaped from the castle, and, climbing as fast as he could down the beanstalk, got safe home to his mother's cottage.

The little brown hen laid so many golden eggs that Jack and his mother had now more money than they could spend. But Jack was always thinking about the beanstalk; and one day he crept out of the window again, and climbed up, and up, and up, and up, until he reached the top.

This time, you may be sure, he was careful not to be seen; so he crept round to the back of the castle, and when the giant's wife went out he slipped into the kitchen and hid himself in the oven. In came the giant, roaring louder than ever:

"Fee, fi, fo, fum,
I smell the blood of an Englishman;
Be he alive, or be he dead,
I'll grind his bones to make my bread!"

But the giantess was quite sure that she had seen no little boys that morning; and after grumbling a great deal, the giant sat down to breakfast. Even then he was not quite satisfied, for every now and again he would say:

"Fee, fi, fo, fum,
I smell the blood of an Englishman;"

and once he got up and looked in the kettle. But, of course, Jack was in the oven all the time!

When the giant had finished, he called out: "Wife, bring me the golden harp!" So she brought in the golden harp, and placed it on the table. "Sing!" said the giant; and the harp at once began to sing the most beautiful songs that ever were heard. It sang so sweetly that the giant soon fell fast asleep; and then Jack crept quietly out of the oven, and going on tiptoe to the table, seized hold of the golden harp. But the harp at once called out: "Master! master!" and the giant woke up just in time to catch sight of Jack running out of the kitchen-door.

With a fearful roar, he seized his oak-tree club, and dashed after Jack, who held the harp tight, and ran faster than he had ever run before. The giant, brandishing his club, and taking terribly long strides, gained on Jack at every instant, and he would have been caught if the giant hadn't slipped over a boulder. Before he could pick himself up, Jack began to climb down the beanstalk, and when the giant arrived at the edge he was nearly half-way to the cottage. The giant began to climb down too; but as soon as Jack saw him coming, he called out: "Mother, bring me an axe!" and the widow hurried out with a chopper. Jack had no sooner reached the ground than he cut the beanstalk right in two. Down came the giant with a terrible crash, and that, you may be sure, was the end of him. What became of the giantess and the castle nobody knows. But Jack and his mother grew very rich, and lived happy ever after.

❧ ❧ ❧

HOW TO TELL A TRUE PRINCESS

THERE was once upon a time a Prince who wanted to marry a Princess, but she must be a true Princess. So he traveled through the whole world to find one, but there was always something against each. There were plenty of Princesses, but he could not find out if they were true Princesses. In every case there was some little defect, which showed the genuine article was not yet found. So he came home again in very low spirits, for he had wanted very much to have a true Princess. One night there was a dreadful storm; it thundered and lightened and the rain streamed down in torrents. It was fearful! There was a knocking heard at the palace gate, and the old King went to open it.

There stood a Princess outside the gate; but oh, in what a sad plight she was from the rain and the storm! The water was running down from her hair and her dress into the points of her shoes and out at the heels again. And yet she said she was a true Princess!

"Well, we shall soon find out!" thought the old Queen. But she said nothing and went into the sleeping-room, took off all the bedclothes, and laid a pea on the bottom of the bed. Then she put twenty mattresses on top of the pea and twenty eider-down quilts on the top of the mattresses. And this was the bed in which the princess was to sleep.

The next morning she was asked how she had slept.

"Oh, very badly!" said the Princess. "I scarcely closed my eyes all night! I am sure I don't know what was in the bed. I lay on something so hard that my whole body is black and blue. It is dreadful!"

Now they perceived that she was a true Princess, because she had felt the pea through the twenty mattresses and the twenty eider-down quilts.

No one but a true Princess could be so sensitive.

So the Prince married her, for now he knew that at last he had got hold of a true Princess. And the pea was put into the Royal Museum, where it is still to be seen if no one has stolen it. Now, this is a true story.

❧ ❧ ❧

THE SLEEPING BEAUTY

ONCE upon a time long ago—so long, indeed, that even the very oldest people now alive could not remember it—there lived a King and Queen in a beautiful palace, a great white

PRINCE FLORIMOND FINDS THE SLEEPING BEAUTY.

marble palace, with wide halls and high towers, and a golden roof that flashed in the sun.

And all round the palace, for miles and miles, there were lovely gardens and pleasure-grounds, with terraces and green lawns, and ancient trees where the birds would sit and sing all day and all night long, and more flowers than you could ever think of if you were to think a whole summer through. There were peacocks and birds of paradise on the broad lawns, and pretty slender brown deer in the shady glades, and gold and silver fishes in the ponds and fountains, and great red and yellow fruits ripened in the orchards.

There was everything there that heart could wish—except just one, and that was the one thing in all the world that this King and Queen wanted to make them perfectly happy. For there was no little child to run and play about the sunny gardens and pick the flowers, and pet the birds and beasts that wandered there. And this would often make them very sad.

But at last, after many years, they had their wish, and a little baby daughter was born to them—a tiny child with a face like a blush rosebud, eyes like violets, and a little red mouth like the pimpernel flowers that grow in the cornfields and by the wayside in summer-time.

Now, you can easily think how glad this King and Queen were, and what great rejoicings were made over all the country.

Bonfires as big as haystacks were kept burning all night, fat oxen were roasted whole in the market-place of every town, the church-bells were rung and rung again until the ringers were out of breath and their arms were aching, and every little child in the kingdom was given a beautiful present for the baby Princess's sake.

In the palace, of course, all was bustle and hurry to make ready for the christening-feast; the maids were busy putting flowers all about the halls and chambers, and sprinkling the shining floors with sweet-smelling leaves and petals.

For the most important guests invited to this christening were seven very powerful fairies, and you know, I am sure, how particular fairies are about what they eat and drink. Not that they are greedy; but they are used to such delicate food that even the very best of ours seems strange to them. So the Queen was very anxious that they should be pleased; for they had been asked to be godmothers to the baby Princess, and she wanted them to be in a good humor so that they should be kind to her little one.

It was a beautiful summer afternoon, and the roses on the palace terrace were nodding their heads sleepily in the warm breeze, when the fairies' chariots came into sight, sailing through the blue sky like a flight of bright-winged butterflies.

They were all good fairies, and had known the King and Queen all their lives long, and as they had not seen them for some time there was a great deal to talk about and much news to tell. And, dear me! how pleased they were with the baby! They all agreed that she was the prettiest little darling they had ever seen—almost as pretty as a real fairy baby—and *that* was a compliment indeed, I can tell you.

And when they went in to the great banqueting-hall and sat down to table, they were even more delighted than at first. For each one of them there was a set of six golden dinner things—knife, spoon, fork, cup, dish, and plate—made on purpose as a present for each, and all different. One was set with pearls, another with diamonds, the third with rubies, the fourth with opals, the fifth with amethysts, the sixth with emeralds, the seventh with sapphires; and nobody could tell which was the most beautiful.

They were just going to begin, and everybody was as happy as happy could be, when, all of a sudden, there was a clashing of brazen claws and a rushing of wings, and something like a black cloud seemed to pass before the tall windows and darken all the room, so that the guests could hardly see their plates. Then the great doors burst open with a terrible bang, and an old fairy in a long trailing black gown, with her face almost hidden in a black hood, jumped out of a black chariot drawn by fierce griffins, and stalked up to the table.

The King turned pale, and the Queen nearly fainted away, for this was the spiteful fairy Tormentilla, who lived all alone, an immense distance away from everywhere and everyone, in a dismal black stone castle in the middle of a desert. The poor

Queen had been so happy and so busy that she had forgotten all about her, and never sent her an invitation.

However, they all tried to make the best of it, and another chair was brought, and another place laid for Tormentilla; and both the King and Queen told her over and over again how very, very sorry they were not to have asked her.

It was all in vain. Nothing could please her; she would eat and drink nothing, and she sat, scowling and looking angrily at the other fairies' jeweled cups and dishes, until the feast was over, and it was time to give the presents.

Then they all went into the great tapestried room where the tiny Princess lay sleeping in her mother-o'-pearl cradle, and the seven fairies began to say what they would each give her.

The first stepped forward and said: "She shall always be as good as gold"; the second: "She shall be the cleverest Princess in the world"; the third: "She shall be the most beautiful"; the fourth: "She shall be the happiest"; the fifth: "She shall have the sweetest voice that was ever heard"; the sixth: "Everyone shall love her." And then the wicked old cross fairy strode over to the cradle with long quick steps, and said, shaking her black crooked stick at the King and Queen: "*And I say that she shall prick her hand with a spindle and die of the wound!*"

At this the Queen fell on her knees and begged and prayed Tormentilla to call back her cruel words; but suddenly the seventh fairy, the youngest of all, who knew Tormentilla well, and had hidden herself behind the curtains for fear that some such thing might happen, came out and said:

"Do not cry so, dear Queen; I cannot quite undo my cousin's wicked enchantment, but I can promise you that your daughter shall not die, but only fall asleep for a hundred years. And, when these are past and gone, a Prince shall come and awaken her with a kiss."

So the King and Queen dried their tears and thanked the kind fairy Heartsease for her goodness; and all the fairies went back to their homes, and things went on much as usual in the palace. But you can imagine how careful the Queen was of her little girl; and the King made a law that every spindle in the country must be destroyed, and that no more should be made, and that anyone who had a spindle should be heavily punished, if not executed at once.

Well, the years went by happily enough until the Princess Miranda was almost eighteen years old, and all that the six fairies had promised came true, for she was the best and the prettiest and the cleverest Princess in all the world, and everybody loved her. And, indeed, by this time Tormentilla's spiteful words were almost forgotten.

"Poor old thing," the Queen would sometimes say, "she was so angry at having been left out that she did not know what she was saying. Of course, she did not really mean it."

Now, the King and Queen had to go away for a few days to a great entertainment that one of their richest nobles was giving at his country house; and, as the Princess did not wish to go, they left her behind with her ladies-in-waiting in the beautiful old palace. For the first two days she amused herself very well, but on the third she missed her father and mother so much that, to pass the time till they came back, she began exploring all the old lumber-rooms and out-of-the-way attics in the palace, and laughing at the dusty furniture and queer curiosities she found there.

At last she found herself at the top of a narrow winding stairway in a tall turret that seemed even older than all the rest of the palace. And when she lifted the latch of the door in front of her she saw a little low chamber with curiously painted walls, and there sat a little old, old woman in a high white cap, spinning at a wheel.

For some time she stood at the door, watching the old woman curiously; she could not imagine what she was doing, for the Princess had never seen a spinning-wheel in her life before, because, as I told you, the King had ordered them all to be destroyed.

Now, it happened that the poor old woman who lived in this tower had never heard the King's command, for she was so deaf that if you shouted until you were hoarse she would never have been able to understand you.

"What pretty work you are doing there, Goody? And why does that wheel go whirr, whirr, whirr?" said the Princess.

The old woman neither answered nor looked up, for, ot course, she did not hear.

So the Princess stepped into the room and laid her hand upon the old woman's shoulder.

Goody started then, looked up, and rubbed her eyes.

"Deary, deary me!" cried she, in a high, cracked voice. "And who may you be, my pretty darling?"

"I'm the Princess Miranda," screamed the maiden in her ear, but the old woman only shook her head—she could hear nothing.

Then the Princess pointed to the spindle, and made the old woman understand that she wanted to try if she could work it.

So Goody nodded, and laughed, and got up from her seat, and the Princess sat down and took the spindle in her hand. But no sooner did she touch it than she pricked the palm of her hand with the point, and sank down in a swoon.

Immediately a deep silence fell on all around. The little bird that only a moment before had been singing so sweetly upon the window-sill hushed his song. The distant hum of voices from the courtyard beneath ceased; even Goody stopped short in the directions she was giving the Princess, and neither moved hand nor foot towards the poor little maid, and all because she had fallen fast asleep as she stood.

Below in the castle it was just the same. The King and Queen, who had that moment returned from their journey and were enquiring for their daughter, fell asleep before the lady-in-waiting could answer them, and as to the lady herself she had begun to snore—in a ladylike manner, of course—before you could have winked your eye.

The soldiers and men-at-arms slumbered as they stood. The page-boy fell asleep with his mouth wide open, and a fly that had just been going to settle on his nose fell asleep too in mid-air.

Although the sun had been shining brightly when the Princess took the spindle in her hand, no sooner did she prick herself with the point than deep shadows darkened the sunny rooms and gardens.

It was just as though night had overtaken them, but there

was no one in or near the palace to heed whether it were dark or light.

This sudden darkness had been caused by a magic wood which had sprung up all around the palace and its grounds. It was at least half a mile thick, and was composed of thorns and prickly plants, through which it seemed impossible for anyone to penetrate. It was so thick and high that it hid even the topmost towers of the enchanted castle, and no one outside could have dreamed that such a castle lay behind it.

Well, and so the years went on, and on, and on, until a hundred years had passed, and the palace and the story of it were all but forgotten. And it happened that a King's son from a neighboring country came hunting that way with his men, and horses, and dogs. And in the excitement of the chase he rode on and on until he became separated from his servants and attendants, and found himself in a part of the country where he had never been before. In vain he tried to retrace his steps: he only seemed to wander farther away in the wrong direction.

Presently he came to a woodcutter's cottage, and dismounted to ask his way. An old, old man lived in this hut, and after he had directed the Prince as to the best way back, the young man pointed to a thick wood ahead, and asked what lay beyond it. Then the old man told him that there was a legend that beyond the wood was an enchanted palace where a beautiful Princess had lain sleeping for a hundred years, and whom a Prince was to awaken with a kiss.

Directly the Prince Florimond heard this, nothing would serve but he must go there and see for himself if the tale were true. So he rode and he rode until he came to the edge of the wood, and there he got off his horse and began to push his way through the thorny thicket. It was hard work indeed, for the briars were so strong and so sharp that you would never believe that anyone could get past them, and they closed up behind him as he went.

But he was strong and brave, and after a time the way became easier, until at last he came to the palace.

There everyone was sleeping—the sentinels and soldiers in the court-yard, the cooks in the kitchen, and pages and lords-

and ladies-in-waiting in the corridors and chambers; and, in the great throne-room the King and Queen on their golden and ivory thrones.

Prince Florimond passed on, wondering more and more, till he came at length to the narrow staircase which led to the little tower in which the Princess had fallen asleep. He mounted this, and then came the greatest wonder of all—the beautiful sleeping lady, in her glistening white robes. She was so beautiful that to see her almost took away his breath; and, falling on his knees, he bent to kiss her cheek. And as he kissed her, she opened her lovely blue eyes and said, smiling: "Oh! Prince, have you come at last? I have had such pleasant dreams."

Then she sat up laughing and rubbing her eyes, and gave him her hand, and they went hand in hand together down the stairs and along the corridors, till they came to the throne-room. And there were the King and Queen rubbing their eyes too, and they kissed their daughter and welcomed the Prince most gladly.

And, all at the same time, the whole palace was awake. Cocks crowed, dogs barked, the cats began to mew, the spits to turn, the clocks to strike, the soldiers presented arms, the heralds blew their trumpets, the head cook boxed a little scullion's ears, the butler went on drinking his half-finished tankard of wine, the first lady-in-waiting finished winding her skein of silk.

Everything, in short, went on exactly as though the spell had lasted a hundred seconds instead of years. To be sure, Princess Miranda's pretty white dress was just such a one as Prince Florimond's great-grandmother might have worn. But that gave them something to laugh at.

And now my story is done, for I need hardly tell you that the Prince and Princess were married amid great rejoicings, and lived happily ever after; and that the seven fairy godmothers danced at the wedding. So all ended well, and what more could anyone wish?

OLD-FASHIONED POEMS

THE MAN IN THE MOON

Said the Raggedy Man on a hot afternoon,
"My!
Sakes!
What a lot o' mistakes
Some little folks makes on the Man in the Moon!
But people that's been up to see him like Me,
And calls on him frequent and intimutly,
Might drop a few hints that would interest you
Clean!
Through!
If you wanted 'em to—
Some actual facts that might interest you!

"O the Man in the Moon has a crick in his back;
Whee!
Whimm!
Ain't you sorry for him?
And a mole on his nose that is purple and black;
And his eyes are so weak that they water and run
If he dares to *dream* even he looks at the sun,—
So he jes' dreams of stars, as the doctors advise—
My!
Eyes!
But isn't he wise—
To jes' dream of stars, as the doctors advise?

"And the Man in the Moon has a boil on his ear—
Whee!
Whing!
What a singular thing!
I know! but these facts are authentic, my dear,—
There's a boil on his ear; and a corn on his chin,—
He calls it a dimple—but dimples stick in—
Yet it might be a dimple turned over, you know!
Whang!
Ho!
Why certainly so!—
It might be a dimple turned over, you know:

"And the Man in the Moon has a rheumatic knee,
Gee!
Whizz!
What a pity that is!
And his toes have worked round where his heels
ought to be.
So whenever he wants to go North he goes South,
And comes back with the porridge crumbs all
round his mouth,
And he brushes them off with a Japanese fan,
Whing!
Whann!
What a marvelous man!
What a very remarkably marvelous man!

"And the Man in the Moon," sighed the Raggedy
Man,
"Gits!
So!
Sullonesome, you know!
Up there by himself since creation began!—
That when I call on him and then come away,
He grabs me and holds me and begs me to stay,—

Till—well, if it was n't for *Jimmy-cum-Jim*,
Dadd!
Limb!
I'd go pardners with him!
Jes' jump my bob here and be pardners with him!"

JAMES WHITCOMB RILEY

(From "The Raggedy Man," copyright 1907. *Used by special permission of the publishers, The Bobbs-Merrill Company.)*

☘ ☘ ☘

SAGE COUNSEL

The lion is the beast to fight,
He leaps along the plain,
And if you run with all your might,
He runs with all his mane.
I'm glad I'm not a Hottentot,
But if I were, with outward cal-lum
I'd either faint upon the spot
Or hie me up a leafy pal-lum.

The chamois is the beast to hunt;
He's fleeter than the wind,
And when the chamois is in front,
The hunter is behind.
The Tyrolese make famous cheese
And hunt the chamois o'er the chaz-zums
I'd choose the former if you please,
For precipices give me spaz-zums.

The polar bear will make a rug
Almost as white as snow;
But if he gets you in his hug,
He rarely lets you go.

And Polar ice looks very nice,
With all the colors of a pris-sum;
But, if you'll follow my advice,
Stay home and learn your catechis-sum.

ARTHUR THOMAS QUILLER-COUCH

☙ ☙ ☙

LIMERICKS

There was an Old Man in a tree,
Who was horribly bored by a Bee;
When they said, "Does it buzz?" he replied,
"Yes, it does!
It's a regular brute of a Bee."

There was an Old Man on some rocks,
Who shut his Wife up in a box:
When she said, "Let me out," he exclaimed,
"Without doubt
You will pass all your life in that box."

There was an Old Man who said "How
Shall I flee from this horrible Cow?
I will sit on this stile, and continue to smile,
Which may soften the heart of that Cow."

There was an Old Man who said, "Hush!
I perceive a young bird in this bush!"
When they said, "Is it small?" he replied, "Not
at all;
It is four times as big as the bush!"

There was once an Old Man with a beard,
Who said, "It is just as I feared!—
Two Owls and a Hen,
Four Larks and a Wren
Have all built their nests in my beard."

There was an old person of Ware
Who rode on the back of a bear;
When they said, "Does it trot?"
He said, "Certainly not,
It's a Moppsikon Floppsikon bear."

There was a young lady in blue,
Who said, "Is it you? Is it you?"
When they said, "Yes, it is," she replied only,
"Whizz!"
That ungracious young lady in blue.

EDWARD LEAR

MORE LIMERICKS

There was a small boy of Quebec,
Who was buried in snow to his neck;
When they said. "Are you friz?"
He replied, "Yes, I is—
But we don't call this cold in Quebec."

RUDYARD KIPLING

There was a young lady of Niger
Who smiled as she rode on a Tiger;
They came back from the ride
With the lady inside,
And the smile on the face of the Tiger.

There was a young maid who said, "Why
Can't I look in my ear with my eye?
If I give my mind to it,
I'm sure I can do it—
You never can tell till you try."

ANONYMOUS

THE DEAD DOLL

You needn't be trying to comfort me—I tell you
my dolly is dead!
There's no use in saying she isn't, with a crack
like that in her head.
It's just like you said it wouldn't hurt much to
have my tooth out, that day;
And then, when the man 'most pulled my head off,
you hadn't a word to say.

And I guess you must think I'm a baby, when you
say you can mend it with glue:
As if I didn't know better than that! Why, just
suppose it was you?
You might make her look all mended—but what
do I care for looks?
Why, glue's for chairs and tables, and toys and
the backs of books!

My dolly! my own little daughter! Oh, but it's
the awfullest crack!
It just makes me sick to think of the sound when
her poor head went whack
Against that horrible brass thing that holds up
the little shelf.
Now, Nursey, what makes you remind me? I
know that I did it myself!

I think you must be crazy—you'll get her another
head!
What good would forty heads do her? I tell you
my dolly is dead!
And to think I hadn't quite finished her elegant
new spring hat!
And I took a sweet ribbon of hers last night to tie
on that horrid cat!

When my mamma gave me that ribbon—I was
playing out in the yard—
She said to me, most expressly, "Here's a ribbon
for Hildegarde."
And I went and put it on Tabby, and Hildegarde
saw me do it;
But I said to myself, "Oh, never mind, I don't believe she knew it!"

But I know that she knew it now, and I just believe, I do,
That her poor little heart was broken, and so her
head broke too.
Oh, my baby! my little baby! I wish my head
had been hit!
For I've hit it over and over, and it hasn't
cracked a bit.

But since the darling is dead, she'll want to be
buried, of course:
We will take my little wagon, Nurse, and you
shall be the horse;
And I'll walk behind and cry, and we'll put her
in this, you see—
This dear little box—and we'll bury her there out
under the maple-tree.

And papa will make me a tombstone, like the one
he made for my bird;
And he'll put what I tell him on it—yes, every
single word!
I shall say: "Here lies Hildegarde, a beautiful
doll, who is dead;
She died of a broken heart, and a dreadful crack
in her head."

MARGARET VANDERGRIFT

LITTLE THINGS

Little drops of water
  Little grains of sand,
Make the mighty ocean,
  And the pleasant land.

Thus the little moments,
  Humble though they be,
Make the mighty ages
  Of eternity.

Thus our little errors
  Lead the soul away
From the path of virtue,
  Off in sin to stray.

Little deeds of kindness,
  Little words of love,
Make our earth an Eden,
  Like the heaven above.

Ascribed to Julia A. F. Carney

❧ ❧ ❧

THE GOLDEN RULE

To do to others as I would
  That they should do to me,
Will make me gentle, kind, and good,
  As children ought to be.

Unknown

❧ ❧ ❧

DO THE BEST YOU CAN

If I was a cobbler it should be my pride
  The best of all cobblers to be;
If I was a tinker, no tinker beside
  Should mend an old kettle like me.

Unknown

THE VOICE OF SPRING

I am coming, I am coming!
Hark! the little bee is humming;
See, the lark is soaring high
In the blue and sunny sky;
And the gnats are on the wing,
Wheeling round in airy ring.

See, the yellow catkins cover
All the slender willows over!
And on the banks of mossy green
Star-like primroses are seen;
And, their clustering leaves below,
White and purple violets grow.

Hark! the new-born lambs are bleating
And the cawing rooks are meeting
In the elms,—a noisy crowd;
All the birds are singing loud;
And the first white butterfly
In the sunshine dances by.

Look around thee, look around!
Flowers in all the fields abound;
Every running stream is bright;
All the orchard trees are white;
And each small and waving shoot
Promises sweet flowers and fruit.

❧ ❧ ❧

THE LARK AND THE ROOK

"Good night, Sir Rook!" said a little lark.
"The daylight fades; it will soon be dark;

I've bathed my wings in the sun's last ray;
I've sung my hymn to the parting day;
So now I haste to my quiet nook
In yon dewy meadow—good night, Sir Rook!"

"Good night, poor Lark," said his titled friend
With a haughty toss and a distant bend;
"I also go to my rest profound,
But not to sleep on the cold, damp ground.
The fittest place for a bird like me
Is the topmost bough of yon tall pine-tree.

"I opened my eyes at peep of day
And saw you taking your upward way,
Dreaming your fond romantic dreams,
An ugly speck in the sun's bright beams;
Soaring too high to be seen or heard;
And I said to myself: 'What a foolish bird!'

"I trod the park with a princely air,
I filled my crop with the richest fare;
I cawed all day 'mid a lordly crew,
And I made more noise in the world than you!
The sun shone forth on my ebon wing;
I looked and wondered—good night, poor
thing!"

"Good night, once more," said the lark's sweet voice.
"I see no cause to repent my choice;
You build your nest in the lofty pine,
But is your slumber more sweet than mine?
You make more noise in the world than I,
But whose is the sweeter minstrelsy?"

UNKNOWN

THANKSGIVING DAY

Over the river and through the wood,
To grandfather's house we go;
The horse knows the way
To carry the sleigh
Through the white and drifted snow.

Over the river and through the wood—
Oh, how the wind does blow!
It stings the toes
And bites the nose,
As over the ground we go.

Over the river and through the wood,
To have a first-rate play.
Hear the bells ring,
"Ting-a-ling-ding!"
Hurrah for Thanksgiving Day!

Over the river and through the wood
Trot fast, my dapple-gray!
Spring over the ground,
Like a hunting-hound!
For this is Thanksgiving Day.

Over the river and through the wood,
And straight through the barn-yard gate.
We seem to go
Extremely slow,—
It is so hard to wait!

Over the river and through the wood—
Now grandmother's cap I spy!
Hurrah for the fun!
Is the pudding done?
Hurrah for the pumpkin-pie?

LYDIA MARIA CHILD

THE MAGPIE'S NEST

A FABLE

When the Arts in their infancy were,
  In a fable of old 'tis express'd
A wise magpie constructed that rare
  Little house for young birds, call'd a nest.

This was talk'd of the whole country round;
  You might hear it on every bough sung,
"Now no longer upon the rough ground
  Will fond mothers brood over their young:"

"For the magpie with exquisite skill
  Has invented a moss-cover'd cell
Within which a whole family will
  In the utmost security dwell."

UNKNOWN

❧ ❧ ❧

THE FAIRIES OF THE CALDON LOW

A MIDSUMMER LEGEND

"And where have you been, my Mary,
  And where have you been from me?"
"I've been to the top of the Caldon Low,
  The midsummer-night to see."

"And what did you see, my Mary,
  All up on the Caldon Low?"
"I saw the glad sunshine come down,
  And I saw the merry winds blow."

"And what did you hear, my Mary,
All up on the Caldon hill?"
"I heard the drops of the water made,
And the ears of the green corn fill."

"Oh! tell me all, my Mary—
All, all that ever you know;
For you must have seen the fairies,
Last night on the Caldon Low."

"Then take me on your knee, mother;
And listen, mother of mine:
A hundred fairies danced last night,
And the harpers they were nine;

"And their harp-strings rung so merrily
To their dancing feet so small;
But oh! the words of their talking
Were merrier far than all."

"And what were the words, my Mary,
That then you heard them say?"
"I'll tell you all, my mother;
But let me have my way.

"Some of them played with the water,
And rolled it down the hill;
'And this,' they said, 'shall speedily turn
The poor old miller's mill;

"'For there has been no water
Ever since the first of May;
And a busy man will the miller be
At dawning of the day.

"'Oh! the miller, how he will laugh
When he sees the mill-dam rise!
The jolly old miller, how he will laugh
Till the tears fill both his eyes!'

"And some they seized the little winds
  That sounded over the hill;
And each put a horn unto his mouth,
  And blew both loud and shrill;

"'And there,' they said, 'the merry winds go
  Away from every horn;
And they shall clear the mildew dank
  From the blind old widow's corn.

"'Oh! the poor, blind widow,
  Though she has been blind so long,
She'll be blithe enough when the mildew's gone,
  And the corn stands tall and strong.'

"And some they brought the brown lint-seed,
  And flung it down from the Low;
'And this,' they said, 'by sunrise,
  In the weaver's croft shall grow.

"'Oh! the poor, lame weaver,
  How will he laugh outright
When he sees his dwindling flax-field
  All full of flowers by night!'

"And then outspoke a brownie,
  With a long beard on his chin;
'I have spun up all the tow,' said he,
  'And I want some more to spin.

"'I've spun a piece of hempen cloth,
  And I want to spin another;
A little sheet for Mary's bed,
  And an apron for her mother.

"With that I could not help but laugh,
  And I laughed out loud and free;
And then on the top of the Caldon Low
  There was no one left but me.

"And on the top of the Caldon Low
The mists were cold and gray,
And nothing I saw but the mossy stones
That round about me lay.

"But, coming down from the hill-top,
I heard afar below,
How busy the jolly miller was,
And how the wheel did go.

"And I peeped into the widow's field,
And, sure enough, were seen
The yellow ears of the mildewed corn,
All standing stout and green.

"And down by the weaver's croft I stole,
To see if the flax were sprung;
And I met the weaver at his gate,
With the good news on his tongue.

"Now this is all I heard, mother,
And all that I did see;
So, pr'ythee, make my bed, mother,
For I'm tired as I can be."

Mary Howitt

☙ ☙ ☙

THE LAND OF STORY-BOOKS

At evening when the lamp is lit,
Around the fire my parents sit;
They sit at home and talk and sing,
And do not play at anything.

Now, with my little gun, I crawl
All in the dark along the wall,
And follow round the forest track
Away behind the sofa back.

There, in the night, where none can spy,
All in my hunter's camp I lie,
And play at books that I have read
Till it is time to go to bed.

These are the hills, these are the woods,
These are my starry solitudes;
And there the river by whose brink
The roaring lions come to drink.

I see the others far away
As if in firelit camp they lay,
And I, like to an Indian scout,
Around their party prowled about.

So, when my nurse comes in for me,
Home I return across the sea,
And go to bed with backward looks
At my dear land of Story-books.

ROBERT LOUIS STEVENSON

❧ ❧ ❧

A VISIT FROM ST. NICHOLAS

'T was the night before Christmas, when all through the house
Not a creature was stirring, not even a mouse;
The stockings were hung by the chimney with care,
In hopes that St. Nicholas soon would be there;
The children were nestled all snug in their beds,
While visions of sugar-plums danced in their heads;

And mamma in her kerchief, and I in my cap,
Had just settled our brains for a long winter's nap,—
When out on the lawn there arose such a clatter,
I sprang from my bed to see what was the matter.
Away to the window I flew like a flash,
Tore open the shutters and threw up the sash.
The moon on the breast of the new-fallen snow
Gave a lustre of midday to objects below;
When what to my wondering eyes should appear,
But a miniature sleigh and eight tiny reindeer,
With a little old driver, so lively and quick
I knew in a moment it must be St. Nick.
More rapid than eagles his coursers they came,
And he whistled and shouted, and called them by name:
"Now, Dasher! now, Dancer! now, Prancer and Vixen!
On, Comet! on, Cupid, on, Donder and Blitzen!
To the top of the porch, to the top of the wall!
Now dash away, dash away, dash away all!"
As dry leaves that before the wild hurricane fly,
When they meet with an obstacle, mount to the sky,
So up to the house-top the coursers they flew,
With the sleigh full of toys,—and St. Nicholas too.
And then in a twinkling I heard on the roof
The prancing and pawing of each little hoof.
As I drew in my head, and was turning around,
Down the chimney St. Nicholas came with a bound.
He was dressed all in fur from his head to his foot,
And his clothes were all tarnished with ashes and soot;
A bundle of toys he had flung on his back,
And he looked like a pedler just opening his pack.
His eyes how they twinkled! his dimples how merry!
His cheeks were like roses, his nose like a cherry;
His droll little mouth was drawn up like a bow,
And the beard on his chin was as white as the snow.
The stump of a pipe he held tight in his teeth,
And the smoke it encircled his head like a wreath.
He had a broad face and a little round belly
That shook, when he laughed, like a bowl full of jelly.

He was chubby and plump—a right jolly old elf;
And I laughed, when I saw him, in spite of myself.
A wink of his eye and a twist of his head
Soon gave me to know I had nothing to dread.
He spoke not a word, but went straight to his work,
And filled all the stockings; then turned with a jerk,
And laying his finger aside of his nose,
And giving a nod, up the chimney he rose.
He sprang to his sleigh, to his team gave a whistle,
And away they all flew like the down of a thistle;
But I heard him exclaim, ere he drove out of sight,
"Happy Christmas to all, and to all a good-night!"

CLEMENT CLARKE MOORE

❧ ❧ ❧

LITTLE ORPHANT ANNIE

Little Orphant Annie's come to our house to stay,
An' wash the cups and saucers up, an' brush the crumbs away,
An' shoo the chickens off the porch, an' dust the hearth, an' sweep,
An' make the fire, an' bake the bread, an' earn her board-an'-keep;
An' all us other children, when the supper things is done,
We set around the kitchen fire an' has the mostest fun
A-list'nin' to the witch-tales 'at Annie tells about.
An' the Gobble-uns 'at gits you
Ef you
Don't
Watch
Out!

Onc't they was a little boy wouldn't say his
prayers,—
So when he went to bed at night, away up stairs,
His Mammy heerd him holler, an' his Daddy heerd
him bawl,
An' when they turn't the kivers down, he wasn't
there at all!
An' they seeked him in the rafter-room, an' cubby-
hole, an press,
An' seeked him up the chimbly-flue, an' ever'-
wheres, I guess;
But all they ever found was thist his pants an'
roundabout!
An' the Gobble-uns git you
Ef you
Don't
Watch
Out!

An' one time a little girl 'ud allus laugh an' grin,
An' make fun of ever' one, an' all her blood an'
kin;
An' onc't when they was "company," an' ole
folks was there,
She mocked 'em an' shocked 'em, an' said she
didn't care!
An' thist as she kicked her heels, an' turn't to run
an' hide,
They was two great big black Things a-standin'
by her side,
An' they snatched her through the ceilin' 'fore she
knowed what she's about!
An' the Gobble-uns'll git you
Ef you
Don't
Watch
Out!

An' little Orphant Annie says, when the blaze is
blue,
An' the lampwick sputters, an' the wind goes
woo-oo!
An' you hear the crickets quit, an' the moon is
gray,
An' the lightnin'-bugs in dew is all squenched
away,—
You better mind yer parents, and yer teachers
fond and dear,
An' churish them 'at loves you, an' dry the or-
phant's tear,
An' he'p the pore an' needy ones 'at clusters all
about,
Er the Gobble-uns'll git you
Ef you
Don't
Watch
Out!

JAMES WHITCOMB RILEY

(From "Riley Child Rhymes," copyright 1899. Used by special permission of the publishers, The Bobbs-Merrill Company.)

❧ ❧ ❧

THE CHATTERBOX

From morning to night 't was Lucy's delight
To chatter and talk without stopping;
There was not a day but she rattled away,
Like water forever a-dropping!

As soon as she rose, while she put on her clothes,
'Twas vain to endeavor to still her;
Nor once did she lack to continue her clack,
Till again she lay down on her pillow.

You'll think now, perhaps, there would have been gaps,
If she had n't been wonderful clever;
That her sense was so great, and so witty her pate
That it would be forthcoming forever.

But that's quite absurd; for have you not heard,
Much tongue and few brains are connected,
That they are supposed to think least who talk most,
And their wisdom is always suspected?

While Lucy was young, had she bridled her tongue
With a little good sense and exertion,
Who knows but she might have been our delight,
Instead of our jest and aversion?

ANN TAYLOR

THE VOICE OF SPRING

I come, I come! ye have called me long;
I come o'er the mountains, with light and song.
Ye may trace my step o'er the waking earth
By the winds which tell of the violet's birth,
By the primrose stars in the shadowy grass,
By the green leaves opening as I pass.

I have breathed on the South, and the chestnut-flowers
By thousands have burst from the forest bowers,
And the ancient graves and the fallen fanes
Are veiled with wreathes on Italian plains;
But it is not for me, in my hour of bloom,
To speak of the ruin or the tomb!

I have looked o'er the hills of the stormy North,
And the larch has hung all his tassels forth;

The fisher is out on the sunny sea,
And the reindeer bounds o'er the pastures free,
And the pine has a fringe of softer green,
And the moss looks bright, where my step has been.

I have sent through the wood-paths a glowing sigh,
And called out each voice of the deep blue sky,
From the night-bird's lay through the starry time,
In the groves of the soft Hesperian clime,
To the swan's wild note by the Iceland lakes,
When the dark fir-branch into verdure breaks.

From the streams and founts I have loosed the chain;
They are sweeping on to the silvery main,
They are flashing down from the mountain brows,
They are flinging spray o'er the forest boughs,
They are bursting fresh from their sparry caves,
And the earth resounds with the joy of waves.

FELICIA DOROTHEA HEMANS

THE HISTORY LESSON

There was a monkey climbed up a tree,
When he fell down, then down fell he.

There was a crow sat on a stone,
When he was gone, then there was none.

There was an old wife did eat an apple,
When she had eat two, she had eat a couple.

There was a horse going to the mill,
When he went on, he stood not still.

There was a butcher cut his thumb,
When it did bleed, then blood did come.

There was a lackey ran a race,
When he ran fast, he ran apace.

There was a cobbler clouting shoon,
When they were mended, they were done.

There was a chandler making candle,
When he them strip, he did them handle.

There was a navy went into Spain,
When it returned, it came again.

ANONYMOUS

❧ ❧ ❧

SONG OF LIFE

A traveller on a dusty road
  Strewed acorns on the lea;
And one took root and sprouted up,
  And grew into a tree.
Love sought its shade at evening-time,
  To breathe its early vows;
And Age was pleased, in heights of noon,
  To bask beneath its boughs.
The dormouse loved its dangling twigs,
  The birds sweet music bore—
It stood a glory in its place,
  A blessing evermore.

A little spring had lost its way
  Amid the grass and fern;
A passing stranger scooped a well
  Where weary men might turn.

He walled it in, and hung with care
  A ladle on the brink;
He thought not of the deed he did,
  But judged that Toil might drink.
He passed again; and lo! the well,
  By summer never dried,
Had cooled ten thousand parchéd tongues,
  And saved a life beside.

A nameless man, amid the crowd
  That thronged the daily mart,
Let fall a word of hope and love,
  Unstudied from the heart,
A whisper on the tumult thrown,
  A transitory breath,
It raised a brother from the dust,
  It saved a soul from death.
O germ! O fount! O word of love!
  O thought at random cast!
Ye were but little at the first,
  But mighty at the last.

CHARLES MACKAY

☙ ☙ ☙

THE GOOD TIME COMING

There 's a good time coming, boys.
  A good time coming:
We may not live to see the day,
But earth shall glisten in the ray
  Of the good time coming.
Cannon-balls may aid the truth,
  But thought's a weapon stronger;
We'll win our battle by its aid;—
  Wait a little longer.

There's a good time coming, boys,
  A good time coming:
The pen shall supersede the sword,
And Right, not Might, shall be the lord
  In the good time coming.
Worth, not Birth, shall rule mankind,
  And be acknowledged stronger;
The proper impulse has been given;—
  Wait a little longer.

There's a good time coming, boys
  A good time coming:
War in all men's eyes shall be
A monster of iniquity
  In the good time coming.
Nations shall not quarrel then,
  To prove which is the stronger;
Nor slaughter men for glory's sake;—
  Wait a little longer.

There's a good time coming, boys,
  A good time coming:
Hateful rivalries of creed
Shall not make their martyrs bleed
  In the good time coming.
Religion shall be shorn of pride,
  And flourish all the stronger;
And Charity shall trim her lamp;—
  Wait a little longer.

There's a good time coming, boys,
  A good time coming:
And a poor man's family
Shall not be his misery
  In the good time coming.
Every child shall be a help
  To make his right arm stronger;
The happier he, the more he has:—
  Wait a little longer.

There's a good time coming, boys,
  A good time coming:
Little children shall not toil
Under, or above, the soil
  In the good time coming;
But shall play in healthful fields,
  Till limbs and mind grow stronger;
And every one shall read and write;—
  Wait a little longer.

There's a good time coming, boys,
  A good time coming:
The people shall be temperate,
And shall love instead of hate,
  In the good time coming.
They shall use, and not abuse,
  And make all virtue stronger;
The reformation has begun;—
  Wait a little longer.

There's a good time coming, boys,
  A good time coming:
Let us aid it all we can,
Every woman, every man,
  The good time coming:
Smallest helps, if rightly given,
  Make the impulse stronger;
'T will be strong enough one day;—
  Wait a little longer.

CHARLES MACKAY

☘ ☘ ☘

WINDY NIGHTS

Whenever the moon and stars are set,
    Whenever the wind is high,
All night long in the dark and wet,
    A man goes riding by,

Late at night when the fires are out,
Why does he gallop and gallop about?

Whenever the trees are crying aloud,
And ships are tossed at sea,
By, on the highway, low and loud,
By at the gallop goes he.
By at the gallop he goes, and then
By he comes back at the gallop again.

ROBERT LOUIS STEVENSON

☙ ☙ ☙

THE WONDERFUL WORLD

Great, wide, beautiful, wonderful World,
With the wonderful water round you curled,
And the wonderful grass upon your breast,
World, you are beautifully drest.

The wonderful air is over me,
And the wonderful wind is shaking the tree—
It walks on the water, and whirls the mills,
And talks to itself on the top of the hills.

You friendly Earth, how far do you go,
With the wheat-fields that nod and the rivers
that flow,
With cities and gardens, and cliffs and isles,
And people upon you for thousands of miles?

Ah! you are so great, and I am so small,
I hardly can think of you, World, at all;
And yet, when I said my prayers to-day,
My mother kissed me, and said, quite gay,

"If the wonderful World is great to you,
And great to father and mother, too,
You are more than the Earth, though you are
such a dot!
You can love and think, and the Earth cannot!"

William Brighty Rands

❧ ❧ ❧

HARK! HARK! THE LARK

Hark! hark! the lark at heaven's gate sings,
And Phœbus 'gins arise,
His steeds to water at those springs
On chaliced flowers that lies;

And winking Mary-buds begin
To ope their golden eyes;
With every thing that pretty bin,
My lady sweet, arise;
Arise, arise.

William Shakespeare

❧ ❧ ❧

JOG ON, JOG ON

Jog on, jog on, the foot-path way,
And merrily hent the stile-a;
A merry heart goes all the day,
Your sad tires in a mile-a.

William Shakespeare

SWEET STORY OF OLD

I think when I read that sweet story of old,
When Jesus was here among men,
How He call'd little children as lambs to His fold,
I should like to have been with them then.

I wish that His hands had been placed on my head,
That His arm had been thrown around me,
And that I might have seen His kind look when He said,
"Let the little ones come unto me."

Yet still to His footstool in prayer I may go,
And ask for a share in His love;
And if I thus earnestly seek Him below,
I shall see Him and hear Him above;

In that beautiful place He has gone to prepare
For all who are washed and forgiven;
And many dear children shall be with Him there,
For of such is the kingdom of heaven.

But thousands and thousands who wander and fall,
Never heard of that heavenly home;
I wish they could know there is room for them all,
And that Jesus has bid them to come.

JEMIMA LUKE

☙ ☙ ☙

MY SHADOW

I have a little shadow that goes in and out with me,
And what can be the use of him is more than I can see,
He is very, very like me from the heels up to the head;
And I see him jump before me, when I jump into my bed.

The funniest thing about him is the way he likes to grow—
Not at all like proper children, which is always very slow;
For he sometimes shoots up taller like an india-rubber ball,
And he sometimes gets so little that there's none of him at all.

He hasn't got a notion of how children ought to play,
And can only make a fool of me in every sort of way.
He stays so close beside me, he's a coward you can see;
I'd think shame to stick to nursie as that shadow sticks to me!

One morning, very early, before the sun was up,
I rose and found the shining dew on every buttercup;
But my lazy little shadow, like an arrant sleepy-head,
Had stayed at home behind me and was fast asleep in bed!

ROBERT LOUIS STEVENSON

☙ ☙ ☙

BY COOL SILOAM'S SHADY RILL

By cool Siloam's shady rill
  How sweet the lily grows!
How sweet the breath beneath the hill
  Of Sharon's dewy rose!

Lo, such the child whose early feet
  The paths of peace have trod;
Whose secret heart, with influence sweet,
  Is upward drawn to God.

By cool Siloam's shady rill
  The lily must decay;
The rose that blooms beneath the hill
  Must shortly fade away.

And soon, too soon, the wintry hour
  Of man's maturer age
Will shake the soul with sorrow's power,
  And stormy passion's rage.

O Thou, whose infant feet were found
Within thy Father's shrine,
Whose years, with changeless virtue crowned,
Were all alike divine;

Dependent on thy bounteous breath,
We seek thy grace alone,
In childhood, manhood, age, and death,
To keep us still thine own.

Reginald Heber

☙ ☙ ☙

THE WIND IN A FROLIC

The wind one morning sprang up from sleep,
Saying, "Now for a frolic! now for a leap!
Now for a madcap galloping chase!
I'll make a commotion in every place!"
So it swept with a bustle right through a great town,
Creaking the signs, and scattering down
Shutters, and whisking, with merciless squalls,
Old women's bonnets and gingerbread stalls.
There never was heard a much lustier shout,
As the apples and oranges tumbled about;
And the urchins, that stand with their thievish eyes
Forever on watch, ran off each with a prize.
Then away to the fields it went blustering and humming,
And the cattle all wondered whatever was coming.
It plucked by their tails the grave, matronly cows,
And tossed the colts' manes all about their brows,
Till, offended at such a familiar salute,
They all turned their backs and stood silently mute.
So on it went, capering and playing its pranks;
Whistling with reeds on the broad river banks;
Puffing the birds, as they sat on the spray,
Or the traveler grave on the King's highway.
It was not too nice to bustle the bags
Of the beggar, and flutter his dirty rags,

'T was so bold that it feared not to play its joke
With the doctor's wig, and the gentleman's cloak.
Through the forest it roared, and cried gayly, "Now,
You sturdy old oaks, I'll make you bow!"
And it made them bow without more ado,
Or it cracked their great branches through and through.
  Then it rushed like a monster o'er cottage and farm,
Striking their inmates with sudden alarm;
And they ran out like bees in a midsummer swarm.
There were dames with their kerchiefs tied over their caps,
To see if their poultry were free from mishaps;
The turkeys, they gobbled, the geese screamed aloud,
And the hens crept to roost in a terrified crowd;
There was rearing of ladders, and logs laying on,
Where the thatch from the roof threatened soon to be gone.
  But the wind had passed on, and had met in a lane
With a schoolboy, who panted and struggled in vain,
For it tossed him, and twirled him, then passed, and he stood
With his hat in a pool, and his shoe in the mud.

William Howitt

THE GRAVES OF A HOUSEHOLD

They grew in beauty, side by side,
  They filled one home with glee;
Their graves are severed far and wide,
  By mount, and stream, and sea.

The same fond mother bent at night
  O'er each fair, sleeping brow;
She had each folded flower in sight:
  Where are those sleepers now?

One, midst the forest of the West,
  By a dark stream is laid;
The Indian knows his place of rest,
  Far in the cedar shade.

The sea, the blue, lone sea, hath one;
He lies where pearls lie deep;
He was the loved of all, yet none
O'er his low bed may weep.

One sleeps where southern vines are dressed
Above the noble slain;
He wrapped the colors round his breast
On a blood-red field of Spain.

And one—o'er her the myrtle showers
Its leaves by soft winds fanned;
She faded midst Italian flowers—
The last of that fair band.

And parted thus, they rest who played
Beneath the same green tree;
Whose voices mingled as they prayed
Around one parent knee.

They that with smiles lit up the hall,
And cheered with song the hearth;
Alas for love! if thou wert all,
And naught beyond, O earth!

Felicia Dorothea Hemans

WE ARE SEVEN

. . . A simple child
That lightly draws its breath,
And feels its life in every limb,
What should it know of death?

I met a little cottage-girl:
She was eight years old, she said;
Her hair was thick with many a curl
That clustered round her head.

She had a rustic, woodland air,
  And she was wildly clad;
Her eyes were bright, and very fair—
  Her beauty made me glad.

"Sisters and brothers, little maid,
  How many may you be?"
"How many? Seven in all," she said,
  And wond'ring looked at me.

"And where are they? I pray you tell."
  She answered, "Seven are we;
And two of us at Conway dwell,
  And two are gone to sea.

"Two of us in the churchyard lie,
  My sister and my brother;
And, in the churchyard cottage, I
  Dwell near them with my mother."

"You say that two at Conway dwell,
  And two are gone to sea,
Yet ye are seven?—I pray you tell,
  Sweet maid, how this may be?"

Then did the little maid reply,
  "Seven boys and girls are we;
Two of us in the churchyard lie,
  Beneath the churchyard tree."

"You run about, my little maid,
  Your limbs they are alive:
If two are in the churchyard laid,
  Then ye are only five."

"Their graves are green, they may be seen,"
  The little maid replied;
"Twelve steps or more from my mother's door,
  And they are side by side.

"My stockings there I often knit,
My kerchief there I hem;
And there upon the ground I sit—
I sit and sing to them.

"And often after sunset, sir,
When it is light and fair,
I take my little porringer,
And eat my supper there.

"The first that died was little Jane;
In bed she moaning lay,
Till God released her of her pain,
And then she went away.

"So in the churchyard she was laid;
And when the grass was dry,
Together round her grave we played,
My brother John and I.

"And when the ground was white with snow,
And I could run and slide,
My brother John was forced to go,
And he lies by her side."

"How many are you, then," said I,
"If they two are in heaven?"
The little maiden did reply,
"O master! we are seven."

"But they are dead; these two are dead!
Their spirits are in heaven!"
'T was throwing words away; for still
The little maid would have her will,
And said, "Nay, we are seven!"

William Wordsworth

THE BETTER LAND

"I hear thee speak of the better land;
Thou call'st its children a happy band;
Mother! oh, where is that radiant shore?
Shall we not seek it and weep no more?
Is it where the flower of the orange blows,
And the fireflies dance through the myrtle boughs?"—
"Not there, not there my child!"

"Is it where the feathery palm trees rise,
And the date grows ripe under sunny skies?
Or midst the green islands of glittering seas,
Where fragrant forests perfume the breeze,
And strange bright birds on their starry wings
Bear the rich hues of all glorious things?"—
"Not there, not there, my child!"

"Is it far away, in some region old,
Where the rivers wander o'er sands of gold?
Where the burning rays of the ruby shine,
And the diamond lights up the secret mine,
And the pearl gleams forth from the coral strand?
Is it there, sweet mother, that better land?"—
"Not there, not there, my child!"

"Eye hath not seen it, my gentle boy;
Ear hath not heard its deep songs of joy;
Dreams cannot picture a world so fair,—
Sorrow and death may not enter there;
Time doth not breathe on its fadeless bloom;
For beyond the clouds and beyond the tomb,
It is there, it is there, my child!"

FELICIA DOROTHEA HEMANS

THE JUVENILE ORATOR

You'd scarce expect one of my age
To speak in public, on the stage;
And if I chance to fall below
Demosthenes or Cicero,
Don't view me with a critic's eye,
But pass my imperfections by.

Large streams from little fountains flow;
Tall oaks from little acorns grow;
And though I now am small and young,
Of judgment weak, and feeble tongue,
Yet all great learned men—like me—
Once learned to read their A, B, C.

And why may not Columbia's soil
Rear men as great as Britain's isle,
Exceed what Greece and Rome have done,
Or any land beneath the sun?

May n't Massachusetts prove as great
As any other sister state?
Or, where's the town, go far or near,
That does not find a rival here?
Or, where 's the boy but three feet high
Who's made improvement more than I?

Those thoughts inspire my youthful mind
To be the greatest of mankind;
Great, not like Cæsar, stained with blood;
But only great, as I am good.

DAVID EVERETT

THE FOX AND THE CROW

A FABLE

The fox and the crow,
In prose, I well know,
Many good little girls can rehearse:
Perhaps it will tell
Pretty nearly as well,
If we try the same fable in verse.

In a dairy a crow,
Having ventured to go,
Some food for her young ones to seek,
Flew up in the trees,
With a fine piece of cheese,
Which she joyfully held in her beak.

A fox, who lived by,
To the tree saw her fly,
And to share in the prize made a vow;
For having just dined,
He for cheese felt inclined,
So he went and sat under the bough.

She was cunning, he knew,
But so was he too,
And with flattery adapted his plan;
For he knew if she'd speak,
It must fall from her beak,
So, bowing politely, began.

"'T is a very fine day"
(Not a word did she say):
"The wind, I believe, ma'am, is south:
A fine harvest for peas:"
He then looked at the cheese,
But the crow did not open her mouth.

Sly Reynard, not tired,
Her plumage admired,
"How charming! how brilliant its hue!
The voice must be fine,
Of a bird so divine,
Ah, let me just hear it, pray do.

"Believe me, I long
To hear a sweet song!"
The silly crow foolishly tries:
She scarce gave one squall,
When the cheese she let fall,
And the fox ran away with the prize.

MORAL

Ye innocent fair,
Of coxcombs beware,
To flattery never give ear;
Try well each pretense,
And keep to plain sense,
And then you have little to fear.

LITTLE B. (TAYLOR?)

❧ ❧ ❧

THE USE OF FLOWERS

God might have bade the earth bring forth
Enough for great and small,
The oak tree and the cedar tree,
Without a flower at all.

We might have had enough, enough
For every want of ours,
For luxury, medicine, and toil,
And yet have had no flowers.

The ore within the mountain mine
Requireth none to grow;
Nor doth it need the lotus flower
To make the river flow.

The clouds might give abundant rain,
The nightly dews might fall,
And the herb that keepeth life in man
Might yet have drunk them all.

Then wherefore, wherefore were they made,
All dyed with rainbow light,
All fashioned with supremest grace,
Upspringing day and night,—

Springing in valleys green and low,
And on the mountain high,
And in the silent wilderness,
Where no man passes by?

Our outward life requires them not,
Then wherefore had they birth?—
To minister delight to man,
To beautify the earth;

To comfort man, to whisper hope
Whene'er his faith is dim;
For Whoso careth for the flowers
Will much more care for him.

MARY HOWITT

CONTENTED JOHN

One honest John Tomkins, a hedger and ditcher,
Although he was poor, did not want to be richer;
For all such vain wishes in him were prevented
By a fortunate habit of being contented.

Though cold was the weather, or dear was the food,
John never was found in a murmuring mood;
For this he was constantly heard to declare,—
What he could not prevent he would cheerfully bear.

"For why should I grumble and murmur?" he said;
"If I cannot get meat, I can surely get bread;
And, though fretting may make my calamities deeper,
It can never cause bread and cheese to be cheaper."

If John was afflicted with sickness or pain,
He wished himself better, but did not complain,
Nor lie down and fret in despondence and sorrow,
But said that he hoped to be better to-morrow.

If any one wronged him or treated him ill,
Why, John was good-natured and sociable still;
For he said that revenging the injury done
Would be making two rogues when there need be but one.

And thus honest John, though his station was humble,
Passed through this sad world without even a grumble;
And I wish that some folks, who are greater and richer,
Would copy John Tomkins, the hedger and ditcher.

JANE TAYLOR

THE OLD MAN'S COMFORTS, AND HOW HE GAINED THEM

"You are old, Father William," the young man cried;
"The few locks which are left you are gray;
You are hale, Father William—a hearty old man:
Now tell me the reason, I pray."

"In the days of my youth," Father William replied,
"I remembered that youth would fly fast,
And abused not my health and my vigor at first,
That I never might need them at last."

"You are old, Father William," the young man cried,
"And pleasures with youth pass away;
And yet you lament not the days that are gone:
Now tell me the reason, I pray."

"In the days of my youth," Father William replied,
"I remembered that youth could not last;
I thought of the future, whatever I did,
That I never might grieve for the past."

"You are old, Father William," the young man cried,
"And life must be hastening away;
You are cheerful, and love to converse upon death:
Now tell me the reason, I pray."

"I am cheerful, young man," Father William replied;
"Let the cause thy attention engage:
In the days of my youth I remembered my God;
And he hath not forgotten my age."

Robert Southey

☙ ☙ ☙

THE FROST

The frost looked forth on a still, clear night,
And whispered, "Now I shall be out of sight;
So through the valley and over the height
I'll silently take my way.
I will not go on like that blustering train,
The wind and the snow, the hail and the rain,
That make so much bustle and noise in vain,
But I'll be as busy as they!"

He flew up, and powdered the mountain's crest;
He lit on the trees, and their boughs he dressed
With diamonds and pearls;—and over the breast
Of the quivering lake he spread

A bright coat of mail, that it need not fear
The glittering point of many a spear
That he hung on its margin, far and near,
  Where a rock was rearing its head.

He went to the windows of those who slept,
And over each pane, like a fairy crept;
Wherever he breathed—wherever he stepped—
  Most beautiful things were seen
By morning's first light! There were flowers and trees,
With bevies of birds and swarms of bright bees;
There were cities—temples, and towers; and these,
  All pictured in silvery sheen!

But one thing he did that was hardly fair—
He peeped in the cupboard, and finding there
That none had remembered for him to prepare,
  "Now, just to set them a-thinking,
I'll bite their rich basket of fruit," said he,
"This burly old pitcher—I'll burst it in three!
And the glass with the water they've left for me
  Shall 'tchick!' to tell them I'm drinking!"

HANNAH FLAGG GOULD

❧ ❧ ❧

THE BATTLE OF BLENHEIM

It was a summer evening,
  Old Kaspar's work was done,
And he before his cottage door
  Was sitting in the sun,
And by him sported on the green
His little grandchild Wilhelmine.

She saw her brother Peterkin
  Roll something large and round,
Which he beside the rivulet
  In playing there had found;

He came to ask what he had found,
That was so large and smooth and round.

Old Kaspar took it from the boy,
  Who stood expectant by;
And then the old man shook his head,
  And with a natural sigh,
"'T is some poor fellow's skull," said he,
"Who fell in the great victory.

"I find them in the garden,
  For there's many hereabout;
And often, when I go to plow
  The plowshare turns them out!
For many thousand men," said he,
"Were slain in that great victory."

"Now tell us what 't was all about,"
  Young Peterkin he cries;
While little Wilhelmine looks up
  With wonder-waiting eyes;
"Now tell us all about the war,
And what they killed each other for."

"It was the English," Kaspar cried,
  "Who put the French to rout;
But what they killed each other for
  I could not well make out.
But everybody said," quoth he,
"That 't was a famous victory.

"My father lived at Blenheim then,
  Yon little stream hard by;
They burnt his dwelling to the ground,
  And he was forced to fly:
So with his wife and child he fled,
Nor had he where to rest his head.

"With fire and sword the country round
  Was wasted far and wide,
And many a childing mother then
  And new-born baby died:
But things like that, you know, must be
At every famous victory.

"They say it was a shocking sight
  After the field was won;
For many thousand bodies here
  Lay rotting in the sun:
But things like that, you know, must be
After a famous victory.

"Great praise the Duke of Marlbro' won,
  And our good Prince Eugene."
"Why 't was a very wicked thing!"
  Said little Wilhelmine.
"Nay—nay—my little girl," quoth he,
"It was a famous victory.

"And everybody praised the Duke
  Who this great fight did win."
"And what good came of it at last?"
  Quoth little Peterkin.
"Why, that I cannot tell," said he,
"But 't was a famous victory."

Robert Southey

❧ ❧ ❧

THE CHAMELEON

A FABLE

FROM M. DE LAMOTTE

Oft has it been my lot to mark
A proud, conceited, talking spark,
With eyes, that hardly served at most
To guard their master 'gainst a post;

Yet round the world the blade has been
To see whatever could be seen,
Returning from his finished tour,
Grown ten times perter than before;
Whatever word you chance to drop,
The traveled fool your mouth will stop:
"Sir, if my judgment you'll allow,
I've seen—and sure I ought to know,"
So begs you'd pay a due submission,
And acquiesce in his decision.

Two travelers of such a cast,
As o'er Arabia's wilds they passed
And on their way in friendly chat,
Now talked of this, and then of that,
Discoursed awhile, 'mongst other matter,
Of the chameleon's form and nature.
"A stranger animal," cries one,
"Sure never lived beneath the sun.
A lizard's body, lean and long,
A fish's head, a serpent's tongue,
Its foot with triple claw disjoined;
And what a length of tail behind!
How slow its pace; and then its hue—
Who ever saw so fine a blue?"

"Hold, there," the other quick replies,
"'T is *green*, I saw it with these eyes,
As late with open mouth it lay,
And warmed it in the sunny ray:
Stretched at its ease, the beast I viewed
And saw it eat the air for food."
"I've seen it, sir, as well as you,
And must again affirm it blue;
At leisure I the beast surveyed,
Extending in the cooling shade."
"'T is green, 't is green, sir I assure ye!"
"Green!" cries the other in a fury—

"Why, sir!—d'ye think I've lost my eyes?"
"'T were no great loss," the friend replies,
"For, if they always serve you thus,
You'll find them of but little use."

So high at last the contest rose,
From words they almost came to blows;
When luckily came by a third—
To him the question they referred,
And begged he'd tell 'em, if he knew,
Whether the thing was green or blue.
"Sirs," cries the umpire, "cease your pother!
The creature's neither one nor t' other.
I caught the animal last night,
And viewed it o'er by candlelight:
I marked it well—'t was black as jet—
You stare—but sirs, I've got it yet,
And can produce it." "Pray, sir, do:
I'll lay my life the thing is blue."
"And I'll be sworn, that when you've seen
The reptile, you'll pronounce him green."
"Well, then, at once to ease the doubt,"
Replies the man, "I'll turn him out:
And when before your eyes I've set him,
If you don't find him black, I'll eat him."
He said: then full before their sight
Produced the beast, and lo!—'t was white.

Both stared, the man looked wondrous wise—
"My children," the chameleon cries,
(Then first the creature found a tongue,)
"You are all right, and all are wrong:
When next you talk of what you view,
Think others see as well as you;
Nor wonder, if you find that none
Prefers your eyesight to his own."

JAMES MERRICK

THE BLACKBERRY GIRL

"Why, Phebe, are you come so soon?
Where are your berries, child?
You cannot, sure, have sold them all,
You had a basket piled."

"No, mother, as I climbed the fence,
The nearest way to town,
My apron caught upon the stake,
And so I tumbled down.

"I scratched my arm and tore my hair,
But still did not complain;
And had my blackberries been safe,
Should not have cared a grain.

"But when I saw them on the ground,
All scattered by my side,
I picked my empty basket up,
And down I sat and cried.

"Just then a pretty little Miss
Chanced to be walking by;
She stopped, and looking pitiful,
She begged me not to cry.

"'Poor little girl, you fell,' said she,
'And must be sadly hurt;'
'Oh, no,' I cried; 'but see my fruit,
All mixed with sand and dirt.'

"'Well, do not grieve for that,' she said;
'Go home, and get some more.'
'Ah, no, for I have stripped the vines,
These were the last they bore.

"'My father, Miss, is very poor,
And works in yonder stall;
He has so many little ones,
He cannot clothe us all.

"'I always longed to go to church,
But never could I go;
For when I asked him for a gown,
He always answered, "No.

"'"There's not a father in the world
That loves his children more;
I'd get you one with all my heart,
But, Phebe, I am poor."

"'But when the blackberries were ripe,
He said to me one day,
"Phebe, if you will take the time
That's given you for play,

"'"And gather blackberries enough,
And carry them to town,
To buy your bonnet and your shoes,
I'll try to get a gown."

"'Oh, Miss, I fairly jumped for joy,
My spirits were so light;
And so, when I had leave to play,
I picked with all my might.

"'I sold enough to get my shoes,
About a week ago;
And these, if they had not been spilt,
Would buy a bonnet, too.

"'But now they're gone, they all are gone,
And I can get no more,
And Sundays I must stay at home,
Just as I did before.'

"And, mother, then I cried again
As hard as I could cry;
And looking up, I saw a tear
Was standing in her eye.

"She caught her bonnet from her head,
'Here, here,' she cried, 'take this!'
'Oh, no, indeed—I fear your ma
Would be offended, Miss.'

"'My ma! no, never; she delights
All sorrow to beguile;
And 't is the sweetest joy she feels,
To make the wretched smile.

"'She taught me when I had enough,
To share it with the poor;
And never let a needy child,
Go empty from the door.

"'So take it, for you need not fear
Offending her, you see;
I have another, too, at home,
And one's enough for me.'

"So then I took it—here it is—
For pray what could I do?
And, mother, I shall love that Miss
As long as I love you."

UNKNOWN

MABEL ON MIDSUMMER DAY

A STORY OF THE OLDEN TIME

PART I

"Arise, my maiden, Mabel,"
The mother said; "arise,
For the golden sun of midsummer
Is shining in the skies.

"Arise, my little maiden,
For thou must speed away,
To wait upon thy grandmother
This livelong summer day.

"And thou must carry with thee
This wheaten cake so fine,
This new-made pat of butter,
This little flask of wine;

"And tell the dear old body,
This day I cannot come,
For the goodman went out yestermorn,
And he is not come home.

"And more than this, poor Amy
Upon my knee doth lie;
I fear me, with this fever pain
The little child will die!

"And thou canst help thy grandmother
The table thou canst spread;
Canst feed the little dog and bird;
And thou canst make her bed.

"And thou canst fetch the water
From the lady-well hard by;
And thou canst gather from the wood
The fagots brown and dry;

"Canst go down to the lonesome glen,
To milk the mother ewe;
This is the work, my Mabel,
That thou wilt have to do.

"But listen now, my Mabel,
This is midsummer day,
When all the fairy people
From elfland come away.

"And when thou 'rt in the lonesome glen,
  Keep by the running burn,
And do not pluck the strawberry flower,
  Nor break the lady-fern.

"But think not of the fairy folk,
  Lest mischief should befall;
Think only of poor Amy,
  And how thou lov'st us all.

"Yet keep good heart, my Mabel,
  If thou the fairies see,
And give them kindly answer
  If they should speak to thee.

"And when into the fir-wood
  Thou goest for fagots brown,
Do not, like idle children,
  Go wandering up and down.

"But fill thy little apron,
  My child, with earnest speed;
And that thou break no living bough
  Within the wood take heed.

"For they are spiteful brownies
  Who in the wood abide;
So be thou careful of this thing,
  Lest evil should betide.

"But think not, little Mabel,
  Whilst thou art in the wood,
Of dwarfish, willful brownies,
  But of the Father good.

"And when thou goest to the spring
  To fetch the water thence,
Do not disturb the little stream,
  Lest this should give offense.

"For the queen of all the fairies,
  She loves that water bright;
I've seen her drinking there myself
  On many a summer night.

"But she's a gracious lady,
  And her thou need'st not fear;
Only disturb thou not the stream,
  Nor spill the water clear."

"Now all this I will heed, mother,
  Will no word disobey,
And wait upon the grandmother
  This livelong summer day."

PART II

Away tripped little Mabel,
  With the wheaten cake so fine,
With the new-made pat of butter,
  And the little flask of wine.

And long before the sun was hot,
  And the summer mist had cleared,
Beside the good old grandmother
  The willing child appeared.

And all her mother's message
  She told with right good-will,
How that the father was away,
  And the little child was ill.

And then she swept the hearth up clean,
  And then the table spread;
And next she fed the dog and bird;
  And then she made the bed.

"And go now," said the grandmother,
  "Ten paces down the dell,
And bring in water for the day,—
  Thou know'st the lady-well."

The first time that good Mabel went,
  Nothing at all saw she,
Except a bird, a sky-blue bird,
  That sat upon a tree.

The next time that good Mabel went,
  There sat a lady bright
Beside the well,—a lady small,
  All clothed in green and white.

A courtesy low made Mabel,
  And then she stooped to fill
Her pitcher at the sparkling spring,
  But no drop did she spill.

"Thou art a handy maiden,"
  The fairy lady said;
"Thou hast not spilt a drop, nor yet
  The fairy spring troubled!

"And for this thing which thou hast done,
  Yet mayst not understand,
I give to thee a better gift
  Than houses or than land.

"Thou shalt do well whate'er thou dost,
  As thou hast done this day;
Shalt have the will and power to please,
  And shalt be loved alway."

Thus having said, she passed from sight,
  And naught could Mabel see,
But the little bird, the sky-blue bird,
  Upon the leafy tree.

"And now go," said the grandmother,
  "And fetch in fagots dry;
All in the neighboring fir-wood
  Beneath the trees they lie."

Away went kind, good Mabel,
  Into the fir-wood near,
Where all the ground was dry and brown,
  And the grass grew thin and sear.

She did not wander up and down,
  Nor yet a live branch pull,
But steadily of the fallen boughs
  She picked her apron full.

And when the wildwood brownies
  Came sliding to her mind,
She drove them thence, as she was told,
  With home thoughts sweet and kind.

But all that while the brownies
  Within the fir-wood still,
They watched her how she picked the wood,
  And strove to do no ill.

"And, oh, but she is small and neat,"
  Said one; "'t were shame to spite
A creature so demure and meek,
  A creature harmless quite!"

"Look only," said another,
  "At her little gown of blue;
At her kerchief pinned about her head,
  And at her little shoe!"

"Oh, but she is a comely child,"
  Said a third; "and we will lay
A good-luck penny in her path,
  A boon for her this day,—
Seeing she broke no living wood;
  No live thing did affray!"

With that the smallest penny,
  Of the finest silver ore,
Upon the dry and slippery path,
  Lay Mabel's feet before.

With joy she picked the penny up,
  The fairy penny good;
And with her fagots dry and brown
  Went wandering from the wood.

"Now she has that," said the brownies,
  "Let flax be ever so dear,
'T will buy her clothes of the very best,
  For many and many a year!"

"And go now," said the grandmother,
  "Since falling is the dew,
Go down unto the lonesome glen,
  And milk the mother ewe!"

All down into the lonesome glen,
  Through copses thick and wild,
Through moist rank grass, by trickling streams,
  Went on the willing child.

And when she came to the lonesome glen,
  She kept beside the burn,
And neither plucked the strawberry flower
  Nor broke the lady fern.

And while she milked the mother ewe
  Within this lonesome glen,
She wished that little Amy
  Were strong and well again.

And soon as she thought this thought,
  She heard a coming sound,
As if a thousand fairy folk
  Were gathering all around.

And then she heard a little voice,
  Shrill as the midge's wing,
That spake aloud,—"A human child
  Is here; yet mark this thing,—

"The lady-fern is all unbroke,
  The strawberry flower unta'en!
What shall be done for her who still
  From mischief can refrain?"

"Give her a fairy cake!" said one;
  "Grant her a wish!" said three;
"The latest wish that she hath wished,"
  Said all, "whate'er it be!"

Kind Mabel heard the words they spake,
  And from the lonesome glen
Unto the good old grandmother
  Went gladly back again.

Thus happened it to Mabel
  On that midsummer day,
And these three fairy blessings
  She took with her away.

'T is good to make all duty sweet,
  To be alert and kind;
'T is good, like little Mabel,
  To have a willing mind.

MARY HOWITT

LLEWELLYN AND HIS DOG

The spearmen heard the bugle sound,
  And cheer'ly smiled the morn;
And many a brach, and many a hound,
  Attend Llewellyn's horn.

And still he blew a louder blast,
  And gave a louder cheer;
"Come, Gelert! why art thou the last
  Llewellyn's horn to hear?

"Oh, where does faithful Gelert roam,
  The flower of all his race?
So true, so brave—a lamb at home,
  A lion in the chase."

That day Llewellyn little loved
  The chase of hart or hare,
And scant and small the booty proved,
  For Gelert was not there.

Unpleased, Llewellyn homeward hied,
  When, near the portal seat,
His truant Gelert he espied,
  Bounding his lord to greet.

But when he gained the castle door,
  Aghast the chieftain stood;
The hound was smeared with gouts of gore,
  His lips and fangs ran blood!

Llewellyn gazed with wild surprise;
  Unused such looks to meet,
His fav'rite checked his joyful guise,
  And crouched, and licked his feet.

Onward in haste Llewellyn passed
  (And on went Gelert too),
And still, where'er his eyes were cast,
  Fresh blood gouts shocked his view!

O'erturned his infant's bed he found,
  The blood-stained cover rent;
And all around the walls and ground
  With recent blood besprent.

He called his child—no voice replied;
  He searched with terror wild;
Blood! blood! he found on every side,
  But nowhere found his child!

"Hell-hound! by thee my child's devoured!"
  The frantic father cried;
And to the hilt his vengeful sword
  He plunged in Gelert's side.

His suppliant, as to earth he fell,
  No pity could impart;
But still his Gelert's dying yell
  Passed heavy o'er his heart.

Aroused by Gelert's dying yell,
  Some slumberer wakened nigh;
What words the parent's joy can tell,
  To hear his infant cry!

Concealed beneath a mangled heap,
  His hurried search had missed,
All glowing from his rosy sleep,
  His cherub boy he kissed!

Nor scratch had he, nor harm, nor dread,
  But the same couch beneath
Lay a great wolf, all torn and dead,—
  Tremendous still in death!

Ah, what was then Llewellyn's pain!
  For now the truth was clear;
The gallant hound the wolf had slain,
  To save Llewellyn's heir.

Vain, vain was all Llewellyn's woe;
  "Best of thy kind, adieu!
The frantic deed which laid thee low
  This heart shall ever rue!"

And now a gallant tomb they raised,
  With costly sculpture decked;
And marbles storied with his praise
  Poor Gelert's bones protect.

Here never could the spearmen pass,
  Or forester, unmoved,
Here oft the tear-besprinkled grass
  Llewellyn's sorrow proved.

And here he hung his horn and spear,
  And oft, as evening fell,
In fancy's piercing sounds would hear
  Poor Gelert's dying yell.

William Robert Spencer

❧ ❧ ❧

THE SNOWBIRD'S SONG

The ground was all covered with snow one day,
And two little sisters were busy at play,
When a snowbird was sitting close by on a tree,
And merrily singing his chick-a-de-dee,
    Chick-a-de-dee, chick-a-de-dee,
And merrily singing his chick-a-de-dee.

He had not been singing that tune very long,
Ere Emily heard him, so loud was his song:
"Oh, sister, look out of the window," said she;
"Here's a dear little bird singing chick-a-de-dee.
    Chick-a-de-dee, etc.

"Oh, mother, do get him some stockings and shoes,
And a nice little frock, and a hat if he choose;
I wish he'd come into the parlor and see
How warm we would make him, poor chick-a-de-dee."
    Chick-a-de-dee, etc.

"There is one, my dear child, though I cannot tell who,
Has clothed me already, and warm enough too.
Good morning! Oh, who are so happy as we?"
And away he went singing his chick-a-de-dee.
Chick-a-de-dee, etc.

FRANCIS C. WOODWORTH

FOR A' THAT AND A' THAT

Is there for honest poverty
Wha hangs his head, and a' that?
The coward slave, we pass him by;
We dare be poor for a' that.
For a' that, and a' that,
Our toils obscure, and a' that;
The rank is but the guinea's stamp,—
The man's the gowd for a' that.

What though on hamely fare we dine,
Wear hoddin gray, and a' that?
Gie fools their silks, and knaves their wine,—
A man's a man for a' that.
For a' that, and a' that,
Their tinsel show, and a' that;
The honest man, though e'er sae poor,
Is king o' men for a' that.

Ye see yon birkie ca'd a lord,
Wha struts, and stares, and a' that—
Though hundreds worship at his word,
He's but a coof for a' that;
For a' that, and a' that,
His riband, star, and a' that;
The man of independent mind,
He looks and laughs at a' that.

A prince can mak a belted knight,
  A marquis, duke, and a' that;
But an honest man's aboon his might,—
  Guid faith, he maunna fa' that!
For a' that, and a' that;
  Their dignities, and a' that,
The pith o' sense, and pride o' worth,
  Are higher ranks than a' that.

Then let us pray that come it may,—
  As come it will for a' that,—
That sense and worth, o'er a' the earth,
  May bear the gree, and a' that.
For a' that, and a' that,
  It's coming yet, for a' that,—
When man to man, the warld o'er,
  Shall brothers be for a' that!

ROBERT BURNS

FABLES

FABLES FROM ÆSOP

THE GOOSE THAT LAID GOLDEN EGGS

THERE was a man who once had a very handsome goose, that always laid golden eggs. Now, he thought there must be gold inside of her, so he wrung her neck straightway, and found she was exactly like all other geese. He thought to find riches, and lost the little he had.

The fable teaches that one who has anything should be content with it, and avoid covetousness, lest he lose what he has.

☙ ☙ ☙

THE BOYS AND THE FROGS

A company of idle boys were watching some frogs by the side of a pond, and as fast as any of the frogs lifted their heads the boys would pelt them down again with stones.

"Boys," said one of the frogs, "you forget that, though this may be fun for you, it is death to us."

☙ ☙ ☙

THE LION AND THE MOUSE

A mouse happened to run into the mouth of a sleeping lion, who roused himself, caught him, and was just about eating him, when the little fellow begged him to let him go, saying, "If I am saved, I shall be everlastingly grateful." So, with a smile, the lion let him off. It befell him not long after to be saved by the mouse's gratitude, for when he was caught by some hunters and bound by ropes to a tree, the mouse, hearing his roaring groans, came and gnawed the ropes, and set him free, saying, "You laughed at me once, as if you could receive no return from me, but now, you see, it is you who have to be grateful to me."

The story shows that there come sudden changes of affairs, when the most powerful owe everything to the weakest.

❧ ❧ ❧

THE FOX AND THE GRAPES

A hungry fox discovered some bunches of grapes hanging from a vine high up a tree, and, as he gazed, longed to get at them, and could not; so he left them hanging there and went off muttering, "They're sour grapes."

❧ ❧ ❧

THE FROG AND THE OX

An ox, grazing in a swampy meadow, chanced to set his foot among a parcel of young frogs, and crushed nearly the whole brood to death. One that escaped ran off to his mother with the dreadful news. "O mother," said he, "it was a beast—such a big four-footed beast, that did it!" "Big?" quoth the old frog, "How big? was it as big"—and she puffed herself out—"as big as this?" "Oh, a great deal bigger than that." "Well, was it so big?" and she swelled herself out yet more. "Indeed, mother, but it was; and if you were to burst yourself, you would never reach half its size." The old frog made one more trial, determined to be as big as the ox, and burst herself, indeed.

❧ ❧ ❧

THE CAT, THE MONKEY, AND THE CHESTNUTS

A cat and a monkey were sitting one day in the chimney corner watching some chestnuts which their master had laid down to roast in the ashes. The chestnuts had begun to burst with the heat, and the monkey said to the cat, "It is plain that your paws were made especially for pulling out those chestnuts. Do you reach forth and draw them out. Your paws are, indeed, exactly like our master's hands." The cat was greatly flattered by this speech, and reached forward for the tempting chestnuts, but scarcely had he touched the hot ashes than he drew back with a cry, for he had burnt his paw; but he tried again, and managed to pull one chestnut out; then he pulled another, and a third, though each time he singed the hair on his paws. When he could pull no more out he turned about and found that the monkey had taken the time to crack the chestnuts and eat them.

THE COUNTRY MAID AND HER MILKPAIL

A country maid was walking slowly along with a pail of milk upon her head, and thinking thus:

"The money for which I shall sell this milk will buy me three hundred eggs. These eggs, allowing for what may prove addled, will produce at least two hundred and fifty chickens. The chickens will be fit to carry to market about Christmas, when poultry always brings a good price, so that by May-day I shall have money enough to buy a new gown. Let me see—green suits me; yes, it shall be green. In this dress I will go to the fair, where all the young fellows will want me for a partner, but I shall refuse every one of them." By this time she was so full of her fancy that she tossed her head proudly, when over went the pail, which she had entirely forgotten, and all the milk was spilled on the ground.

Moral. Don't count your chickens before they are hatched.

THE ASS IN THE LION'S SKIN

The Ass once dressed himself in the Lion's skin and went about frightening all the little beasts. Now he happened on the Fox, and tried to frighten him too; but the Fox chanced to hear

THE TORTOISE AND THE HARE.

THE FOX WITHOUT A TAIL.

him speak, and said: "Well, to be sure, I should have been frightened too, if I hadn't heard you bray, and seen your ears sticking out."

So there are some men who make themselves appear very fine outwardly, but are betrayed as soon as they begin to talk.

☙ ☙ ☙

THE TORTOISE AND THE HARE

What a dull, heavy creature," says the Hare, "is this Tortoise!" "And yet," says the Tortoise, "I'll run with you for a wager." "Done," says the Hare, and then they asked the Fox to be the judge. They started together, and the Tortoise kept jogging on still, till he came to the end of the course. The Hare laid himself down midway and took a nap; "for," says he, "I can catch up with the Tortoise when I please." But it seems he overslept himself, for when he came to wake, though he scudded away as fast as possible, the Tortoise had got to the post before him and won the wager.

Slow and steady wins the race.

☙ ☙ ☙

THE VAIN JACKDAW

A jackdaw picked up some beautiful feathers left by the peacocks on the ground. He stuck them into his own tail, and, thinking himself too fine to mix with the other daws, strutted off to the peacocks, expecting to be welcomed as one of themselves.

The peacocks at once saw through his disguise, and, despising him for his foolishness and conceit, began to peck him, and soon he was stripped of all his borrowed plumes.

Very much ashamed, the jackdaw went sadly home, meaning to join his old friends as if nothing had happened. But they, remembering how he had scorned them before, chased him away and would have nothing to do with him.

"If you had been content," said one, "to remain as nature

made you, instead of trying to be what you are not, you would have neither been punished by your betters nor despised by your equals."

❧ ❧ ❧

THE FOX WITHOUT A TAIL

A fox lost his tail in escaping from a steel trap. When he began to go about again, he found that every one looked down upon or laughed at him. Not liking this, he thought to himself that if he could persuade the other foxes to cut off their tails, his own loss would not be so noticeable.

Accordingly he called together the foxes and said: "How is it that you still wear your tails? Of what use are they? They are in the way, they often get caught in traps, they are heavy to carry and not pretty to look upon. Believe me, we are far better without them. Cut off your tails, my friends, and you will see how much more comfortable it is. I for my part have never enjoyed myself so much nor found life so pleasant as I have since I lost mine."

Upon this, a sly old fox, seeing through the trick, cried, "It seems to me, my friend, that you would not be so anxious for us to cut off our tails, if you had not already lost yours."

❧ ❧ ❧

THE WOLF IN SHEEP'S CLOTHING

A wolf put on the skin of a sheep, and getting in among the flock by means of this disguise, killed many of the sheep. The shepherd, who wondered why so many of his flock had disappeared, at last discovered the deceit. He fastened a rope cunningly round the pretended sheep's neck, led him to a tree, and there hanged him.

Some other shepherds passing that way and seeing what they thought was a sheep hanging from a tree, said, "What, brother! Surely you do not hang sheep?"

"No," answered the shepherd, "but I hang wolves when I catch them dressed up in sheep's skins!"

Then he showed them their mistake, and they praised the justice of the deed he had done.

☙ ☙ ☙

THE CROW AND THE PITCHER

A crow, whose throat was parched and dry with thirst, saw a pitcher in the distance. In great joy he flew to it, but found that it held only a little water, and even that was too near the bottom to be reached, for all his stooping and straining. Next he tried to overturn the pitcher, thinking that he would at least be able to catch some of the water as it trickled out. But this he was not strong enough to do. In the end he found some pebbles lying near, and by dropping them one by one into the pitcher, he managed at last to raise the water up to the very brim, and thus was able to quench his thirst.

☙ ☙ ☙

THE MAN, HIS SON, AND HIS ASS

A man and his son were leading their ass to market. A girl, seeing them, cried, "Why walk when you can ride?" On hearing this, the man set his son upon the ass.

Going further, they heard an old man say, "Shame for the young to ride while old people walk!" Thereupon the man made his son get down and rode himself.

Presently they met some women who cried, "Look at the poor tired son and lazy father!" Hearing this, the man took his son up beside him and so they rode into the town.

There a young man called to them, "Two men on one beast! It seems to me you are more fit to carry the ass than he is to carry you."

Then they got down, tied the beast's legs to a pole, and carried him thus till they came to a bridge. As they went, the children shouted so loudly that the ass took fright—kicked his legs free, and jumped over the bridge into the river.

Thus having lost his ass, the man went home, crying, "Try to please everybody and you will please nobody, not even yourself!"

FABLES OF INDIA

ADAPTED BY P. V. RAMASWAMI RAJU

THE CAMEL AND THE PIG

A CAMEL said, "Nothing like being tall! See how tall I am." A pig who heard these words said, "Nothing like being short; see how short I am!"

The camel said, "Well, if I fail to prove the truth of what I said, I will give you my hump."

The pig said, "If I fail to prove the truth of what I have said, I will give up my snout."

"Agreed!" said the camel.

"Just so!" said the pig.

They came to a garden inclosed by a low wall without any opening. The camel stood on this side the wall, and, reaching the plants within by means of his long neck, made a breakfast on them. Then he turned jeeringly to the pig, who had been standing at the bottom of the wall, without even having a look at the good things in the garden, and said, "Now, would you be tall or short?"

Next they came to a garden inclosed by a high wall, with a wicket gate at one end. The pig entered by the gate, and, after having eaten his fill of the vegetables within, came out, laughing at the poor camel, who had had to stay outside, because he was too tall to enter the garden by the gate, and said, "Now, would you be tall or short?"

Then they thought the matter over, and came to the conclusion that the camel should keep his hump and the pig his snout, observing:

"Tall is good, where tall would do;
Of short, again, 't is also true!"

THE MAN AND HIS PIECE OF CLOTH

A man in the East, where they do not require as much clothing as in colder climates, gave up all worldly concerns and retired to a wood, where he built a hut and lived in it.

His only clothing was a piece of cloth which he wore round his waist. But, as ill-luck would have it, rats were plentiful in the wood, so he had to keep a cat. The cat required milk to keep it, so a cow had to be kept. The cow required tending, so a cow-boy was employed. The boy required a house to live in, so a house was built for him. To look after the house a maid had to be engaged. To provide company for the maid a few more houses had to be built, and people invited to live in them. In this manner a little township sprang up.

The man said, "*The further we seek to go from the world and its cares, the more they multiply!*"

☙ ☙ ☙

THE SEA, THE FOX, AND THE WOLF

A fox that lived by the seashore once met a wolf that had never seen the sea. The wolf said, "What is the sea?"

"It is a great piece of water by my dwelling," said the fox.

"Is it under your control?" asked the wolf.

"Certainly," said the fox.

"Will you show me the sea, then?" said the wolf.

"With pleasure," said the fox. So the fox led the wolf to the sea, and said to the waves, "Now go back,"—they went back. "Now come up,"—and they came up! Then the fox said to the waves, "My friend, the wolf, has come to see you, so you will come up and go back till I bid you stop;" and the wolf saw, with wonder, the waves coming up and going back.

He said to the fox, "May I go into the sea?"

"As far as you like. Don't be afraid, for, at a word, the sea would go or come as I bid, and as you have already seen."

The wolf believed the fox, and followed the waves rather far from the shore. A great wave soon upset him, and threw up his carcass on the shore. The fox made a hearty breakfast on it, saying, "*The fool's ear was made for the knave's tongue.*"

❧ ❧ ❧

THE BIRDS AND THE LIME

A fowler in the East once went to a wood, scattered some grain on the ground, spread a net over it with some lime in it, and was watching from a distance to see what luck would attend his efforts.

A great many birds assembled on the trees around the net, and said, "What fine corn that is! We can seldom hope to get anything like it."

An owl that was close by said, "How nice that white thing in the net is!"

"What is it?" said the birds.

"Why, it is our best friend in the world; it is lime. When it holds us in its embrace, we can never hope to get away."

The birds left the place at once. Said the fowler, "*A clever bird knows the lime!*"

❧ ❧ ❧

THE RAVEN AND THE CATTLE

One evening, as some cattle were wending their way home, a raven rode on the horns of a bull in the herd; and as he approached the cottage, cried to the farmer, "Friend, my work for the day is over; you may now take charge of your cattle."

"What was your work?" asked the farmer.

"Why," said the raven, "the arduous task of watching these cattle and bringing them home."

"Am I to understand you have been doing all the work for me?" said the farmer.

"Certainly," said the raven, and flew away with a laugh.

Quoth the farmer with surprise, "*How many there are that take credit for things which they have never done!*"

❧ ❧ ❧

TINSEL AND LIGHTNING

A piece of tinsel on a rock once said to a pebble, "You see how bright I am! I am by birth related to the lightning."

"Indeed!" said the pebble; "then accept my humble respects."

Some time after, a flash of lightning struck the rock, and the tinsel lost all its brilliancy by the scorching effects of the flash.

"Where is your brilliancy now?" said the pebble.

"Oh, it is gone to the skies," said the tinsel, "for I have lent it to the lightning that came down a moment ago to borrow it of me."

"Dear me!" said the pebble; "*how many fibs doth good bragging need!*"

❧ ❧ ❧

THE ASS AND THE WATCH-DOG

A watch-dog in a village was barking all night to keep thieves off from his master's house. An ass, who observed this, thought that the dog amused himself by barking. So he brayed all night. When the day dawned, the owner of the ass thought the poor animal had been suffering from some disorder. Therefore he sent for the village doctor, and laid the case before him.

The doctor examined the animal closely, and said, "Friend, you must brand this ass forthwith, else he will soon go into fits and die."

The ass said, "I assure you nothing is wrong with me; I simply amused myself last night."

"Oh, no," said the inexorable leech; "I know what the wily brute means. He would rather die, and make you the loser, than be branded and recover his health."

So they bound the ass with ropes, and branded him all over with red-hot irons. Some time after the ass moved out to see how the village had fared during his illness. The dog asked why he had been branded. The ass narrated the story. Quoth the dog, "*He that mistakes work for amusement must pay for his error.*"

❧ ❧ ❧

THE LARK AND ITS YOUNG ONES

A child went up to a lark, and said, "Good lark, have you any young ones?"

"Yes, child, I have," said the lark; "and they are very pretty ones indeed!" Then she pointed to them, and said, "This is Fair Wing, that is Tiny Bill, and that other is Bright Eye."

The child said, "Yes, at home, we are three—myself and my two sisters, Jane and Alice; and mamma says we are pretty little children, and that she is very fond of us."

To this the little larks replied, "Oh yes, mamma is very fond of us too."

Then the child said, "Good lark, will you send home Tiny Bill to play with me?" Before the lark could reply, Bright Eye said, "Yes, if you will send little Alice to play with us in our nest."

The child said, "Oh, Alice will be so sorry to leave home, and come away from mamma!"

Bright Eye said, "Tiny Bill will be so sorry to leave our nest, and go away from mamma!"

The child was abashed, and went home, saying, "*Ah, every one is fond of home!*"

❧ ❧ ❧

THE TWO GEMS

A despot in the East once said to his fawning courtiers, "He that goes round my kingdom in the shortest possible time shall have one of these two gems."

A courtier went round the King, and said, "Sire, may I have the prize?"

"How so?" said the King.

"Why, you are the kingdom, are you not?" said the courtier.

The despot was so well pleased with the courtier that he gave him both the gems.

The other courtiers said, in a whisper, "*Flatterers prey upon fools.*"

FAIRY TALES AND LAUGHTER STORIES

SCANDINAVIAN STORIES

THE HARDY TIN SOLDIER

BY HANS CHRISTIAN ANDERSEN

THERE were once five-and-twenty tin soldiers; they were all brothers, for they had all been born of one old tin spoon. They shouldered their muskets, and looked straight before them; their uniform was red and blue, and very splendid. The first thing they had heard in the world, when the lid was taken off their box, had been the words "Tin soldiers!" These words were uttered by a little boy, clapping his hands: the soldiers had been given to him, for it was his birthday; and now he put them upon the table. Each soldier was exactly like the rest; but one of them had been cast last of all, and there had not been enough tin to finish him; but he stood as firmly upon his one leg as the others on their two; and it was just this Soldier who became remarkable.

On the table on which they had been placed stood many other playthings, but the toy that attracted most attention was a neat castle of cardboard. Through the little windows one could see straight into the hall. Before the castle some little trees were placed round a little looking-glass, which was to represent a clear lake. Waxen swans swam on this lake, and were mirrored in it. This was all very pretty; but the prettiest of all was a little lady, who stood at the open door of the castle; she was also cut out in paper, but she had a dress of the clearest gauze, and a little narrow blue ribbon over her shoulders, that looked like a scarf; and in the middle of this ribbon was a shining tinsel rose as big as her whole face. The little lady stretched out both her arms, for she was a dancer; and then she lifted one leg so high that the Tin Soldier could not see it at all, and thought that, like himself, she had but one leg.

"That would be the wife for me," thought he; "but she is very grand. She lives in a castle, and I have only a box, and there are five-and-twenty of us in that. It is no place for her. But I must try to make acquaintance with her."

And then he lay down at full length behind a snuff-box which was on the table; there he could easily watch the little dainty lady, who continued to stand upon one leg without losing her balance.

When the evening came all the other tin soldiers were put into their box, and the people in the house went to bed. Now the toys began to play at "visiting," and at "war," and "giving balls." The tin soldiers rattled in their box, for they wanted to join, but could not lift the lid. The nutcracker threw somersaults, and the pencil amused itself on the table: there was so much noise that the canary woke up, and began to speak too, and even in verse. The only two who did not stir from their places were the Tin Soldier and the Dancing Lady: she stood straight up on the point of one of her toes, and stretched out both her arms; and he was just as enduring on his one leg; and he never turned his eyes away from her.

Now the clock struck twelve—and, bounce! the lid flew off the snuff-box; but there was no snuff in it, but a little black Goblin: you see, it was a trick.

"Tin Soldier!" said the Goblin, "don't stare at things that don't concern you."

But the Tin Soldier pretended not to hear him.

"Just you wait till to-morrow!" said the Goblin.

But when the morning came, and the children got up, the Tin Soldier was placed in the window; and whether it was the Goblin or the draught that did it, all at once the window flew open, and the Soldier fell head over heels out of the third story. That was a terrible passage! He put his leg straight up, and stuck with helmet downward and his bayonet between the paving-stones.

The servant-maid and the little boy came down directly to look for him, but though they almost trod upon him, they could not see him. If the Soldier had cried out "Here I am!" they would have found him; but he did not think it fitting to call out loudly, because he was in uniform.

Now it began to rain; the drops soon fell thicker, and at last it came down into a complete stream. When the rain was past, two street boys came by.

"Just look!" said one of them: "there lies a Tin Soldier. He must come out and ride in the boat."

And they made a boat out of a newspaper, and put the Tin Soldier in the middle of it, and so he sailed down the gutter, and the two boys ran beside him and clapped their hands. Goodness preserve us! how the waves rose in that gutter, and how fast the stream ran! But then it had been a heavy rain. The paper boat rocked up and down, and sometimes turned round so rapidly that the Tin Soldier trembled; but he remained firm, and never changed countenance, and looked straight before him, and shouldered his musket.

All at once the boat went into a long drain, and it became as dark as if he had been in his box.

"Where am I going now?" he thought. "Yes, yes, that's the Goblin's fault. Ah! if the little lady only sat here with me in the boat, it might be twice as dark for what I should care."

Suddenly there came a great Water Rat, which lived under the drain.

"Have you a passport?" said the Rat. "Give me your passport."

But the Tin Soldier kept silence, and held his musket tighter than ever. The boat went on, but the Rat came after it. Hu! how he gnashed his teeth, and called out to the bits of straw and wood.

"Hold him! hold him! He hasn't paid toll—he hasn't shown his passport!"

But the stream became stronger and stronger. The Tin Soldier could see the bright daylight where the arch ended; but he heard a roaring noise, which might well frighten a bolder man. Only think—just where the tunnel ended, the drain ran

A VOICE SAID ALOUD. "THE TIN SOLDIER!"

into a great canal; and for him that would have been as dangerous as for us to be carried down a great waterfall.

Now he was already so near it that he could not stop. The boat was carried out, the poor Tin Soldier stiffening himself as much as he could, and no one could say that he moved an eyelid. The boat whirled round three or four times, and was full of water to the very edge—it must sink. The Tin Soldier stood up to his neck in water, and the boat sank deeper and deeper, and the paper was loosened more and more; and now the water closed over the soldier's head. Then he thought of the pretty little Dancer, and how he should never see her again; and it sounded in the Soldier's ears:

> "Farewell, farewell, thou warrior brave,
> For this day thou must die!"

And now the paper parted, and the Tin Soldier fell out; but at that moment he was snapped up by a great fish.

Oh, how dark it was in that fish's body! It was darker yet than in the drain tunnel; and then it was very narrow too. But the Tin Soldier remained unmoved, and lay at full length shouldering his musket.

The fish swam to and fro; he made the most wonderful movements, and then became quite still. At last something flashed through him like lightning. The daylight shone quite clear, and a voice said aloud, "The Tin Soldier!" The fish had been caught, carried to market, bought, and taken into the kitchen, where the cook cut him open with a large knife. She seized the Soldier round the body with both her hands and carried him into the room, where all were anxious to see the remarkable man who had traveled about in the inside of a fish; but the Tin Soldier was not at all proud. They placed him on the table, and there—no! What curious things may happen in the world. The Tin Soldier was in the very room in which he had been before! he saw the same children, and the same toys stood on the table; and there was the pretty castle with the graceful little Dancer. She was still balancing herself on one leg, and held the other extended in the air. She was hardy too. That moved the Tin Soldier; he was very nearly weeping tin tears, but that would not have been proper. He looked at her, but they said nothing to each other.

Then one of the little boys took the Tin Soldier and flung him into the stove. He gave no reason for doing this. It must have been the fault of the Goblin in the snuff-box.

The Tin Soldier stood there quite illuminated, and felt a heat that was terrible; but whether this heat proceeded from the real fire or from love he did not know. The colors had quite gone off from him; but whether that had happened on the journey, or had been caused by grief, no one could say. He looked at the little lady, she looked at him, and he felt that he was melting; but he still stood firm, shouldering his musket. Then suddenly the door flew open, and the draught of air caught the Dancer, and she flew like a sylph just into the stove to the Tin Soldier, and flashed up in a flame, and she was gone. Then the Tin Soldier melted down into a lump; and when the servant-maid took the ashes out next day, she found him in the shape of a little tin heart. But of the Dancer nothing remained but the tinsel rose, and that was burned as black as a coal.

☙ ☙ ☙

THE FIR TREE

BY HANS CHRISTIAN ANDERSEN

OUT in the forest stood a pretty little Fir Tree. It had a good place; it could have sunlight, air there was in plenty, and all around grew many larger comrades—pines as well as firs. But the little Fir Tree wished ardently to become greater. It did not care for the warm sun and the fresh air; it took no notice of the peasant children, who went about talking together, when they had come out to look for strawberries and raspberries. Often they came with a whole pot-full, or had strung berries on a straw; then they would sit down by the little Fir Tree and say, "How pretty and small that one is!" and the Fir Tree did not like to hear that at all.

Next year he had grown a great joint, and the following year he was longer still, for in fir trees one can always tell by the number of rings they have how many years they have been growing.

"Oh, if I were only as great a tree as the other!" sighed the little Fir, "then I would spread my branches far around, and look out from my crown into the wide world. The birds would then build nests in my boughs, and when the wind blew I could nod just as grandly as the others yonder."

It took no pleasure in the sunshine, in the birds, and in the red clouds that went sailing over him morning and evening.

When it was winter, and the snow lay all around, white and sparkling, a hare would often come jumping along, and spring right over the little Fir Tree. Oh! this made him so angry. But two winters went by, and when the third came the little Tree had grown so tall that the hare was obliged to run round it.

"Oh! to grow, to grow, and become old; that's the only fine thing in the world," thought the Tree.

In the autumn woodcutters always came and felled a few of the largest trees; that was done this year too, and the little Fir Tree, that was now quite well grown, shuddered with fear, for the great stately trees fell to the ground with a crash, and their branches were cut off, so that the trees looked quite naked, long, and slender—they could hardly be recognized. But then they were laid upon wagons, and horses dragged them away out of the wood. Where were they going? What destiny awaited them?

In the spring, when the Swallows and the Stork came, the Tree asked them, "Do you know where they were taken? Did you not meet them?"

The Swallows knew nothing about it, but the Stork looked thoughtful, nodded his head, and said:

"Yes, I think so. I met many new ships when I flew out of Egypt; on the ships were stately masts; I fancy these were the trees. They smelt like fir. I can assure you they're stately—very stately."

"Oh that I were only big enough to go over the sea! What kind of thing is this sea, and how does it look?"

"It would take too long to explain all that," said the Stork, and he went away.

"Rejoice in thy youth," said the Sunbeams; "rejoice in thy fresh growth, and in the young life that is within thee."

And the Wind kissed the Tree, and the Dew wept tears upon it; but the Fir Tree did not understand that.

When Christmas-time approached, quite young trees were felled, sometimes trees which were neither so old nor so large as this Fir Tree, that never rested, but always wanted to go away. These young trees, which were always the most beautiful, kept all their branches; they were put upon wagons, and horses dragged them away out of the wood.

"Where are they all going?" asked the Fir Tree. "They are not greater than I—indeed, one of them was much smaller. Why do they keep all their branches? Whither are they taken?"

"We know that! We know that!" chirped the Sparrows. "Yonder in the town we looked in at the windows. We know where they go. Oh! they are dressed up in the greatest pomp and splendor that can be imagined. We have looked in at the windows, and have perceived that they are planted in the middle of a warm room, and adorned with the most beautiful things—gilt apples, honey-cakes, playthings, and many hundred of candles."

"And then?" asked the Fir Tree, and trembled through all its branches. "And then? What happens then?"

"Why, we have not seen anything more. But it was incomparable."

"Perhaps I may be destined to tread this glorious path one day!" cried the Fir Tree, rejoicingly. "That is even better than traveling across the sea. How painfully I long for it! If it were only Christmas now! Now I am great and grown up, like the rest who were led away last year. Oh, if I were only on the carriage! If I were only in the warm room, among all the pomp and splendor! And then? Yes, then something even better will come, something far more charming, or else why should they adorn me so? There must be something grander, something greater still to come; but what? Oh! I'm suffering, I'm longing! I don't know myself what is the matter with me!"

"Rejoice in us," said Air and Sunshine. "Rejoice in thy fresh youth here in the woodland."

But the Fir Tree did not rejoice at all, but it grew and grew;

winter and summer it stood there, green, dark green. The people who saw it said, "That's a handsome tree!" and at Christmas time it was felled before any one of the others. The axe cut deep into its marrow, and the tree fell to the ground with a sigh; it felt a pain, a sensation of faintness, and could not think at all of happiness, for it was sad at parting from its home, from the place where it had grown up; it knew that it should never again see the dear old companions, the little bushes and flowers all around—perhaps not even the birds. The parting was not at all agreeable.

The Tree only came to itself when it was unloaded in a yard, with other trees, and heard a man say:

"This one is famous; we only want this one!"

Now two servants came in gay liveries, and carried the Fir Tree into a large, beautiful parlor. All around the walls hung pictures, and by the great stove stood large Chinese vases with lions on the covers; there were rocking-chairs, silken sofas, great tables covered with picture books, and toys worth a hundred times a hundred dollars, at least the children said so. And th[illegible] Fir Tree was put into a great tub filled with sand; but no[illegible] could see that it was a tub, for it was hung round wit[illegible] cloth, and stood on a large, many-colored carpet. O[illegible] Tree trembled! What was to happen now? Th[illegible] the young ladies also, decked it out. On one [illegible] little nets, cut out of colored paper; every [illegible] sweetmeats; golden apples and walnuts hu[illegible] grew there, and more than a hundred litt[illegible] and blue, were fastened to the differen[illegible] looked exactly like real people—the tre[illegible] before—swung among the foliage, and [illegible] the tree was fixed a tinsel star. It wa[illegible] splendid.

"This evening," said all, "this ev[illegible]

"Oh," thought the Tree, "that[illegible] Oh, that the lights may be soon lit up[illegible] I wonder if trees will come out of the[illegible] the sparrows fly against the panes?[illegible] stand adorned in summer and wi[illegible]

Yes, he did not guess badly. But he had a complete backache from mere longing, and the backache is just as bad for a Tree as the headache for a person.

At last the candles were lighted. What a brilliance, what splendor! The Tree trembled so in all its branches that one of the candles set fire to a green twig, and it was scorched.

"Heaven preserve us!" cried the young ladies; and they hastily put the fire out.

Now the Tree might not even tremble. Oh, that was terrible! It was so afraid of setting fire to some of its ornaments, and it was quite bewildered with all the brilliance. And now the folding doors were thrown open, and a number of children rushed in as if they would have overturned the whole Tree; the older people followed more deliberately. The little ones stood quite silent, but only for a minute; then they shouted till the room rang: they danced gleefully round the Tree, and one present after another was plucked from it.

"What are they about?" thought the Tree. "What's going to be done?"

And the candles burned down to the twigs, and as they [illegible] down they were extinguished, and then the children [illegible]ermission to plunder the Tree. Oh! they rushed [illegible] that every branch cracked again: if it had not [illegible] the top and by the golden star to the ceiling, [illegible]en down.

[illegible]anced about with their pretty toys. No [illegible]ee except one old man, who came up and [illegible]nches, but only to see if a fig or an apple [illegible]

[illegible]" shouted the children; and they drew [illegible]he tree; and he sat down just beneath [illegible]e in the green wood," said he, "and [illegible]vantage of listening to my tale. But [illegible] you hear the story of Ivede-Avede, [illegible] who fell downstairs, and still was [illegible]rried the Princess?"

[illegible]ome, "Klumpey-Dumpey!" cried [illegible] crying and shouting. Only the

Fir Tree was quite silent, and thought, "Shall I not be in it? Shall I have nothing to do in it?" But he had been in the evening's amusement, and had done what was required of him.

And the fat man told about Klumpey-Dumpey who fell downstairs, and yet was raised to honor and married the Princess. And the children clapped their hands, and cried, "Tell another! tell another!" for they wanted to hear about Ivede-Avede; but they only got the story of Klumpey-Dumpey. The Fir Tree stood quite silent and thoughtful; never had the birds in the wood told such a story as that. Klumpey-Dumpey fell downstairs and yet came to honor and married the Princess!

"Yes, so it happens in the world!" thought the Fir Tree, and believed it must be true, because that was such a nice man who told it. "Well, who can know? Perhaps I shall fall downstairs, too, and marry a Princess!" And it looked forward with pleasure to being adorned again, the next evening, with candles and toys, gold and fruit. "To-morrow I shall not tremble," it thought.

"I will rejoice in all my splendor. To-morrow I shall here the story of Klumpey-Dumpey again, and perhaps that of Ivede-Avede, too."

And the Tree stood all night quiet and thoughtful.

In the morning the servants and the chambermaid came in.

"Now my splendor will begin afresh," thought the Tree. But they dragged him out of the room, and upstairs to the garret, and here they put him in a dark corner where no daylight shone.

"What's the meaning of this?" thought the Tree. "What am I to do here? What is to happen?"

And he leaned against the wall, and thought, and thought. And he had time enough, for days and nights went by, and nobody came up; and when at length some one came, it was only to put some great boxes in a corner. Now the Tree stood quite hidden away, and the supposition is that it was quite forgotten.

"Now it's winter outside," thought the Tree. "The earth is hard and covered with snow, and people cannot plant me; therefore I suppose I'm to be sheltered here until spring comes. How considerate that is! How good people are! If it were only not so dark here, and so terribly solitary!—not even a little hare? That was pretty out there in the wood, when the snow lay thick and the hare sprang past; yes, even when he jumped over me; but then I did not like it. It is terribly lonely up here!"

"Piep! piep!" said a little Mouse, and crept forward, and then came another little one. They smelt at the Fir Tree, and then slipped among the branches.

"It's horribly cold," said the two little Mice, "or else it would be comfortable here. Don't you think so, you old Fir Tree?"

"I'm not old at all," said the Fir Tree. "There are many much older than I."

"Where do you come from?" asked the Mice. "And what do you know?" They were dreadfully inquisitive. "Tell us about the most beautiful spot on earth. Have you been there? Have you been in the store room, where cheeses lie on the shelves, and hams hang from the ceiling, where one dances on tallow candles, and goes in thin and comes out fat?"

"I don't know that," replied the Tree; "but I know the wood, where the sun shines and the birds sing."

And then it told all about its youth.

And the little Mice had never heard anything of the kind; and they listened and said:

"What a number of things you have seen! How happy you must have been!"

"I?" replied the Fir Tree; and it thought about what it had told. "Yes, those were really quite happy times." But then he told of the Christmas Eve, when he had been hung with sweetmeats and candles.

"Oh!" said the little Mice, "how happy you have been, you old Fir Tree!"

"I'm not old at all," said the Tree. "I only came out of the wood this winter. I'm only rather backward in my growth."

"What splendid stories you can tell!" said the little Mice.

And next night they came with four other little Mice, to

hear what the Tree had to relate; and the more it said, the more clearly did it remember everything, and thought, "Those were quite merry days! But they may come again. Klumpey-Dumpey fell downstairs and yet he married the Princess. Perhaps I may marry a Princess too?" And then the Fir Tree thought of a pretty little Birch Tree that grew out in the forest: for the Fir Tree, that Birch was a real Princess.

"Who's Klumpey-Dumpey?" asked the little Mice.

And then the Fir Tree told the whole story. It could remember every single word; and the little Mice were ready to leap to the very top of the tree with pleasure. Next night a great many more Mice came, and on Sunday two Rats even appeared; but these thought the story was not pretty, and the little Mice were sorry for that, for now they also did not like it so much as before.

"Do you only know one story?" asked the Rats.

"Only that one," replied the Tree. "I heard that on the happiest evening of my life; I did not think then how happy I was."

"That's a very miserable story. Don't you know any about bacon and tallow candles—a store-room story?"

"No," said the Tree.

"Then we'd rather not hear you," said the Rats.

And they went back to their own people. The little Mice at last stayed away also; and then the Tree sighed and said:

"It was very nice when they sat round me, the merry little Mice, and listened when I spoke to them. Now that's past too. But I shall remember to be pleased when they take me out."

But when did that happen? Why, it was one morning that people came and rummaged in the garret; the boxes were put away, and the Tree brought out; they certainly threw him rather roughly on the floor, but a servant dragged him away at once to the stairs, where the daylight shone.

"Now life is beginning again!" thought the Tree.

It felt the fresh air and the first sunbeams, and now it was out in the courtyard. Everything passed so quickly that the Tree quite forgot to look at itself, there was so much to look at all round. The courtyard was close to a garden, and here everything was blooming; the roses hung fresh and fragrant over the little paling, the linden trees were in blossom, and the swallows cried, "Quinze-wit! quinze-wit! my husband's come!" But it was not the Fir Tree that they meant.

"Now I shall live!" said the Tree, rejoicingly, and spread its branches far out; but, alas! they were all withered and yellow; and it lay in the corner among nettles and weeds. The tinsel star was still upon it, and shone in the bright sunshine.

In the courtyard a couple of the merry children were playing who had danced round the tree at Christmas time, and had rejoiced over it. One of the youngest ran up and tore off the golden star.

"Look what is sticking to the ugly old fir tree!" said the child, and he trod upon the branches till they cracked again under his boots.

And the Tree looked at all the blooming flowers and the splendor of the garden, and then looked at itself, and wished it had remained in the dark corner of the garret; it thought of its fresh youth in the wood, of the merry Christmas Eve, and of the little Mice which had listened so pleasantly to the story of Klumpey-Dumpey.

"Past! past!" said the old Tree. "Had I but rejoiced when I could have done so! Past! past!"

And the servant came and chopped the Tree into little pieces; a whole bundle lay there; it blazed brightly under the great brewing kettle, and it sighed deeply, and each sigh was like a little shot; and the children who were at play there ran up and seated themselves at the fire, looked into it, and cried "Puff! puff!" But at each explosion, which was a deep sigh, the Tree thought of a summer day in the woods, or of a winter night there, when the stars beamed; he thought of Christmas Eve and of Klumpey-Dumpey, the only story he had ever heard or knew how to tell; and then the Tree was burned.

The boys played in the garden, and the youngest had on his breast a golden star, which the Tree had worn on its happiest evening. Now that was past, and the Tree's life was past, and the story is past too: past! past!—and that's the way with all stories.

THE DARNING-NEEDLE

BY HANS CHRISTIAN ANDERSEN

THERE was once a Darning-needle, who thought herself so fine, she imagined she was an embroidering-needle.

"Take care, and mind you hold me tight!" she said to the Fingers that took her out. "Don't let me fall! If I fall on the ground I shall certainly never be found again, for I am so fine!"

"That's as it may be," said the Fingers; and they grasped her round the body.

"See, I'm coming with a train!" said the Darning-needle, and she drew a long thread after her, but there was no knot in the thread.

The Fingers pointed the needle just at the cook's slipper, in which the upper leather had burst, and was to be sewn together.

"That's vulgar work," said the Darning-needle. "I shall never get through. I'm breaking! I'm breaking!" And she really broke. "Did I not say so?" said the Darning-needle; "I'm too fine!"

"Now it's quite useless," said the Fingers; but they were obliged to hold her fast, all the same; for the cook dropped some sealing-wax upon the needle, and pinned her handkerchief together with it in front.

"So, now I'm a breast-pin!" said the Darning-needle. "I knew very well that I should come to honor; when one is something, one comes to something!"

And she laughed quietly to herself—and one can never see when a darning-needle laughs. There she sat, as proud as if she were in a state coach, and looked all about her.

"May I be permitted to ask if you are of gold?" she inquired of the pin, her neighbor. "You have a very pretty appearance and a peculiar head, but it is only little. You must take pains to grow, for it's not every one that has sealing-wax dropped upon him."

And the Darning-needle drew herself up so proudly that she fell out of the handkerchief right into the sink, which the cook was rinsing out.

"Now we're going on a journey," said the Darning-needle. "If I only don't get lost!"

But she really was lost.

"I'm too fine for this world," she observed, as she lay in the gutter. "But I know who I am, and there's always something in that!"

So the Darning-needle kept her proud behavior, and did not lose her good humor. And things of many kinds swam over her, chips and straws and pieces of old newspapers.

"Only look how they sail!" said the Darning-needle. "They don't know what is under them! I'm here, I remain firmly here. See, there goes a chip thinking of nothing in the world but of himself—of a chip! There's a straw going by now. How he turns! how he twirls about! Don't think only of yourself, you might easily run up against a stone. There swims a bit of newspaper. What's written upon it has long been forgotten, and yet it gives itself airs. I sit quietly and patiently here. I know who I am, and I shall remain what I am."

One day something lay close beside her that glittered splendidly; then the Darning-needle believed that it was a diamond; but it was a bit of broken bottle; and because it shone the Darning-needle spoke to it, introducing herself as a breast-pin.

"I suppose you are a diamond?" she observed.

"Why, yes, something of that kind."

And then each believed the other to be a very valuable thing; and they began speaking about the world, and how very conceited it was.

"I have been in a lady's box," said the Darning-needle, "and this lady was a cook. She had five fingers on each hand, and I never saw anything so conceited as those five fingers. And yet they were only there that they might take me out of the box and put me back into it."

"Were they of good birth?" asked the Bit of Bottle.

"No, indeed," replied the Darning-needle: "but very haughty. There were five brothers, all of the finger family. They kept very proudly together though they were of different lengths: the outermost, the thumbling, was short and fat; he walked out in front of the ranks, and only had one joint in his back, and could only make a single bow; but he said that if he were hacked off a man, that man was useless for service in war. Dainty-mouth, the second finger, thrust himself into sweet and sour, pointed to sun and moon, and gave the impression when they wrote. Longman, the third, looked at all the others over his shoulder. Goldborder, the fourth, went about with a golden belt round his waist; and little Playman did nothing at all, and was proud of it. There was nothing but bragging among them, and therefore I went away."

"And now we sit here and glitter!" said the Bit of Bottle.

At that moment more water came into the gutter, so that it overflowed, and the Bit of Bottle was carried away.

"So he is disposed of," observed the Darning-needle. "I remain here. I am too fine. But that's my pride, and my pride is honorable." And proudly she sat there, and had many great thoughts. "I could almost believe I had been born of a sunbeam, I'm so fine! It really appears as if the sunbeams were always seeking for me under the water. Ah! I'm so fine that my mother cannot find me. If I had my old eye, which broke off, I think I should cry; but, no, I should not do that; it's not genteel to cry."

One day a couple of street boys lay grubbing in the gutter, where they sometimes found old nails, farthings, and similar treasures. It was dirty work, but they took great delight in it.

"Oh!" cried one, who had pricked himself with the Darning-needle, "there's a fellow for you!"

"I'm not a fellow; I'm a young lady!" said the Darning-needle.

But nobody listened to her. The sealing-wax had come off, and she had turned black; but black makes one look slender, and she thought herself finer even than before.

"Here comes an eggshell sailing along!" said the boys; and they stuck the Darning-needle fast in the eggshell.

"White walls, and black myself! that looks well," remarked the Darning-needle. "Now one can see me. I only hope

I shall not be seasick!" But she was not seasick at all. "It is good against seasickness, if one has a steel stomach, and does not forget that one is a little more than an ordinary person! Now my seasickness is over. The finer one is, the more one can bear."

"Crack!" went the eggshell, for a wagon went over her.

"Good Heavens, how it crushes one!" said the Darning-needle. "I'm getting seasick now—I'm quite sick."

But she was not really sick, though the wagon went over her; she lay there at full length, and there she may lie.

☙ ☙ ☙

THUMBELINA

BY HANS CHRISTIAN ANDERSEN

SHE had a little house of her own, a little garden too, this woman of whom I am going to tell you, but for all that she was not quite happy.

"If only I had a little child of my own," she said, "how the walls would ring with her laughter, and how the flowers would brighten at her coming. Then, indeed, I should be quite happy."

And an old witch heard what the woman wished, and said, "Oh, but that is easily managed. Here is a barley-corn. Plant it in a flower-pot and tend it carefully, and then you will see what will happen."

The woman was in a great hurry to go home and plant the barley-corn, but she did not forget to say "thank you" to the old witch. She not only thanked her, she even stayed to give her six silver pennies.

Then she hurried away to her home, took a flower-pot and planted her precious barley-corn.

And what do you think happened? Almost before the corn was planted, up shot a large and beautiful flower. It was still unopened. The petals were folded closely together, but it looked like a tulip. It really was a tulip, a red and yellow one, too.

The woman loved flowers. She stooped and kissed the

beautiful bud. As her lips touched the petals, they burst open, and oh! wonder of wonders! there, in the very middle of the flower, there sat a little child. Such a tiny, pretty little maiden she was.

They called her Thumbelina. That was because she was no bigger than the woman's thumb.

And where do you think she slept? A little walnut shell, lined with blue, that was her cradle.

When she slept little Thumbelina lay in her cradle on a tiny heap of violets, with the petal of a pale pink rose to cover her.

And where do you think she played? A table was her playground. On the table the woman placed a plate of water. Little Thumbelina called that her lake.

Round the plate were scented flowers, the blossoms lying on the edge, while the pale green stalks reached thirstily down to the water.

In the lake floated a large tulip leaf. This was Thumbelina's little boat. Seated there she sailed from side to side of her little lake, rowing cleverly with two white horse hairs. As she rowed backwards and forwards she sang softly to herself. The woman listening heard, and thought she had never known so sweet a song.

And now such a sad thing happened.

In through the broken window-pane hopped a big toad, oh! such an ugly big toad. She hopped right on to the table, where Thumbelina lay dreaming in her tiny cradle, under the pale pink rose leaf.

She peeped at her, this ugly old toad.

"How beautiful the little maiden is," she croaked. "She will make a lovely bride for my handsome son." And she lifted the little cradle, with Thumbelina in it, and hopped out through the broken window-pane, down into the garden.

At the foot of the garden was a broad stream. Here, under the muddy banks lived the old toad with her son.

How handsome she thought him! But he was really very ugly. Indeed, he was exactly like his mother.

When he saw little Thumbelina in her tiny cradle, he croaked with delight.

"Do not make so much noise," said his mother, "or you will wake the tiny creature. We may lose her if we are not careful. The slightest breeze would waft her far away. She is as light as gossamer."

Then the old toad carried Thumbelina out into the middle of the stream. "She will be safe here," she said, as she laid her gently on one of the leaves of a large water lily, and paddled back to her son.

"We will make ready the best rooms under the mud," she told him, "and then you and the little maiden will be married."

Poor little Thumbelina! She had not seen the ugly big toad yet, nor her ugly son.

When she woke up early in the morning, how she wept! Water all around her! How could she reach the shore? Poor little Thumbelina!

Down under the mud the old toad was very busy, decking the best room with buttercups and buds of water-lilies to make it gay for her little daughter-in-law, Thumbelina.

"Now we will go to bring her little bed and place it ready," said the old toad, and together she and her son swam out to the leaf where little Thumbelina sat.

"Here is my handsome son," she said, "he is to be your husband," and she bowed low in the water, for she wished to be very polite to the little maiden.

"Croak, croak," was all the young toad could say, as he looked at his pretty little bride.

Then they took away the tiny little bed, and Thumbelina was left all alone.

How the tears stained her pretty little face! How fast they fell into the stream! Even the fish as they swam hither and thither thought, "How it rains to-day," as the tiny drops fell thick and fast.

They popped up their heads and saw the forlorn little maiden.

"She shall not marry the ugly toad," they said, as they looked with eager eyes at the pretty child. "No, she shall not marry the ugly toad."

But what could the little fish do to help Thumbelina?

Oh! they were such clever little fish!

They found the green stem which held the leaf on which Thumbelina sat. They bit it with their little sharp teeth, and they never stopped biting, till at last they bit the green stem through; and away, down the stream, floated the leaf, carrying with it little Thumbelina.

"Free, free!" she sang, and her voice tinkled as a chime of fairy bells. "Free, free!" she sang merrily as she floated down the stream, away, far away out of reach of the ugly old toad and her ugly son.

And as she floated on, the little wild birds sang round her, and on the banks the little wild harebells bowed to her.

Butterflies were flitting here and there in the sunshine. A pretty little white one fluttered on to the leaf on which sat Thumbelina. He loved the tiny maiden so well that he settled down beside her.

Now she was quite happy! Birds around her, flowers near her, and the water gleaming like gold in the summer sunshine. What besides could little Thumbelina wish?

She took off her sash and threw one end of it round the butterfly. The other end she fastened firmly to the leaf. On and on floated the leaf, the little maiden and the butterfly.

Suddenly a great cockchafer buzzed along. Alas! he caught sight of little Thumbelina. He flew to her, put his claw round her tiny waist and carried her off, up on to a tree.

Poor little Thumbelina! How frightened she was! How grieved she was, too, for had she not lost her little friend the butterfly?

Would he fly away, she wondered, or would her sash hold him fast?

The cockchafer was charmed with the little maiden. He placed her tenderly on the largest leaf he could find. He gathered honey for her from the flowers, and as she sipped it, he sat near and told her how beautiful she looked.

But there were other chafers living in the tree, and when they came to see little Thumbelina, they said, "She is not pretty at all."

"She has only two legs," said one.

"She has no feelers," said another.

Some said she was too thin, others that she was too fat, and then they all buzzed and hummed together, "How ugly she is, how ugly she is!" But all the time little Thumbelina was the prettiest, daintiest little maiden that ever lived.

And now the cockchafer who had flown off with little Thumbelina thought he had been rather foolish to admire her.

He looked at her again. "Pretty? No, after all she was not very pretty." He would have nothing to do with her, and away he and all the other chafers flew. Only first they carried little Thumbelina down from the tree and placed her on a daisy. She wept because she was so ugly—so ugly that the chafers could not live with her. But all the time, you know, she was the prettiest little maiden in the world.

She was living all alone in the wood now, but it was summer and she could not feel sad or lonely while the warm golden sunshine touched her so gently, while the birds sang to her, and the flowers bowed to her.

Yes, little Thumbelina was happy. She ate honey from the flowers, and drank dew out of the golden buttercups and danced and sang the livelong day.

But summer passed away and autumn came. The birds began to whisper of flying to warmer countries, and the flowers began to fade and hang their heads, and as autumn passed away, winter came, cold, dreary winter.

Thumbelina shivered with cold. Her little frock was thin and old. She would certainly be frozen to death, she thought, as she wrapped herself up in a withered leaf.

Then the snow began to fall, and each snowflake seemed to smother her. She was so very tiny.

Close to the wood lay a corn-field. The beautiful golden grain had been carried away long ago, now there was only dry short stubble. But to little Thumbelina the stubble was like a great forest.

She walked through the hard field. She was shaking with cold. All at once she saw a little door just before her. She looked again—yes, it was a door.

The field-mouse had made a little house under the stubble,

and lived so cosily there. She had a big room full of corn, and she had a kitchen and pantry as well.

"Perhaps I shall get some food here," thought the cold and hungry little maiden, as she stood knocking at the door, just like a tiny beggar child. She had had nothing to eat for two long days. Oh, she was very hungry!

"What a tiny thing you are!" said the field-mouse, as she opened the door and saw Thumbelina. "Come in and dine with me."

How glad Thumbelina was, and how she enjoyed dining with the field-mouse.

She behaved so prettily that the old field-mouse told her she might live with her while the cold weather lasted. "And you shall keep my room clean and neat, and you shall tell me stories," she added.

That is how Thumbelina came to live with the field-mouse and to meet Mr. Mole.

"We shall have a visitor soon," said the field-mouse. "My neighbor, Mr. Mole, comes to see me every week-day. His house is very large, and he wears a beautiful coat of black velvet. Unfortunately, he is blind. If you tell him your prettiest stories he may marry you."

Now the mole was very wise and very clever, but how could little Thumbelina ever care for him. Why, he did not love the sun, nor the flowers, and he lived in a house underground. No, Thumbelina did not wish to marry the mole.

However she must sing to him when he came to visit his neighbor the field-mouse. When she had sung "Ladybird, Ladybird, fly away home," and "Boys and girls come out to play," the mole was charmed, and thought he would like to marry the little maiden with the beautiful voice.

Then he tried to be very agreeable. He invited the field-mouse and Thumbelina to walk along the underground passage he had dug between their houses. Mr. Mole was very fond of digging underground.

As it was dark the mole took a piece of tinder-wood in his mouth and led the way. The tinder-wood shone like a torch in the dark passage.

A little bird lay in the passage, a little bird who had not flown away when the flowers faded and the cold winds blew.

It was dead, the mole said.

When he reached the bird, the mole stopped and pushed his nose right up through the ceiling to make a hole, through which the daylight might shine.

There lay the swallow, his wings pressed close to his side. His little head and legs drawn in under his feathers. He had died of cold.

"Poor little swallow!" thought Thumbelina. All wild birds were her friends. Had they not sung to her and fluttered round her all the long glad summer days?

But the mole kicked the swallow with his short legs. "That one will sing no more," he said roughly. "It must be sad to be born a bird and to be able only to sing and fly. I am thankful none of my children will be birds," and he proudly smoothed down his velvet coat.

"Yes," said the field-mouse; "what can a bird do but sing? When the cold weather comes it is useless."

Thumbelina said nothing. Only when the others moved on, she stooped down and stroked the bird gently with her tiny hand, and kissed its closed eyes.

That night the little maiden could not sleep. "I will go to see the poor swallow again," she thought.

She got up out of her tiny bed. She wove a little carpet out of hay. Down the long underground passage little Thumbelina walked, carrying the carpet. She reached the bird at last, and spread the carpet gently round him. She fetched warm cotton and laid it over the bird.

"Even down on the cold earth he will be warm now," thought the gentle little maiden.

"Farewell," she said sadly, "farewell, little bird! Did you sing to me through the long summer days, when the leaves were green and the sky was blue? Farewell, little swallow!" and she stooped to press her tiny cheeks against the soft feathers.

As she did so, she heard—what could it be? Pit, pat, pit, pat! Could the bird be alive? Little Thumbelina listened still. Yes, it was the beating of the little bird's heart that she heard.

He had not been dead after all, only frozen with cold. The little carpet and the covering the little maid had brought warmed the bird. He would get well now.

What a big bird he seemed to Thumbelina! She was almost afraid now, for she was so tiny. She was tiny, but she was brave. Drawing the covering more closely round the poor swallow, she brought her own little pillow, that the bird's head might rest softly.

Thumbelina stole out again the next night. "Would the swallow look at her," she wondered.

Yes, he opened his eyes, and looked at little Thumbelina, who stood there with a tiny torch of tinder-wood.

"Thanks, thanks, little Thumbelina," he twittered feebly. "Soon I shall grow strong and fly out in the bright sunshine once more; thanks, thanks, little maiden."

"Oh! but it is too cold, it snows and freezes, for now it is winter," said Thumbelina. "Stay here and be warm, and I will take care of you," and she brought the swallow water in a leaf.

And the little bird told her all his story,—how he had tried to fly to the warm countries, and how he had torn his wing on a blackthorn bush and fallen to the ground. But he could not tell her how he had come to the underground passage.

All winter the swallow stayed there, and Thumbelina was often in the long passage, with her little torch of tinder-wood. But the mole and the field-mouse did not know how Thumbelina tended and cared for the swallow.

At last spring came, and the sun sent its warmth down where the swallow lay in the underground passage.

Little Thumbelina opened the hole which the mole had made in the ceiling, and the sunshine streamed down on the swallow and the little girl.

How the swallow longed to soar away, up and up, to be lost to sight in the blue, blue sky!

"Come with me, little Thumbelina," said the swallow, "come with me to the blue skies and the green woods."

But Thumbelina remembered how kind the field-mouse had been to her when she was cold and hungry, and she would not leave her.

"Farewell! farewell! then, little maiden," twittered the swallow as he flew out and up, up into the sunshine.

Thumbelina loved the swallow dearly. Her eyes were full of tears as she watched the bird disappearing till he was only a tiny speck of black.

And now sad days came to little Thumbelina.

The golden corn was once more waving in the sunshine above the house of the field-mouse, but Thumbelina must not go out lest she lose herself among the corn.

Not go out in the bright sunshine! Oh, poor little Thumbelina!

"You must get your wedding clothes ready this summer," said the field-mouse. "You must be well provided with linen and worsted. My neighbor the mole will wish a well-dressed bride."

The mole had said he wished to marry little Thumbelina before the cold winter came again.

So Thumbelina sat at the spinning-wheel through the long summer days, spinning and weaving with four little spiders to help her.

In the evening the mole came to visit her. "Summer will soon be over," he said, "and we shall be married."

But oh! little Thumbelina did not wish the summer to end.

Live with the dull old mole, who hated the sunshine, who would not listen to the song of the birds—live underground with him! Little Thumbelina wished the summer would never end.

The spinning and weaving were over now. All the wedding clothes were ready. Autumn was come.

"Only four weeks and the wedding-day will have come," said the field-mouse.

And little Thumbelina wept.

"I will not marry the tiresome old mole," she said.

"I shall bite you with my white tooth if you talk such nonsense," said the field-mouse. "Among all my friends not one of them has such a fine velvet coat as the mole. His cellars are full and his rooms are large. You ought to be glad to marry so well," she ended.

"Was there no escape from the underground home?" little Thumbelina wondered.

The wedding-day came. The mole arrived to fetch his little bride.

How could she say good-by for ever to the beautiful sunshine?

"Farewell, farewell!" she cried, and waved her little hands towards the glorious sun.

"Farewell, farewell!" she cried, and threw her tiny arms round a little red flower growing at her feet.

"Tell the dear swallow, when he comes again," she whispered to the flower, "tell him I will never forget him."

"Tweet, tweet!" what was that Thumbelina heard? "Tweet, tweet!" Could it be the swallow?

The flutter of wings was round her. Little Thumbelina looked. How glad she was, for there, indeed, was the little bird she had tended and cared for so long. She told him, weeping, she must not stay. She must marry the mole and live underground, and never see the sun, the glorious sun.

"Come with me, come with me, little Thumbelina," twittered the swallow. "You can sit on my back, and I will fly with you to warmer countries, far from the tiresome old mole. Over mountains and seas we will fly to the country where the summer never ends, and the sunlight always shines."

Then little Thumbelina seated herself on her dear swallow's back, and put her tiny feet on his outstretched wing. She tied herself firmly with her little sash to the strongest feather of the bird.

And the swallow soared high into the air. High above forests and lakes, high above the big mountains that were crested with snow, he soared.

And little Thumbelina shivered as she felt the cold air, but soon she crept under the bird's warm feathers, and only pushed out her little head to see the beauty all around her.

They had reached the warm countries now. The sun was more brilliant here, the flowers more radiant.

On and on flew the swallow, till he came to a white marble palace. Half-ruined it was, and vine leaves trailed up the long slender pillars. And among the broad, green leaves many a swallow had built his nest, and one of these nests belonged to Thumbelina's little swallow.

"This is my home," said the bird, "but you shall live in one of these brilliant flowers, in the loveliest of them all."

And little Thumbelina clapped her hands with joy.

The swallow flew with her to a stately sunflower, and set her carefully on one of the broad yellow petals.

But think, what was her surprise! In the very heart of the flower stood a little Prince, fair and transparent as crystal. On his head he wore a crown of gold, on his shoulders a pair of delicate wings, and he was small, every bit as small as Thumbelina. He was the spirit of the flower.

For you know in each flower there is a spirit—a tiny little boy or girl, but this little Prince was King of all the flower spirits.

The little King thought Thumbelina the loveliest maiden he had ever seen. He took off his golden crown and placed it on the tiny head of the little maid, and in a silvery voice he asked, "Will you be my bride, little Thumbelina, and reign with me over the flower spirits?"

How glad Thumbelina was!

The little King wished to marry her. Yes, she would be his little Queen.

Then out of each blossom stepped tiny little children. They came to pay their homage to little Thumbelina.

Each one brought her a present, and the most beautiful of all the presents was a pair of wings, delicate as gossamer. And when they were fastened on the shoulders of the little Queen, she could fly from flower to flower.

And the swallow sat on his nest above, and sang his sweetest bridal song for the wedding of little Thumbelina.

❧ ❧ ❧

THE TINDER-BOX

BY HANS CHRISTIAN ANDERSEN

A STORY about a tinder-box? Yes, but then it was such a wonderful one! Why, it must certainly have been a magic box!

It belonged to an old witch, this tinder-box, but it had been left right down inside a tree by the ugly old witch's grandmother. But get it again she must, for she knew it really was a magic tinder-box.

But how could she get it?

Ah! here was her chance.

Tramp, tramp; right, left, right, left. She heard the steps come nearer and nearer. She looked! There was a soldier coming along; tramp, tramp.

She could see him now, with a knapsack on his back, and his sword at his side.

The soldier had been to the wars and was coming home.

"Good evening," said the witch, as he came close to her. "Good evening; what a bright sword you wear, and what a big knapsack! You shall have as much money as you wish for yourself!"

"Thank you, old witch," said the soldier. But he did not tell her that she did not look as though she had much money to spare. He was too wise to say anything but, "Thank you, old witch."

"Do you see that big tree?" she said, and she pointed to one that stood close by the wayside. "It is hollow inside. Climb up to the top, and you will see a hole. It is large. You must creep through it and let yourself down, right down under the tree. Tie a rope round your waist, and I will haul you up again when you call."

"But what am I to do under the tree?" asked the soldier.

"What are you to do? Why, did I not tell you you should have money. It is there, under the tree, copper, silver, gold. Gold!" cried the witch, in a rough and eager voice. "When you come to the bottom of the tree there is a large passage. It is quite light, indeed it is ablaze with light. More than a hundred lamps are burning. There you will see three doors. The keys are in the keyholes. Unlock the doors and walk in. In the first room in the middle of the floor, is a big box. On the top of it sits a dog. He has big eyes, they are as big as saucers, but do not let that trouble you. You shall have my blue checked apron. Spread it on the floor. Go forward quickly, seize the dog and place him on it. After that is done, you can open the box, and take out as much money as you wish. It is true the box holds only copper coins, but if you would rather have silver, just walk into the next room. There sits another dog, on another box, with big eyes, eyes as big as—oh, as big as mill-wheels, but never mind that. Place the dog on my apron, then open the box and take as much silver as you wish. But if you would rather have gold, why, then open the third door. There you will see another dog, sitting on another box. This one is tremendous, quite gigantic, and he has eyes, oh! such great, rolling eyes! They are as large as the Round Tower. He is a dog indeed, but do not let that trouble you. Place him on my blue checked apron and he will not hurt you. Then take gold, as much gold as ever you wish."

"Splendid!" said the soldier. You see he had been to the wars and was a brave man. "Splendid! But what am I to give you, old witch? You will wish something, I am quite certain of that."

"No," said the witch: "I do not wish one single coin. But I do wish my old tinder-box. My grandmother left it behind her, the last time she went down the tree."

"Well, tie the rope round my waist," said the soldier.

"Here it is," said the witch, "and here is my blue checked apron. It is very important."

Up the tree climbed the soldier, into the tree he crept through the hole at the top, and down, down the hollow inside he slipped, and there he was, in a wide passage, lighted, as the witch had said, by a hundred burning lamps.

The soldier unlocked the first door he saw. There sat the dog with eyes as big as saucers, staring at him in great surprise.

"I must obey my orders," thought the soldier.

He placed the witch's apron on the floor, seized the dog bravely, and placed him on the apron.

Then he opened the box. It was full of copper coins. He crammed as many as he could into his pocket, shut the lid, placed the dog again on the box, and passed on to the second door.

He unlocked it. Yes! there sat another dog on another box, with great eyes, as big as mill-wheels.

"If you stare at me so hard, you will hurt your eyes," said

the soldier, and thought what a joke he had made. Then he seized the dog, placed it on the witch's apron, and raised the lid of the second box.

Silver, every coin was silver! The soldier threw away all his copper coins in a great hurry. He must have silver. He stuffed his pockets and his knapsack with the silver coins, and clapped his hands. He was rich now.

On he went to the third room. He unlocked it. There indeed was another box and another dog, and oh, horrible! the soldier almost shut his eyes. The dog had eyes, great big rolling eyes, eyes as large as the Round Tower. And they would not keep still. No, round and round they rolled.

But the soldier was brave; he had been to the wars.

"Good evening," he said, and he lifted his hat respectfully, for never before in all his life, had he seen so big, so enormous a creature.

Then he walked straight up to the dog. Could he lift him? Yes, he took the immense animal in his arms, set him on the witch's apron, and opened the third box.

Gold! It was full of gold. He would be able to buy the whole town, and all the sugar-plums, and all the tin soldiers, and all the rocking-horses and whips in the world.

The soldier was delighted. He threw away his silver money. Silver! He did not want silver. Here was gold, gold!

He filled his pockets and his knapsack, but he could not bear to stop there. No, he crammed his cap and his boots so full that he could hardly walk. He was really rich at last. He shut the lid, placed the dog again on the box, and went out of the room, along the passage.

Then he shouted up the tree, "Halloo, old witch! haul me up again."

"Have you got the tinder-box?" said the witch.

"Oh, that I had quite forgotten," answered the soldier, and back he went to fetch it.

When he came back the witch took the rope and hauled and hauled, till there was the soldier, once more, safe on the high road, just as he was before, only now he was rich, so rich that he had become very bold.

He had gold in his pockets, gold in his knapsack, gold in his cap, gold in his boots.

"What are you going to do with the tinder-box, just tell me that?" said the soldier.

"That is no business of yours," said the witch. "You have the gold, give me the tinder-box!"

"Rubbish!" said the soldier. He had grown rude as well as rich, you see. "Rubbish—take your choice—tell me at once what you mean to do with the tinder-box, or I will draw my sword and cut off your head."

"I won't tell you," screamed the witch.

Then the soldier cut off her head, and the poor witch lay there dead. But the soldier did not stay to look at her. In a great hurry he took all his gold and tied it up in the blue checked apron.

He slung it across his shoulder, put the tinder-box in his pocket, and marched off to town.

How grand he felt! What heaps of gold he had in his bundle!

When the soldier reached the town he walked straight to the finest hotel, and asked for the best rooms, and for dinner ordered all his favorite puddings and fruits.

The servant who cleaned his boots tossed her head. "Shabby boots for a rich man to wear," she said.

But next day the soldier had bought himself very grand new boots, and gay clothing, so that no one could possibly call him shabby.

Shabby! No, he was a great man now, and people crowded round this rich fellow, told him all the sights there were to be seen in their city, all about their King too, and the beautiful Princess, his daughter.

"I should like to see her, this wonderful Princess," said the soldier.

"But you cannot see her," they told him. "She lives, the beautiful Princess, in a great copper castle, with walls and towers all round. Only the King visits her there, for it was once foretold that she would marry a common soldier, and that our King does not wish."

"I must see her once, just once," thought the soldier. But how was he going to find the way into the castle, that was the question?

Meanwhile he led a merry life. He drove about in the King's Park; he went to the theater; he gave money to the poor, because he remembered how miserable it was to have no money in his own pocket.

The soldier was always gaily dressed now. He had a great many friends who said he was a real gentleman, and that pleased him very much.

And so he went on day after day, spending money and giving money, but getting none, till at last the gold came to an end. He had only two copper coins left: he was only a poor soldier once more.

Leaving the grand hotel he went to live in a small room. He found a tiny attic, just under a roof, up, oh! so many stairs. Here he lived, mending his own clothes, brushing his own boots. He had no visitors, for his grand friends would not take the trouble to walk up so many stairs to his little attic.

Hungry? Yes, he was hungry too, and as he had no money to buy even a farthing candle, he had to sit alone in the dark.

One evening he suddenly thought of the witch's tinder-box. Surely in it there were matches.

The soldier opened it eagerly. Yes, there lay the matches. He seized one and struck it on the tinder-box.

No sooner had he done this, than the door burst suddenly open, and there, there, staring at him, stood the dog with eyes as big as saucers.

"What does my master command?" asked the dog.

"No wonder the old witch wished the tinder-box for her very own," thought the soldier. Aloud he said to the dog, "Fetch me some money," and the dog instantly vanished to do his master's bidding.

He was back in a moment, and lo! in his mouth was a big bag, full of pennies.

"Why, this is a magic box," said the soldier. "I have a treasure indeed." And so he had, for listen! Strike the box once, the dog with eyes as large as saucers appeared. Strike it twice and the dog with eyes as big as mill-wheels appeared. Strike it thrice and there appeared the monster dog with eyes that rolled round and round and were as large as the Round Tower itself. All three dogs did the soldier's bidding.

Now the soldier could have gold again. Gold as much as ever he wished.

He moved once more to the grand rooms in the fine hotel. He had gay clothes again; and now, strangely enough, all his friends came to see him and liked him as much as ever.

One evening the soldier's thoughts wandered away to the beautiful Princess, the beautiful Princess who was shut up so safely in the great copper palace.

"It is ridiculous that no one sees the Princess," thought the soldier. "I want to see her, and I shall."

He pulled out his tinder-box, struck a light, and lo! there stood the dog with eyes as large as saucers.

"It is the middle of the night," said the soldier, "but I must see the Princess, if it is only for a moment."

The dog bounded out of the door, and before the soldier had time to wonder what he would do or say if the beautiful Princess really appeared, there she was.

Yes, there she was, fast asleep on the dog's back. She was beautiful, so beautiful that the soldier was quite sure that she was a real Princess. He stooped and kissed her hand. She was so beautiful he could not help it. Then off ran the dog, back to the copper palace with the Princess.

"I had such a strange dream last night," the Princess told the King and Queen at breakfast next morning. "I dreamed that an enormous dog came and carried me off to a soldier, and the soldier kissed my hand. It was a strange dream," she murmured.

"The Princess must not be left alone to-night," said the Queen. "She may be frightened if she dreams again." And she told an old dame who lived at court to sit in the Princess's room at night.

But what would the Queen have said if she had known that what the Princess told them was no dream, but something that had really and truly happened.

Well, that evening the soldier thought he would like to see the Princess again.

He struck a light, and there stood one of his obedient dogs.

"Bring the Princess," ordered the soldier, and the dog vanished to do his master's will.

The old dame sat beside the Princess's bed. She had heard all about the Princess's dream.

"Was she dreaming herself now?" she wondered. She pinched herself.—No, she was wide awake, yet she saw a dog, a real dog with eyes as large as saucers, in front of her.

The dog seized the Princess, and ran off; but although he ran very quickly, the old dame found time to put on her goloshes before she followed.

How she panted along! How she ran, the faithful old dame! She was just in time to see the Princess on the dog's back disappear into a large house.

"I shall mark the house, so that I may know it in the morning," she thought. And she took a piece of white chalk and made a great white cross on the door.

Then she walked home and slept.

Soon afterwards the dog carried the Princess back to the copper palace, and noticed the great white cross on the door of the hotel where his master lived.

And what do you think he did? Oh, he was a wise dog. He took a piece of chalk, and he put a great white cross on every door in the town.

Early next morning the King and Queen and all the lords and ladies of the court were astir. They had heard the old dame's story, and were going to see the house with the great white cross.

They had scarcely started, when the King's eyes fell on a great white cross! "Here it is," cried the King eagerly.

"What nonsense you talk, my dear! it is here," said the Queen, for almost at the same moment she too had seen a door with a great white cross.

Then all the lords and ladies cried: "It is here, it is here," as one after another they saw doors marked with great white crosses. The hubbub was terrible, and the poor old dame was quite bewildered. How could she tell which door she had marked? It was quite useless. The dog had perplexed everybody, and they went back to the copper palace knowing no more than when they left it.

But the Queen was a clever woman. She could do more than just sit very properly on a throne.

The same evening, she took her big gold scissors and cut up a large piece of silk into small pieces. These she sewed together into a pretty little bag. Then she filled the bag with the finest grains of wheat. With her own hands she tied the bag round the Princess's waist, after which she took her gold scissors again and cut a tiny little hole in the bag, a hole just big enough to let the grains of wheat drop out whenever the Princess moved.

That night the dog came again and carried the Princess off to the soldier, and the soldier wished he were a Prince, for then he would marry this beautiful Princess.

Now although the dog had very big eyes, eyes as large as saucers, he did not notice the tiny grains of wheat as they dropped out all along the road from the palace to the soldier's window. Under the window the dog stopped and climbed up the wall with the Princess, into the soldier's room.

The next morning the King and Queen followed the little grains of wheat and very easily found out where the Princess had been.

Then the soldier was seized and put into prison.

Oh, how dark and tiresome it was! But it was worse than that one day, when they told him he was to be hanged, "hanged to-morrow," they told him.

What a fright the soldier was in, and, worst of all, he had left his tinder-box at the hotel.

Morning came! Through the narrow bars of his little window the soldier could see the people all hurrying out of town. They were going to see him hanged.

He heard the drums, he saw the soldiers marching along. He wished he were marching with them. Alas, alas! that could never be now—

A little shoemaker's apprentice, with a leather apron, came running along. He was in such a hurry that he lost one of his slippers. It fell close under the soldier's window, as he sat peering out through the narrow bars.

The soldier called to the boy, "There is no hurry, for I am still here. Nothing will happen till I go. I will give you twopence if you will run to the house where I used to live and fetch me my tinder-box. You must run all the way."

The shoemaker's boy thought he would like to earn twopence, and off he raced to bring the tinder-box.

He found it. "A useless little box," he said to himself, but back he raced with it to the soldier; and then—what do you think happened?

Outside the town the scaffold had been raised, the soldiers were drawn up round it, as well as crowds of people.

The King and Queen were there too, seated on a magnificent throne, exactly opposite the judges and councilors.

The rope was being put round the soldier's neck, when he turned to the King and Queen and earnestly entreated one last favor—only to be allowed to smoke one pipe of tobacco.

What a harmless request! How could the King refuse so harmless a request?

"Yes," said his Majesty, "you may smoke one pipe of tobacco."

The soldier took out his tinder-box, struck a match, once, twice, thrice, and lo! there before him stood the three enormous dogs, waiting his commands.

"Help me," shouted the soldier; "do not let me be hanged."

At once the three terrible dogs rushed at the judges and councilors, tossed them high into the air, so that as they fell they were broken into pieces.

The King began to speak; perhaps he was going to forgive the soldier, but no one knows what he was going to say, for the biggest dog gave him no time to finish his sentence.

He rushed at the King and Queen, flung them high into the air, so that when they fell down, they too were broken all to pieces.

Then the soldiers and the people, who were all terribly frightened, shouted in a great hurry, "Brave soldier, you shall be our King, and the beautiful Princess shall be our Queen!"

And while they led the soldier to the royal carriage the great big dogs bounded along in front.

Little boys whistled gaily, and the guards presented arms.

Then the Princess was sent for, and made Queen, which she liked much better than living shut up in a copper palace. And the wedding feast lasted for eight whole days, and the three monster wizard dogs sat at the table, staring around them with all their eyes.

❧ ❧ ❧

BOOTS AND HIS BROTHERS

BY GEORGE WEBBE DASENT

ONCE on a time there was a man who had three sons, Peter, Paul, and John. John was Boots, of course, because he was the youngest. I can't say the man had anything more than these three sons, for he had n't one penny to rub against another; and so he told his sons over and over again they must go out into the world and try to earn their bread, for there at home there was nothing to be looked for but starving to death.

Now, near the man's cottage was the King's palace, and, you must know, just against the King's windows a great oak had sprung up, which was so stout and big that it took away all the light from the King's palace. The King had said he would give many, many dollars to the man who could fell the oak, but no one was man enough for that, for as soon as ever one chip of the oak's trunk flew off, two grew in its stead. A well, too, the King would have dug, which was to hold water for the whole year; for all his neighbors had wells, but he hadn't any, and that he thought a shame. So the King said he would give to any one who could dig him such a well as would hold water for a whole year round, both money and goods; but no one could do it, for the King's palace lay high, high up on a hill, and they had dug only a few inches before they came upon the living rock.

But as the King had set his heart on having these two

things done, he had it given out far and wide, in all the churches of his kingdom, that he who could fell the big oak in the King's courtyard, and get him a well that would hold water the whole year round, should have the Princess and half the kingdom. Well, you may easily know there was many a man who came to try his luck; but for all their hacking and hewing, and all their digging and delving, it was no good. The oak got bigger and stouter at every stroke, and the rock didn't get softer, either. So one day those three brothers thought they'd set off and try too, and their father hadn't a word against it; for even if they didn't get the Princess and half the kingdom, it might happen they might get a place somewhere with a good master; and that was all he wanted. So when the brothers said they thought of going to the palace, their father said "yes" at once. So Peter, Paul, and Jack went off from their home.

Well, they hadn't gone far before they came to a fir-wood, and up along one side of it rose a steep hillside, and as they went, they heard something hewing and hacking away up on the hill among the trees.

"I wonder, now, what it is that is hewing away up yonder," said Jack.

"You're always so clever with your wonderings," said Peter and Paul both at once. "What wonder is it, pray, that a woodcutter should stand and hack up on a hillside?"

"Still, I'd like to see what it is, after all," said Jack; and up he went.

"Oh, if you're such a child, 'twill do you good to go and take a lesson," bawled out his brothers after him.

But Jack didn't care for what they said; he climbed the steep hillside towards where the noise came, and when he reached the place, what do you think he saw? Why, an axe that stood there hacking and hewing, all of itself, at the trunk of a fir.

"Good-day!" said Jack. "So you stand here all alone and hew, do you?"

"Yes; here I've stood and hewed and hacked a long, long time, waiting for you," said the Axe.

"Well, here I am at last," said Jack, as he took the axe, pulled it off its handle, and stuffed both head and handle into his wallet.

So when he got down again to his brothers, they began to jeer and laugh at him.

"And now, what funny thing was it you saw up yonder on the hillside?" they said.

"Oh, it was only an axe we heard," said Jack.

So when they had gone a bit farther, they came under a steep spur of rock, and up there they heard something digging and shoveling.

"I wonder now," said Jack, "what it is digging and shoveling up yonder at the top of the rock."

"Ah, you're always so clever with your wonderings," said Peter and Paul again; "as if you'd never heard a woodpecker hacking and pecking at a hollow tree."

"Well, well," said Jack, "I think it would be a piece of fun just to see what it really is."

And so off he set to climb the rock, while the others laughed and made game of him. But he didn't care a bit for that; up he climbed, and when he got near the top, what do you think he saw? Why, a spade that stood there digging and delving.

"Good-day!" said Jack. "So you stand here all alone, and dig and delve!"

"Yes, that's what I do," said the Spade, "and that's what I've done this many a long day, waiting for you."

"Well, here I am," said Jack again, as he took the spade and knocked it off its handle, and put it into his wallet, and then down again to his brothers.

"Well, what was it, so rare and strange," said Peter and Paul, "that you saw up there at the top of the rock?"

"Oh," said Jack, "nothing more than a spade; that was what we heard."

So they went on again a good bit, till they came to a brook. They were thirsty, all three, after their long walk, and so they lay down beside the brook to have a drink.

"I wonder now," said Jack, "where all this water comes from."

"I wonder if you're right in your head," said Peter and Paul in one breath. "If you're not mad already, you'll go mad very soon, with your wonderings. Where the brook comes from, indeed! Have you never heard how water rises from a spring in the earth?"

"Yes; but still I've a great fancy to see where this brook comes from," said Jack.

So up alongside the brook he went, in spite of all that his brothers bawled after him. Nothing could stop him. On he went. So, as he went up and up, the brook got smaller and smaller, and at last, a little way farther on, what do you think he saw? Why, a great walnut, and out of that the water trickled.

"Good-day!" said Jack again. "So you lie here, and trickle and run down all alone?"

"Yes, I do," said the Walnut; "and here have I trickled and run this many a long day, waiting for you."

"Well, here I am," said Jack, as he took up a lump of moss, and plugged up the hole, that the water mightn't run out. Then he put the walnut into his wallet, and ran down to his brothers.

"Well, now," said Peter and Paul, "have you found out where the water comes from? A rare sight it must have been!"

"Oh, after all, it was only a hole it ran out of," said Jack; and so the others laughed and made game of him again, but Jack didn't mind that a bit.

"After all, I had the fun of seeing it," said he.

So when they had gone a bit farther they came to the King's palace; but as every one in the kingdom had heard how they might win the Princess and half the realm, if they could only fell the big oak and dig the King's well, so many had come to try their luck that the oak was now twice as stout and big as it had been at first, for two chips grew for every one they hewed out with their axes, as I dare say you all bear in mind. So the King had now laid it down as a punishment that if any one tried and couldn't fell the oak, he should be put on a barren island, and both his ears were to be clipped off. But the two brothers didn't let themselves be scared by that; they were quite sure they could fell the oak, and Peter, as he was eldest, was to try his hand first; but it went with him as with all the rest who had hewn at the oak; for every chip he cut out, two grew in its place. So the King's men seized him, and clipped off both his ears, and put him out on the island.

Now Paul, he was to try his luck, but he fared just the same; when he had hewn two or three strokes, they began to see the oak grow, and so the King's men seized him too, and clipped his ears, and put him out on the island; and his ears they clipped closer, because they said he ought to have taken a lesson from his brother.

So now Jack was to try.

"If you *will* look like a marked sheep, we're quite ready to clip your ears at once, and then you'll save yourself some bother," said the King, for he was angry with him for his brothers' sake.

"Well, I'd like to just try first," said Jack, and so he got leave. Then he took his axe out of his wallet and fitted it to its handle.

"Hew away!" said he to his axe; and away it hewed, making the chips fly again, so that it wasn't long before down came the oak.

When that was done, Jack pulled out his spade, and fitted it to its handle.

"Dig away!" said he to the spade; and so the spade began to dig and delve till the earth and rock flew out in splinters, and so he had the well soon dug out, you may think.

And when he had got it as big and deep as he chose, Jack took out his walnut and laid it in one corner of the well, and pulled the plug of moss out.

"Trickle and run," said Jack, and so the nut trickled and ran, till the water gushed out of the hole in a stream, and in a short time the well was brimful.

Then Jack had felled the oak which shaded the King's palace, and dug a well in the palace-yard, and so he got the Princess and half the kingdom, as the King had said; but it was lucky for Peter and Paul that they had lost their ears, else they had heard each hour and day how every one said, "Well, after all, Jack wasn't so much out of his mind when he took to wondering."

THE HUSBAND WHO WAS TO MIND THE HOUSE

BY GEORGE WEBBE DASENT

ONCE on a time there was a man so surly and cross he never thought his wife did anything right in the house. So one evening, in haymaking time, he came home, scolding and swearing, and showing his teeth and making a dust.

"Dear love, don't be so angry; there's a good man," said his goody; "to-morrow let's change our work. I'll go out with the mowers and mow, and you shall mind the house at home."

Yes, the husband thought that would do very well. He was quite willing, he said.

So, early next morning, his goody took a scythe over her neck, and went out into the hayfield with the mowers and began to mow; but the man was to mind the house, and do the work at home.

First of all he wanted to churn the butter; but when he had churned a while he got thirsty, and went down to the cellar to tap a barrel of ale. So, just when he had knocked in the bung, and was putting the tap into the cask, he heard overhead the pig come into the kitchen. Then off he ran up the cellar steps, with the tap in his hand, as fast as he could, to look after the pig, lest it should upset the churn; but when he got up, and saw the pig had already knocked the churn over, and stood there, routing and grunting amongst the cream which was running all over the floor, he got so wild with rage that he quite forgot the ale-barrel, and ran at the pig as hard as he could. He caught it, too, just as it ran out of doors, and gave it such a kick that piggy lay for dead on the spot. Then all at once he remembered he had the tap in his hand; but when he got down to the cellar, every drop of ale had run out of the cask.

Then he went into the dairy and found enough cream left to fill the churn again, and so he began to churn, for butter they must have at dinner. When he had churned a bit, he remembered that their milking cow was still shut up in the stable, and hadn't had a bit to eat or a drop to drink all the morning, though the sun was high. Then all at once he thought 'twas too far to take her down to the meadow, so he'd just get her up on the housetop—for the house, you must know, was thatched with sods, and a fine crop of grass was growing there. Now their house lay close up against a steep down, and he thought if he laid a plank across to the thatch at the back he'd easily get the cow up.

But still he couldn't leave the churn, for there was his little babe crawling about on the floor, and "if I leave it," he thought, "the child is sure to upset it." So he took the churn on his back, and went out with it; but then he thought he'd better first water the cow before he turned her out on the thatch; so he took up a bucket to draw water out of the well; but, as he stooped down at the well's brink, all the cream ran out of the churn over his shoulders, and so down into the well.

Now it was near dinner-time, and he hadn't even got the butter yet; so he thought he'd best boil the porridge, and filled the pot with water, and hung it over the fire. When he had done that, he thought the cow might perhaps fall off the thatch and break her legs or her neck. So he got up on the house to tie her up. One end of the rope he made fast to the cow's neck, and the other he slipped down the chimney and tied round his own thigh; and he had to make haste, for the water now began to boil in the pot, and he had still to grind the oatmeal.

So he began to grind away; but while he was hard at it, down fell the cow off the housetop after all, and as she fell she dragged the man up the chimney, by the rope. There he stuck fast; and as for the cow, she hung half-way down the wall, swinging between heaven and earth, for she could neither get down nor up.

And now the goody had waited seven lengths and seven breadths for her husband to come and call them home to dinner; but never a call they had. At last she thought she'd waited long enough, and went home. But when she got there and saw the cow hanging in such an ugly place, she ran up and cut the rope in two with her scythe. But as she did this, down came her husband out of the chimney; and so when his old dame came inside the kitchen, there she found him standing on his head in the porridge-pot.

☙ ☙ ☙

BUTTERCUP

BY GEORGE WEBBE DASENT

ONCE on a time there was an old wife who sat and baked. Now you must know that this old wife had a little son, who was so plump and fat, and so fond of good things, that they called him Buttercup; she had a dog, too, whose name was Goldtooth, and as she was baking, all at once Goldtooth began to bark.

"Run out, Buttercup, there's a dear!" said the old wife, "and see what Goldtooth is barking at."

So the boy ran out, and came back crying out,—

"Oh, Heaven help us! here comes a great big witch, with her head under her arm, and a bag at her back."

"Jump under the kneading-trough and hide yourself," said his mother.

So in came the old hag.

"Good day," said she.

"God bless you!" said Buttercup's mother.

"Isn't your Buttercup at home to-day?" asked the hag.

"No, that he isn't. He's out in the wood with his father, shooting grouse."

"Plague take it," said the hag, "for I had such a nice little silver knife I wanted to give him."

"Pip, pip! here I am," said Buttercup under the kneading-trough, and out he came.

"I'm so old and stiff in the back," said the hag, "you must creep into the bag and fetch it out for yourself."

But when Buttercup was well into the bag, the hag threw it over her back and strode off, and when they had gone a good bit of the way, the old hag got tired and asked,

"How far is it off to Snoring?"

"Half a mile," answered Buttercup.

So the hag put down the sack on the road, and went aside by herself into the wood, and lay down to sleep. Meantime Buttercup set to work and cut a hole in the sack with his knife; then he crept out and put a great root of a fir-tree into the sack, and ran home to his mother.

When the hag got home and saw what there was in the sack, you may fancy she was in a fine rage.

Next day the old wife sat and baked again, and her dog began to bark, just as he did the day before.

"Run out, Buttercup, my boy," said she, "and see what Goldtooth is barking at."

"Well, I never!" cried Buttercup, as soon as he got out; "if there isn't that ugly old beast coming again with her head under her arm and a great sack at her back."

"Under the kneading-trough with you and hide," said his mother.

"Good day!" said the hag; "is your Buttercup at home to-day?"

"I'm sorry to say he isn't," said his mother; "he's out in the wood with his father, shooting grouse."

"What a bore!" said the hag; "here I have a beautiful little silver spoon I want to give him."

"Pip, pip! here I am," said Buttercup, and crept out.

"I'm so stiff in the back," said the old witch, "you must creep into the sack and fetch it out for yourself."

So when Buttercup was well into the sack, the hag swung it over her shoulders and set off home as fast as her legs could carry her. But when they had gone a good bit she grew weary, and asked,

"How far is it off to Snoring?"

"A mile and a half," answered Buttercup.

So the hag set down the sack, and went aside into the wood to sleep a bit, but while she slept Buttercup made a hole in the sack and got out, and put a great stone into it. Now, when the old witch got home, she made a great fire on the hearth, and put a big pot on it, and got everything ready to boil Buttercup; but when she took the sack, and thought she was going to turn out Buttercup into the pot, down plumped the stone and made a hole in the bottom of the pot, so that the water ran out and quenched the fire. Then the old hag was in a dreadful rage, and said, "If he makes himself ever so heavy next time, he shan't take me in again."

The third day everything went just as it had gone twice before; Goldtooth began to bark, and Buttercup's mother said to him,

"Do run out and see what our dog is barking at."

So out he went, but he soon came back crying out,

"Heaven save us! Here comes the old hag again with her head under her arm and a sack at her back."

"Jump under the kneading-trough and hide," said his mother.

"Good day!" said the hag, as she came in at the door; "is your Buttercup at home to-day?"

"You're very kind to ask after him," said his mother; "but he's out in the wood with his father, shooting grouse."

"What a bore, now," said the old hag; "here have I got such a beautiful little silver fork for him."

"Pip, pip! here I am," said Buttercup, as he came out from under the kneading-trough.

"I'm so stiff in the back," said the hag, "you must creep into the sack and fetch it out for yourself."

But when Buttercup was well inside the sack the old hag swung it across her shoulders, and set off as fast as she could. This time she did not turn aside to sleep by the way, but went straight home with Buttercup in the sack, and when she reached her house it was Sunday.

So the old hag said to her daughter:

"Now you must take Buttercup and kill him, and boil him nicely till I come back, for I'm off to church to bid my guests to dinner."

So, when all in the house were gone to church, the daughter

was to take Buttercup and kill him, but then she didn't know how to set about it at all.

"Stop a bit," said Buttercup; "I'll soon show you how to do it; just lay your head on the chopping-block, and you'li soon see."

So the poor silly thing laid her head down, and Buttercup took an axe and chopped her head off, just as if she had been a chicken. Then he laid her head in the bed, and popped her body into the pot, and boiled it so nicely; and when he had done that, he climbed up on the roof, and dragged up with him the fir-tree root and the stone, and put one over the door, and the other at the top of the chimney.

So when the household came back from church, and saw the head on the bed, they thought it was the daughter who lay there asleep; and then they thought they would just taste the broth.

"Good, by my troth!
Buttercup broth,"

said the old hag.

"Good, by my troth!
Daughter broth,"

said Buttercup down the chimney, but no one heeded him.

So the old hag's husband, who was every bit as bad as she, took the spoon to have a taste.

"Good, by my troth!
Buttercup broth,"

said he.

"Good, by my troth!
Daughter broth,"

said Buttercup down the chimney pipe.

Then they all began to wonder who it could be that chattered so, and ran out to see. But when they came out at the door, Buttercup threw down on them the fir-tree root and the stone, and broke all their heads to bits. After that he took all the gold and silver that lay in the house, and went home to his mother, and became a rich man.

GERMAN STORIES

SEVEN AT ONE BLOW

BY WILHELM AND JAKOB GRIMM

A TAILOR sat in his workroom one morning, stitching away busily at a coat for the Lord Mayor. He whistled and sang so gaily that all the little boys who passed the shop on their way to school thought what a fine thing it was to be a tailor, and told one another that when they grew to be men they'd be tailors, too.

"How hungry I feel, to be sure!" cried the little man, at last; "but I'm far too busy to trouble about eating. I must finish his lordship's coat before I touch a morsel of food," and he broke once more into a merry song.

"Fine new jam for sale," sang out an old woman, as she walked along the street.

"Jam! I can't resist such a treat," said the tailor; and, running to the door, he shouted, "This way for jam, dame; show me a pot of your very finest."

The woman handed him jar after jar, but he found fault with all. At last he hit upon some to his liking.

"And how many pounds will you take, sir?"

"I'll take four ounces," he replied, in a solemn tone, "and mind you give me good weight."

The old woman was very angry, for she had expected to sell several pounds, at least; and she went off grumbling, after she had weighed out the four ounces.

"Now for a feed!" cried the little man, taking a loaf from the cupboard as he spoke. He cut off a huge slice, and spread the jam on quite half an inch thick; then he suddenly remembered his work.

"It will never do to get jam on the Lord Mayor's coat, so I'll finish it off before I take even one bite," said he. So he picked up his work once more, and his needle flew in and out like lightning.

I am afraid the Lord Mayor had some stitches in his garment that were quite a quarter of an inch long.

The tailor glanced longingly at his slice of bread and jam once or twice, but when he looked the third time it was quite covered with flies, and a fine feast they were having off it.

This was too much for the little fellow. Up he jumped, crying:

"So you think I provide bread and jam for you, indeed! Well, we'll very soon see! Take that!" and he struck the flies such a heavy blow with a duster that no fewer than seven lay dead upon the table, while the others flew up to the ceiling in great haste.

"Seven at one blow!" said the little man with great pride. "Such a brave deed ought to be known all over the town, and it won't be my fault if folks fail to hear of it."

So he cut out a wide belt, and stitched on it in big golden letters the words "Seven at one blow." When this was done he fastened it round him, crying:

"I'm cut out for something better than a tailor, it's quite clear. I'm one of the world's great heroes, and I'll be off at once to seek my fortune."

He glanced round the cottage, but there was nothing of value to take with him. The only thing he possessed in the world was a small cheese.

"You may as well come, too," said he, stowing away the cheese in his pocket, "and now I'm off."

When he got into the street the neighbors all crowded round him to read the words on his belt.

"Seven at one blow!" said they to one another. "What a blessing he's going; for it wouldn't be safe to have a man about us who could kill seven of us at one stroke."

You see, they didn't know that the tailor had only killed flies; they took it to mean men.

He jogged along for some miles until he came to a hedge, where a little bird was caught in the branches.

"Come along," said the tailor; "I'll have you to keep my cheese company"; so he caught the bird and put it carefully into his pocket with the cheese.

Soon he reached a lofty mountain, and he made up his mind to climb it and see what was going on at the other side. When he reached the top, there stood a huge giant, gazing down into the valley below.

"Good day," said the tailor.

The giant turned round, and seeing nobody but the little tailor there, he cried with scorn:

"And what might you be doing here, might I ask? You'd best be off at once."

"Not so fast, my friend," said the little man; "read this."

"Seven at one blow," read the giant, and he began to wish he'd been more civil.

"Well, I'm sure nobody would think it to look at you," he replied; "but since you are so clever, do this," and he picked up a stone and squeezed it until water ran out.

"Do that! Why, it's mere child's play to me," and the man took out his cheese and squeezed it until the whey ran from it. "Now who is cleverer?" asked the tailor. "You see, I can squeeze milk out, while you only get water."

The giant was too surprised to utter a word for a few minutes; then, taking up another stone, he threw it so high into the air that for a moment they couldn't see where it went; then down it fell to the ground again.

"Good!" said the tailor; "but I'll throw a stone that won't come back again at all."

Taking the little bird from his pocket, he threw it into the air, and the bird, glad to get away, flew right off and never returned.

This sort of thing didn't suit the giant at all, for he wasn't used to being beaten by any one.

"Here's something that you'll never manage," said he to the little man. "Just come and help me to carry this fallen oak-tree for a few miles."

"Delighted!" said the tailor, "and I'll take the end with the branches, for it's sure to be heavier."

"Agreed," replied the giant, and he lifted the heavy trunk on to his shoulder, while the tailor climbed up among the branches at the other end, and sang with all his might, as though carrying a tree was nothing to him.

The poor giant, who was holding the tree-trunk and the little tailor as well, soon grew tired.

"I'm going to let it fall!" he shouted, and the tailor jumped down from the branches, and pretended he had been helping all the time.

"The idea of a man your size finding a tree too heavy to carry!" laughed the little tailor.

"You are a clever little fellow, and no mistake," replied the giant, "and if you'll only come and spend the night in our cave, we shall be delighted to have you."

"I shall have great pleasure in coming, my friend," answered the little tailor, and together they set off for the giant's home.

There were seven more giants in the cave, and each one of them was eating a roasted pig for his supper. They gave the little man some food, and then showed him a bed in which he might pass the night. It was so big that, after tossing about for half an hour in it, the tailor thought he would be more comfortable if he slept in the corner, so he crept out without being noticed.

In the middle of the night the giant stole out of bed and went up to the one where he thought the little man was fast asleep. Taking a big bar of iron, he struck such a heavy blow at it that he woke up all the other giants.

"Keep quiet, friends," said he. "I've just killed the little scamp."

The tailor made his escape as soon as possible, and he journeyed on for many miles, until he began to feel very tired, so he lay down under a tree, and was soon fast asleep. When he awoke, he found a big crowd of people standing round him. Up walked one very wise-looking old man, who was really the King's prime minister.

"Is it true that you have killed seven at one blow?" he asked.

"It is a fact," answered the little tailor.

"Then come with me to the King, my friend, for he's been searching for a brave man like you for some time past. You are to be made captain of his army, and the King will give you a fine house to live in."

"That I will," replied the little man. "It is just the sort of thing that will suit me, and I'll come at once."

He hadn't been in the King's service long before every one grew jealous of him. The soldiers were afraid that, if they offended him, he would make short work of them all, while the members of the King's household didn't fancy the idea of making such a fuss over a stranger.

So the soldiers went in a body to the King and asked that another captain should be put over them, for they were afraid of this one.

The King didn't like to refuse, for fear they should all desert, and yet he didn't dare get rid of the captain, in case such a strong and brave man should try to have his revenge.

At last the King hit upon a plan. In some woods close by there lived two giants, who were the terror of the country side; they robbed all the travelers, and if any resistance was offered they killed the men on the spot.

Sending for the little tailor, he said:

"Knowing you to be the bravest man in my kingdom, I want to ask a favor of you. If you will kill these two giants, and bring me back proof that they are dead, you shall marry the Princess, my daughter, and have half my kingdom. You shall also take one hundred men to help you, and you are to set off at once."

"A hundred men, your Majesty! Pray, what do I want with a hundred men? If I can kill seven at one blow, I needn't be afraid of two. I'll kill them fast enough, never fear."

The tailor chose ten strong men, and told them to await him on the border of the wood, while he went on quite alone. He could hear the giants snoring for quite half an hour before he reached them, so he knew in which direction to go.

He found the pair fast asleep under a tree, so he filled his pockets with stones and climbed up into the branches over their heads. Then he began to pelt one of the giants with the missiles, until after a few minutes one of the men awoke. Giving the other a rough push, he cried:

"If you strike me like that again, I'll know the reason why."

"I didn't touch you," said the other giant crossly, and they were soon fast asleep once more.

Then the tailor threw stones at the other man, and soon he awoke as the first had done.

"What did you throw that at me for?" said he.

"You are dreaming," answered the other, "I didn't throw anything."

No sooner were they fast asleep again, than the little man began to pelt them afresh.

Up they both sprang, and seizing each other, they began to fight in real earnest. Not content with using their fists, they tore up huge trees by the roots, and beat each other until very soon the pair lay dead on the ground.

Down climbed the little tailor, and taking his sword in his hand he plunged it into each giant, and then went back to the edge of the forest where the ten men were waiting for him.

"They are as dead as two door nails," shouted the little man. "I don't say that I had an easy task, for they tore up trees by their roots to try to protect themselves with, but, of course, it was no good. What were two giants to a man who has slain seven at one blow?"

But the men wouldn't believe it until they went into the forest and saw the two dead bodies, lying each in a pool of blood, while the ground was covered with uprooted trees.

Back they went to the King, but instead of handing over half his kingdom, as he had promised, his Majesty told the little tailor that there was still another brave deed for him to do before he got the Princess for his bride.

"Just name it, then; I'm more than ready," was the man's reply.

"You are to kill the famous unicorn that is running wild in the forest and doing so much damage. When this is done you shall have your reward at once."

"No trouble at all, your Majesty. I'll get rid of him in a twinkling."

He made the ten men wait for him at the entrance to the wood as they had done the first time, and taking a stout rope and a saw he entered the forest alone.

Up came the unicorn, but just as it was about to rush at the man he darted behind a big tree.

The unicorn dashed with such force against the tree that its horn was caught quite fast and it was kept a prisoner.

Taking his rope, he tied it tightly round the animal, and, after sawing off the horn, back he went to the palace, leading the unicorn by his side.

But even then the King was not satisfied, and he made the little tailor catch a wild boar that had been seen wandering in the woods.

He took a party of huntsmen with him, but again he made them wait on the outskirts of the forest while he went on by himself.

The wild boar made a dash at the little tailor; but the man was too quick for it. He slipped into a little building close by, with the animal at his heels. Then, catching sight of a small window, he forced his way out into the forest again, and while the boar, who was too big and clumsy to follow, stood gazing at the spot where he had disappeared, the tailor ran round and closed the door, keeping the animal quite secure inside. Then he called the hunters, who shot the boar and carried the body back to the palace.

This time the King was obliged to keep his promise; so the little tailor became a Prince, and a grand wedding they had, too.

When they had been married for about a couple of years, the Princess once overheard her husband talking in his sleep.

"Boy, if you have put a patch on that waistcoat, take the Lord Mayor's coat home at once, or I'll box your ears," he said.

"Oh, dear," cried the Princess, "to think that I've married a common tailor! Whatever can I do to get rid of him?"

So she told her father the story, and the King said she need not worry, for he would find a way out of the difficulty. She was to leave the door open that night, and while the tailor was sleeping, the King's servants should steal into the room, bind the tailor, and take him away to be killed.

The Princess promised to see that everything was in readiness, and she tripped about all day with a very light heart.

She little knew that one of the tailor's servants had overheard their cruel plot, and carried the news straight to his master.

That night, when the Princess thought her husband was sleeping fast, she crept to the door and opened it.

To her great terror, the tailor began to speak.

"Boy, take the Lord Mayor's coat home, or I'll box your ears. Haven't I killed seven at one blow? Haven't I slain two giants, a unicorn, and a wild boar? What do I care for the men who are standing outside my door at this moment?"

At these words off flew the men as though they had been shot from a gun, and no more attempts were ever made on his life. So the Princess had to make the best of a bad job.

He lived on and when the old King died he ascended the throne in his stead. So the brave little tailor became ruler over the whole kingdom; and his motto throughout his whole life was, "Seven at one blow."

☙ ☙ ☙

ONE EYE, TWO EYES, THREE EYES

BY WILHELM AND JAKOB GRIMM

THERE was once a woman who had three daughters, of whom the eldest was named "One Eye," because she had only one eye in the middle of her forehead. The second had two eyes, like other people, and she was called "Two Eyes." The youngest had three eyes, two like her second sister, and one in the middle of her forehead, like the eldest, and she bore the name of "Three Eyes."

Now because little Two Eyes looked just like other people, her mother and sisters could not endure her. They said to her, "You are not better than common folks, with your two eyes; you don't belong to us."

So they pushed her about, and threw all their old clothes to her for her to wear, and gave her only the pieces that were left to eat, and did everything that they could to make her miserable.

TWO-EYES, THE GOAT, AND THE MAGIC TABLE.

It so happened that little Two Eyes was sent into the fields to take care of the goats, and she was often very hungry, although her sisters had as much as they liked to eat. So one day she seated herself on a mound in the field, and began to weep and cry so bitterly that two little rivulets flowed from her eyes. Once, in the midst of her sorrow she looked up, and saw a woman standing near her who said, "What are you weeping for, little Two Eyes?"

"I cannot help weeping," she replied; "for because I have two eyes, like other people, my mother and sisters cannot bear me; they push me about from one corner to another and make me wear their old clothes, and give me nothing to eat but what is left, so that I am always hungry. To-day they gave me so little that I am nearly starved."

"Dry up your tears, little Two Eyes," said the wise woman; "I will tell you something to do which will prevent you from ever being hungry again. You have only to say to your own goat:

"'Little goat, if you're able,
Pray deck out my table,'

and immediately there will be a pretty little table before you full of all sorts of good things for you to eat, as much as you like. And when you have had enough, and you do not want the table any more, you need only say:

"'Little goat, when you're able,
Remove my nice table,'

and it will vanish from your eyes."

Then the wise woman went away. "Now," thought little Two Eyes, "I will try if what she says is true, for I am hungry," so she said:

"Little goat, if you're able,
Come and deck my pretty table."

The words were scarcely spoken, when a beautiful little table stood really before her; it had a white cloth and plates, and knives and forks, and silver spoons, and such a delicious dinner, smoking hot as if it had just come from the kitchen.

Then little Two Eyes sat down and said the shortest grace she knew—"Pray God be our guest for all time. Amen"—before she allowed herself to taste anything. But oh, how she did enjoy her dinner! and when she had finished, she said, as the wise woman had taught her:

"Little goat, when you're able,
Remove my nice table."

In a moment, the table and everything upon it had disappeared. "That is a pleasant way to keep house," said little Two Eyes, and felt quite contented and happy. In the evening, when she went home with the goat, she found an earthenware dish with some scraps which her sisters had left for her, but she did not touch them. The next morning she went away with the goat, leaving them behind where they had been placed for her. The first and second times that she did so, the sisters did not notice it; but when they found it happened every day, they said one to the other, "There is something strange about little Two Eyes, she leaves her supper every day, and all that has been put for her has been wasted; she must get food somewhere else."

So they determined to find out the truth, and they arranged that when Two Eyes took her goat to the field, One Eye should go with her to take particular notice of what she did, and discover if anything was brought for her to eat and drink.

So when Two Eyes started with her goat, One Eye said to her, "I am going with you to-day to see if the goat gets her food properly while you are watching the rest."

But Two Eyes knew what she had in her mind. So she drove the goat into the long grass, and said, "Come, One Eye, let us sit down here and rest, and I will sing to you."

One Eye seated herself, and, not being accustomed to walk so far, or to be out in the heat of the sun, she began to feel tired, and as little Two Eyes kept on singing, she closed her one eye and fell fast asleep.

When Two Eyes saw this, she knew that One Eye could not betray her, so she said:

"Little goat, if you are able,
Come and deck my pretty table."

She seated herself when it appeared, and ate and drank very quickly, and when she had finished she said:

"Little goat, when you are able,
Come and clear away my table."

It vanished in the twinkling of an eye; and then Two Eyes woke up One Eye, and said: "Little One Eye, you are a clever one to watch goats; for, while you are asleep, they might be running all over the world. Come, let us go home!"

So they went to the house, and little Two Eyes again left the scraps on the dish untouched, and One Eye could not tell her mother whether little Two Eyes had eaten anything in the field; for she said to excuse herself, "I was asleep."

The next day the mother said to Three Eyes, "You must go to the field this time, and find out whether there is anyone who brings food to little Two Eyes; for she must eat and drink secretly."

So when little Two Eyes started with her goat, Three Eyes followed and said, "I am going with you to-day, to see if the goats are properly fed and watched."

But Two Eyes knew her thoughts; so she led the goat through the long grass to tire Three Eyes, and at last she said, "Let us sit down here and rest, and I will sing to you, Three Eyes."

She was glad to sit down, for the walk and the heat of the sun had really tired her; and, as her sister continued her song, she was obliged to close two of her eyes, and they slept, but not the third. In fact, Three Eyes was wide awake with one eye, and heard and saw all that Two Eyes did; for poor little Two Eyes, thinking she was asleep, said her speech to the goat, and the table came with all the good things on it, and was carried away when Two Eyes had eaten enough; and the cunning Three Eyes saw it all with her one eye. But she pretended to be asleep when her sister came to wake her and told her she was going home.

That evening, when little Two Eyes again left the supper they placed aside for her, Three Eyes said to her mother, "I know where the proud thing gets her good eating and drinking;" and then she described all she had seen in the field. "I saw it all with one eye," she said; "for she had made my other two eyes close with her fine singing, but luckily the one in my forehead remained open."

Then the envious mother cried out to poor little Two Eyes, "You wish to have better food than we, do you? You shall lose your wish!" She took up a butcher's knife, went out, and stuck the good little goat in the heart, and it fell dead.

When little Two Eyes saw this, she went out into the field, seated herself on a mound, and wept most bitter tears.

Presently the wise woman stood again before her, and said, "Little Two Eyes, why do you weep?"

"Ah!" she replied, "I must weep. The goat, who every day spread my table so beautifully, has been killed by my mother, and I shall have again to suffer from hunger and sorrow."

"Little Two Eyes," said the wise woman, "I will give you some good advice. Go home, and ask your sister to give you the heart of the slaughtered goat, and then go and bury it in the ground in front of the house-door."

On saying this the wise woman vanished.

Little Two Eyes went home quickly, and said to her sister, "Dear sister, give me some part of my poor goat. I don't want anything valuable; only give me the heart."

Her sister laughed, and said: "Of course you can have that if you don't want anything else."

So little Two Eyes took the heart; and in the evening, when all was quiet, buried it in the ground outside the house-door, as the wise woman had told her to do.

The next morning, when they all rose and looked out of the window, there stood a most wonderful tree, with leaves of silver and apples of gold hanging between them. Nothing in the wide world could be more beautiful or more costly. They none of them knew how the tree could come there in one night, excepting little Two Eyes. She supposed it had grown up from the heart of the goat; for it stood over where she had buried it in the earth.

Then said the mother to little One Eye, "Climb up, my child, and break off some of the fruit from the tree."

One Eye climbed up, but when she tried to catch a branch

and pluck one of the apples, it escaped from her hand, and so it happened every time she made the attempt, and, do what she would, she could not reach one.

"Three Eyes," said the mother, "climb up, and try what you can do; perhaps you will be able to see better with your three eyes than One Eye can."

One Eye slid down from the tree, and Three Eyes climbed up. But Three Eyes was not more skilful; with all her efforts she could not draw the branches, nor the fruit, near enough to pluck even a leaf, for they sprang back as she put out her hand.

At last the mother was impatient, and climbed up herself, but with no more success, for, as she appeared to grasp a branch, or fruit, her hand closed upon thin air.

"May I try?" said little Two Eyes; "perhaps I may succeed."

"You, indeed!" cried her sisters; "you, with your two eyes, what can you do?"

But Two Eyes climbed up, and the golden apples did not fly back from her when she touched them, but almost laid themselves on her hand, and she plucked them one after another, till she carried down her own little apron full.

The mother took them from her, and gave them to her sisters, as she said little Two Eyes did not handle them properly, but this was only from jealousy, because little Two Eyes was the only one who could reach the fruit, and she went into the house feeling more spiteful to her than ever.

It happened that while all three sisters were standing under the tree together a young knight rode by. "Run away, quick, and hide yourself, little Two Eyes; hide yourself somewhere, for we shall be quite ashamed for you to be seen." Then they pushed the poor girl, in great haste, under an empty cask, which stood near the tree, and several of the golden apples that she had plucked along with her.

As the knight came nearer they saw he was a handsome man; and presently he halted, and looked with wonder and pleasure at the beautiful tree with its silver leaves and golden fruit.

At last he spoke to the sisters, and asked: "To whom does this beautiful tree belong? If a man possessed only one branch he might obtain all he wished for in the world."

"This tree belongs to us," said the two sisters, "and we will break off a branch for you if you like." They gave themselves a great deal of trouble in trying to do as they offered; but all to no purpose, for the branches and the fruit evaded their efforts, and sprung back at every touch.

"This is wonderful," exclaimed the knight, "that the tree should belong to you, and yet you are not able to gather even a branch."

They persisted, however, in declaring that the tree was their own property. At this moment little Two Eyes, who was angry because her sisters had not told the truth, caused two of the golden apples to slip out from under the cask, and they rolled on till they reached the feet of the knight's horse. When he saw them, he asked in astonishment where they came from.

The two ugly maidens replied that they had another sister, but they dared not let him see her, for she had only two eyes, like common people, and was named little Two Eyes.

But the knight felt very anxious to see her, and called out, "Little Two Eyes, come here." Then came Two Eyes, quite comforted, from the empty cask, and the knight was astonished to find her so beautiful.

Then he said: "Little Two Eyes, can you break off a branch of the tree for me?"

"Oh yes," she replied, "I can, very easily, for the tree belongs to me." And she climbed up, and, without any trouble, broke off a branch with its silver leaves and golden fruit and gave it to the knight.

He looked down at her as she stood by his horse, and said: "Little Two Eyes, what shall I give you for this?"

"Ah!" she answered, "I suffer from hunger and thirst, and sorrow, and trouble, from early morning till late at night; if you would only take me with you, and release me, I should be so happy."

Then the knight lifted the little maiden on his horse, and rode home with her to his father's castle. There she was given beautiful clothes to wear, and as much to eat and drink as she wished, and as she grew up the young knight loved her so dearly that they were married with great rejoicings.

Now, when the two sisters saw little Two Eyes carried away by the handsome young knight, they were overjoyed at their good fortune. "The wonderful tree belongs to us now," they said; "even if we cannot break off a branch, yet everybody who passes will stop to admire it, and make acquaintance with us, and, who knows? we may get husbands after all."

But when they rose the next morning, lo! the tree had vanished, and with it all their hopes. And on this very morning, when little Two Eyes looked out of her chamber window of the castle, she saw, to her great joy, that the tree had followed her.

Little Two Eyes lived for a long time in great happiness; but she heard nothing of her sisters, till one day two poor women came to the castle, to beg for alms. Little Two Eyes saw them, and, looking earnestly in their faces, she recognized her two sisters, who had become so poor that they were obliged to beg their bread from door to door.

But the good sister received them most kindly, and promised to take care of them and give them all they wanted. And then they did indeed repent and feel sorry for having treated her so badly in their youthful days.

❧ ❧ ❧

THE MUSICIANS OF BREMEN

BY WILHELM AND JAKOB GRIMM

A CERTAIN man had a donkey that had served him faithfully for many long years, but whose strength was so far gone that at last he was quite unfit for work. So his master began to consider how much he could make of the donkey's skin, but the beast, perceiving that no good wind was blowing, ran away along the road to Bremen. "There," thought he, "I can be town musician." When he had run some way, he found a hound lying by the roadside, yawning like one who was very tired. "What are you yawning for now, you big fellow?" asked the ass.

"Ah," replied the hound, "because every day I grow older and weaker; I cannot go any more to the hunt, and my master has well-nigh beaten me to death, so that I took to flight; and now I do not know how to earn my bread."

"Well, do you know," said the ass, "I am going to Bremen, to be town musician there; suppose you go with me and take a share in the music. I will play on the lute, and you shall beat the kettledrums." The dog was satisfied, and off they set.

Presently they came to a cat, sitting in the middle of the path, with a face like three rainy days! "Now, then, old shaver, what has crossed you?" asked the ass.

"How can one be merry when one's neck has been pinched like mine?" answered the cat. "Because I am growing old, and my teeth are all worn to stumps, and because I would rather sit by the fire and spin, than run after mice, my mistress wanted to drown me; and so I ran away. But now good advice is dear, and I do not know what to do."

"Go with us to Bremen. You understand nocturnal music, so you can be town musician." The cat consented, and went with them. The three vagabonds soon came near a farmyard, where, upon the barn door, the cock was sitting crowing with all his might. "You crow through marrow and bone," said the ass; "what do you do that for?"

"That is the way I prophesy fine weather," said the cock; "but because grand guests are coming for the Sunday, the housewife has no pity, and has told the cook-maid to make me into soup for the morrow; and this evening my head will be cut off. Now I am crowing with a full throat as long as I can."

"Ah, but you, Red-comb," replied the ass, "rather come away with us. We are going to Bremen, to find there something better than death; you have a good voice, and if we make music together it will have full play."

The cock consented to this plan, and so all four traveled on together. They could not, however, reach Bremen in one day, and at evening they came into a forest, where they meant to pass the night. The ass and the dog laid themselves down under a large tree, the cat and the cock climbed up into the branches, but the latter flew right to the top, where he was most safe. Before he went to sleep he looked all round the four quarters, and soon thought he saw a little spark in the distance; so, calling his companions, he said they were not far from a house, for he saw a light. The ass said: "If it is so, we had better get up and go farther, for the pasturage here is very bad"; and the dog continued: "Yes, indeed! a couple of bones with some meat on would be very acceptable!" So they made haste toward the spot where the light was, and which shone now brighter and brighter, until they came to a well-lighted robber's cottage. The ass, as the biggest, went to the window and peeped in. "What do you see, Gray-horse?" asked the cock. "What do I see?" replied the ass; "a table laid out with savory meats and drinks, with robbers sitting around enjoying themselves."

"That would be the right sort of thing for us," said the cock.

"Yes, yes, I wish we were there," replied the ass. Then these animals took counsel together how they should contrive to drive away the robbers, and at last they thought of a way. The ass placed his forefeet upon the window ledge, the hound got on his back, the cat climbed up upon the dog, and, lastly, the cock flew up and perched upon the head of the cat. When this was accomplished, at a given signal they commenced together to perform their music: the ass brayed, the dog barked, the cat mewed, and the cock crew; and they made such a tremendous noise, and so loud, that the panes of the window were shivered! Terrified at these unearthly sounds, the robbers got up with great precipitation, thinking nothing less than that some spirits had come, and fled off into the forest, so the four companions immediately sat down at the table, and quickly ate up all that was left, as if they had been fasting for six weeks.

As soon as they had finished, they extinguished the light, and each sought for himself a sleeping-place, according to his nature and custom. The ass laid himself down upon some straw, the hound behind the door, the cat upon the hearth, near the warm ashes, and the cock flew up on a beam which ran across the room. Weary with their long walk, they soon went to sleep.

At midnight the robbers perceived from their retreat that no light was burning in their house, and all appeared quiet; so the captain said: "We need not have been frightened into fits"; and, calling one of the band, he sent him forward to reconnoiter. The messenger, finding all still, went into the kitchen to strike a light, and, taking the glistening, fiery eyes of the cat for live coals, he held a lucifer match to them, expecting it to take fire. But the cat, not understanding the joke, flew in his face, spitting and scratching, which dreadfully frightened him, so that he made for the back door; but the dog, who laid there, sprang up and bit his leg; and as he limped upon the straw where the ass was stretched out, it gave him a powerful kick with its hind foot. This was not all, for the cock, awaking at the noise, clapped his wings, and cried from the beam: "Cock-a-doodle-doo, cock-a-doodle-do!"

Then the robber ran back as well as he could to his captain, and said: "Ah, my master, there dwells a horrible witch in the house, who spat on me and scratched my face with her long nails; and then before the door stands a man with a knife, who chopped at my leg; and in the yard there lies a black monster, who beat me with a great wooden club; and besides all, upon the roof sits a judge, who called out, 'Bring the knave up, do!' so I ran away as fast as I could."

After this the robbers dared not again go near their house; but everything prospered so well with the four town musicians of Bremen, that they did not forsake their situation! And there they are to this day, for anything I know.

☙ ☙ ☙

THE FISHERMAN AND HIS WIFE

BY WILHELM AND JAKOB GRIMM

THERE was once a fisherman who lived with his wife in a miserable little hovel close to the sea. He went to fish every day, and he fished and fished, and at last one day, when he was sitting looking deep down into the shining water, he felt something on his line. When he hauled it up there was a great flounder on the end of the line. The flounder said to him: "Look here, fisherman, don't you kill me; I am no common flounder, I am an enchanted prince! What good will it do you to kill me? I sha'n't be good to eat; put me back into the water, and leave me to swim about."

"Well," said the fisherman, "you need not make so many words about it. I am quite ready to put back a flounder that can talk." And so saying, he put back the flounder into the shining water, and it sank down to the bottom, leaving a streak of blood behind it.

Then the fisherman got up and went back to his wife in the hovel. "Husband," she said, "hast thou caught nothing to-day?"

"No," said the man; "all I caught was one flounder, and he said he was an enchanted prince, so I let him go swim again."

"Didst thou not wish for anything then?" asked the good wife.

"No," said the man; "what was there to wish for?"

"Alas!" said his wife; "isn't it bad enough always to live in this wretched hovel? Thou mightest at least have wished for a nice clean cottage. Go back and call him; tell him I want a pretty cottage; he will surely give us that!"

"Alas," said the man, "what am I to go back there for?"

"Well," said the woman, "it was thou who caught him and let him go again; for certain he will do that for thee. Be off now!"

The man was still not very willing to go, but he did not want to vex his wife, and at last he went back to the sea.

He found the sea no longer bright and shining, but dull and green. He stood by it and said:

"Flounder, flounder in the sea,
Prythee, hearken unto me:
My wife, Ilsebil, will have her own way
Whatever I wish, whatever I say."

The flounder came swimming up, and said: "Well, what do you want?"

"Alas!" said the man; "I had to call you, for my wife said I ought to have wished for something, as I caught you. She doesn't want to live in our miserable hovel any longer; she wants a pretty cottage."

"Go home again, then," said the flounder; "she has her wish fully."

The man went home and found his wife no longer in the old hut, but a pretty little cottage stood in its place, and his wife was sitting on a bench by the door.

She took him by the hand, and said: "Come and look in here—isn't this much better?"

They went inside and found a pretty sitting-room, and a bedroom with a bed in it, a kitchen, and a larder furnished with everything of the best in tin and brass, and every possible requisite. Outside there was a little yard with chickens and ducks, and a little garden full of vegetables and fruit.

"Look!" said the woman, "is not this nice?"

"Yes," said the man; "and so let it remain. We can live here very happily."

"We will see about that," said the woman, and with that they ate something and went to bed.

Everything went well for a week or more, and then said the wife: "Listen, husband; this cottage is too cramped, and the garden is too small. The flounder might have given us a bigger house. I want to live in a big stone castle. Go to the flounder, and tell him to give us a castle."

"Alas, wife!" said the man; "the cottage is good enough for us; what should we do with a castle?"

"Never mind," said his wife; "do thou but go to the flounder, and he will manage it."

"Nay, wife," said the man; "the flounder gave us the cottage. I don't want to go back; as likely as not he'll be angry."

"Go, all the same," said the woman. "He can do it easily enough, and willingly into the bargain. Just go!"

The man's heart was heavy, and he was very unwilling to go. He said to himself: "It's not right." But at last he went.

He found the sea was no longer green; it was still calm, but dark violet and gray. He stood by it and said:

"Flounder, flounder in the sea,
Prythee, hearken unto me:
My wife, Ilsebil, will have her own way
Whatever I wish, whatever I say."

"Now, what do you want?" said the flounder.

"Alas," said the man, half scared, "my wife wants a big stone castle."

"Go home again," said the flounder; "she is standing at the door of it."

Then the man went away, thinking he would find no house, but when he got back he found a great stone palace, and his wife standing at the top of the steps, waiting to go in.

She took him by the hand and said, "Come in with me."

With that they went in and found a great hall paved with marble slabs, and numbers of servants in attendance, who opened the great doors for them. The walls were hung with beautiful tapestries, and the rooms were furnished with golden chairs and tables, while rich carpets covered the floors, and crystal chandeliers hung from the ceilings. The tables groaned under every kind of delicate food and the most costly wines. Outside the house there was a great courtyard, with stabling for horses, and cows, and many fine carriages. Beyond this there was a great garden filled with the loveliest flowers, and fine fruit trees. There was also a park, half a mile long, and in it were stags and hinds, and hares, and everything of the kind one could wish for.

"Now," said the woman, "is not this worth having?"

"Oh, yes," said the man; "and so let it remain. We will live in this beautiful palace and be content."

"We will think about that," said his wife, "and sleep upon it."

With that they went to bed.

Next morning the wife woke up first; day was just dawning, and from her bed she could see the beautiful country around her. Her husband was still asleep, but she pushed him with her elbow, and said, "Husband, get up and peep out of the window. See here, now, could we not be king over all this land? Go to the flounder. We will be king."

"Alas, wife," said the man, "what should we be king for? I don't want to be king."

"Ah," said his wife, "if thou wilt not be king, I will. Go to the flounder. I will be king."

"Alas, wife," said the man, "whatever dost thou want to be king for? I don't like to tell him."

"Why not?" said the woman. "Go thou must. I will be king."

So the man went; but he was quite sad because his wife would be king.

"It is not right," he said; "it is not right."

When he reached the sea, he found it dark, gray, and rough, and evil-smelling. He stood there and said:

"Flounder, flounder in the sea,
Prythee, hearken unto me:
My wife, Ilsebil, will have her own way
Whatever I wish, whatever I say."

"Now, what does she want?" said the flounder.

"Alas," said the man, "she wants to be king now."

"Go back. She is king already," said the flounder.

So the man went back, and when he reached the palace he found that it had grown much larger, and a great tower had been added, with handsome decorations. There was a sentry at the door, and numbers of soldiers were playing drums and trumpets. As soon as he got inside the house, he found everything was marble and gold; and the hangings were of velvet, with great golden tassels. The doors of the saloon were thrown wide open and he saw the whole court assembled. His wife was sitting on a lofty throne of gold and diamonds; she wore a golden crown, and carried in one hand a scepter of pure gold. On each side of her stood her ladies in a long row, each one a head shorter than the next.

He stood before her, and said, "Alas, wife, art thou now king?"

"Yes," she said; "now I am king."

He stood looking at her for some time, and then he said, "Ah, wife, it is a fine thing for thee to be king; now we will not wish to be anything more."

"Nay, husband," she answered, quite uneasily, "I find the time hangs very heavy on my hands. I can't bear it any longer. Go back to the flounder. King I am, but I must also be emperor."

"Alas, wife," said the man, "why dost thou now want to be emperor?"

"Husband," she answered, "go to the flounder. Emperor I will be."

"Alas, wife," said the man, "emperor he can't make thee, and I won't ask him. There is only one emperor in the country; and emperor the flounder cannot make thee, that he can't."

"What?" said the woman. "I am king, and thou art but my husband. To him thou must go, and that right quickly. If he can make a king, he can also make an emperor. Emperor I will be, so quickly go."

He had to go, but he was quite frightened. And as he went, he thought, "This won't end well; emperor is too shameless. The flounder will make an end of the whole thing."

With that he came to the sea, but now he found it quite black, and heaving up from below in great waves. It tossed to and fro, and a sharp wind blew over it, and the man trembled. So he stood there, and said:

"Flounder, flounder in the sea,
Prythee, hearken unto me:
My wife, Ilsebil, will have her own way
Whatever I wish, whatever I say."

"What does she want now?" said the flounder.

"Alas, flounder," he said, "my wife wants to be emperor."

"Go back," said the flounder. "She is emperor."

So the man went back, and when he got to the door, he found that the whole palace was made of polished marble, with alabaster figures and golden decorations. Soldiers marched up and down before the doors, blowing their trumpets and beating their drums. Inside the palace, counts, barons, and dukes walked about as attendants, and they opened to him the doors, which were of pure gold.

He went in, and saw his wife sitting on a huge throne made of solid gold. It was at least two miles high. She had on her head a great golden crown, set with diamonds, three yards high. In one hand she held the scepter, and in the other the ball of empire. On each side of her stood the gentlemen-at-arms in two rows, each one a little smaller than the other, from giants two miles high, down to the tiniest dwarf no bigger than my little finger. She was surrounded by princes and dukes.

Her husband stood still, and said, "Wife, art thou now emperor?"

"Yes," said she; "now I am emperor."

Then he looked at her for some time, and said, "Alas, wife, how much better off art thou for being emperor?"

"Husband," she said, "what art thou standing there for? Now I am emperor, I mean to be pope! Go back to the flounder."

"Alas, wife," said the man, "what wilt thou not want? Pope thou canst not be. There is only one pope in Christendom. That's more than the flounder can do."

"Husband," she said, "pope I will be; so go at once. I must be pope this very day."

"No, wife," he said, "I dare not tell him. It's no good; it's too monstrous altogether. The flounder cannot make thee pope."

"Husband," said the woman, "don't talk nonsense. If he can make an emperor, he can make a pope. Go immediately. I am emperor, and thou art but my husband, and thou must obey."

So he was frightened, and went; but he was quite dazed. He shivered and shook, and his knees trembled.

A great wind arose over the land, the clouds flew across the sky, and it grew as dark as night; the leaves fell from the trees, and the water foamed and dashed upon the shore. In the distance the ships were being tossed to and fro on the waves, and he heard them firing signals of distress. There was still a little patch of blue in the sky among the dark clouds, but toward the south they were red and heavy, as in a bad storm. In despair, he stood and said:

"Flounder, flounder in the sea,
Prythee, hearken unto me:
My wife, Ilsebil, will have her own way
Whatever I wish, whatever I say."

"Now, what does she want?" said the flounder.

"Alas" said the man, "she wants to be pope."

"Go back. Pope she is," said the flounder.

So back he went, and he found a great church, surrounded with palaces. He pressed through the crowd, and inside he found thousands and thousand of lights, and his wife, entirely clad in gold, was sitting on a still higher throne, with three golden crowns upon her head, and she was surrounded with priestly state. On each side of her were two rows of candles, the biggest as thick as a tower, down to the tiniest little taper. Kings and emperors were on their knees before her, kissing her shoe.

"Wife," said the man, looking at her, "art thou now pope?"

"Yes," said she; "now I am pope."

So there he stood gazing at her, and it was like looking at a shining sun.

"Alas, wife," he said, "art thou better off for being pope?" At first she sat as stiff as a post, without stirring. Then he said, "Now, wife, be content with being pope; higher thou canst not go."

"I will think about that," said the woman, and with that they both went to bed. Still she was not content, and could not sleep for her inordinate desires. The man slept well and soundly, for he had walked about a great deal in the day; but his wife could think of nothing but what further grandeur she could demand. When the dawn reddened the sky, she raised herself up in bed and looked out of the window, and when she saw the sun rise she said:

"Ha! can I not cause the sun and the moon to rise? Husband!" she cried, digging her elbow into his side, "wake up and go to the flounder. I will be lord of the universe."

Her husband, who was still more than half asleep, was so shocked that he fell out of bed. He thought he must have heard wrong. He rubbed his eyes and said:

"Alas, wife, what didst thou say?"

"Husband," she said, "if I cannot be lord of the universe, and cause the sun and moon to set and rise, I shall not be able to bear it. I shall never have another happy moment."

She looked at him so wildly that it caused a shudder to run through him.

"Alas, wife," he said, falling on his knees before her, "the flounder can't do that. Emperor and pope he can make, but that is indeed beyond him. I pray thee, control thyself and remain pope."

Then she flew into a terrible rage. Her hair stood on end; she panted for breath, and screamed:

"I won't bear it any longer; wilt thou go?"

Then he pulled on his trousers and tore away like a madman. Such a storm was raging that he could hardly keep his feet; houses and trees quivered and swayed, mountains trembled, and the rocks rolled into the sea. The sky was pitchy black; it thundered and lightened, and the sea ran in black waves, mountains high, crested with white foam. He shrieked out, but could hardly make himself heard:

"Flounder, flounder in the sea,
Prythee, hearken unto me:
My wife, Ilsebil, will have her own way
Whatever I wish, whatever I say."

"Now, what does she want?" asked the flounder.

"Alas," he said, "she wants to be Lord of the Universe."

"Now she must go back to her old hovel," said the flounder; "and there you will find her."

And there they are to this very day!

☙ ☙ ☙

LITTLE SNOW-WHITE

BY WILHELM AND JAKOB GRIMM

ONCE upon a time it was the middle of winter; the flakes of snow were falling like feathers from the sky; a Queen sat at a window sewing, and the frame of the window was made of black ebony. As she was sewing and looking out of the window at the snow, she pricked her finger with the needle, and three drops of blood fell upon the snow. And the red looked pretty upon the white snow, and she thought to herself:

"Would that I had a child as white as snow, as red as blood, and as black as the wood of the window-frame!" Soon after that she had a little daughter, who was as white as snow, and as red as blood, and her hair was as black as ebony; so she was called Little Snow-white. And when the child was born, the Queen died.

A year after, the King took to himself another wife. She was beautiful but proud, and she could not bear to have any one else more beautiful. She had a wonderful Looking-glass, and when she stood in front of it, and looked at herself in it, and said:

"Looking-glass, Looking-glass, on the wall,
Who in this land is the fairest of all?"

the Looking-glass answered:

"Thou, O Queen, art the fairest of all!"

At last she was well pleased, for she knew the Looking-glass spoke the truth.

Now Snow-white grew up, and became more and more beautiful; and when she was seven years old she was as beautiful as the day, and more beautiful than the Queen herself. And once when the queen asked her Looking-glass:

"Looking-glass, Looking-glass, on the wall,
Who in this land is the fairest of all?"

it answered:

"Thou art fairer than all who are here, Lady Queen,
But more beautiful by far is Snow-white, I ween."

Then the Queen was angry, and turned green with envy. From that hour, whenever she looked at Snow-white, her breath came and went, she hated the girl so much.

And envy grew higher and higher in her heart like a weed, so that she had no peace day or night. She called a huntsman, and said:

"Take the child away into the wood; I will no longer have her in my sight. Kill her, and bring me back her heart as a token." The huntsman did as he was told, and took her away; but when he had drawn his knife, and was about to pierce Snow-white's little heart, she began to weep, and said:

"Ah, dear huntsman, leave me my life! I will run away into the wild wood, and never come home again."

And as she was so beautiful the huntsman had pity on her and said:

"Run away, then, you poor child." The wild beasts will soon kill her, thought he; and yet it seemed as if a stone had been rolled from his heart, since it was no longer needful for him to kill her. As a young boar just then came running by he stabbed it, and cut out its heart and took it to the Queen as a proof that the child was dead. The cook had to salt this, and the wicked Queen ate it, and thought she had eaten the heart of Snow-white.

But now the poor child was all alone in the great wood, and so afraid that she started at every bush, and did not know what to do. Then she began to run, and ran over sharp stones and through thorns, and the wild beasts ran past her, but did her no harm.

She ran as long as her feet would go, until it was almost evening; then she saw a little cottage, and went into it to rest herself. Everything in the cottage was small, but neater and cleaner than can be told. There was a table on which was a white cover, and seven little plates, and by each plate was a little spoon; there were seven little knives and forks, and seven little mugs. Against the wall stood seven little beds side by side, covered with snow-white coverlets.

Little Snow-white was so hungry and thirsty that she ate some fruit and bread from each plate, and drank a drop of milk out of each mug, for she did not wish to take all from one only. Then, as she was so tired, she lay down on one of the little beds, but none of them suited ner; one was too long, another too short; but at last she found the seventh one was just right, and so she stayed in it, said her prayers, and went to sleep.

When it was quite dark the owners of the cottage came back;

LITTLE SNOW-WHITE AND THE PEDDLER-WOMAN.

they were seven dwarfs who dug in the hills for gold. They lit their seven candles, and as it was now light within the cottage they could see that some one had been there, for everything was not in the same order in which they had left it.

The first said, "Who has been sitting on my chair?"

The second, "Who has been eating off my plate?"

The third, "Who has been taking some of my bread?"

The fourth, "Who has been eating my fruit?"

The fifth, "Who has been using my fork?"

The sixth, "Who has been cutting with my knife?"

The seventh, "Who has been drinking out of my mug?"

Then the first looked round and saw that there was a little hole in his bed, and he said:

"Who has been getting into my bed?" The others came up and each called out:

"Somebody has been lying in my bed too." But the seventh, when he looked at his bed, saw little Snow-white, who was lying asleep there. And he called the others, who came running up, and they cried out with wonder, and brought their seven little candles and let the light fall on little Snow-white.

"Oh, heavens! oh, heavens!" cried they, "what a lovely child!" and they were so glad that they did not wake her, but let her sleep on in the bed. And the seventh dwarf slept with the others, one hour with each, and so got through the night.

When it was morning little Snow-white awoke, and was afraid when she saw the seven dwarfs. But they were friendly and asked her what her name was.

"My name is Snow-white," she answered.

"How have you come to our house?" said the dwarfs. Then she told them that the Queen had wished to have her killed, but that the huntsman had spared her life; she had run for the whole day, until at last she had found their house. The dwarfs said:

"If you will take care of our house, cook, make the beds, wash, sew, and knit; and if you will keep everything neat and clean, you can stay with us, and you shall want for nothing."

"Yes," said Snow-white, "with all my heart," and she stayed with them. She kept the house in order for them; in the mornings they went to the hills and looked for gold; in the evenings they came back, and then their supper had to be ready. The girl was alone the whole day, so the good dwarfs warned her and said:

"Beware of the Queen; she will soon know that you are here; be sure to let no one come in."

But the Queen, thinking she had eaten Snow-white's heart, began to suppose she was again the first and most beautiful person in the world; and she went to her Looking-glass and said:

"Looking-glass, Looking-glass, on the wall,
Who in this land is the fairest of all?"

And the Glass answered:

"O Queen, thou art fairest of all I see,
But over the hills, where the seven dwarfs dwell,
Snow-white is still alive and well,
And no one else is so fair as she."

And so she thought and thought again how she might kill Snow-white, for so long as she was not the fairest in the whole land, envy let her have no rest. And when she had at last thought of something to do, she painted her face and dressed herself like an old peddler-woman, and no one could have known her. Then she went over the seven hills to the seven dwarfs, and knocked at the door and cried:

"Pretty things to sell, very cheap, very cheap." Little Snow-white looked out of the window and called out:

"Good-day, my good woman, what have you to sell?"

"Good things, pretty things," she answered; "stay-laces of all colors," and she pulled out one which was woven of bright silk.

"I may let the good old woman in," thought Snow-white, and she unbolted the door and bought the pretty laces.

"Child," said the old woman, "what a fright you look! Come, I will lace you properly for once."

Snow-white stood before her, and let herself be laced with the new laces. But the old woman laced so quickly and laced so tightly that Snow-white lost her breath and fell down as if dead. "Now I am the most beautiful," said the Queen to herself, and ran away.

Not long after, in the evening, the seven dwarfs came home, but how shocked they were when they saw their dear little Snow-white lying on the ground! She did not stir or move, and seemed to be dead. They lifted her up, and, as they saw that she was laced too tightly, they cut the laces; then she began to breathe a little, and after a while came to life again. When the dwarfs heard what had happened they said:

"The old peddler-woman was no one else than the wicked Queen; take care and let no one come in when we are not with you."

But the wicked woman, when she was at home again, went in front of the Glass and asked:

> "Looking-glass, Looking-glass, on the wall,
> Who in this land is the fairest of all?"

And it answered as before:

> "O Queen, thou art fairest of all I see,
> But over the hills, where the seven dwarfs dwell,
> Snow-white is still alive and well,
> And no one else is so fair as she."

When she heard that, all her blood rushed to her heart with fear, for she saw plainly that little Snow-white was again alive.

"But now," she said, "I will think of something that shall put an end to you," and so she made a comb that was full of poison. Then she took the shape of another old woman. So she went over the seven hills to the seven dwarfs, knocked at the door, and cried, "Good things to sell, cheap, cheap!" Little Snow-white looked out and said:

"Go away; I cannot let any one come in."

"I suppose you can look," said the old woman, and pulled the comb out and held it up. It pleased the girl so well that she let herself be coaxed and opened the door. When they had made a bargain the old woman said, "Now I will comb you properly for once." Poor little Snow-white had no fear, and let the old woman do as she pleased, but hardly had she put the comb in her hair than the poison worked, and the girl fell down senseless.

"You piece of beauty," said the wicked woman, "you are done for now," and she went away.

But as good luck would have it, it was almost evening, and the seven dwarfs soon came home. When they saw Snow-white lying as if dead upon the ground, they knew at once the Queen had been there, and they looked and found the comb. Scarcely had they taken it out when Snow-white came to herself, and told them what had happened. Then they warned her once more to be upon her guard and to open the door to no one.

The Queen, at home, went in front of the Glass, and said:

"Looking-glass, Looking-glass, on the wall,
Who in this land is the fairest of all?"

Then it answered as before:

"O Queen, thou art fairest of all I see,
But over the hills, where the seven dwarfs dwell,
Snow-white is still alive and well,
And no one else is so fair as she."

When she heard the Glass speak thus she trembled and shook with rage.

"Snow-white shall die," she cried, "even if it costs me my life!"

She went into a quiet, secret, lonely room, where no one ever came, and there she made an apple full of poison. It was white with a red cheek, so that every one who saw it longed for it; but whoever ate a piece of it must surely die.

When the apple was ready she painted her face, and dressed herself up as a country-woman, and so she went over the seven hills to the seven dwarfs. She knocked at the door. Snow-white put her head out of the window and said:

"I cannot let any one in; the seven dwarfs have told me not to."

"It is all the same to me," said the woman. "I shall soon get rid of my apples. There, I will give you one."

"No," said Snow-white, "I dare not take anything."

"Are you afraid of poison?" said the old woman. "Look, I will cut the apple in two pieces; you eat the red cheek, and I will eat the white." The apple was so cunningly made that only the red cheek was poisoned. Snow-white longed for the fine apple, and when she saw that the woman ate part of it she could stand it no longer, and stretched out her hand and took the other half. But harldy had she a bit of it in her mouth when she fell down dead. Then the Queen looked at her with a dreadful look, and laughed aloud and said:

"White as snow, red as blood, black as ebony-wood! This time the dwarfs cannot wake you up again."

And when she asked of the Looking-glass at home:

"Looking-glass, Looking-glass, on the wall,
Who in this land is fairest of all?"

it answered at last:

"O Queen, in this land thou art fairest of all."

Then her envious heart had rest, so far as an envious heart can have rest.

When the dwarfs came home in the evening, they found Snow-white lying upon the ground; she breathed no longer, and was dead. They lifted her up, unlaced her, combed her hair, washed her with water and wine, but it was all of no use; the poor child was dead, and stayed dead. They laid her upon a bier, and all seven of them sat round it and wept for her, and wept three whole days.

Then they were going to bury her, but she still looked as if she were living, and still had her pretty red cheeks. They said:

"We could not bury her in the dark ground," and they had a coffin of glass made, so that she could be seen from all sides, and they laid her in it, and wrote her name upon it in golden letters, and that she was a King's daughter. Then they put the coffin out upon the hill, and one of them always stayed by it and watched it. And birds came too, and wept for Snow-white; first an owl, then a raven, and last a dove.

And now Snow-white lay a long, long time in the coffin, and she did not change, but looked as if she were asleep; for she was as white as snow, as red as blood, and her hair was as black as ebony.

It happened that a King's son came into the wood, and went to the dwarfs' house to spend the night. He saw the coffin on the hill, and the beautiful Snow-white within it, and read what was written upon it in golden letters. Then he said to the dwarfs:

"Let me have the coffin, I will give you whatever you want for it." But the dwarfs answered:

"We will not part with it for all the gold in the world." Then he said:

"Let me have it as a gift, for I cannot live without seeing Snow-white. I will honor and prize her as the dearest thing I have." As he spoke in this way the good dwarfs took pity upon him, and gave him the coffin.

And now the King's son had it carried away by his servants on their shoulders. And it happened that they stumbled over a tree-stump, and with the shock the piece of apple which Snow-white had bitten off came out of her throat. And before long she opened her eyes, lifted up the lid of the coffin, sat up, and was once more alive.

"Oh, heavens, where am I?" she cried. The King's son, full of joy, said:

"You are with me," and told her what had happened, and said, "I love you more than everything in the world; come with me to my father's palace; you shall be my wife."

Snow-white was willing, and went with him, and their wedding was held with great show and splendor. The wicked Queen was also bidden to the feast. When she had put on her beautiful clothes, she went before the Looking-glass, and said:

"Looking-glass, Looking-glass, on the wall,
Who in this land is the fairest of all?"

The Glass answered:

"O Queen, of all here the fairest art thou,
But the young Queen is fairer by far I trow."

Then the wicked woman gave a scream, and was so wretched, so utterly wretched, that she knew not what to do. At first she would not go to the wedding at all, but she had no peace, and must go to see the young Queen. And when she went in she knew Snow-white; and she stood still with rage and fear, and could not stir. But iron slippers had already been put upon the fire, and they were brought in with tongs, and set before her. Then she was forced to put on the red hot shoes, and dance until she dropped down dead.

❧ ❧ ❧

THE GOOSE-GIRL

BY WILHELM AND JAKOB GRIMM

AN old Queen had a beautiful daughter, who was betrothed to a young Prince of a neighboring kingdom. When the time for the marriage came near, it was arranged that she was to travel to his country accompanied only by her waiting-maid. Her mother, the Queen, provided her with many costly robes and jewels, such as a Princess about to marry the Prince of a great kingdom would require. She also gave her a horse named Falada, which had the gift of speech.

Just before the Princess started on her journey, the Queen pricked her finger, and dropped three drops of blood upon a handkerchief. "Take this," she told her daughter, "and guard it carefully. It will serve you when in danger."

The Princess took the handkerchief, and embraced her mother. They shed many tears at parting, but at last the Princess mounted the wonderful horse and started on the journey. When she and the maid had ridden for some time, they came to a stream of clear, cold water. Being very thirsty, the Princess asked the maid to bring her a drink in the golden cup. The maid insolently replied that she might get the water for herself, as she did not intend to serve her any longer. The Princess was so thirsty that she dismounted and drank from the stream. As she bent over to place her lips to the water, she said to herself, "O, Heaven! what am I to do?" The three drops of blood upon the handkerchief made answer:

"If she knew this, for thy sake
Thy queen-mother's heart would break."

When the Princess had slaked her thirst, she mounted her horse and resumed her journey, and being gentle and forgiving, she soon forgot the maid's rudeness. The sun shone on them fiercely, and the road was filled with dust, so that they had not gone far before the Princess again became thirsty. When they came to a brook, she called to the maid:

"Pray fetch me a drink in my golden cup."

The maid's answer was even more insolent than before. "If you are thirsty, get down and drink. I do not mean to serve you any longer."

The Princess's throat was parched, so she dismounted and drank from the stream, at the same time murmuring, "O, Heaven! what am I to do?" The three drops of blood again replied:

"If she knew this, for thy sake
Thy queen-mother's heart would break."

As she raised her head from the water, the handkerchief bearing the three drops of blood fell unnoticed from her dress and floated down the stream. The maid, however, had observed the loss with no small satisfaction. Without the three drops of blood, the Princess was completely in her power, and the traitorous servant immediately took advantage of her helplessness. She obliged the Princess to disrobe and exchange the royal dress for her own mean one. After making her swear, on fear of death, never to betray the secret, the maid mounted Falada and left her own horse for the Princess.

Falada bore the false Princess to the palace; but the horse had noted all, and bided his time. The Prince came out to meet them, and took the impostor bride to the royal chamber, while the true one was left waiting in the court below. Seeing her there, forlorn and beautiful, the old King inquired of the bride who it was she had thus left outside.

"Only a woman who kept me company," she carelessly replied. "Give her some work to content her."

The King could think of nothing suitable for such as she; but lacking something better to offer, sent her to help the boy Curdken herd geese. So it happened that the real bride became a goose-girl.

The false bride at length remembered Falada's gift of speech and became alarmed lest he should betray the secret of her treachery. She told the Prince that the horse which had brought her was vicious and had given her much trouble, and that she desired his head cut off immediately. The Prince at once granted her request, and gave orders that Falada be beheaded.

When the real Princess heard the sad news, she dried her tears and sought the executioner. She could not save her dear Falada from his doom, but with the aid of a gold piece she persuaded the slaughterer to nail his head over the great gate through which she had to pass on her way to and from the goose-pasture.

The next morning, when she and Curdken drove their geese under the gate, the Princess wrung her hands and cried:

"O Falada, hang you there?"

And the head replied to her:

"'Tis Falada, Princess fair.
If she knew this, for thy sake
Thy queen-mother's heart would break."

When she had driven the geese to the field, she sat down and loosed her golden hair. Curdken, seeing it shining in the sun, caught at it to pull some out. Whereupon she sang:

"Wind, blow gently here, I pray,
And take Curdken's hat away.
Keep him chasing o'er the wold,
While I bind my hair of gold."

When Curdken had recovered his hat and returned to where she was sitting, her hair was plaited, and he could get none of it. This made him very angry all day.

The next morning they again came to the gate where Falada's head was nailed, and the goose-girl said as before:

"O Falada, hang you there?"

And the head as before replied to her:

"'Tis Falada, Princess fair.
If she knew this, for thy sake
Thy queen-mother's heart would break."

Again she passed on with the geese and Curdken under the gate, and when she came to the field where they were herded, sat down and loosed her hair. The sun shone upon it, and Curdken again caught at its golden threads. The goose-girl called to the wind:

"Wind, blow gently here, I pray,
And take Curdken's hat away.
Keep him chasing o'er the wold,
While I bind my hair of gold."

The wind did as she asked, and Curdken ran so far for his hat that when he returned the golden hair was plaited and bound about her head.

Curdken was sullen all day long, and when at night they had driven the geese home, he complained to the King:

"The goose-girl so teases me that I will no longer herd the geese with her."

When asked how she had offended, he told the King that she spoke every morning to the horse's head that was over the gate, and that the head replied and called her Princess. He also related how the goose-girl sat in the sun and combed her golden hair, while she sent him chasing for his hat.

The King bade Curdken go the next day with his flock as usual. When morning came the King arose early and stood in the shadow of the town-gate. He heard the goose-girl say, "O Falada, hang you there?" and he heard the head make answer:

"'Tis Falada, Princess fair.
If she knew this, for thy sake
Thy queen-mother's heart would break."

Then the King followed on to the field, where he hid behind a bush and watched them herd the geese. After a time the goose-girl undid her glittering hair; and as Curdken snatched at it, the King heard her say:

"Wind, blow gently here, I pray,
And take Curdken's hat away.
Keep him chasing o'er the wold,
While I bind my hair of gold."

The wind came at her bidding, and carried the herd-boy's hat across the fields; while she combed the shining hair and made it fast.

The King quietly returned to the palace, and that night he sent for the goose-girl. He told her he had watched her at the gate and in the field, and asked her the meaning of her strange actions.

"O King! I may not tell; for I have sworn, if my life were spared, to speak to no one of my woes," she replied.

The King pleaded with her, but she was firm; and at last he told her to tell her troubles to the iron stove, since she would not confide in him. When he had left her, she fell upon her knees before the stove and poured forth her sorrows:

"Here am I, the daughter of a Queen, doomed to the lowly service of a goose-girl, while the false waiting-maid steals my treasures and my bridegroom."

She sobbed and wept, until the King, who had stood outside and heard all, came in and bade her dry her eyes. He ordered her arrayed in royal robes; and then she appeared as lovely as the sun. The Prince was summoned; and the old King told him the story, and showed him the true bride. She was so beautiful that the Prince knelt at her feet in admiration, and knew her to be the real Princess.

A great banquet was given, to which many guests were invited. On one side of the Prince sat the false bride, and on the other the real Princess, who was so radiantly lovely that the maid did not know her. The King at last asked the waiting-maid what punishment should be dealt to a traitor.

Not knowing that she was passing sentence on herself, the waiting-maid's answer was as cruel as she was wicked. Said she:

"Let her be put into a barrel, and drawn by two white horses, up hill and down, till she is dead."

When the wicked maid had been punished according to her own decree, the Princess was wedded to the young Prince, and reigned with him for many happy years over the kingdom where she had first served as a goose-girl.

THE GOLDEN BIRD

BY WILHELM AND JAKOB GRIMM

THERE was once a King who had a beautiful pleasure-garden behind his palace, in which grew a tree that bore golden apples. As fast as the apples ripened they were counted, but the next day one was always missing.

This was made known to the King, who commanded that a watch should be kept every night under the tree. Now, the King had three sons, and he sent the eldest into the garden when night was coming on; but at midnight he fell fast asleep, and in the morning another apple was missing. The following night the second son had to watch, but he did not succeed any better, and again another apple was missing in the morning. Now came the turn of the youngest son, who was eager to go; but the King did not rely much upon him, and thought he would watch even worse than his brothers; however, at last he consented.

The youth threw himself on the ground under the tree and watched steadily, without letting sleep master him. As twelve o'clock struck, something rustled in the air, and he saw a bird fly by in the moonlight, whose feathers were of shining gold. The bird alighted on the tree and was just picking off one of the apples when the young Prince shot a bolt at it. Away flew the bird, but the arrow had knocked off one of its feathers, which was of the finest gold. The youth picked it up and showed it to the King next morning, and told him all he had seen in the night.

Thereupon the King assembled his council, and each one declared that a single feather like this one was of greater value than the whole kingdom.

"However valuable this feather may be," said the King, "one will not be of much use to me—I must have the whole bird."

So the eldest son went forth on his travels, to look for the wonderful bird, and he had no doubt that he would be able to find it.

When he had gone a short distance, he saw a fox sitting close to the edge of the forest, so he drew his bow to shoot. But the fox cried out: "Do not shoot me, and I will give you a piece of good advice! You are now on the road to the golden bird, and this evening you will come to a village where two inns stand opposite to each other—one will be brilliantly lighted, and great merriment will be going on inside; do not, however, go in, but rather enter the other, even though it appears but a poor place to you."

"How can such a ridiculous animal give me rational advice?" thought the young Prince, and shot at the fox, but missed it, so it ran away with its tail in the air. The King's son then walked on, and in the evening he came to a village where the two inns stood: in one there was dancing and singing, but the other was quiet, and had a very mean and wretched appearance.

"I should be an idiot," thought he to himself, "if I were to go to this gloomy old inn while the other is so bright and cheerful." Therefore, he went into the merry one, lived there in rioting and revelry, and so forgot the golden bird, his father, and all good behavior.

As time passed away, and the eldest son did not return home, the second son set out on his travels to seek the golden bird. Like the eldest brother, he met with the fox, and did not follow the good advice it gave him. He likewise came to the two inns, and at the window of the noisy one his brother stood entreating him to come in. This he could not resist, so he went in, and began to live a life of pleasure only.

Again a long time passed by without any news, so the youngest Prince wished to try his luck, but his father would not hear of it. At last, for the sake of peace, the King was obliged to consent, for he had no rest as long as he refused. The fox was again sitting at the edge of the forest, and once more it begged for its own life and gave its good advice. The youth was good-hearted, and said:

"Have no fear, little fox; I will not do thee any harm."

"Thou wilt never repent of thy good nature," replied the fox, "and in order that thou mayest travel more quickly, get up behind on my tail."

Scarcely had the youth seated himself, when away went the fox over hill and dale, so fast that the Prince's hair whistled in the wind. When they came to the village, the youth dismounted, and following the fox's advice, he turned at once into the shabby-looking inn, where he slept peacefully through the night. The next morning, when the Prince went into the fields, the fox was already there, and said:

"I will tell thee what further thou must do. Go straight on, and thou wilt come to a castle before which a whole troop of soldiers will be lying asleep. Go right through the midst of them into the castle, and thou wilt come to a chamber where is hanging a wooden cage containing a golden bird. Close by stands an empty golden cage, for show; but be careful that thou dost not take the bird out of its ugly cage and put it in the splendid one, or it will be very unlucky for thee."

With these words the fox once more stretched out its tail, and the King's son sat upon it again, and away they went over hill and dale, with their hair whistling in the wind.

When they arrived at the castle, the Prince found everything as the fox had said, and he soon discovered the room in which the golden bird was sitting in its wooden cage; by it stood a golden one; while three golden apples were lying about the room. But the Prince thought it would be silly to put such a lovely bird in so ugly and common a cage; so, opening the door, he placed it in the golden cage. In an instant the bird set up a piercing shriek, which awakened all the soldiers, who rushed in and made him prisoner.

The next morning he was brought before a judge, who at once condemned him to death. Still, the King said his life should be spared on one condition, and that was, that he brought him the golden horse, which ran faster than the wind; and if he succeeded he should also receive the golden bird as a reward.

The young Prince set out on his journey, but he sighed and felt very sorrowful, for where was he to find the golden horse? All at once, he saw his old friend, the fox, sitting by the wayside.

"Ah!" exclaimed the fox, "thou seest now what has happened through not listening to me. But be of good courage; I will look after thee, and tell thee how thou mayest discover the horse. Thou must travel straight along this road until thou comest to a castle; the horse is there in one of the stables. Thou wilt find a stable boy lying before the stall, but he will be fast asleep and snoring, so thou wilt be able to lead out the golden horse quite quietly. But there is one thing thou must be careful about, and that is to put on the shabby old saddle of wood and leather, and not the golden one which hangs beside it—otherwise everything will go wrong with thee." Then the fox stretched out his tail, the Prince took a seat upon it, and away they went over hill and dale, with their hair whistling in the wind.

Everything happened as the fox had said. The Prince came to the stable where the golden horse was standing, but, as he was about to put on the shabby old saddle, he thought to himself, "It does seem a shame that such a lovely animal should be disgraced with this. The fine saddle is his by right; it must go on."

Scarcely had the golden saddle rested on the horse's back when it began to neigh loudly. This awakened the stable boy, who awakened the grooms, who rushed in and seized the Prince and made him a prisoner. The following morning he was brought to trial and condemned to death, but the King promised him his life, as well as the golden horse, if the youth could find the beautiful daughter of the King of the golden castle. Once more, with a heavy heart, the Prince set out on his journey, and by great good fortune he soon came across the faithful fox.

"I really should have left thee to the consequences of thy folly," said the fox; "but as I feel great compassion for thee, I will help thee out of thy new misfortune. The path to the castle lies straight before thee; thou wilt reach it about the evening. At night, when everything is quiet, the lovely Princess will go to the bath-house, to bathe there. As soon as she enters, thou must spring forward and give her a kiss; then she will follow thee wherever thou carest to lead her; only be careful that she does not take leave of her parents, or everything will go wrong."

Then the fox stretched out his tail, the Prince seated himself on it, and away they both went over hill and dale, their hair whistling in the wind.

When the King's son came to the golden palace, everything happened as the fox had predicted. He waited until midnight, and when everyone was soundly asleep the beautiful Princess went into the bath-house, so he sprang forward and kissed her. The Princess then said she would joyfully follow him, but she besought him with tears in her eyes to allow her to say farewell to her parents. At first he withstood her entreaties, but as she wept still more, and fell at his feet, he at last yielded.

Scarcely was the maiden at the bedside of her father, when he awoke, and so did everyone else in the palace; so the foolish youth was captured and put into prison.

On the following morning the King said to him: "Thy life is forfeited, and thou canst only find mercy if thou clearest away the mountain that lies before my windows, and over which I cannot see, but it must be removed within eight days. If thou dost succeed thou shalt have my daughter as a reward."

So the Prince commenced at once to dig and to shovel away the earth without cessation, but when after seven days he saw how little he had been able to accomplish, and that all his labor was as nothing, he fell into a great grief and gave up all hope.

On the evening of the seventh day, however, the fox appeared. "Thou dost not deserve that I should take thy part or befriend thee, but do thou go away and lie down to sleep, and I will do the work for thee."

And the next morning, when he awoke and looked out of the window, the mountain had disappeared! Then the Prince, quite overjoyed, hastened to the King and told him that the conditions were fulfilled, so that the King, whether he would or not, was obliged to keep his word and give him his daughter.

Then these two went away together, and it was not long before the faithful fox came to them.

"Thou hast indeed gained the best of all," said he; "but to the maiden of the golden castle belongs also the golden horse."

"How can I get it?" enquired the youth.

THE PRINCE STARTS HOMEWARD WITH HIS TREASURE.

"I will tell thee," answered the fox; "first of all, take the lovely Princess to the King who sent you to the golden palace. There will then be unheard-of joy; they will gladly lead the golden horse to thee and give it thee. Mount it instantly, and give your hand to everyone at parting, and last of all to the Princess. Grasp her hand firmly; make her spring into the saddle behind thee, and then gallop away; no one will be able to overtake thee, for the golden horse runs faster than the wind."

This was all happily accomplished, and the King's son carried off the beautiful Princess on the golden horse. The fox did not remain behind, and spoke thus to the young Prince:

"Now I will help thee to find the golden bird. When thou comest near the castle where the bird is to be found, let the Princess dismount, and I will take her under my protection. Then ride on the golden horse to the courtyard of the palace, where thy coming will cause great joy, and they will fetch the golden bird for thee. Directly the cage is in thy hands, gallop back to us and fetch the maiden again."

When this plot was successfully carried out, and the Prince was about to ride home with his treasure, the fox said, "Now must thou reward me for all my services."

"What is it that thou dost desire?" enquired the Prince.

"When we come to yonder wood, thou must shoot me dead and cut off my head and paws."

"That would be a fine sort of gratitude," said the King's son; "that I cannot possibly promise thee."

"Then," replied the fox, "if thou wilt not, I must leave thee; but before I go I will give thee again some good advice. Beware of two things—buy no gallows'-flesh, and see that thou dost not sit on the brink of a well!"

With this the fox ran off into the forest.

"Ah!" thought the young Prince, "that is a wonderful animal with very whimsical ideas! Who would buy gallows'-flesh, and when have I ever had the slightest desire to sit on the brink of a well?"

So he rode on with the beautiful maiden, and his path led

him once more through the village in which his two brothers had stopped. Here there was great tumult and lamentation, and when he asked what it all meant, he was told that two men were going to be hanged. When he came nearer, he saw that they were his two brothers, who had committed every kind of wicked folly and had squandered all their money. Then the young Prince asked if they could not be freed.

"Supposing you do pay for them," the people answered, "where is the good of wasting your money in order to free such villains?"

Nevertheless, he did not hesitate, but paid for them, and when the brothers were freed they all rode away together. They came to the forest where they first encountered the fox, and as it was cool and pleasant away from the burning sun, the two brothers said:

"Let us sit and rest a little by this well, and eat and drink something."

The young Prince consented, and while they were all talking together he quite forgot the fox's warning, and suspected no evil.

But suddenly the two brothers threw him backwards into the well, and, seizing the maiden, the horse, and the golden bird, they went home to their father.

"We not only bring you the golden bird," said they, "but we have also found the golden palace."

There was great rejoicing, but the horse would not eat, neither would the bird sing, and the maiden only sat and wept.

But the youngest brother had not perished. By good fortune the well was dry, and he had fallen on soft moss without hurting himself, but he could not get out again.

Even in this misfortune the faithful fox did not desert him, but came springing down to him and scolded him for not following his advice.

"Still I cannot forsake thee," said he, "and I will help to show thee daylight once more."

Then he told him to seize hold of his tail and hold on tightly; and so saying, he lifted him up in the air.

"Even now thou art not out of danger," said the fox, "for

thy brothers were not certain of thy death, and have set spies to watch for thee in the forest, who will certainly kill thee if they see thee."

There was an old man sitting by the wayside with whom the young Prince changed clothes, and, thus disguised, he reached the court of the King.

No one recognized him, but the golden bird began to sing, and the golden horse commenced to eat, and the lovely maiden ceased to weep.

The King was astonished and asked: "What does this all mean?"

Then said the maiden: "I know not, but I was so sad, and now I feel light-hearted; it is as if my true husband had returned."

Then she told him all that had happened, although the other brothers had threatened to kill her if she betrayed them.

The King then summoned all the people in the castle before him: and there came with them the young Prince dressed as a beggar in his rags, but the maiden recognized him instantly and fell upon his neck.

So the wicked brothers were seized and executed, but the young Prince married the lovely Princess and was made his father's heir.

But what became of the poor fox?

Long afterwards the young Prince went again into the forest, and there he met once more with the fox, who said:

"Thou hast now everything in the world thou canst desire, but to my misfortunes there can be no end, although it is in thy power to release me from them."

So he entreated the Prince to shoot him dead and cut off his head and feet.

At last the Prince consented to do so, and scarcely was the deed done than the fox was changed into a man, who was no other than the brother of the beautiful Princess, at last released from the spell that had bound him.

So now nothing was wanting to the happiness of the Prince and his bride as long as they lived.

FRENCH STORIES

BEAUTY AND THE BEAST

ADAPTED BY E. NESBIT

ONCE upon a time there was a rich merchant, who had three daughters. They lived in a very fine house in a beautiful city, and had many servants in grand liveries to wait upon them. All their food was served on gold and silver dishes, and their gowns were made of the richest stuff sewn with jewels.

The two eldest were called Marigold and Dressalinda. Never a day passed but these two went out to some feast or junketing; but Beauty, the youngest, loved to stay at home and keep her old father company.

Now, it happened that misfortune came upon the merchant. Ships of his which were sailing the high seas laden with merchandise of great price, were wrecked, and in one day he found that he was no longer the richest merchant in the city, but a very poor man.

There was still left to him a little house in the country, and to this, when everything else had been sold, he retired. His three daughters, of course, went with him.

Marigold and Dressalinda were very cross to think that they had lost all their money, and after being so rich and sought after, they must now live in a miserable cottage.

But Beauty's only thought was to cheer her old father, and while her two sisters sat on wooden chairs and cried and bewailed themselves, Beauty lighted the fire and got the supper ready, for the merchant was now so poor that he could not even keep a servant.

And so it went on. The two eldest sisters would do nothing but sulk in corners, while Beauty swept the floors and washed the dishes, and did her best to make the poor cottage pleasant

They led their sister a dreadful life too, with their complaints, for not only did they refuse to do anything themselves, but they said that everything she did was done wrong. But Beauty bore all their unkindness patiently, for her father's sake.

In this way a whole year went by, and then one day a letter came for the merchant.

He hastened to find his daughters, for he was anxious to tell them the good news contained in the letter.

"My dear children," he said, "at last our luck has turned. This letter says that one of the ships supposed to have been lost has come safely home to port, and if that be so, we need no longer live in poverty. We shall not be so rich as before, but we shall have enough to keep us in comfort. Get me my traveling-cloak, Beauty. I will set out at once to claim my ship. And now tell me, girls, what shall I bring you when I come back?"

"A hundred pounds," said Marigold, without hesitating an instant.

"I want a new silk dress," said Dressalinda, "an apple-green one, sewn with seed-pearls, and green shoes with red heels, and a necklace of emeralds, and a box of gloves."

"And what shall I bring for you, my Beauty?" asked the father, as his little daughter helped him to put on his traveling-cloak.

"Oh, bring me a rose," said Beauty hastily.

Her father kissed her fondly, and set out.

"You silly girl," said Marigold, "you just want our father to think you are more unselfish than we are—that's what you want! A rose, indeed!"

"Indeed, sister," said Beauty, "that was not the reason. I thought our father would have enough to do in seeing to the safety of his ship, without being troubled to do shopping for me."

But the sisters were very much offended, and went off to sit in their own room to talk of the fine things they would have when their father came back.

In the meantime the merchant went his way to the city, full of hope and great plans as to what he would do with his money.

But when he got there, he found that some one had played a trick on him, and no ship of his had come into harbor, so he was just as badly off as before.

He spent the whole day looking about to make sure there was no truth in the letter he had received, and it was beginning to get dusk when he started out, with a sad heart, to make the journey home again. He was tired and miserable, and he had tasted no food since he left home in the morning.

It was quite dark by the time he came to the great wood through which he had to pass to get to his cottage, and when he saw a light shining through the trees, he decided not to go to his home that night, but to make his way towards the light in the wood and ask for food and shelter.

He expected to find a woodcutter's cottage, but what was his surprise, as he drew near to the light, to find that it came from the windows of a large and beautiful palace!

He knocked at the gates, but no one answered, and presently, driven by hunger and cold, he made bold to enter, and mounted the marble steps into the great hall.

All the way he never saw a soul. There was a big fire in the hall, and when he had warmed himself, he set out to look for the master of the house. But he did not look far, for behind the first door he opened was a cosy little room with supper set for one, a supper the mere look of which made you hungry.

So the merchant sat down as bold as you please, and made a very hearty supper, after which he again thought he would look for the master of the house.

He started off and opened another door, but there he saw a bed, merely to look at which made you sleepy, so he said to himself:

"This is some fairies' work. I had better not look any farther for the master of the house."

And with that he tumbled into bed, and, being very tired, he went to sleep at once, and slept like a top till it was time to get up in the morning.

When he awoke he was quite surprised to find himself in such a soft and comfortable bed, but presently he remembered all that had happened to him.

"I must be going," he said to himself, "but I wish I could thank my host for my good rest and my good supper."

When he got out of bed he found he had something else to be grateful for, for on the chair by the bedside lay a fine suit of new clothes, marked with his name, and with ten gold pieces in every pocket. He felt quite a different man when he had put on the suit of blue and silver, and jingled the gold pieces of money in his pockets.

When he went downstairs, he found a good breakfast waiting for him in the little room where he had supped the night before, and when he had made a good meal, he thought he would go for a stroll in the garden.

Down the marble steps he went, and when he came to the garden, he saw that it was full of roses, red and white and pink and yellow, and the merchant looked at them, and remembered Beauty's wish.

"Oh, my poor daughters," he said, "what a disappointment it will be to them to know that my ship has not come home after all, but Beauty at any rate can have what she wanted."

So he stretched out his hand and plucked the biggest red rose within his reach.

As the stalk snapped in his fingers, he started back in terror, for he heard an angry roar, and the next minute a dreadful Beast sprang upon him. It was taller than any man, and uglier than any animal, but, what seemed most dreadful of all to the merchant, it spoke to him with a man's voice, after it had roared at him with the Beast's.

"Ungrateful wretch!" said the Beast. "Have I not fed you, lodged you, and clothed you, and now you must repay my hospitality by stealing the only thing I care for, my roses?"

"Mercy! mercy!" cried the merchant.

"No," said the Beast, "you must die!" The poor merchant fell upon his knees and tried to think of something to say to soften the heart of the cruel Beast; and at last he said, "Sir, I only stole this rose because my youngest daughter asked me to bring her one. I did not think, after all you have given me, that you would grudge me a flower."

"Tell me about this daughter of yours," said the Beast suddenly. "Is she a good girl?"

"The best and dearest in the world," said the old merchant. And then he began to weep, to think that he must die and leave his Beauty alone in the world, with no one to be kind to her.

"Oh!" he cried, "what will my poor children do without me?"

"You should have thought of that before you stole the rose," said the Beast. "However, if one of your daughters loves you well enough to suffer instead of you, she may. Go back and tell them what has happened to you, but you must give me your promise that either you, or one of your daughters, shall be at my palace door in three months' time from to-day."

The wretched man promised.

"At any rate," he thought, "I shall have three months more of life."

Then the Beast said, "I will not let you go empty-handed."

So the merchant followed him back into the palace. There, on the floor of the hall, lay a great and beautiful chest of wrought silver.

"Fill this with any treasures that take your fancy," said the Beast.

And the merchant filled it up with precious things from the Beast's treasure-house.

"I will send it home for you," said the Beast, shutting down the lid.

And so, with a heavy heart, the merchant went away; but as he went through the palace gate, the Beast called to him that he had forgotten Beauty's rose, and at the same time held out to him a large bunch of the very best.

The merchant put these into Beauty's hand when she ran to meet him at the door of their cottage.

"Take them, my child," he said, "and cherish them, for they have cost your poor father his life."

And with that he sat down and told them the whole story. The two elder sisters wept and wailed, and of course blamed Beauty for all that had happened.

"If it had not been for your wanting a rose, our father would have left the palace in safety, with his new suit and his gold pieces; but your foolishness has cost him his life."

"No," said Beauty, "it is *my* life that shall be sacrificed, for when the three months are over, I shall go to the Beast, and he may kill me if he will, but he shall never hurt my dear father."

The father tried hard to persuade her not to go, but she had made up her mind, and at the end of the three months she set out for the Beast's palace.

Her father went with her, to show her the way. As before, he saw the lights shining through the wood, knocked and rang in vain at the great gate, warmed himself at the fire in the big hall, and then found the little room with the supper on the table that made you hungry to look at. Only this time the table was laid for two.

"Come, father dear," said Beauty, "take comfort. I do not think the Beast means to kill me, or surely he would not have given me such a good supper."

But the next moment the Beast came into the room. Beauty screamed and clung to her father.

"Don't be frightened," said the Beast gently, "but tell me, do you come here of your own free will?"

"Yes," said Beauty, trembling.

"You are a good girl," said the Beast, and then, turning to the old man, he told him that he might sleep there for that night, but in the morning he must go and leave his daughter behind him.

They went to bed and slept soundly, and the next morning the father departed, weeping bitterly.

Beauty, left alone, tried not to feel frightened. She ran here and there through the palace, and found it more beautiful than anything she had ever imagined.

The most beautiful set of rooms in the palace had written over the doors, "Beauty's Rooms," and in them she found books and music, canary-birds and Persian cats, and everything that could be thought of to make the time pass pleasantly.

"Oh, dear!" she said; "if only I could see my poor father I should be almost happy."

As she spoke, she happened to look at a big mirror, and in it she saw the form of her father reflected, just riding up to the door of his cottage.

That night, when Beauty sat down to supper, the Beast came in.

"May I have supper with you?" said he.

"That must be as you please," said Beauty.

So the Beast sat down to supper with her, and when it was finished, he said:

"I am very ugly, Beauty, and I am very stupid, but I love you; will you marry me?"

"No, Beast," said Beauty gently.

The poor Beast sighed and went away.

And every night the same thing happened. He ate his supper with her, and then asked her if she would marry him. And she always said, "No, Beast."

All this time she was waited on by invisible hands, as though she had been a queen. Beautiful music came to her ears without her being able to see the musicians, but the magic looking-glass was best of all, for in it she could see whatever she wished. As the days went by, and her slightest wish was granted, almost before she knew what she wanted, she began to feel that the Beast must love her very dearly, and she was very sorry to see how sad he looked every night when she said "No" to his offer of marriage.

One day, she saw in her mirror that her father was ill, so that night she said to the Beast:

"Dear Beast, you are so good to me, will you let me go home to see my father? He is ill, and he thinks that I am dead. Do let me go and cheer him up, and I will promise faithfully to return to you."

"Very well," said the Beast kindly, "but don't stay away more than a week, for if you do, I shall die of grief, because I love you so dearly."

"How shall I reach home?" said Beauty; "I do not know the way."

Then the Beast gave her a ring, and told her to put it on her finger when she went to bed, turn the ruby towards the palm of her hand, and then she would wake up in her father's cottage. When she wanted to come back, she was to do the same thing.

So in the morning, when she awoke, she found herself at her father's house, and the old man was beside himself with joy to see her safe and sound.

But her sisters did not welcome her very kindly, and when they heard how kind the Beast was to her, they envied her her good luck in living in a beautiful palace, whilst they had to be content with a cottage.

"I wish we had gone," said Marigold. "Beauty always gets the best of everything."

"Tell us all about your grand palace," said Dressalinda, "and what you do, and how you spend your time."

So Beauty, thinking it would amuse them to hear, told them, and their envy increased day by day. At last Dressalinda said to Marigold:

"She has promised to return in a week. If we could only make her forget the day, the Beast might be angry and kill her, and then there would be a chance for us."

So on the day before she ought to have gone back, they put some poppy juice in a cup of wine which they gave her, and this made her so sleepy that she slept for two whole days and nights. At the end of that time her sleep grew troubled, and she dreamed that she saw the Beast lying dead among the roses in the beautiful gardens of his paiace; and from this dream she awoke crying bitterly.

Although she did not know that a week and two days had gone by since she left the Beast, yet after that dream she at once turned the ruby towards her palm, and the next morning there she was, sure enough, in her bed in the Beast's palace.

She did not know where his rooms in the palace were, but she felt she could not wait till supper-time before seeing him, so she ran hither and thither, calling his name. But the palace was empty, and no one answered her when she called.

Then she ran through the gardens, calling his name again and again, but still there was silence.

"Oh! what shall I do if I cannot find him?" she said. "I shall never be happy again."

Then she remembered her dream, and ran to the rose garden, and there, sure enough, beside the basin of the big fountain, lay the poor Beast without any sign of life in him.

Beauty flung herself on her knees beside him.

"Oh, dear Beast," she cried, "and are you really dead? Alas! alas! then I, too, will die, for I cannot live without you."

Immediately the Beast opened his eyes, sighed, and said: "Beauty, will you marry me?"

And Beauty, beside herself with joy when she found that he was still alive, answered:

"Yes, yes, dear Beast, for I love you dearly."

At these words the rough fur dropped to the ground, and in place of the Beast stood a handsome Prince, dressed in a doublet of white and silver, like one made ready for a wedding. He knelt at Beauty's feet and clasped her hands.

"Dear Beauty," he said, "nothing but your love could have disenchanted me. A wicked fairy turned me into a Beast, and condemned me to remain one until some fair and good maiden should love me well enough to marry me, in spite of my ugliness and stupidity. Now, dear one, the enchantment is broken; let us go back to my palace. You will find that all my servants—who, too, have been enchanted, and have waited on you all this long time with invisible hands—will now become visible."

So they returned to the palace, which by this time was crowded with courtiers, eager to kiss the hands of the Prince and his bride. And the Prince whispered to one of his attendants, who went out, and in a very little time came back with Beauty's father and sisters.

The sisters were condemned to be changed into statues, and to stand at the right and left of the palace gates until their hearts should be softened, and they should be sorry for their unkindness to their sister. But Beauty, happily married to her Prince, went secretly to the statues every day and wept over them.

And by her tears their stony hearts were softened, and they were changed into flesh and blood again, and were good and kind for the rest of their lives.

And Beauty and the Beast, who was a Beast no more, but a handsome Prince, lived happily ever after.

And indeed I believe they are living happily still, in the beautiful land where dreams come true.

❧ ❧ ❧

THE WHITE CAT

BY THE COMTESSE D'AULNOY

THERE was once a King who had three sons, and because they were all so good and so handsome, he could not make up his mind to which of them to give his kingdom. For he was growing an old man, and began to think it would soon be time for him to let one of them reign in his stead.

So he determined to set them a task to perform, and whichever should be the most successful was to have the kingdom as his reward.

It was some time before he could decide what the task should be. But at last he told them that he had a fancy for a very beautiful little dog, and that they were all to set out to find one for him. They were to have a whole year in which to search, and were all to return to the castle on the same day, and present the various dogs they had chosen at the same hour.

The three Princes were greatly surprised by their father's sudden fancy for a little dog, but when they heard that whichever of them brought back the prettiest little animal was to succeed his father on the throne, they made no further objection, for it gave the two younger sons a chance they would not otherwise have had of being King.

So they bade their father good-bye, and after agreeing to be back at the castle at the same hour, and on the same day, when a year should have passed away, the three brothers all started together.

A great number of lords and servants accompanied them out

of the city, but when they had ridden about a league they sent everyone back, and after embracing one another affectionately, they all set out to try their luck in different directions.

The two eldest met with many adventures on their travels, but the youngest saw the most wonderful sights of all.

He was young and handsome, and as clever as a Prince should be, besides being brave.

Wherever he went he enquired for dogs, and hardly a day passed without his buying several, big and little, greyhounds, spaniels, lap-dogs, and sheep-dogs—in fact, every kind of dog that you could think of, and very soon he had a troop of fifty or sixty trotting along behind him, one of which he thought would surely win the prize.

So he journeyed on from day to day, not knowing where he was going, until one night he lost his way in a thick dark forest, and after wandering many weary miles in the wind and rain he was glad to see at last a bright light shining through the trees. He thought he must be near some woodcutter's cottage, but what was his surprise when he found himself before the gateway of a splendid castle!

At first he hesitated about entering, for his garments were travel stained, and he was drenched with rain, so that no one could have possibly taken him for a Prince. All the beautiful little dogs he had taken so much trouble to collect had been lost in the forest, and he was thoroughly weary and disheartened.

However, something seemed to bid him enter the castle, so he pulled the bell. Immediately the gateway flew open, and a number of beautiful white hands appeared, and beckoned to him to cross the courtyard and enter the great hall.

Here he found a splendid fire blazing, beside which stood a comfortable arm-chair; the hands pointed invitingly towards it, and as soon as the Prince had seated himself they proceeded to take off his wet, muddy clothes, and dress him in a magnificent suit of silk and velvet.

When he was ready, the hands led him into a brilliantly-lighted room, in which was a table spread for supper. At the end of the room was a raised platform, upon which a number of cats were seated, all playing different musical instruments.

THE CASTLE OF THE WHITE CAT.

The Prince began to think he must be dreaming, when the door opened, and a lovely little White Cat came in. She wore a long black veil, and was accompanied by a number of cats, dressed in black, and carrying swords.

She came straight up to the Prince, and in a sweet, sad little voice bade him welcome. Then she ordered supper to be served, and the whole company sat down together.

They were waited upon by the mysterious hands, but many of the dishes were not to the Prince's liking. Stewed rats and mice may be a first-rate meal for a cat, but the Prince did not feel inclined to try them.

However, the White Cat ordered the hands to serve the Prince with the dishes he liked best, and at once, without his even mentioning his favorite food, he was supplied with every dainty he could think of.

After the Prince had satisfied his hunger, he noticed that the Cat wore a bracelet upon her paw, in which was set a miniature of himself; but when he questioned her about it, she sighed, and seemed so sad that, like a well-behaved Prince, he said no more about the matter.

Soon after supper, the hands conducted him to bed, when he at once fell fast asleep, and did not awaken until late the next morning. On looking out of his window, he saw that the White Cat and her attendants were about to start out on a hunting expedition.

As soon as the hands had dressed him in a hunting-suit of green, he hurried down to join his hostess.

The hands led him up to a wooden horse, and seemed to expect him to mount. At first the Prince was inclined to be angry, but the White Cat told him so gently that she had no better steed to offer him, that he at once mounted, feeling very much ashamed of his ill-humor.

They had an excellent day's sport. The White Cat, who rode a monkey, proved herself a clever huntress, climbing the tallest trees with the greatest ease, and without once falling from her steed.

Never was there a pleasanter hunting party, and day after day the time passed so happily away that the Prince forgot all about the little dog he was searching for, and even forgot his own home and his father's promise.

At length the White Cat reminded him that in three days he must appear at court, and the Prince was terribly upset to think that he had now no chance of winning his father's kingdom. But the White Cat told him that all would be well, and giving him an acorn, bade him mount the wooden horse and ride away.

The Prince thought she must be mocking him, but when she held the acorn to his ear, he heard quite plainly a little dog's bark.

"Inside this acorn," she said, "is the prettiest little dog in the world. But be sure you do not open the fruit until you are in the King's presence."

The Prince thanked her, and having bidden her a sorrowful farewell, mounted his wooden steed and rode away.

Before he reached the castle, he met his two brothers, who made fine fun of the wooden horse, and also of the big ugly dog which trotted by his side.

They imagined this to be the one their brother had brought back from his travels, hoping that it would gain the prize.

When they reached the palace, everyone was loud in praise of the two lovely little dogs the elder brothers had brought back with them, but when the youngest opened his acorn and showed a tiny dog, lying upon a white satin cushion, they knew that this must be the prettiest little dog in the world.

However, the King did not feel inclined to give up his throne just yet, so he told the brothers that there was one more task they must first perform: they must bring him a piece of muslin so fine that it would pass through the eye of a needle.

So once more the brothers set out upon their travels. As for the youngest, he mounted his wooden horse and rode straight back to his dear White Cat.

She was delighted to welcome him, and when the Prince told her that the King had now ordered him to find a piece of muslin fine enough to go through the eye of a needle, she smiled at him very sweetly, and told him to be of good cheer.

"In my palace I have some very clever spinners," she said, "and I will set them to work upon the muslin."

The Prince had begun to suspect by this time that the White Cat was no ordinary pussy, but whenever he begged her to tell him her history, she only shook her head mournfully and sighed.

Well, the second year passed away as quickly as the first, and the night before the day on which the three Princes were expected at their father's court, the White Cat gave the young Prince a walnut, telling him that it contained the muslin. Then she bade him good-by, and he mounted the wooden horse and rode away.

This time the young Prince was so late that his brothers had already begun to display their pieces of muslin to the King when he arrived at the castle gates. The materials they had brought were of extremely fine texture, and passed easily through the eye of a darning-needle, but through the small needle the King had provided they would *not* pass. Then the youngest Prince stepped into the great hall and produced his walnut. He cracked it carefully, and found inside a hazel-nut. This when cracked held a cherrystone, inside the cherrystone was a grain of wheat, and in the wheat a millet-seed. The Prince himself began to mistrust the White Cat, but he instantly felt a cat's claw scratch him gently, so he persevered, opened the millet-seed, and found inside a beautiful piece of soft white muslin that was four hundred ells long at the very least. It passed with the greatest ease through the eye of the smallest needle in the kingdom, and the Prince felt that now the prize must be his.

But the old King was still very loth to give up ruling, so he told the Princes that before any one of them could become King he must find a Princess to marry him who would be lovely enough to grace her high station; and whichever of the Princes brought home the most beautiful bride should *really* have the kingdom for his own.

Of course, the Prince went back to the White Cat, and told her how very unfairly his father had behaved to him. She comforted him as best she could, and told him not to be afraid, for she would introduce him to the loveliest Princess the sun had ever shone upon.

The appointed time passed happily away, and one evening the White Cat reminded the Prince that on the next day he must return home.

"Alas!" said he, "where shall I find a Princess now? The time is so short that I cannot even look for one."

Then the White Cat told him that if only he would do as she bade him all would be well.

"Take your sword, cut off my head and my tail, and cast them into the flames," she said.

The Prince declared that on no account would he treat her so cruelly; but she begged him so earnestly to do as she asked that at last he consented.

No sooner had he cast the head and the tail into the fire than a beautiful Princess appeared where the body of the cat had been. The spell that had been cast upon her was broken, and at the same time her courtiers and attendants, who had also been changed into cats, hastened in in their proper forms again, to pay their respects to their mistress.

The Prince at once fell deeply in love with the charming Princess, and begged her to accompany him to his father's court as his bride.

She consented, and together they rode away. During the journey, the Princess told her husband the story of her enchantment.

She had been brought up by the fairies, who treated her with great kindness until she offended them by falling in love with the young man whose portrait the Prince had seen upon her paw, and who exactly resembled him.

Now, the fairies wished her to marry the King of the Dwarfs, and were so angry when she declared she would marry no one but her own true love, that they changed her into a White Cat as a punishment.

When the Prince and his bride reached the court, all were bound to acknowledge that the Princess was by far the loveliest lady they had ever seen.

So the poor old King felt that now he would be obliged to give up his kingdom. But the Princess knelt by his side, kissed his hand gently, and told him that there was no reason for him to cease ruling, for she was rich enough to give a mighty kingdom to each of his elder sons, and still have three left for herself and her dear husband.

SHE·WAS HAP-PY ALL·DAY·
LONG IN FAI-RY LAND
K·C

So everyone was pleased, and there was great rejoicing and feasting in the King's palace, and they all lived happily ever after.

❧ ❧ ❧

THE STORY OF PRETTY GOLDILOCKS

THERE was once a Princess so lovely that no one could see her without loving her. Her hair fell about her shoulders in waving masses, and because it was the color of gold, she was called Pretty Goldilocks. She always wore a crown of flowers, and her dresses were embroidered with pearls and diamonds.

The fame of her beauty reached a young King, who determined to marry her, although he had never seen her. He sent an ambassador to ask her hand in marriage; and so confident was he that the Princess would return with him, that he made every preparation to receive her. The ambassador arrived at the palace of the Princess with a hundred horses and as many servants. With great ceremony, he presented the King's gifts of pearls and diamonds, together with his message. The Princess, however, did not favor the King's suit, and sent back his gifts with a polite refusal. When the ambassador returned without the Princess, every one blamed him for his failure; and the King's disappointment was so great that no one could console him.

Now at the King's court was a young man so handsome and clever that he was called Charming. Every one loved him, except some who were envious because he was the King's favorite. One day Charming rashly remarked that if the King had sent *him* for the Princess, she would have come back with him. His enemies at once went to the King and used the remark to influence him against Charming.

"He thinks himself so handsome that the Princess could not have resisted him, although she refused his King," they told his Majesty.

The boastful words so offended the King that he ordered Charming to be shut up in the tower, where he had only straw to lie on and bread and water to eat. In this miserable state he languished for some time, not knowing why he had been imprisoned. One day the King happened to be passing the tower and heard him exclaim:

"I am the King's most faithful subject; how have I incurred his displeasure?" Then, in spite of the protests of Charming's enemies, the King ordered the tower-door opened and Charming brought forth. His old favorite sadly knelt and kissed his hand, saying:

"Sire, how have I offended?"

The King told him of the boast his enemies had repeated.

"True, Sire, I did say that had I been sent to plead your cause, it would not have failed for lack of eloquence. Could the Princess see you as my tongue would picture you, I would not return without her."

The King at once saw that he had been deceived, and restored Charming to favor. While at supper that night, he confided to him that he was as much in love with Goldilocks as ever, and could not be reconciled to her answer.

"Do you think," asked the King, "that she could be induced to change her mind?"

Charming replied that he was at the King's service and willing to undertake the task of winning the Princess for him. The King was delighted and offered him a splendid escort, but he asked only for a good horse.

Early the next day he set forth, with a resolute heart and the King's letter to the Princess. One day when he had ridden a great distance, he dismounted and sat down under a tree that grew beside a river. He took from his pocket a little book, in which he jotted down some happy thoughts that he meant to use in his plea to the Princess. Not far from where he sat, a golden carp was springing from the water to catch flies, and a bound too high landed it on the grass at Charming's feet. It panted helplessly, and would have died had he not taken pity on it and thrown it back into the river. It sank out of sight, but presently returned to the surface long enough to say:

"Thank you, Charming, for saving my life. Some day I

may repay you." Naturally, he was greatly surprised at so much politeness from a fish.

A few days later, while riding along his way, he saw a raven pursued by an eagle. In a moment more the eagle would have overtaken the raven, had not Charming aimed his arrow in time and killed the pursuer. The raven perched on a tree near by and croaked its gratitude:

"You have rescued me from a dreadful fate," it said. "Some day I will repay you."

A day or two afterward, in the dusk of early morning, he heard the distressful cries of an owl. Hunting about, he found the unfortunate bird caught in a net which some birdcatchers had spread. "Why will men persecute and torment harmless creatures!" exclaimed Charming, as he set the bird free. The owl fluttered above his head, saying:

"You have saved me from the fowlers, who would have killed me. I am not ungrateful, and some day I will repay you!" After that it flew swiftly away.

Charming at last reached the palace of the Princess, and asked an audience. His name so pleased her that she at once received him. He was ushered into the presence of the Princess, who sat on a throne of gold and ivory. Her satin dress was embroidered with jewels, and her golden hair was confined by a crown of flowers. Soft music and perfume filled the air, and Charming was so awed by all this splendor that at first he could not speak. Recovering himself in a moment, he told of his mission, and set forth the good qualities of the King in such glowing terms that the Princess listened.

"You have argued so eloquently," replied she, "that I regret to deny you; but I have made a vow not to marry, until the ambassador can return to me a ring which I lost in the river a month ago. I valued it more than all my other jewels, and nothing but its recovery can persuade me to your suit."

Charming could urge no more, but offered an embroidered scarf and his little dog Frisk as tokens of devotion. These were declined, so bowing low, he reluctantly took leave of the Princess. He believed that she had but used this means to put him off, and his disappointment was so great that he could not sleep.

In the morning he and Frisk were walking by the riverside when the dog ran to the water's edge, barking furiously. Joining the little animal, he saw that his excitement was caused by a golden carp which came swimming swiftly toward them. In its mouth was a beautiful ring which it laid in Charming's hand.

"You saved my life by the willow-tree," said the carp, "and I now repay you by giving to you the Princess's ring."

Charming lost no time in presenting it to the Princess and claiming his reward.

"What fairy aids you?" asked the Princess.

"Only my wish to serve you," Charming replied.

"Alas!" said the Princess, "I cannot marry until Galifron, the giant, is dead. Because I would not take him for my husband, he persecutes my subjects and lays waste my land."

"Princess, I will bring back the giant's head to you or die in your defense," bravely declared Charming.

The Princess and all the people tried to dissuade him, but he mounted his horse and rode off, accompanied only by his little dog, Frisk. He traveled straight to the giant's castle. All about it were strewn the bones of Galifron's victims. Inside the castle the giant was singing in a terrible voice:

"Little children I love to eat;
Their bones are tender, their flesh is sweet.
I do not care, I eat so many,
If their hair be straight, or if they haven't any."

Charming called out loudly in reply:

"Be not so boastful, Galifron,
Till you've met a knight, who
May be good to feed upon,
But is here to fight you."

The giant appeared at the door, club in hand. When he saw Charming fearlessly awaiting him, he came toward him in a terrible rage. But before he could wield his club, a raven lit on his head and pecked at his eyes, so that he dropped his weapon and was at Charming's mercy. When the valiant knight had killed the giant, the raven croaked from a tree near by:

"You saved me from the eagle, and I in turn have saved you from the giant."

Charming cut off the head of the giant, and carried it back with him to the Princess. Then the people shouted until they were hoarse, and welcomed him as a great hero.

"Your enemy is dead," Charming told the Princess. "Will you now make my master the happiest of kings?"

"There is," replied the reluctant Princess, "some water which gives eternal health and beauty to those who drink it. I would regret to leave my kingdom without possessing some of it; but no one has dared to brave the two dragons that guard the cavern where the fountain is to be found."

"You do not need the water, Princess; but my life is yours to command," gallantly replied Charming; and he set out at once on the perilous mission.

When he came to the mouth of the cavern, black smoke issued forth; and presently he perceived the terrible form of a dragon, from whose mouth and eyes fire was darting. Bidding good-by to faithful Frisk, he grasped his sword in one hand and the crystal flask which the Princess had given him in the other. Just then he heard his name called twice, and, looking back, he saw an owl flying toward him.

"I can enter the gloomy cavern without danger," the owl said. "Give the flask to me, and I will repay the debt I owe you for having saved me from the net."

Charming gladly surrendered the flask to the owl, who in a short time returned it to him filled with the precious water.

The Princess this time consented to marry the King, and after many preparations she and Charming started for his kingdom. The journey was made so entertaining for the Princess that she one day said to Charming:

"Why did I not make you King, and remain in my own country?" Charming replied that he must have considered his duty to his King, even before a happiness so great.

The King, with presents of rich jewels and a splendid escort, met them on the way to the palace. The marriage was celebrated with great pomp, and Charming stood first in the King's favor. His good fortune, however, did not continue long, for envious enemies pointed out to the King that the Princess was never happy unless Charming was near. The unhappy knight was again put into prison, where he was cruelly chained and fed on bread and water.

When Goldilocks learned this, she wept and implored the King to set him free. "But for him I never would have been here," she said. "Did he not perform every task I required, even that of getting for me the water whereby I shall never grow old?"

The Princess's grief only made the King more jealous, but he determined to make use of this wonderful water of which sne had told. It so happened that one of the Princess's ladies had broken the crystal flask and spilled all of the water. Not daring to confess, she put another in its place that exactly resembled it in appearance. This, however, contained a deadly poison. When the King bathed his face with it, he fell into a sleep from which he never awoke.

There was great confusion in the palace when the King was found dead. Frisk ran immediately to Charming and told him the news. In a short time Goldilocks also appeared, unlocked his chains, and set him free.

"You shall be my husband," said she, "and I will make you King."

Charming fell at her feet and expressed his gratitude and joy. They were married soon afterward, and they reigned together for many happy years.

❧ ❧ ❧

TOADS AND DIAMONDS

A BAD-TEMPERED widow had two daughters. The eldest was like her mother, both in feature and disposition, while the youngest resembled her father. She was sweet-natured always, and as pretty as she was amiable.

The widow doted on the daughter who was so like herself, but had no love for the other, whom she compelled to work hard all day, and to live upon the leavings of her elder sister. Among her other hard tasks, she was obliged to carry water every day from a great distance.

One day when she had just filled her pitcher at the fountain, an old woman asked to drink from it. "With all my heart," replied the pretty girl. Glad to show a kindness to one old and infirm, she held the pitcher while the woman slaked her thirst.

Now, this was not a trembling old peasant, as she appeared, but a fairy who rewarded good deeds. "Your face is pretty and your heart is gentle," said she. "For your kindness to a poor old woman, I will make you a gift. Every time you speak, from your mouth shall come a flower or a jewel."

When the girl reached home her mother scolded her for her long absence. "Pardon me for being away so long," she sweetly replied. As she spoke some pearls and diamonds issued from her lips.

"What is this I see, child?" asked the astonished widow.

The forlorn girl was so happy to be called child by her mother that she eagerly related her experience with the old woman at the fountain, while, with her words, dropped precious stones and roses. The widow immediately called her favorite daughter to her.

"Fanny, wouldst thou have the same gift as thy sister?" asked she. "Go thou to the fountain and fetch water. And if an old woman asks thee for a drink, mind thou treat her civilly."

The girl refused to perform the menial task, until the widow lost patience and drove her to it. Finally, she took the silver tankard and sullenly obeyed. No sooner was she at the fountain than from the wood came a lady most handsomely attired, who asked the haughty girl for a drink from her pitcher.

"I have not come here to serve you," she rudely replied, "but take the pitcher and help yourself, for all I care. I would have you know that I am as good as you."

The lady was the fairy, who had taken the appearance of a

princess to see how far the girl's insolence would go. "I will make you a gift," she said, "to equal your discourtesy and ill breeding. Every time you speak, there shall come from your mouth a snake or a toad."

The girl ran home to her mother, who met her at the door. "Well, daughter," she said, impatient to hear her speak. When she opened her mouth, to the mother's horror, two vipers and two toads sprang from it. "This is the fault of your wretched sister," the unhappy mother cried. She ran to beat the poor younger sister, who fled to the forest to escape the cruel blows. When she was past pursuit, she threw herself upon the green grass and wept bitterly.

The King's son, returning from the hunt, found her thus, and asked the cause of her tears.

"My mother has driven me from my home," she told him. She was so pretty that he fell in love with her at once, and pressed her to tell him more. She then related to him the whole story, while pearls and diamonds kept falling from her lips. Enraptured, he took her to the King, who gave his consent to their immediate marriage.

Meanwhile the ugly and selfish sister had made herself so disagreeable that even her own mother turned against her. She, too, was driven forth into the forest, where she died miserable and alone.

ENGLISH STORIES

THE HISTORY OF TOM THUMB

ADAPTED BY ERNEST RHYS

IT is said that in the days of the famed Prince Arthur, who was king of Britain, in the year 516 there lived a great magician, called Merlin, the most learned and skilful enchanter in the world at that time.

This great magician, who could assume any form he pleased, was traveling in the disguise of a poor beggar, and being very much fatigued, he stopped at the cottage of an honest plowman to rest himself, and ask for some refreshment.

The countryman gave him a hearty welcome, and his wife, who was a very good-hearted, hospitable woman, soon brought him some milk in a wooden bowl, and some coarse brown bread on a platter.

Merlin was much pleased with this homely repast and the kindness of the plowman and his wife; but he could not help seeing that though everything was neat and comfortable in the cottage, they seemed both to be sad and much cast down. He therefore questioned them on the cause of their sadness, and learned that they were miserable because they had no children.

The poor woman declared, with tears in her eyes, that she should be the happiest creature in the world if she had a son; and although he was no bigger than her husband's thumb, she would be satisfied.

Merlin was so much amused with the idea of a boy no bigger than a man's thumb, that he made up his mind to pay a visit to the queen of the fairies, and ask her to grant the poor woman's wish. The droll fancy of such a little person among the human race pleased the fairy queen too, greatly, and she promised Merlin that the wish should be granted. Accordingly, in a short time after, the plowman's wife had a son, who, wonderful to relate, was not a bit bigger than his father's thumb.

The fairy queen, wishing to see the little fellow thus born into the world, came in at the window while the mother was sitting up in bed admiring him. The queen kissed the child, and giving it the name of Tom Thumb, sent for some of the fairies, who dressed her little favorite as she bade them.

"An oak-leaf hat he had for his crown;
His shirt of web by spiders spun;
With jacket wove of thistle's down;
His trousers were of feathers done.
His stockings, of apple-rind, they tie
With eyelash from his mother's eye:
His shoes were made of mouses' skin,
Tann'd with the downy hair within."

It is remarkable that Tom never grew any larger than his father's thumb, which was only of an ordinary size; but as he got older he became very cunning and full of tricks. When he was old enough to play with the boys, and had lost all his own cherry-stones, he used to creep into the bags of his playfellows, fill his pockets, and, getting out unseen, would again join in the game.

One day, however, as he was coming out of a bag of cherry-stones, where he had been pilfering as usual, the boy to whom it belonged chanced to see him. "Ah, ha! my little Tommy," said the boy, "so I have caught you stealing my cherry-stones at last, and you shall be rewarded for your thievish tricks." On saying this, he drew the string tight round his neck, and gave the bag such a hearty shake, that poor little Tom's legs, thighs, and body were sadly bruised. He roared out with the pain, and begged to be let out, promising never to be guilty of such bad practices again.

A short time afterwards his mother was making a batter pudding, and Tom being very anxious to see how it was made, climbed up to the edge of the bowl; but unfortunately his foot slipped and he plumped over head and ears into the batter, unseen by his mother, who stirred him into the pudding-bag, and put him in the pot to boil.

The batter had filled Tom's mouth, and prevented him from

crying; but, on feeling the hot water, he kicked and struggled so much in the pot, that his mother thought that the pudding was bewitched, and, instantly pulling it out of the pot, she threw it to the door. A poor tinker, who was passing by, lifted up the pudding, and, putting it into his budget, he then walked off. As Tom had now got his mouth cleared of the batter, he then began to cry aloud, which so frightened the tinker that he flung down the pudding and ran away. The pudding being broke to pieces by the fall, Tom crept out covered over with the batter, and with difficulty walked home. His mother, who was very sorry to see her darling in such a woful state, put him into a tea-cup, and soon washed off the batter; after which she kissed him, and laid him in bed.

Soon after the adventure of the pudding, Tom's mother went to milk her cow in the meadow, and she took him along with her. As the wind was very high, fearing lest he should be blown away, she tied him to a thistle with a piece of fine thread. The cow soon saw the oak-leaf hat, and, liking the look of it, took poor Tom and the thistle at one mouthful. While the cow was chewing the thistle Tom was afraid of her great teeth, which threatened to crush him to pieces, and he roared out as loud as he could, "Mother, mother!"

"Where are you, Tommy, my dear Tommy?" said his mother.

"Here, mother," replied he, "in the cow's mouth."

His mother began to cry and wring her hands; but the cow, surprised at the odd noise in her throat, opened her mouth and let Tom drop out. Fortunately his mother caught him in her apron as he was falling to the ground, or he would have been dreadfully hurt. She then put Tom in her bosom and ran home with him.

Tom's father made him a whip of a barley straw to drive the cattle with, and having one day gone into the fields, he slipped a foot and rolled into the furrow. A raven, which was flying over, picked him up, and flew with him to the top of a giant's castle that was near the sea-side, and there left him.

Tom was in a dreadful state, and did not know what to do; but he was soon more dreadfully frightened; for old Grumbo the giant came up to walk on the terrace, and seeing Tom, he took him up and swallowed him like a pill.

The giant had no sooner swallowed Tom than he began to repent what he had done; for Tom began to kick and jump about so much that he felt very uncomfortable, and at last threw him up again into the sea. A large fish swallowed Tom the moment he fell into the sea, which was soon after caught, and bought for the table of King Arthur. When they opened the fish in order to cook it, everyone was astonished at finding such a little boy, and Tom was quite delighted to be out again. They carried him to the King, who made Tom his dwarf, and he soon grew a great favorite at court; for by his tricks and gambols he not only amused the King and Queen, but also all the Knights of the Round Table.

It is said that when the King rode out on horseback, he often took Tom along with him, and if a shower came on, he used to creep into his Majesty's waistcoat pocket, where he slept till the rain was over.

King Arthur one day asked Tom about his parents, wishing to know if they were as small as he was, and whether rich or poor. Tom told the King that his father and mother were as tall as any of the sons about court, but rather poor. On hearing this, the King carried Tom to his treasury, the place where he kept all his money, and told him to take as much money as he could carry home to his parents, which made the poor little fellow caper with joy. Tom went immediately to fetch a purse, which was made of a water-bubble, and then returned to the treasury, where he got a silver three-penny piece to put into it.

Our little hero had some trouble in lifting the burden upon his back; but he at last succeeded in getting it placed to his mind, and set forward on his journey. However, without meeting with any accident and after resting himself more than a hundred times by the way, in two days and two nights he reached his father's house in safety.

Tom had traveled forty-eight hours with a huge silver-piece on his back, and was almost tired to death, when his mother ran out to meet him, and carried him into the house.

Tom's parents were both happy to see him, and the more so

as he had brought such an amazing sum of money with him; but the poor little fellow was excessively wearied, having traveled half a mile in forty-eight hours, with a huge silver threepenny-piece on his back. His mother, in order to recover him, placed him in a walnut shell by the fireside, and feasted him for three days on a hazel-nut, which made him very sick; for a whole nut used to serve him a month.

Tom was soon well again; but as there had been a fall of rain, and the ground was very wet, he could not travel back to King Arthur's Court; therefore his mother, one day when the wind was blowing in that direction, made a little parasol of cambric paper, and tying Tom to it, she gave him a puff into the air with her mouth, which soon carried him to the King's palace.

Just at the time when Tom came flying across the court-yard, the cook happened to be passing with the King's great bowl of porridge, which was a dish his Majesty was very fond of; but unfortunately the poor little fellow fell plump into the middle of it, and splashed the hot porridge about the cook's face.

The cook, who was an ill-natured fellow, being in a terrible rage at Tom for frightening and scalding him with the porridge, went straight to the King, and said that Tom had jumped into the royal porridge, and thrown it down out of mere mischief. The King was so enraged when he heard this, that he ordered Tom to be seized and tried for high treason; and there being no person who dared to plead for him, he was condemned to be beheaded immediately.

On hearing this dreadful sentence pronounced, poor Tom fell a-trembling with fear, but, seeing no means of escape, and observing a miller close to him gaping with his great mouth, as country boobies do at a fair, he took a leap, and fairly jumped down his throat. This exploit was done with such activity that not one person present saw it, and even the miller did not know the trick which Tom had played upon him. Now, as Tom had disappeared, the court broke up, and the miller went home to his mill.

When Tom heard the mill at work he knew he was clear

of the court, and therefore he began to roll and tumble about, so that the poor miller could get no rest, thinking he was bewitched; so he sent for a doctor. When the doctor came, Tom began to dance and sing; and the doctor, being as much frightened as the miller, sent in haste for five other doctors and twenty learned men.

When they were debating about this extraordinary case, the miller happened to yawn, when Tom, seizing the chance, made another jump, and alighted safely upon his feet on the middle of the table.

The miller, who was very much provoked at being tormented by such a little pigmy creature, fell into a terrible rage, and, laying hold of Tom, ran to the King with him; but his Majesty, being engaged with state affairs, ordered him to be taken away, and kept in custody till he sent for him.

The cook was determined that Tom should not slip out of his hands this time, so he put him into a mouse-trap, and left him to peep through the wires. Tom had remained in the trap a whole week, when he was sent for by King Arthur, who pardoned him for throwing down the porridge, and took him again into favor. On account of his wonderful feats of activity, Tom was knighted by the King, and went under the name of the renowned Sir Thomas Thumb. As Tom's clothes had suffered much in the batter-pudding, the porridge, and the insides of the giant, miller, and fishes, his Majesty ordered him a new suit of clothes, and to be mounted as a knight.

"Of Butterfly's wings his shirt was made.
His boots of chicken's hide;
And by a nimble fairy blade,
Well learned in the tailoring trade,
His clothing was supplied—
A needle dangled by his side;
A dapper mouse he used to ride,
Thus strutted Tom in stately pride!"

It was certainly very diverting to see Tom in this dress, and mounted on the mouse, as he rode out a-hunting with the King and nobility, who were all ready to expire with laughter at Tom and his fine prancing charger.

One day, as they were riding by a farmhouse, a large cat, which was lurking about the door, made a spring, and seized both Tom and his mouse. She then ran up a tree with them, and was beginning to devour the mouse; but Tom boldly drew his sword, and attacked the cat so fiercely that she let them both fall, when one of the nobles caught him in his hat, and laid him on a bed of down, in a little ivory cabinet.

The queen of the fairies came soon after to pay Tom a visit, and carried him back to Fairyland, where he lived several years. During his residence there, King Arthur, and all the persons who knew Tom, had died; and as he was desirous of being again at court, the fairy queen, after dressing him in a suit of clothes, sent him flying through the air to the palace, in the days of King Thunstone, the successor of Arthur. Every one flocked round to see him, and being carried to the King, he was asked who he was—whence he came—and where he lived? Tom answered:

"My name is Tom Thumb,
From the fairies I've come.
When King Arthur shone,
His Court was my home.
In me he delighted,
By him I was knighted;
Did you never hear of Sir Thomas Thumb?"

The King was so charmed with this address that he ordered a little chair to be made, in order that Tom might sit upon his table, and also a palace of gold, a span high, with a door an inch wide, to live in. He also gave him a coach, drawn by six small mice.

The Queen was so enraged at the honor paid to Sir Thomas that she resolved to ruin him, and told the King that the little knight had been saucy to her.

The King sent for Tom in great haste, but being fully aware of the danger of royal anger, he crept into an empty snail-shell, where he lay for a long time, until he was almost starved with hunger; but at last he ventured to peep out, and seeing a fine large butterfly on the ground, near his hiding-place, he approached very cautiously, and getting himself placed astride on it, was immediately carried up into the air. The butterfly flew with him from tree to tree and from field to field, and at last he returned to the court, where the King and nobility all strove to catch him; but at last poor Tom fell from his seat into a watering-pot, in which he was almost drowned.

When the Queen saw him she was in a rage, and said he should be beheaded; and he was again put into a mouse-trap until the time of his execution.

However, a cat, observing something alive in the trap, patted it about till the wires broke, and set Thomas at liberty.

The King received Tom again into favor, which he did not live to enjoy, for a large spider one day attacked him; and although he drew his sword and fought well, yet the spider's poisonous breath at last overcame him:

"He fell dead on the ground where he stood,
And the spider suck'd every drop of his blood."

King Thunstone and his whole court were so sorry at the loss of their little favorite, that they went into mourning, and raised a fine white marble monument over his grave, with the following epitaph:

"Here lies Tom Thumb, King Arthur's knight,
Who died by a spider's cruel bite,
He was well known in Arthur's Court,
Where he afforded gallant sport;
He rode at tilt and tournament,
And on a mouse a-hunting went.
Alive he filled the Court with mirth;
His death to sorrow soon gave birth.
Wipe, wipe your eyes, and shake your head
And cry—Alas! Tom Thumb is dead!"

☙ ☙ ☙

JACK THE GIANT-KILLER

ADAPTED BY JOSEPH JACOBS

WHEN good King Arthur reigned, there lived near the Land's End of England, in the county of Cornwall, a farmer who had one only son called Jack. He was brisk and of ready, lively wit, so that nobody or nothing could worst him.

In those days the Mount of Cornwall was kept by a huge giant named Cormoran. He was eighteen feet in height, and about three yards round the waist, of a fierce and grim countenance, the terror of all the neighboring towns and villages. He lived in a cave in the midst of the Mount, and whenever he wanted food he would wade over to the mainland, where he would furnish himself with whatever came in his way. Everybody at his approach ran out of their houses, while he seized on their cattle, making nothing of carrying half-a-dozen oxen on his back at a time; and as for their sheep and hogs, he would tie them round his waist like a bunch of tallow-dips. He had done this for many years, so that all Cornwall was in despair.

One day Jack happened to be at the town hall when the magistrates were sitting in council about the giant. He asked, "What reward will be given to the man who kills Cormoran?" "The giant's treasure," they said, "will be the reward." Quoth Jack, "Then let me undertake it."

So he got a horn, shovel, and pickaxe, and went over to the Mount in the beginning of a dark winter's evening, when he fell to work, and before morning had dug a pit twenty-two feet deep, and nearly as broad, covering it over with long sticks and straw. Then he strewed a little mold over it, so that it appeared like plain ground. Jack then placed himself on the opposite side of the pit, farthest from the giant's lodging, and, just at the break of day, he put the horn to his mouth, and blew. This noise roused the giant, who rushed from his cave, crying: "You incorrigible villain, are you come here to disturb my rest? You shall pay dearly for this. Satisfaction I will have, and this it shall be, I will take you whole and broil you for breakfast." He had no sooner uttered this, than he tumbled into the pit, and made the very foundations of the Mount to shake. "Oh Giant," quoth Jack, "where are you now? Oh, faith, you are gotten now into a tight place, where I will surely plague you for your threatening words; what do you think now of broiling me for your breakfast? Will no other diet serve you but poor Jack?" Then having tantalized the giant for a while, he gave him a most weighty knock with his pickaxe on the very crown of his head, and killed him on the spot.

Jack then filled up the pit with earth, and went to search the cave, which he found contained much treasure. When the magistrates heard of this they made a declaration he should henceforth be termed:

JACK THE GIANT-KILLER

and presented him with a sword and a belt, on which were written these words embroidered in letters of gold:

"Here's the right valiant Cornish man,
Who slew the giant Cormoran."

The news of Jack's victory soon spread over all the West of England, so that another giant, named Blunderbore, hearing of it, vowed to be revenged on Jack, if ever he should light on him. This giant was the lord of an enchanted castle situated in the midst of a lonesome wood. Now Jack, about four months afterwards, walking near this wood in his journey to Wales, being weary, seated himself near a pleasant fountain and fell fast asleep. While he was sleeping, the giant, coming there for water, discovered him, and knew him to be the far-famed Jack the Giant-killer by the lines written on the belt. Without ado, he took Jack on his shoulders and carried him towards his castle. Now, as they passed through a thicket, the rustling of the boughs awakened Jack, who was strangely surprised to find himself in the clutches of the giant. His terror was only begun, for, on entering the castle, he saw the ground strewed with human bones, and the giant told him his own would ere long be among them. After this the giant locked poor Jack in an immense chamber, leaving him there while he went to fetch another giant, his brother, living in the same wood, who might share in the meal on Jack.

After waiting some time Jack, on going to the window beheld afar off the two giants coming towards the castle. "Now," quoth Jack to himself, "my death or my deliverance is at hand."

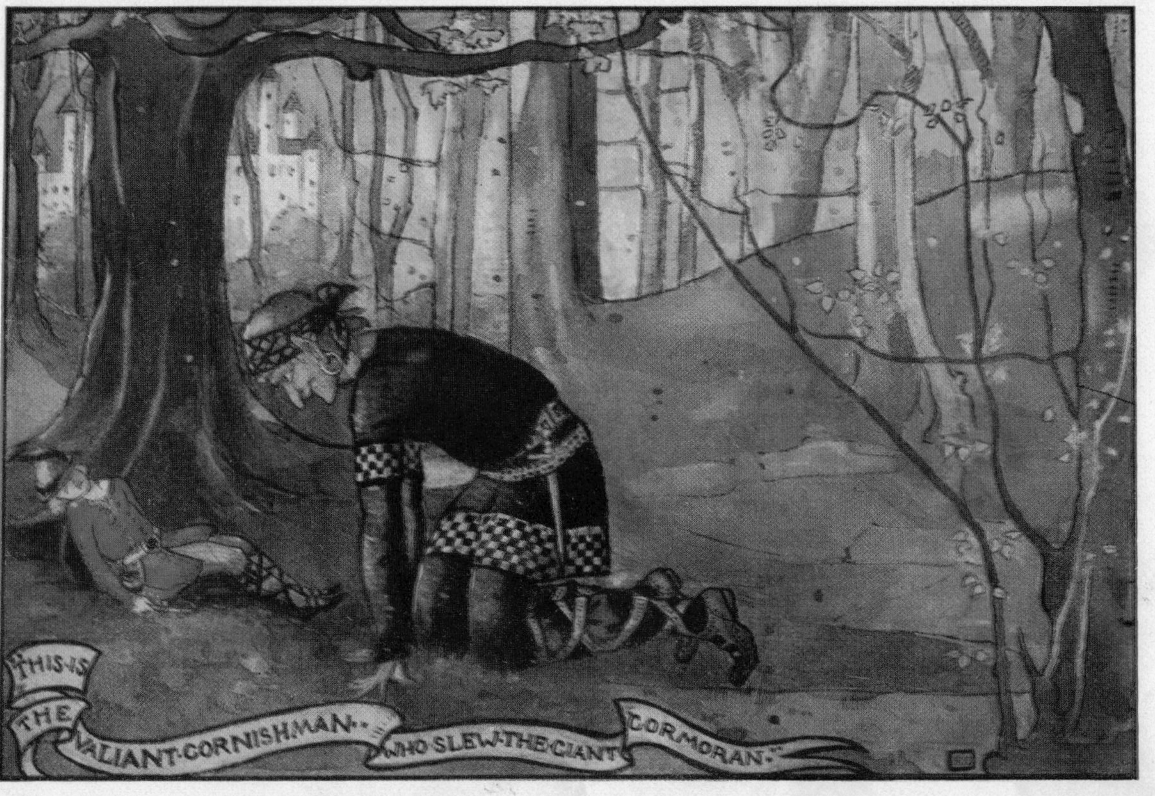
THIS·IS
THE
VALIANT·CORNISHMAN·
WHO·SLEW·THE·GIANT
CORMORAN·

JACK FELL FAST ASLEEP.

Now, there were strong cords in a corner of the room in which Jack was, and two of these he took, and made a strong noose at the end; and while the giants were unlocking the iron gate of the castle he threw the ropes over each of their heads. Then he drew the other ends across a beam, and pulled with all his might, so that he throttled them. Then, when he saw they were black in the face, he slid down the rope, and drawing his sword, slew them both. Then, taking the giant's keys, and unlocking the rooms, he found three fair ladies tied by the hair of their heads, almost starved to death. "Sweet ladies," quoth Jack, "I have destroyed this monster and his brutish brother, and obtained your liberty." This said he presented them with the keys, and so proceeded on his journey to Wales.

Jack made the best of his way by traveling as fast as he could, but lost his road, and was benighted, and could find no habitation until, coming into a narrow valley, he found a large house, and in order to get shelter took courage to knock at the gate. But what was his surprise when there came forth a monstrous giant with two heads; yet he did not appear so fiery as the others were, for he was a Welsh giant, and what he did was by private and secret malice under the false show of friendship. Jack, having told his condition to the giant, was shown into a bedroom, where, in the dead of night, he heard his host in another apartment muttering these words:

"Though here you lodge with me this night,
You shall not see the morning light:
My club shall dash your brains outright!"

"Say'st thou so," quoth Jack; "that is like one of your Welsh tricks, yet I hope to be cunning enough for you." Then, getting out of bed, he laid a log in the bed in his stead, and hid himself in a corner of the room. At the dead time of the night in came the Welsh giant, who struck several heavy blows on the bed with his club, thinking he had broken every bone in Jack's skin. The next morning Jack, laughing in his sleeve, gave him hearty thanks for his night's lodging. "How have you rested?" quoth the giant; "did you not feel anything in the night?" "No," quoth Jack, "nothing but a rat, which gave me two or three slaps with her tail." With that, greatly wondering, the giant led Jack to breakfast, bringing him a bowl containing four gallons of hasty pudding. Being loth to let the giant think it too much for him, Jack put a large leather bag under his loose coat, in such a way that he could convey the pudding into it without its being perceived. Then, telling the giant he would show him a trick, taking a knife, Jack ripped open the bag, and out came all the hasty pudding. Whereupon, saying, "Odds splutters her nails, her can do that trick herself," the monster took the knife, and ripping open his belly, fell down dead.

Now, it happened in these days that King Arthur's only son asked his father to give him a large sum of money, in order that he might go and seek his fortune in the principality of Wales, where lived a beautiful lady possessed with seven evil spirits. The King did his best to persuade his son from it, but in vain; so at last gave way and the Prince set out with two horses, one loaded with money, the other for himself to ride upon. Now, after several days' travel, he came to a market-town in Wales, where he beheld a vast crowd of people gathered together. The Prince asked the reason of it, and was told that they had arrested a corpse for several large sums of money which the deceased owed when he died, The Prince replied that it was a pity creditors should be so cruel, and said, "Go bury the dead, and let his creditors come to my lodging, and there their debts shall be paid." They came, in such great numbers that before night he had only twopence left for himself.

Now Jack the Giant-killer, coming that way, was so taken with the generosity of the Prince, that he desired to be his servant. This being agreed upon, the next morning they set forward on their journey together, when, as they were riding out of the town, an old woman called after the Prince, saying, "He has owed me twopence these seven years; pray pay me as well as the rest." Putting his hand into his pocket, the Prince gave the woman all he had left, so that after their day's food, which cost what small store Jack had by him, they were without a penny between them.

When the sun got low, the King's son said, "Jack, since we have no money, where can we lodge this night?"

But Jack replied, "Master, we'll do well enough, for I have an uncle lives within two miles of this place; he is a huge and monstrous giant with three heads; he'll fight five hundred men in armor, and make them to fly before him."

"Alas!" quoth the Prince, "what shall we do there? He'll certainly chop us up at a mouthful. Nay, we are scarce enough to fill one of his hollow teeth!"

"It is no matter for that," quoth Jack; "I myself will go before and prepare the way for you; therefore stop here and wait till I return." Jack then rode away at full speed, and coming to the gate of the castle, he knocked so loud that he made the neighboring hills resound. The giant roared out at this like thunder, "Who's there?"

Jack answered, "None but your poor cousin Jack."

Quoth he, "What news with my poor cousin Jack?"

He replied, "Dear uncle, bad news, God willing!"

"Prithee," quoth the giant, "what bad news can come to me? I am a giant with three heads, and besides thou knowest I can fight five hundred men in armor, and make them fly like chaff before the wind."

"Oh, but," quoth Jack, "here's the King's son a-coming with a thousand men in armor to kill you and destroy all that you have!"

"Oh, cousin Jack," said the giant, "this is bad news indeed! I will immediately run and hide myself, and thou shalt lock, bolt, and bar me in, and keep the keys until the Prince is gone." Having secured the giant, Jack fetched his master, when they made themselves heartily merry whilst the poor giant lay trembling in a vault under the ground.

Early in the morning Jack furnished his master with a fresh supply of gold and silver, and then sent him three miles forward on his journey, at which time the Prince was pretty well out of the smell of the giant. Jack then returned, and let the giant out of the vault, who asked what he should give him for keeping the castle from destruction. "Why," quoth Jack, "I want nothing but the old coat and cap, together with the old rusty sword and slippers which are at your bed's head."

Quoth the giant: "You know not what you ask; they are the most precious things I have. The coat will keep you invisible, the cap will tell you all you want to know, the sword cuts asunder whatever you strike, and the shoes are of extraordinary swiftness. But you have been very serviceable to me, therefore take them with all my heart." Jack thanked his uncle, and then went off with them. He soon overtook his master and they quickly arrived at the house of the lady the Prince sought, who, finding the Prince to be a suitor, prepared a splendid banquet for him. After the repast was concluded, she told him she had a task for him. She wiped his mouth with a handkerchief, saying, "You must show me that handkerchief to-morrow morning, or else you will lose your head." With that she put it in her bosom. The Prince went to bed in great sorrow, but Jack's cap of knowledge informed him how it was to be obtained. In the middle of the night she called upon her familiar spirit to carry her to Lucifer. But Jack put on his coat of darkness and his shoes of swiftness, and was there as soon as she was. When she entered the place of the demon, she gave the handkerchief to him, and he laid it upon a shelf, whence Jack took it and brought it to his master, who showed it to the lady next day, and so saved his life. On that day, she gave the Prince a kiss and told him he must show her the lips to-morrow morning that she kissed last night, or lose his head.

"Ah!" he replied, "if you kiss none but mine, I will."

"That is neither here nor there," said she; "if you do not, death's your portion!"

At midnight she went as before, and was angry with the demon for letting the handkerchief go. "But now," quoth she, "I will be too hard for the King's son, for I will kiss thee and he is to show me thy lips." Which she did, and Jack, when she was not standing by, cut off Lucifer's head and, brought it under his invisible coat to his master, who the next morning pulled it out by the horns before the lady. This broke the enchantment and the evil spirit left her, and she appeared in all her beauty. They were married the next morning, and soon after went to the Court of King Arthur, where Jack for his many great exploits, was made one of the Knights of the Round Table.

Jack soon went searching for giants again, but he had not ridden far, when he saw a cave, near the entrance of which he beheld a giant sitting upon a block of timber, with a knotted iron club by his side. His goggle eyes were like flames of fire, his countenance grim and ugly, and his cheeks like a couple of large flitches of bacon, while the bristles of his beard resembled rods of iron wire, and the locks that hung down upon his brawny shoulders were like curled snakes or hissing adders. Jack alighted from his horse, and, putting on the coat of darkness, went up close to the giant, and said softly, "Oh! are you there? It will not be long before I take you fast by the beard." The giant all this while could not see him, on account of his invisible coat, so that Jack, coming up close to the monster, struck a blow with his sword at his head, but, missing his aim, he cut off the nose instead. At this, the giant roared like claps of thunder, and began to lay about him with his iron club like one stark mad. But Jack, running behind, drove his sword up to the hilt in the giant's back, so that he fell down dead. This done, Jack cut off the giant's head, and sent it, with his brother's also, to King Arthur, by a wagoner he hired for that purpose.

Jack now resolved to enter the giant's cave in search of his treasure, and, passing along through a great many windings and turnings, he came at length to a large room paved with freestone, at the upper end of which was a boiling caldron, and on the right hand a large table, at which the giant used to dine. Then he came to a window, barred with iron, through which he looked and beheld a vast number of miserable captives, who, seeing him, cried out: "Alas! young man, art thou come to be one amongst us in this miserable den?"

"Ay," quoth Jack, "but pray tell me what is the meaning of your captivity?"

"We are kept here," said one, "till such time as the giants have a wish to feast, and then the fattest among us is slaughtered! And many are the times they have dined upon murdered men!"

"Say you so," quoth Jack, and straightway unlocked the gate and let them free, who all rejoiced like condemned men at sight of a pardon. Then searching the giant's coffers, he shared the gold and silver equally amongst them and took them to a neighboring castle, where they all feasted and made merry over their deliverance.

But in the midst of all this mirth a messenger brought news that Thunderdell, a giant with two heads, having heard of the death of his kinsman, had come from the northern dales to be revenged on Jack, and was within a mile of the castle, the country people flying before him like chaff. But Jack was not a bit daunted, and said, "Let him come! I have a tool to quiet him; and you, ladies and gentlemen, walk out into the garden, and you shall witness this giant Thunderdell's death and destruction."

The castle was situated in the midst of a small island surrounded by a moat thirty feet deep and twenty feet wide, over which lay a drawbridge. So Jack employed men to cut through this bridge on both sides, nearly to the middle; and then, dressing himself in his invisible coat, he marched against the giant with his sword of sharpness. Although the giant could not see Jack, he smelt his approach, and cried out in these words:

"Fee, fi, fo, fum!
I smell the blood of an Englishman!
Be he alive or be he dead,
I'll grind his bones to make me bread!"

"Say'st thou so," said Jack; "then thou art a monstrous miller indeed."

The giant cried out again, "Art thou that villain who killed my kinsmen? Then I will tear thee with my teeth, suck thy blood, and grind thy bones to powder."

"You'll have to catch me first," quoth Jack, and throwing off his invisible coat, so that the giant might see him, and putting on his shoes of swiftness, he ran from the giant, who followed like a walking castle, so that the very foundations of the earth seemed to shake at every step. Jack led him a long dance, in order that the gentlemen and ladies might see; and at last to end the matter, ran lightly over the drawbridge, the giant, in full speed, pursuing him with his club. Then, coming to the middle of the bridge, the giant's great weight broke it down, and he tumbled headlong into the water, where he rolled and wallowed like a whale. Jack, standing by the moat, laughed at him all the while; but though the giant foamed to hear him scoff, and plunged from place to place in the moat, yet he could not get out to be revenged. Jack at length got a cart rope and cast it over the two heads of the giant and drew him ashore by a team of horses, and then cut off both his heads with his sword of sharpness, and sent them to King Arthur.

After some time spent in mirth and pastime, Jack, taking leave of the knights and ladies, set out for new adventures. Through many woods he passed, and came at length to the foot of a high mountain. Here, late at night, he found a lonesome house, and knocked at the door, which was opened by an aged man with a head as white as snow. "Father," said Jack, "can you lodge a benighted traveler that has lost his way?" "Yes," said the old man; "you are right welcome to my poor cottage." Whereupon Jack entered, and down they sat together, and the old man began to speak as follows: "Son, I see by your belt you are the great conqueror of giants, and behold, my son, on the top of this mountain is an enchanted castle; this is kept by a giant named Galligantua, and he, by the help of an old conjurer, betrays many knights and ladies into his castle, where by magic art they are transformed into sundry shapes and forms. But above all, I grieve for a duke's daughter, whom they fetched from her father's garden, carrying her through the air in a burning chariot drawn by fiery dragons. When they secured her within the castle, they transformed her into a white hind. And though many knights have tried to break the enchantment, and work her deliverance, yet no one could accomplish it, on account of two dreadful griffins which are placed at the castle gate and which destroy every one who comes near. But you, my son, may pass by them undiscovered, then on the gates of the castle you will find engraven in large letters how the spell may be broken." Jack gave the old man his hand, and promised that in the morning he would venture his life to free the lady.

In the morning Jack arose and put on his invisible coat and magic cap and shoes, and prepared himself for the fray.

Now, when he had reached the top of the mountain he soon discovered the two fiery griffins, but passed them without fear, because of his invisible coat. When he had got beyond them, he found upon the gates of the castle a golden trumpet hung by a silver chain, under which these lines were engraved:

"Whoever shall this trumpet blow,
Shall soon the giant overthrow,
And break the black enchantment straight;
So all shall be in happy state."

Jack had no sooner read this but he blew the trumpet, at which the castle trembled to its vast foundations, and the giant and conjurer were in horrid confusion, biting their thumbs and tearing their hair, knowing their wicked reign was at an end. Then the giant stooping to take up his club, Jack at one blow cut off his head; whereupon the conjurer, mounting up into the air, was carried away in a whirlwind. Then the enchantment was broken, and all the lords and ladies who had so long been transformed into birds and beasts returned to their proper shapes, and the castle vanished away in a cloud of smoke. This being done, the head of Galligantua was likewise, in the usual manner, conveyed to the Court of King Arthur, where, the very next day, Jack followed, with the knights and ladies who had been delivered. Whereupon, as a reward for his good services, the King prevailed upon the duke to bestow his daughter in marriage on honest Jack. So married they were, and the whole kingdom was filled with joy at the wedding. Furthermore, the King bestowed on Jack a noble castle, with a very beautiful estate thereto belonging, where he and his lady lived in great joy and happiness all the rest of their days.

☙ ☙ ☙

THE THREE SILLIES

ADAPTED BY JOSEPH JACOBS

ONCE upon a time there was a farmer and his wife who had one daughter, and she was courted by a gentleman. Every evening he used to come and see her, and stop to supper at the farmhouse, and the daughter used to be sent down into the cellar to draw the beer for supper. So one evening she had gone down to draw the beer, and she happened to look up at the ceiling while she was drawing, and she saw a mallet stuck in one of the beams. It must have been there a long, long time, but somehow or other she had never noticed it before, and she began a-thinking. And she thought it was very dangerous to have that mallet there, for she said to herself: "Suppose him and me was to be married, and we was to have a son, and he was to grow up to be a man, and come down into the cellar to draw the beer, like as I'm doing now, and the mallet was to fall on his head and kill him, what a dreadful thing it would be!" And she put down the candle and the jug, and sat herself down and began a-crying.

Well, they began to wonder upstairs how it was that she was so long drawing the beer, and her mother went down to see after her, and she found her sitting on the settle crying, and the beer running over the floor. "Why, whatever is the matter?" said her mother. "Oh, mother!" says she, "look at that horrid mallet! Suppose we was to be married, and was to have a son, and he was to grow up, and was to come down to the cellar to draw the beer, and the mallet was to fall on his head and kill him, what a dreadful thing it would be!" "Dear, dear! what a dreadful thing it would be!" said the mother, and she sat her down beside the daughter and started crying too. Then after a bit the father began to wonder that they didn't come back, and he went down into the cellar to look after them himself, and there they two sat crying, and the beer running all over the floor. "Whatever is the matter?" says he. "Why," says the mother, "look at that horrid mallet. Just suppose, if our daughter and her sweetheart was to be married, and was to have a son, and he was to grow up, and was to come down into the cellar to draw the beer, and the mallet was to fall on his head and kill him, what a dreadful thing it would be!" "Dear, dear, dear! so it would!" said the father, and he sat himself down aside of the other two, and started a-crying.

Now the gentleman got tired of stopping up in the kitchen by himself, and at last he went down into the cellar too, to see what they were after; and there they three sat crying side by side, and the beer running all over the floor. And he ran straight and turned the tap. Then he said: "Whatever are you three doing, sitting there crying, and letting the beer run all over the floor?" "Oh!" says the father, "look at that horrid mallet! Suppose you and our daughter was to be married, and was to have a son, and he was to grow up, and was to come down into the cellar to draw the beer, and the mallet was to fall on his head and kill him!" And then they all started crying worse than before. But the gentleman burst out laughing, and reached up and pulled out the mallet, and then he said: "I've traveled many miles, and I never met three such big sillies as you three before; and now I shall start out on my travels again, and when I can find three bigger sillies than you three, then I'll come back and marry your daughter." So he wished them good-by, and started off on his travels, and left them all crying because the girl had lost her sweetheart.

Well, he set out, and he traveled a long way, and at last he came to a woman's cottage that had some grass growing on the roof. And the woman was trying to get her cow to go up a ladder to the grass, and the poor thing durst not go. So the gentleman asked the woman what she was doing. "Why, lookye," she said, "look at all that beautiful grass. I'm going to get the cow on to the roof to eat it. She'll be quite safe, for I shall tie a string round her neck, and pass it down the chimney, and tie it to my wrist as I go about the house, so she can't fall off without my knowing it." "Oh, you poor silly!" said the gentleman, "you should cut the grass and throw it down to the cow!" But the woman thought it was easier to get the cow up the ladder than to get the grass down, so she pushed her and coaxed her and got her up, and tied a string round her neck, and passed it down the chimney, and fastened it to her own wrist. And the gentleman went on his way, but he hadn't gone far when the cow tumbled off the roof, and hung by the string tied round her neck, and it strangled her. And the weight of the cow tied to her wrist pulled the woman up the chimney, and she stuck fast half-way and was smothered in the soot.

Well, that was one big silly.

And the gentleman went on and on, and he went to an inn to

stop the night, and they were so full at the inn that they had to put him in a double-bedded room, and another traveler was to sleep in the other bed. The other man was a very pleasant fellow, and they got very friendly together; but in the morning, when they were both getting up, the gentleman was surprised to see the other hang his trousers on the knobs of the chest of drawers and run across the room and try to jump into them, and he tried over and over again, and couldn't manage it; and the gentleman wondered whatever he was doing it for. At last he stopped and wiped his face with his handkerchief. "Oh dear," he says, "I do think trousers are the most awkwardest kind of clothes that ever were. I can't think who could have invented such things. It takes me the best part of an hour to get into mine every morning, and I get so hot! How do you manage yours?" So the gentleman burst out laughing, and showed him how to put them on; and he was very much obliged to him, and said he never should have thought of doing it that way.

So that was another big silly.

Then the gentleman went on his travels again; and he came to a village, and outside the village there was a pond, and round the pond was a crowd of people. And they had rakes, and brooms, and pitchforks, reaching into the pond; and the gentleman asked what was the matter. "Why," they say, "matter enough! Moon's tumbled into the pond, and we can't rake her out anyhow!" So the gentleman burst out laughing, and told them to look up into the sky, and that it was only the shadow in the water. But they wouldn't listen to him, and abused him shamefully and he got away as quick as he could.

So there were a whole lot of sillies bigger than the three sillies at home. So the gentleman turned back home again and married the farmer's daughter, and if they didn't live happy for ever after, that's nothing to do with you or me.

CELTIC STORIES

KING O'TOOLE AND HIS GOOSE

ADAPTED BY JOSEPH JACOBS

OCH, I thought all the world, far and near, had heerd of King O'Toole—well, well, but the darkness of mankind is untellable! Well, sir, you must know, as you didn't hear it afore, that there was a King, called King O'Toole, who was a fine old King in the old ancient times, long ago; and it was he that owned the churches in the early days. The King, you see was the right sort; he was the real boy, and loved sport as he loved his life, and hunting in particular; and from the rising o' the sun, up he got, and away he went over the mountains after the deer; and fine times they were.

Well, it was all mighty good, as long as the King had his health; but, you see, in the course of time the King grew old, by raison he was stiff in his limbs, and when he got stricken in years, his heart failed him, and he was lost entirely for want o' diversion, because he couldn't go a-hunting no longer; and, by dad the poor King was obliged at last to get a goose to divert him. Oh, you may laugh, if you like, but it's truth I'm telling you; and the way the goose diverted him was this-a-way: You see, the goose used to swim across the lake, and go diving for trout, and catch fish on a Friday for the King, and flew every other day round about the lake, diverting the poor King. All went on mighty well until, by dad, the goose got stricken in years like her master, and couldn't divert him no longer, and then it was that the poor King was lost entirely. The King was walkin' one mornin' by the edge of the lake, lamentin' his cruel fate, and thinking of drowning himself, that could get no diversion in life, when all of a sudden, turning round the corner. whom should he meet but a mighty decent young man coming up to him.

"God save you," says the King to the young man.

"God save you kindly, King O'Toole," says the young man.

"True for you," says the King. "I am King O'Toole," says he, "prince and plennypennytinchery of these parts," says he; "but how came ye to know that?" says he.

"Oh, never mind," says Saint Kavin.

You see it was Saint Kavin, sure enough—the saint himself in disguise, and nobody else. "Oh, never mind," says he, "I know more than that. May I make bold to ask how is your goose, King O'Toole?" says he.

"Blur-an-agers, how came ye to know about my goose?" says the King.

"Oh, no matter; I was given to understand it," says Saint Kavin.

After some more talk the King says, "What are you?"

"I'm an honest man," says Saint Kavin.

"Well, honest man," says the King, "and how is it you make your money so aisy?"

"By makin' old things as good as new," says Saint Kavin.

"Is it a tinker you are?" says the King.

"No," says the saint; "I'm no tinker by trade, King O' Toole; I've a better trade than a tinker," says he—"what would you say," says he, "If I made your old goose as good as new?"

My dear, at the word of making his goose as good as new, you'd think the poor old King's eyes were ready to jump out of his head. With that the King whistled, and down came the poor goose, just like a hound, waddling up to the poor cripple, her master, and as like him as two peas. The minute the saint clapt his eyes on the goose, "I'll do the job for you," says he, "King O'Toole."

"By *Jaminee!*" says King O'Toole, "if you do, I'll say you're the cleverest fellow in the seven parishes."

"Oh, by dad," says St. Kavin, "you must say more nor that—my horn's not so soft all out," says he, "as to repair your old goose for nothing; "what'll you gi' me if I do the job for you?—that's the chat," says Saint Kavin.

"I'll give you whatever you ask," says the King; "isn't that fair?"

"Divil a fairer," says the saint, "that's the way to do business. Now," says he, "this is the bargain I'll make with you, King O'Toole: will you gi' me all the ground the goose flies over, the first offer, after I make her as good as new?"

"I will," says the King.

"You won't go back o' your word?" says Saint Kavin.

"Honor bright!" says King O'Toole, holding out his fist.

"Honor bright!" says Saint Kavin, back again, "it's a bargain. Come here!" says he to the poor old goose—"come here, you unfortunate ould cripple, and it's I that'll make you the sporting bird." With that, my dear, he took up the goose by the two wings—"Criss o' my cross an you," says he, markin' her to grace with the blessed sign at the same minute—and throwing her up in the air, "whew," says he, jist givin' her a blast to help her; and with that, my jewel, she took to her heels, flyin' like one o' the eagles themselves, and cutting as many capers as a swallow before a shower of rain.

Well, my dear, it was a beautiful sight to see the King standing with his mouth open, looking at his poor old goose flying as light as a lark, and better than ever she was; and when she lit at his feet, patted her on the head, and "*Mavourneen,*" says he, "but you are the *darlint* o' the world."

"And what do you say to me," says Saint Kavin, "for making her the like?"

"By Jabers," says the King, "I say nothing beats the art o' man, barring the bees."

"And do you say no more nor that?" says Saint Kavin.

"And that I'm beholden to you," says the King.

"But will you gi' me all the ground the goose flew over?" says Saint Kavin.

"I will," says King O'Toole, "and you're welcome to it," says he, "though it's the last acre I have to give."

"But you'll keep your word true," says the saint.

"As true as the sun," says the King.

"It's well for you, King O'Toole, that you said that word,"

says he; "for if you didn't say that word, the divil the bit o' your goose would ever fly agin."

When the King was as good as his word, Saint Kavin was pleased with him, and then it was that he made himself known to the King. "And," says he, "King O'Toole, you're a dacent man, for I only came here to try you. You don't know me," says he, "because I'm disguised."

"Musha! then," says the King, "who are you?"

"I'm Saint Kavin," said the saint, blessing himself.

"Oh, queen of heaven!" says the King, making the sign of the cross between his eyes, and falling down on his knees before the saint; "is it the great Saint Kavin," says he, "that I've been discoursing all this time without knowing it," says he, "all as one as if he was a lump of a *gossoon?*—and so you're a saint?" says the King.

"I am," says Saint Kavin.

"By Jabers, I thought I was only talking to a dacent boy," says the King.

"Well, you know the difference now," says the saint. "I'm Saint Kavin," says he, "the greatest of all the saints."

And so the King had his goose as good as new, to divert him as long as he lived; and the saint supported him after he came into his property, as I told you, until the day of his death—and that was soon after; for the poor goose thought he was catching a trout one Friday; but, my jewel, it was a mistake he made—and instead of a trout, it was a thieving horse-eel; and instead of the goose killing a trout for the King's supper—by dad, the eel killed the King's goose—and small blame to him; but he didn't ate her, because he darn't ate what Saint Kavin had laid his blessed hands on.

☘ ☘ ☘

THE HAUGHTY PRINCESS

ADAPTED BY PATRICK KENNEDY

THERE was once a very worthy King, whose daughter was the greatest beauty that could be seen far or near, but she was as proud as Lucifer, and no king or prince would she agree to marry.

Her father was tired out at last, and invited every king, and prince, and duke, and earl that he knew or didn't know to come to his court to give her one trial more. They all came, and next day after breakfast they stood in a row in the lawn, and the Princess walked along in the front of them to make her choice. One was fat, and says she: "I won't have you, Beer-barrel!" One was tall and thin, and to him she said, "I won't have you, Ramrod!" To a white-faced man she said, "I won't have you, Pale Death;" and to a red-cheeked man she said, "I won't have you, Cockscomb!" She stopped a little before the last of all, for he was a fine man in face and form. She wanted to find some defect in him, but he had nothing remarkable but a ring of brown curling hair under his chin. She admired him a little, and then carried it off with, "I won't have you, Whiskers!"

So all went away, and the King was so vexed, he said to her, "Now to punish your *impedence*, I'll give you to the first beggarman or singing *sthronshuch* that calls;" and, as sure as the hearth-money, a fellow all over rags, with hair that came to his shoulders, and a bushy red beard all over his face, came next morning, and began to sing before the parlor window.

When the song was over, the hall-door was opened, the singer asked in, the priest brought, and the Princess married to Beardy. She roared and she bawled, but her father didn't mind her. "There," says he to the bridegroom, "is five guineas for you. Take your wife out of my sight, and never let me lay eyes on you or her again."

Off he led her, and dismal enough she was. The only thing that gave her relief was the tones of her husband's voice and his genteel manners. "Whose wood is this?" said she, as they were going through one. "It belongs to the King you called Whiskers yesterday." He gave her the same answer about meadows and cornfields, and at last a fine city. "Ah, what a fool I was!" said she to herself. "He was a fine man, and I might have him for a husband." At last they were coming up to a poor cabin. "Why are you bringing me here?" says the poor lady. "This was my house," said he, "and now it's yours." She began to cry, but she was tired and hungry, and she went in with him.

Ovoch! there was neither a table laid out, nor a fire burning, and she was obliged to help her husband to light it, and boil their dinner, and clean up the place after; and next day he made her put on a stuff gown and a cotton handkerchief. When she had her house readied up, and no business to keep her employed, he brought home sallies [willows], peeled them, and showed her how to make baskets. But the hard twigs bruised her delicate fingers, and she began to cry. Well, then he asked her to mend their clothes, but the needle drew blood from her fingers, and she cried again. He couldn't bear to see her tears, so he bought a creel of earthenware, and sent her to the market to sell them. This was the hardest trial of all, but she looked so handsome and sorrowful, and had such a nice air about her, that all her pans, and jugs, and plates, and dishes were gone before noon, and the only mark of her old pride she showed was a slap she gave a buckeen across the face when he axed her an impudent question.

Well, her husband was so glad, he sent her with another creel the next day; but, faith! her luck was after deserting her. A drunken huntsman came up riding, and his beast got in among her ware, and made *brishe* of every mother's son of 'em. She went home cryin', and her husband wasn't at all pleased. "I see," said he, "you're not fit for business. Come along, I'll get you a kitchen-maid's place in the palace. I know the cook."

So the poor thing was obliged to stifle her pride once more. She was kept very busy, and the footman and the butler would be very impudent about looking for a kiss, but she let a screech out of her the first attempt was made, and the cook gave the fellow such a lambasting with the besom that he made no second offer. She went home to her husband every night, and she carried broken victuals wrapped in papers in her side pockets.

A week after she got service there was great bustle in the kitchen. The King was going to be married, but no one knew who the bride was to be. Well, in the evening the cook filled the Princess's pockets with cold meat and puddens, and, says she, "Before you go, let us have a look at the great doings in the big parlor." So they came near the door to get a peep, and who should come out but the King himself, as handsome as you please, and no other but King Whiskers himself. "Your handsome helper must pay for her peeping," said he to the cook, "and dance a jig with me." Whether she would or no, he held her hand and brought her into the parlor. The fiddlers struck up, and away went *him* with *her*. But they hadn't danced two steps when the meat and the puddens flew out of her pockets. Every one roared out, and she flew to the door, crying piteously. But she was soon caught by the King, and taken into the back parlor. "Don't you know me, my darling?" said he. "I'm both King Whiskers, your husband the ballad-singer, and the drunken huntsman. Your father knew me well enough when he gave you to me, and all was to drive your pride out of you." Well, she didn't know how she was, with fright, and shame, and joy. Love was uppermost, anyhow, for she laid her head on her husband's breast and cried like a child. The maids-of-honor soon had her away and dressed her as fine as hands and pins could do it; and there were her mother and father, too. While the company were wondering what would be the end of the handsome girl and the King, he and his Queen, *who* they didn't know in her fine clothes, came in, and such rejoicings and fine doings as there was, none of us will ever see, anyway.

☙ ☙ ☙

JACK AND HIS MASTER

ADAPTED BY JOSEPH JACOBS

A POOR woman had three sons. The eldest and second eldest were cunning, clever fellows, but they called the youngest Jack the Fool, because they thought he was no better than a simpleton. The eldest got tired of staying at home, and said he'd go look for service. He stayed away a whole year, and then came back one day, dragging one foot after the other, and a poor, wizened face on him, and he was as cross as two sticks. When he was rested and had got something to eat, he told them how he had taken service with the Gray Churl of the Townland of Mischance, and that the agreement was whoever would first say he was sorry for his bargain should get an inch wide of the skin of his back, from shoulder to hips, taken off. If it was the master, he should also pay double wages; if it was the servant, he should get no wages at all. "But the thief," says he, "gave me so little to eat, and kept me so hard at work, that flesh and blood couldn't stand it; and when he asked me once, when I was in a passion, if I was sorry for my bargain, I was mad enough to say I was, and here I am disabled for life."

Vexed enough were the poor mother and brothers; and the second eldest said on the spot he'd go and take service with the Gray Churl, and punish him by all the annoyance he'd give him till he'd make him say he was sorry for his agreement. "Oh, won't I be glad to see the skin coming off the old villain's back!" said he. All they could say had no effect: he started off for the Townland of Mischance, and in a twelvemonth he was back just as miserable and helpless as his brother.

All the poor mother could say didn't prevent Jack the Fool from starting to see if he was able to regulate the Gray Churl. He agreed with him for a year for twenty pounds, and the terms were the same.

"Now, Jack," said the Gray Churl, "if you refuse to do anything you are able to do, you must lose a month's wages."

"I'm satisfied," said Jack; "and if you stop me from doing a thing after telling me to do it, you are to give me an additional month's wages."

"I am satisfied," said the master.

"Or if you blame me for obeying your orders, you must give me the same."

"I am satisfied," said the master again.

The first day that Jack served he was fed very poorly, and was worked to the saddleskirts. Next day he came into the parlor just before the dinner was served up. They were taking the goose off the spit, but, well becomes Jack, he whipped a knife off the dresser, and cut off one side of the breast, one leg and thigh, and one wing, and fell to. In came the master, and began to abuse him for his assurance. "Oh, you know, master, you're to feed me, and wherever the goose goes won't have to be filled again till supper. Are you sorry for our agreement?"

The master was going to cry out he was, but he bethought himself in time. "Oh, no, not at all," said he.

"That's well," said Jack.

Next day Jack was to go clamp turf on the bog. They weren't sorry to have him away from the kitchen at dinner time. He didn't find his breakfast very heavy on his stomach; so he said to the mistress, "I think, ma'am, it will be better for me to get my dinner now, and not lose time coming home from the bog."

"That's true, Jack," said she. So she brought out a good cake, and a print of butter, and a bottle of milk, thinking he'd take them away to the bog. But Jack kept his seat, and never drew rein till bread, butter, and milk had gone down the red lane.

"Now, mistress," said he, "I'll be earlier at my work to-morrow if I sleep comfortably on the sheltery side of a pile of dry peat on dry grass, and not be coming here and going back. So you may as well give me my supper, and be done with the day's trouble." She gave him that, thinking he'd take it to the bog; but he fell to on the spot, and did not leave a scrap to tell tales on him; and the mistress was a little astonished.

He called to speak to the master in the haggard, and said he, "What are servants asked to do in this country after aten their supper?"

"Nothing at all, but to go to bed."

"Oh, very well, sir." He went up on the stable-loft, stripped, and lay down, and some one that saw him told the master. He came up.

"Jack, you anointed scoundrel, what do you mean?"

"To go to sleep, master. The mistress, God bless her, is after giving me my breakfast, dinner, and supper, and yourself told me that bed was the next thing. Do you blame me, sir?"

"Yes, you rascal, I do."

"Hand me out one pound thirteen and fourpence, if you please, sir."

"One divil and thirteen imps, you tinker! what for?"

"Oh, I see, you've forgot your bargain. Are you sorry for it?"

"Oh, ya—NO, I mean. I'll give you the money after your nap."

Next morning early Jack asked how he'd be employed that day. "You are to be holding the plow in that fallow, outside the paddock." The master went over about nine o'clock to see what kind of a plowman was Jack, and what did he see but the little boy driving the bastes, and the sock and coulter of the plow skimming along the sod, and Jack pulling ding-dong agin' the horses.

"What are you doing, you contrary thief?" said the master.

"An' ain't I strivin' to hold this divil of a plow, as you told me; but that ounkrawn of a boy keeps whipping on the bastes in spite of all I say; will you speak to him?"

"No, but I'll speak to you. Didn't you know, you bosthoon, that when I said 'holding the plow,' I meant reddening [plowing up] the ground?"

"Faith, an' if you did, I wish you had said so. Do you blame me for what I have done?"

The master caught himself in time, but he was so stomached [disconcerted], he said nothing.

"Go on and redden the ground now, you knave, as other plowmen do."

"An' are you sorry for our agreement?"

"Oh, not at all, not at all!"

Jack plowed away like a good workman all the rest of the day.

In a day or two the master bade him go and mind the cows in a field that had half of it under young corn. "Be sure, particularly," said he, "to keep Browney from the wheat; while she's out of mischief there's no fear of the rest."

About noon he went to see how Jack was doing his duty, and what did he find but Jack asleep with his face to the sod, Browney grazing near a thorn-tree, one end of a long rope round her horns, and the other end round the tree, and the rest of the beasts all trampling and eating the green wheat. Down came the switch on Jack.

"Jack, you vagabone, do you see what the cows are at?"

"And do you blame me, master?"

"To be sure, you lazy sluggard, I do."

"Hand me out one pound thirteen and fourpence, master. You said if I only kept Browney out of mischief, the rest would do no harm. There she is as harmless as a lamb. Are you sorry for hiring me, master?"

"To be—that is, not at all. I'll give you your money when you go to dinner. Now, understand me; don't let a cow go out of the field nor into the wheat the rest of the day."

"Never fear, master!" and neither did he. But the churl would rather than a great deal he had not hired him.

The next day three heifers were missing, and the master bade Jack go in search of them.

"Where shall I look for them?" said Jack.

"Oh, every place likely and unlikely for them all to be in."

The churl was getting very exact in his words. When he was coming into the yard at dinner time, what work did he find Jack at but pulling armfuls of the thatch off the roof, and peeping into the holes he was making.

"What are you doing there, you rascal?"

"Sure, I'm looking for the heifers, poor things!"

"What would bring them there?"

"I don't think anything could bring them in it; but I looked first into the likely places, that is the cowhouses, and the pastures, and the fields next 'em, and now I'm looking in the unlikeliest place I can think of. Maybe it's not pleasing to you it is."

"And to be sure it isn't pleasing to me, you aggravating goose-cap!"

"Please, sir, hand me one pound thirteen and fourpence before you sit down to your dinner. I'm afraid it's sorrow that's on you for hiring me at all."

"May the div—oh, no; I'm not sorry. Will you begin, if you please, and put in the thatch again, just as if you were doing it for your mother's cabin?"

"Oh, faith I will, sir, with a heart and a half;" and by the time the farmer came out from his dinner, Jack had the roof better than it was before, for he made the boy give him new straw.

Says the master when he came out: "Go, Jack, and look for the heifers, and bring them home."

"And where shall I look for 'em?"

"Go and search for them as if they were your own." The heifers were all in the paddock before sunset.

Next morning says the master: "Jack, the path across the bog to the pasture is very bad; the sheep does be sinking in it every step; go and make the sheep's feet a good path." About an hour after he came to the edge of the bog, and what did he find Jack at but sharpening a carving knife, and the sheep standing or grazing around.

"Is this the way you are mending the path, Jack?" said he.

"Everything must have a beginning, master," said Jack, "and a thing well begun is half done. I am sharpening the knife, and I'll have the feet off every sheep in the flock while you'd be blessing yourself."

"Feet off my sheep, you anointed rogue! and what would you be taking their feet off for?"

"An', sure, to mend the path as you told me. Says you, 'Jack, make a path with the foot of the sheep.'"

"Oh, you fool, I meant make good the path for the sheep's feet."

"It's a pity you didn't say so, master. Hand me out one pound thirteen and fourpence if you don't like me to finish my job."

"Divil do you good with your one pound thirteen and fourpence!"

"It's better pray than curse, master. Maybe you're sorry for your bargain?"

"And to be sure I am—not yet, anyway."

The next night the master was going to a wedding; and says he to Jack, before he set out: "I'll leave at midnight, and I wish you to come and be with me home, for fear I might be overtaken with the drink. If you're there before, you may throw a sheep's eye at me, and I'll be sure to see that they'll give you something for yourself."

About eleven o'clock, while the master was in great spirits, he felt something clammy hit him on the cheek. It fell beside his tumbler, and when he looked at it, what was it but the eye of a sheep. Well, he couldn't imagine who threw it at him, or why it was thrown at him. After a little he got a blow on the other cheek, and still it was by another sheep's eye. Well, he was much vexed, but he thought better to say nothing. In two minutes more, when he was opening his mouth to take a sup, another sheep's eye was slapped into it. He sputtered it out, and cried, "Man o' the house, isn't it a great shame for you to have any one in the room that would do such a nasty thing?"

"Master," says Jack, "don't blame the honest man. Sure it's only myself that was throwin' them sheep's eyes at you, to remind you I was here, and that I wanted to drink the bride and bridegroom's health. You know yourself bade me."

"I know that you are a great rascal; and where did you get the eyes?"

"An' where would I get 'em but in the heads of your own sheep? Would you have me meddle with the bastes of any neighbor, who might put me in the Stone Jug for it?"

"Sorrow on me that ever I had the bad luck to meet with you."

"You're all witness," said Jack, "that my master says he is sorry for having met with me. My time is up. Master, hand me over double wages, and come into the next room, and lay yourself out like a man that has some decency in him, till I take a strip of skin an inch broad from your shoulder to your hip."

Every one shouted out against that; but, says Jack, "You didn't hinder him when he took the same strips from the backs of my two brothers, and sent them home in that state, and penniless, to their poor mother."

When the company heard the rights of the business, they were only too eager to see the job done. The master bawled and roared, but there was no help at hand. He was stripped to his hips, and laid on the floor in the next room, and Jack had the carving-knife in his hand ready to begin.

"Now you cruel old villain," said he, giving the knife a couple of scrapes along the floor: "I'll make you an offer. Give me, along with my double wages, two hundred guineas to support my poor brothers, and I'll do without the strip."

"No!" said he, "I'd let you skin me from head to foot first."

"Here goes, then," said Jack with a grin; but the first little scar he gave, Churl roared out, "Stop your hand; I'll give the money."

"Now, neighbors," said Jack, "you mustn't think worse of me than I deserve. I wouldn't have the heart to take an eye out of a rat itself; I got half a dozen of them from the butcher, and only used three of them."

So all came again into the other room, and Jack was made to sit down, and everybody drank his health, and he drank everybody's health at one offer. And six stout fellows saw himself and the master home, and waited in the parlor while he went up and brought down the two hundred guineas, and double wages for Jack himself. When he got home, he brought the summer along with him to the poor mother and the disabled brothers; and he was no more Jack the Fool in the people's mouths, but "Skin-Churl Jack."

☘ ☘ ☘

HUDDEN AND DUDDEN AND DONALD O'NEARY

ADAPTED BY JOSEPH JACOBS

THERE was once upon a time two farmers, and their names were Hudden and Dudden. They had poultry in their yards, sheep on the uplands, and scores of cattle in the meadow land alongside the river. But for all that they weren't happy, for just between their two farms there lived a poor man by the name of Donald O'Neary. He had a hovel over his head and a strip of grass that was barely enough to keep his one cow, Daisy, from starving, and, though she did her best, it was but seldom that Donald got a drink of milk or a roll of butter from Daisy. You would think there was little here to make Hudden and Dudden jealous, but so it is, the more one has the more one wants, and Donald's neighbors lay awake of nights scheming how they might get hold of his little strip of grass land.

One day Hudden met Dudden, and they were soon grumbling as usual, and all to the tune of, "If only we could get that vagabond, Donald O'Neary, out of the country."

"Let's kill Daisy," said Hudden at last; "if that doesn't make him clear out, nothing will."

No sooner said than agreed; and it wasn't dark before Hudden and Dudden crept up to the little shed where lay poor Daisy, trying her best to chew the cud, though she hadn't had as much grass in the day as would cover your hand. And when Donald came to see if Daisy was all snug for the night, the poor beast had only time to lick his hand once before she died.

Well, Donald was a shrewd fellow, and, downhearted though he was, began to think if he could get any good out of Daisy's death. He thought and he thought, and the next day you might have seen him trudging off early to the fair, Daisy's hide over his shoulder, every penny he had jingling in his pockets. Just before he got to the fair, he made several slits in the hide, put a penny in each slit, walked into the best inn of the town as bold as if it belonged to him, and, hanging the hide up to a nail in the wall, sat down.

"Some of your best whisky," says he to the landlord. But the landlord didn't like his looks. "Is it fearing I won't pay you, you are?" says Donald; "why, I have a hide here that gives me all the money I want." And with that he hit it a whack with his stick, and out hopped a penny. The landlord opened his eyes, as you may fancy.

"What'll you take for that hide?"

"It's not for sale, my good man."

"Will you take a gold piece?"

"It's not for sale, I tell you. Hasn't it kept me and mine for years?" and with that Donald hit the hide another whack, and out jumped a second penny.

Well, the long and the short of it was that Donald let the hide go, and, that very evening, who but he should walk up to Hudden's door?

"Good evening, Hudden. Will you lend me your best pair of scales?"

Hudden stared and Hudden scratched his head, but he lent the scales.

When Donald was safe at home, he pulled out his pocketful of bright gold and began to weigh each piece in the scales. But Hudden had put a lump of butter at the bottom, and so the last piece of gold stuck fast to the scales when he took them back to Hudden.

If Hudden had stared before, he stared ten times more now, and no sooner was Donald's back turned, than he was off as hard as he could pelt to Dudden's.

"Good-evening, Dudden. That vagabond, bad luck to him——"

"You mean Donald O'Neary?"

"And who else should I mean? He's back here weighing out sackfuls of gold."

"How do you know that?"

"Here are my scales that he borrowed, and here's a gold piece still sticking to them."

Off they went together, and they came to Donald's door. Donald had finished making the last pile of ten gold pieces. And he couldn't finish, because a piece had stuck to the scales.

In they walked without an "If you please" or "By your leave."

"Well, *I* never!" that was all *they* could say.

"Good evening, Hudden; good evening, Dudden. Ah! you thought you had played me a fine trick, but you never did me a better turn in all your lives. When I found poor Daisy dead, I thought to myself: 'Well, her hide may fetch something'; and it did. Hides are worth their weight in gold in the market just now."

Hudden nudged Dudden, and Dudden winked at Hudden.

"Good evening, Donald O'Neary."

"Good evening, kind friends."

The next day there wasn't a cow or a calf that belonged to Hudden or Dudden but her hide was going to the fair in Hudden's biggest cart, drawn by Dudden's strongest pair of horses.

When they came to the fair, each one took a hide over his arm, and there they were walking through the fair, bawling out at the top of their voices, "Hides to sell! hides to sell!"

Out came the tanner:

"How much for your hides, my good men?"

"Their weight in gold."

"It's early in the day to come out of the tavern." That was all the tanner said, and back he went to his yard.

"Hides to sell! Fine fresh hides to sell!"

Out came the cobbler:

"How much for your hides, my men?"

"Their weight in gold."

"Is it making game of me you are? Take that for your pains," and the cobbler dealt Hudden a blow that made him stagger.

Up the people came running from one end of the fair to the other. "What's the matter? What's the matter?" cried they.

"Here are a couple of vagabonds selling hides at their weight in gold," said the cobbler.

"Hold 'em fast; hold 'em fast!" bawled the innkeeper, who was the last to come up, he was so fat. "I'll wager it's one of the rogues who tricked me out of thirty gold pieces yesterday for a wretched hide."

It was more kicks than halfpence that Hudden and Dudden got before they were well on their way home again, and they didn't run the slower because all the dogs of the town were at their heels.

Well, as you may fancy, if they loved Donald little before, they loved him less now.

"What's the matter, friends?" said he, as he saw them tearing along, their hats knocked in, and their coats torn off, and their faces black and blue. "Is it fighting you've been? or mayhap you met the police, ill luck to them?"

"We'll police you, you vagabond. It's mighty smart you thought yourself, deluding us with your lying tales."

"Who deluded you? Didn't you see the gold with your own two eyes?"

But it was no use talking. Pay for it he must and should. There was a meal-sack handy, and into it Hudden and Dudden popped Donald O'Neary, tied him up tight, ran a pole through the knot, and off they started for the Brown Lake of the Bog, each with a pole-end on his shoulder, and Donald O'Neary between.

But the Brown Lake was far, the road was dusty, Hudden and Dudden were sore and weary, and parched with thirst. There was an inn by the roadside.

"Let's go in," said Hudden; "I'm dead beat. It's heavy he is for the little he had to eat."

If Hudden was willing, so was Dudden. As for Donald, you may be sure his leave wasn't asked, but he was dumped down at the inn door for all the world as if he had been a sack of potatoes.

"Sit still, you vagabond," said Dudden; "if we don't mind waiting, you needn't."

Donald held his peace, but after a while he heard the glasses clink, and Hudden singing away at the top of his voice.

"I won't have her, I tell you; I won't have her!" said Donald. But nobody heeded what he said.

"I won't have her, I tell you; I won't have her!" said Donald; and this time he said it louder; but nobody heeded what he said.

"I won't have her, I tell you; I won't have her!" said Donald; and this time he said it as loud as he could.

"And who won't you have, may I be so bold as to ask?" said a farmer, who had just come up with a drove of cattle, and was turning in for a glass.

"It's the King's daughter. They are bothering the life out of me to marry her."

"You're the lucky fellow. I'd give something to be in your shoes."

"Do you see that, now! Wouldn't it be a fine thing for a farmer to be marrying a Princess, all dressed in gold and jewels?"

"Jewels, you say? Ah, now, couldn't you take me with you?"

"Well, you're an honest fellow, and as I don't care for the King's danghter, though she's as beautiful as the day, and is covered with jewels from top to toe, you shall have her. Just undo the cord and let me out; they tied me up tight, as they knew I'd run away from her."

Out crawled Donald; in crept the farmer.

"Now lie still, and don't mind the shaking; it's only rumbling over the palace steps you'll be. And maybe they'll abuse you for a vagabond, who won't have the King's daughter; but you needn't mind that. Ah, it's a deal I'm giving up for you, sure as it is that I don't care for the Princess."

"Take my cattle in exchange," said the farmer; and you may guess it wasn't long before Donald was at their tails, driving them homeward.

Out came Hudden and Dudden, and the one took one end of the pole, and the other the other.

"I'm thinking he's heavier," said Hudden.

"Ah, never mind," said Dudden; "it's only a step now to the Brown Lake."

"I'll have her now! I'll have her now!" bawled the farmer from inside the sack.

"By my faith and you shall, though," said Hudden, and he laid his stick across the sack.

"I'll have her! I'll have her!" bawled the farmer, louder than ever.

"Well, here you are," said Dudden, for they were now come to the Brown Lake, and, unslinging the sack, they pitched it plump into the lake.

"You'll not be playing your tricks on us any longer," said Hudden.

"True for you," said Dudden. "Ah, Donald, my boy, it was an ill day when you borrowed my scales!"

Off they went, with a light step and an easy heart, but when they were near home, whom should they see but Donald O'Neary, and all around him the cows were grazing, and the calves were kicking up their heels and butting their heads together.

"Is it you, Donald?" said Dudden. "Faith, you've been quicker than we have."

"True for you, Dudden, and let me thank you kindly; the turn was good, if the will was ill. You'll have heard, like me, that the Brown Lake leads to the Land of Promise. I always put it down as lies, but it is just as true as my word. Look at the cattle."

Hudden stared, and Dudden gaped; but they couldn't get over the cattle; fine, fat cattle they were, too.

"It's only the worst I could bring up with me," said Donald O'Neary; "the others were so fat, there was no driving them. Faith, too, it's little wonder they didn't care to leave, with grass as far as you could see, and as sweet and juicy as fresh butter."

"Ah now, Donald, we haven't always been friends," said Dudden, "but, as I was just saying, you were ever a decent lad, and you'll show us the way, won't you?"

"I don't see that I'm called upon to do that; there is a power more cattle down there. Why shouldn't I have them all to myself?"

"Faith, they may well say, the richer you get, the harder the heart. You always were a neighborly lad, Donald. You wouldn't wish to keep the luck all to yourself?"

"True for you, Hudden, though it's a bad example you set me. But I'll not be thinking of old times. There is plenty for all there, so come along with me."

Off they trudged, with a light heart and an eager step. When they came to the Brown Lake the sky was full of little white clouds, and, if the sky was full, the lake was as full.

"Ah, now, look! there they are!" cried Donald as he pointed to the clouds in the lake.

"Where? where?" cried Hudden, and "Don't be greedy!" cried Dudden, as he jumped his hardest to be up first with the fat cattle. But if he jumped first, Hudden wasn't long behind.

They never came back. Maybe they got too fat, like the cattle. As for Donald O'Neary, he had cattle and sheep all his days to his heart's content.

☘ ☘ ☘

CONNLA OF THE GOLDEN HAIR AND THE FAIRY MAIDEN

ADAPTED BY PATRICK WESTON JOYCE

CONNLA of the Golden Hair was the son of Conn the Hundred-fighter. One day as he stood with his father on the royal Hill of Usna, he saw a lady a little way off, very beautiful, and dressed in strange attire. She approached the spot where he stood; and when she was near, he spoke to her, and asked who she was, and from what place she had come.

The lady replied: "I have come from the Land of the Living—a land where there is neither death nor old age, nor any breach of law. The inhabitants of earth call us Aes-shee, for we have our dwellings within large, pleasant, green hills. We pass our time very pleasantly in feasting and harmless amusements, never growing old; and we have no quarrels or contentions."

The King and his company marveled very much; for though they heard this conversation, no one saw the lady except Connla alone.

"Who is this thou art talking to, my son?" said the King.

And anon she answered for the youth: "Connla is speaking with a lovely, noble-born young lady, who will never die, and who will never grow old. I love Connla of the Golden Hair, and I have come to bring him with me to Moy-mell, the plain of never-ending pleasure. On the day that he comes with me he shall be made King, and he shall reign for ever in Fairyland, without weeping and without sorrow. Come with me, O gentle Connla of the ruddy cheek, the fair, freckled neck, and the golden hair! Come with me, beloved Connla, and thou shalt retain the comeliness and dignity of thy form, free from the wrinkles of old age, till the awful day of judgment."

> "Thy flowing golden hair, thy comely face,
> Thy all majestic form of peerless grace,
> That show thee sprung from Conn's exalted race."

King Conn the Hundred-fighter being much troubled, called then on his druid Coran, to put forth his power against the witchery of the banshee: "O Coran of the mystic arts and of the mighty incantations, here is a contest such as I have never been engaged in since I was made King at Tara—a contest with an invisible lady, who is beguiling my son to Fairyland by her baleful charms. Her cunning is beyond my skill, and I am not able to withstand her power; and if thou, Coran, help

CONNLA AND THE FAIRY MAIDEN

not, my son will be taken away from me by the wiles and witchery of a woman from the fairy hills."

Coran the druid then came forward, and began to chant against the voice of the lady. And his power was greater than hers for that time, so that she was forced to retire.

As she was going away she threw an apple to Connla, who straightway lost sight of her; and the King and his people no longer heard her voice.

The King and the Prince returned with their company to the palace; and Connla remained for a whole month without tasting food or drink except the apple. And though he ate of it each day, it was never lessened, but was as whole and perfect in the end as at the beginning. Moreover, when they offered him aught else to eat or drink he refused it; for while he had his apple he did not deem any other food worthy to be tasted. And he began to be very moody and sorrowful, thinking of the lovely fairy maiden.

At the end of the month, as Connla stood by his father's side among the nobles, on the Plain of Arcomin, he saw the lady approaching him from the west. And when she had come near, she addressed him in this manner: "A glorious seat, indeed, has Connla among wretched, short-lived mortals, awaiting the dreadful stroke of death! But now, the ever-youthful people of Moy-mell, who never feel age, and who fear not death, seeing thee day by day among thy friends, in the assemblies of thy fatherland, love thee with a strange love, and they will make thee King over them if thou wilt come with me."

When the King heard the words of the lady, he commanded his people to call the druid again to him, saying, "Bring my druid Coran to me; for I see that the fairy lady has this day regained the power of her voice."

At this the lady said: "Valiant Conn, fighter of a hundred, the faith of the druids has come to little honor among the upright, mighty, numberless people of this land. When the righteous law shall be restored, it will seal up the lips of the false black demon; and his druids shall no longer have power to work their guileful spells."

Now the King observed, and marveled greatly, that whenever the lady was present his son never spoke one word to any one, even though they addressed him many times. And when the lady had ceased to speak, the King said: "Connla, my son, has thy mind been moved by the words of the lady?"

Connla spake then, and replied, "Father, I am very unhappy; for though I love my people beyond all, I am filled with sadness on account of this lady!"

When Connla had said this, the maiden again addressed him, and chanted these words in a very sweet voice:

"A land of youth, a land of rest,
A land from sorrow free;
It lies far off in the golden west,
On the verge of the azure sea.
A swift canoe of crystal bright,
That never met mortal view—
We shall reach the land ere fall of night,
In that strong and swift canoe;
We shall reach the strand
Of that sunny land,
From druids and demons free;
The land of rest
In the golden west,
On the verge of the azure sea!

"A pleasant land of winding vales, bright streams, and verdurous plains,
Where summer all the live-long year in changeless splendor reigns;
A peaceful land of calm delight, of everlasting bloom;
Old age and death we never know, no sickness, care, or gloom;
The land of youth,
Of love and truth,
From pain and sorrow free,
The land of rest,
In the golden west,
On the verge of the azure sea!

"There are strange delights for mortal men in that island of the west;
The sun comes down each evening in its lovely vales to rest;
And though far and dim
On the ocean's rim
It seems to mortal view,
We shall reach its halls
Ere the evening falls,
In my strong and swift canoe;
And evermore
That verdant shore
Our happy home shall be;
The land of rest,
In the golden west,
On the verge of the azure sea!

"It will guard thee, gentle Connla of the flowing golden hair,
It will guard thee from the druids, from the demons of the air,
My crystal boat will guard thee, till we reach that western shore,
When thou and I in joy and love shall live for evermore:

From the druid's incantation,
From his black and deadly snare,
From the withering imprecation
Of the demon of the air,

"It will guard thee, gentle Connla of the flowing golden hair;
My crystal boat shall guard thee, till we reach that silver strand
Where thou shalt reign in endless joy, the King of the Fairyland!"

When the maiden had ended her chant, Connla suddenly walked away from his father's side, and sprang into the curragh, the gleaming, straight-gliding, strong, crystal canoe. The King and his people saw them afar off, and dimly moving away over the bright sea towards the sunset. They gazed sadly after them, till they lost sight of the canoe over the utmost verge; and no one can tell whither they went, for Connla was never again seen in his native land.

ITALIAN STORIES

PINOCCHIO'S ADVENTURES IN WONDERLAND*

BY CARLO LORENZINI

I

MASTER CHERRY FINDS A QUEER PIECE OF WOOD

THERE was once upon a time . .

"A king!" my little readers will instantly exclaim.

No, children, you are wrong. There was once upon a time a piece of wood.

This wood was not valuable; it was only a common log like those that are burnt in winter in the stoves and fireplaces to make a cheerful blaze and warm the rooms.

I cannot say how it came about, but the fact is, that one fine day this piece of wood was lying in the shop of an old carpenter of the name of Master Antonio. He was, however, called by everybody Master Cherry, on account of the end of his nose, which was always as red and polished as a ripe cherry.

No sooner had Master Cherry set his eyes on the piece of wood than his face beamed with delight; and, rubbing his hands together with satisfaction, he said softly to himself:

"This wood has come at the right moment; it will just do to make the leg of a little table."

Having said this he immediately took a sharp axe with which to remove the bark and the rough surface. Just, however, as he was going to give the first stroke he remained with his arm suspended in the air, for he heard a very small voice saying imploringly: "Do not strike me so hard!"

Picture to yourselves the astonishment of good old Master Cherry!

He turned his terrified eyes all around the room to try and discover where the little voice could possibly have come from, but he saw nobody! He looked under the bench—nobody; he looked into a cupboard that was always shut—nobody; he looked into a basket of shavings and sawdust—nobody; he even opened the door of the shop and gave a glance into the street—and still nobody. Who, then, could it be?

"I see how it is;" he said, laughing and scratching his wig; "evidently that little voice was all my imagination. Let us set to work again."

And taking up the axe he struck a tremendous blow on the piece of wood.

"Oh! oh! you have hurt me!" cried the same little voice dolefully.

This time Master Cherry was petrified. His eyes started out of his head with fright, his mouth remained open, and his tongue hung out almost to the end of his chin like a mask on a fountain. As soon as he had recovered the use of his speech, he began to say, stuttering and trembling with fear:

"But where on earth can that little voice have come from that said 'Oh! oh!?' . . .Here there is certainly not a living soul. Is it possible that this piece of wood can have learnt to cry and to lament like a child? I cannot believe it. This piece of wood here it is; a log for fuel like all others, and thrown on the fire it would about suffice to boil a saucepan of beans. . . .How then? Can anyone be hidden inside it? If anyone is hidden inside, so much the worse for him. I will settle him at once."

So saying he seized the poor piece of wood and commenced beating it without mercy against the walls of the room.

Then he stopped to listen if he could hear any little voice lamenting. He waited two minutes—nothing; five minutes—nothing; ten minutes—still nothing!

"I see how it is," he then said, forcing himself to laugh and pushing up his wig; "evidently, the little voice that said 'Oh! oh!' was all my imagination! Let us to work again."

But all the same he was in a great fright; he tried to sing to give himself a little courage.

Putting the axe aside he took his plane to plane and polish

the bit of wood; but whilst he was running it up and down he heard the same little voice say, laughing:

"Have done! you are tickling me all over!"

This time poor Master Cherry fell down as if he had been struck by lightning. When he at last opened his eyes he found himself seated on the floor.

His face was quite changed; even the end of his nose, instead of being crimson, as it was nearly always, had become blue from fright.

II

GEPPETTO PLANS A WONDERFUL PUPPET

At that moment some one knocked at the door.

"Come in," said the carpenter, without having the strength to rise to his feet.

A lively little old man immediately walked into the shop. His name was Geppetto, but when the boys in the neighborhood wished to put him in a passion they called him by the nickname of Polendina, because his yellow wig greatly resembled a pudding made of Indian corn.

Geppetto was very fiery. Woe to him who called him Polendina! He became furious, and there was no holding him.

"Good day, Master Antonio," said Geppetto; "what are you doing there on the floor?"

"I am teaching the alphabet to the ants."

"Much good may that do you."

"What has brought you to me, neighbor Geppetto?"

"My legs. But to say the truth, Master Antonio, I am come to ask a favor of you."

"Here I am ready to serve you," replied the carpenter getting on his knees.

"This morning an idea came into my head."

"Let us hear it."

"I thought I would make a beautiful wooden puppet that should know how to dance, to fence, and to leap like an acrobat. With this puppet I would travel about the world to earn a piece of bread and a glass of wine. What do you think of it?"

"Bravo, Polendina!" exclaimed the same little voice, and it was impossible to say where it came from.

Hearing himself called Polendina, Geppetto became as red as a turkey-cock from rage, and turning to the carpenter he said in a fury:

"Why do you insult me?"

"Who insults you?"

"You called me Polendina!"

"It was not I!"

"Would you have it then, that it was I? It was you, I say!"

"No!"

"Yes!"

"No!"

"Yes!"

And becoming more and more angry, from words they came to blows, and flying at each other they bit, and fought, and scratched manfully.

When the fight was over Master Antonio was in possession of Geppetto's yellow wig, and Geppetto discovered that the gray wig belonging to the carpenter had remained between his teeth.

"Give me back my wig," screamed Master Antonio.

"And you return me mine, and let us make friends."

The two old men having each recovered his own wig shook hands, and swore that they would remain friends to the end of their lives.

"Well then, neighbor Geppetto," said the carpenter, to prove that peace was made, "what is the favor that you wish of me?"

"I want a little wood to make my puppet; will you give me some?"

Master Antonio was delighted, and he immediately went to the bench and fetched the piece of wood that had caused him so much fear. Just as he was going to give it to his friend the piece of wood gave a shake and wriggling violently out of his hands struck with all its force against the dried-up shins of poor Geppetto.

"Ah! is that the courteous way in which you make your presents, Master Antonio? You have almost lamed me!"

"I swear to you that it was not I!"

"Then you would have it that it was I?"

"The wood is entirely to blame!"

"I know that it was the wood, but it was you that hit my legs with it!"

"I did not hit you with it!"

"Liar!"

"Geppetto, don't insult me or I will call you Polendina!"

"Ass!"

"Polendina!"

"Donkey!"

"Polendina!"

"Baboon!"

"Polendina!"

On hearing himself called Polendina for the third time Geppetto, blind with rage, fell upon the carpenter and they fought desperately.

When the battle was over, Master Antonio had two more scratches on his nose, and his adversary had two buttons less on his waistcoat. Their accounts being thus squared they shook hands, and swore to remain good friends for the rest of their lives.

Geppetto carried off his fine piece of wood, and thanking Master Antonio returned limping to his house.

III

THE PUPPET IS NAMED PINOCCHIO

Geppetto lived in a small ground-floor room that was only lighted from the staircase. The furniture could not have been simpler—a bad chair, a poor bed, and a broken-down table. At the end of the room there was a fireplace with a lighted fire; but the fire was painted, and by the fire was painted a saucepan that was boiling cheerfully, and sending out a cloud of smoke that looked exactly like real smoke.

As soon as he reached home Geppetto took his tools and set to work to cut out and model his puppet.

"What name shall I give him?" he said to himself; "I think I will call him Pinocchio. It is a name that will bring him luck. I once knew a whole family so called. There was Pinocchio the father, Pinocchia the mother, and Pinocchi the children, and all of them did well. The richest of them was a beggar."

Having found a name for his puppet he began to work in good earnest, and he first made his hair, then his forehead and then his eyes.

The eyes being finished, imagine his astonishment when he perceived that they moved and looked fixedly at him.

Geppetto seeing himself stared at by those two wooden eyes, took it almost in bad part, and said in an angry voice:

"Wicked wooden eyes, why do you look at me?"

No one answered.

Then he proceeded to carve the nose; but no sooner had he made it than it began to grow. And it grew, and grew, and grew until in a few minutes it had become an immense nose that seemed as if it would never end.

Poor Geppetto tired himself out with cutting it off. But the more he cut and shortened it, the longer did that impertinent nose become!

The mouth was not even completed when it began to laugh and deride him.

"Stop laughing!" said Geppetto provoked; but he might as well have spoken to the wall.

"Stop laughing, I say!" he roared in a threatening tone.

The mouth then ceased laughing, but put out its tongue as far as it would go.

Geppetto, not to spoil his handiwork, pretended not to see, and continued his labors. After the mouth he fashioned the chin, then the throat, and then the shoulders, the stomach, the arms and the hands.

The hands were scarcely finished when Geppetto felt his wig snatched from his head. He turned round, and what did he see? He saw his yellow wig in the puppet's hand.

"Pinocchio! . . . Give me back my wig instantly!"

But Pinocchio instead of returning it, put it on his own head, and was in consequence nearly smothered.

Geppetto at this insolent and derisive behavior felt sadder and more melancholy than he had ever been in his life before; and turning to Pinocchio he said to him:

"You young rascal! You are not yet completed, and you are already beginning to show want of respect to your father! That is bad, my boy, very bad."

And he dried a tear.

The legs and feet remained to be done.

When Geppetto had finished the feet he received a kick on the point of the nose.

"I deserve it!" he said to himself; "I should have thought of it sooner! Now it is too late!"

He then took the puppet under the arms and placed him on the floor to teach him to walk.

Pinocchio's legs were stiff and he could not move, but Geppetto led him by the hand and showed him how to put one foot before the other.

When his legs became flexible Pinocchio began to walk by himself and to run about the room; until, having gone out of the house door, he jumped into the street and escaped.

Poor Geppetto rushed after him but was not able to overtake him, for that rascal Pinocchio leapt in front of him like a hare, and knocking his wooden feet together against the pavement made as much clatter as twenty pairs of peasant's clogs.

"Stop him! stop him!" shouted Geppetto; but the people in the street, seeing a wooden puppet running like a racehorse stood still in astonishment to look at it, and laughed, and laughed, and laughed, until it beats description. . . .

IV

THE FIRE-EATER FRIGHTENS PINOCCHIO

When Pinocchio came into the little puppet theater, an incident occurred that almost produced a revolution.

I must tell you that the curtain was drawn up, and the play had already begun.

On the stage Harlequin and Punchinello were as usual quarreling with each other, and threatening every moment to come to blows.

The audience, all attention, laughed till they were ill as they listened to the bickerings of these two puppets, who gesticulated and abused each other so naturally that they might have been two reasonable beings, and two persons of the world.

All at once Harlequin stopped short, and turning to the public he pointed with his hand to some one far down in the pit, and exclaimed in a dramatic tone:

"Gods of the firmament! do I dream, or am I awake? But surely that is Pinocchio!"

"It is indeed Pinocchio!" cried Punchinello.

"It is indeed himself!" screamed Miss Rose, peeping from behind the scenes.

"It is Pinocchio! it is Pinocchio!" shouted all the puppets in chorus, leaping from all sides on to the stage. "It is Pinocchio! It is our brother Pinocchio! Long live Pinocchio!"

"Pinocchio, come up here to me," cried Harlequin, "and throw yourself into the arms of your wooden brothers!"

At this affectionate invitation Pinocchio made a leap from the end of the pit into the reserved seats; another leap landed him on the head of the leader of the orchestra, and then he sprang upon the stage.

The embraces, the hugs, the friendly pinches, and the demonstrations of warm brotherly affection that Pinocchio received from the excited crowd of actors and actresses of the puppet dramatic company beat description.

The sight was doubtless a moving one, but the public in the pit, finding that the play was stopped, became impatient, and began to shout "We will have the play—go on with the play!"

It was all breath thrown away. The puppets, instead of continuing the recital, redoubled their noise and outcries, and putting Pinocchio on their shoulders they carried him in triumph before the footlights.

At that moment out came the showman. He was very big

and so ugly that the sight of him was enough to frighten anyone. His beard was as black as ink, and so long that it reached from his chin to the ground. I need only say that he trod upon it when he walked. His mouth was as big as an oven, and his eyes were like two lanterns of red glass with lights burning inside of them. He carried a whip made of snakes and foxes' tails twisted together, which he cracked constantly.

At his unexpected appearance there was a profound silence: no one dared to breathe. A fly might have been heard in the stillness. The poor puppets of both sexes trembled like so many leaves.

"Why have you come to raise a disturbance in my theater?" asked the showman of Pinocchio in the gruff voice of a hob-goblin suffering from a severe cold in the head.

"Believe me, honored sir, that it was not my fault!"

"That is enough! To-night we will settle our accounts."

As soon as the play was over the showman went into the kitchen where a fine sheep, preparing for his supper, was turning slowly on the spit in front of the fire. As there was not enough wood to finish roasting and browning it, he called Harlequin and Punchinello, and said to them:

"Bring that puppet here; you will find him hanging on a nail. It seems to me that he is made of very dry wood, and I am sure that if he was thrown on the fire he would make a beautiful blaze for the roast."

At first Harlequin and Punchinello hesitated; but, appalled by a severe glance from their master, they obeyed. In a short time they returned to the kitchen carrying poor Pinocchio, who was wriggling like an eel taken out of water, and screaming desperately, "Papa! papa! save me! I will not die, I will not die!"

V

FIRE-EATER SNEEZES AND PARDONS PINOCCHIO

The showman Fire-eater—for that was his name—looked, I must say, a terrible man, especially with his black beard that covered his chest and legs like an apron. On the whole, however, he had not a bad heart. In proof of this, when he saw Pinocchio brought before him, struggling and screaming "I will not die, I will not die!" he was quite moved and felt sorry for him. He tried to hold out, but after a little he could stand it no longer and he sneezed violently. When he heard the sneeze, Harlequin, who up to that moment had been in the deepest affliction, and bowed down like a weeping willow, became quite cheerful, and leaning towards Pinocchio he whispered to him softly:

"Good news, brother. The showman has sneezed, and that is a sign that he pities you, and consequently you are saved."

For you must know that whilst most men when they feel compassion for somebody either weep, or at least pretend to dry their eyes, Fire-eater, on the contrary, had the habit of sneezing.

After he had sneezed, the showman, still acting the ruffian, shouted to Pinocchio:

"Have done crying! Your lamentations have given me a pain in my stomach . . . . I feel a spasm, that almost . . . . . Etci! etci!" and he sneezed again twice.

"Bless you!" said Pinocchio.

"Thank you! And your papa and your mamma, are they still alive?" asked Fire-eater.

"Papa, yes: my mamma I have never known."

"Who can say what a sorrow it would be to your poor old father if I was to have you thrown amongst those burning coals! Poor old man! I compassionate him! . . . . Etci! etci! etci!" and he sneezed three times.

"Bless you!" said Pinocchio.

"Thank you! All the same, some compassion is due to me, for you see I have no more wood with which to finish roasting my mutton, and to tell you the truth, under the circumstances you would have been of great use to me! However, I have had pity on you, so I must have patience. Instead of you I will burn under the spit one of the puppets belonging to my company. Ho there, gendarmes!"

At this call two wooden gendarmes immediately appeared.

They were very long and very thin and had on cocked hats, and held unsheathed swords in their hands.

The showman said to them in a hoarse voice:

"Take Harlequin, bind him securely, and then throw him on the fire to burn. I am determined that my mutton shall be well roasted."

Only imagine that poor Harlequin! His terror was so great that his legs bent under him, and he fell with his face on the ground.

At this agonizing sight Pinocchio, weeping bitterly, threw himself at the showman's feet, and bathing his long beard with his tears he began to say in a supplicating voice:

"Have pity, Sir Fire-eater!"

"Here there are no sirs," the showman answered severely.

"Have pity, Sir Knight!"

"Here there are no knights!"

"Have pity, Commander!"

"Here there are no commanders!"

"Have pity, Excellence!"

Upon hearing himself called Excellence the showman began to smile, and became at once kinder and more tractable. Turning to Pinocchio he asked:

"Well, what do you want from me?"

"I implore you to pardon poor Harlequin."

"For him there can be no pardon. As I have spared you he must be put on the fire, for I am determined that my mutton shall be well roasted."

"In that case," cried Pinocchio proudly, rising and throwing away his cap of bread crumb—"in that case I know my duty. Come on, gendarmes! Bind me and throw me amongst the flames. No, it is not just that poor Harlequin, my true friend, should die for me!"

These words, pronounced in a loud heroic voice, made all the puppets who were present cry. Even the gendarmes, although they were made of wood, wept like two newly-born lambs.

Fire-eater at first remained as hard and unmoved as ice, but little by little he began to melt and to sneeze. And having sneezed four or five times, he opened his arms affectionately, and said to Pinocchio:

"You are a good brave boy! Come here and give me a kiss."

Pinocchio ran at once, and climbing like a squirrel up the showman's beard he deposited a hearty kiss on the point of his nose.

"Then the pardon is granted?" asked poor Harlequin in a faint voice that was scarcely audible.

"The pardon is granted!" answered Fire-eater. He then added, sighing and shaking his head:

"I must have patience! To-night I shall have to resign myself to eat the mutton half raw; but another time, woe to him who chances!"

At the news of the pardon all the puppets ran to the stage, and having lighted the lamps and chandeliers as if for a full-dress performance, they began to leap and to dance merrily. At dawn they were still dancing.

VI

THE SHOWMAN BECOMES GENEROUS

The following day Fire-eater called Pinocchio to one side and asked him:

"What is your father's name?"

"Geppetto."

"And what trade does he follow?"

"He is a beggar."

"Does he gain much?"

"Gain much? Why, he has never a penny in his pocket. Only think, to buy a spelling-book for me to go to school, he was obliged to sell the only coat he had to wear—a coat that between patches and darns was not fit to be seen."

"Poor devil! I feel almost sorry for him! Here are five gold pieces. Go at once and take them to him with my compliments."

You can easily understand that Pinocchio thanked the

showman a thousand times. He embraced all the puppets of the company one by one, even to the gendarmes, and beside himself with delight set out to return home.

But he had not gone far when he met on the road a Fox lame in one foot, and a Cat blind in both eyes, who were going along helping each other like good companions in misfortune. The Fox who was lame walked leaning on the Cat, and the Cat who was blind was guided by the Fox.

"Good day, Pinocchio," said the Fox, accosting him politely.

"How do you come to know my name?" asked the puppet.

"I know your father well."

"Where did you see him?"

"I saw him yesterday at the door of his house."

"And what was he doing?"

"He was in his shirt sleeves and shivering with cold."

"Poor papa! But that is over; for the future he shall shiver no more."

"Why?"

"Because I am become a gentleman."

"A gentleman—you!" said the Fox, and he began to laugh rudely and scornfully. The Cat also began to laugh, but to conceal it she combed her whiskers with her forepaws.

"There is little to laugh at," cried Pinocchio angrily. "I am really sorry to make your mouths water, but if you know anything about it, you can see that here are five gold pieces."

And he pulled out the money that Fire-eater had made him a present of.

At the sympathetic ring of the money the Fox with an involuntary movement stretched out the paw that had seemed crippled, and the cat opened wide two eyes that looked like two green lanterns. It is true that she shut them again, and so quickly that Pinocchio observed nothing.

"And now," asked the Fox, "what are you going to do with all that money?"

"First of all," answered the Puppet, "I intend to buy a new coat for my papa, made of gold and silver, and with diamond buttons, and then I will buy a spelling-book for myself."

"For yourself?"

"Yes, indeed, for I wish to go to school to study in earnest."

"Look at me!" said the Fox. "Through my foolish passion for study I have lost a leg."

"Look at me!" said the Cat. "Through my foolish passion for study I have lost the sight of both my eyes."

At that moment a white Blackbird, that was perched on the hedge by the road, began his usual song, and said:

"Pinocchio, don't listen to the advice of bad companions; if you do you will repent it!"

Poor Blackbird! If only he had not spoken! The Cat with a great leap sprang upon him and without even giving him time to say "Oh!" ate him in a mouthful, feathers and all.

Having eaten him and cleaned her mouth she shut her eyes again and feigned blindness as before.

"Poor Blackbird!" said Pinocchio to the Cat. "Why did you treat him so badly?"

"I did it to give him a lesson. He will learn another time not to meddle in other people's conversation."

They had gone almost half-way when the Fox, halting suddenly, said to the puppet:

"Would you like to double your money?"

"In what way?"

"Would you like to make out of your five miserable gold pieces, a hundred, a thousand, two thousand?"

"I should think so! But in what way?"

"The way is easy enough. Instead of returning home you must go with us."

"And where do you wish to take me?"

"To the Land of the Owls."

Pinocchio reflected a moment, and then he said resolutely:

"No, I will not go. I am already close to the house, and I will return home to my papa who is waiting for me. Who can tell how often the poor old man must have sighed yesterday when I did not come back! I have been a bad son, indeed, and the Talking-cricket was right when he said 'Disobedient boys never come to any good in the world.' I have found it to my cost, for many misfortunes have happened to me. Even yesterday in Fire-eater's house I ran the risk . . . . . Oh! it makes me shudder only to think of it."

"Well, then, said the Fox, "you are quite decided to go home? Go, then, and so much the worse for you."

"So much the worse for you!" repeated the Cat.

"Think well of it, Pinocchio, for you are giving a kick to fortune."

"To fortune!" repeated the Cat.

"Between to-day and to-morrow your five gold pieces would have become two thousand."

"Two thousand!" repeated the Cat.

"But how is it possible that they could have become so many?" asked Pinocchio, remaining with his mouth open from astonishment.

"I will explain it to you at once," said the Fox. "You must know that in the Land of the Owls there is a sacred field called by everybody the Field of Miracles. In this field you must dig a little hole, and you put into it, we will say one gold piece. Then you cover up the hole with a little earth; you water it with two pails of water from the fountain, then sprinkle it with two pinches of salt, and when night comes you can go quietly to bed. In the meanwhile, during the night, the gold piece will grow and flower, and in the morning when you return to the field, what do you find? You find a beautiful tree laden with as many gold pieces as an ear of corn has grains in the month of June."

"So that," said Pinocchio, more and more bewildered, "supposing I buried my five gold pieces in that field, how many should I find there the following morning?"

"That is exceedingly easy calculation," replied the Fox, "a calculation that you can make on the ends of your fingers. Suppose that every gold piece gives you an increase of five hundred; multiply five hundred by five, and the following morning will find you with two thousand five hundred shining gold pieces in your pocket."

"Oh! how delightful!" cried Pinocchio, dancing for joy. "As soon as ever I have obtained those gold piecss, I will keep two thousand for myself, and the other five hundred I will make a present of to you two."

"A present to us?" cried the Fox with indignation, and appearing much offended. "What are you dreaming of?"

"What are you dreaming of?" repeated the Cat.

"We do not work," said the Fox, "for dirty interest, we work solely to enrich others."

"Others!" repeated the Cat.

"What good people!" thought Pinocchio to himself; and forgetting there and then his papa, the new coat, the spelling-book, and all his good resolutions, he said to the Fox and the Cat:

"Let us be off at once. I will go with you."

VII

THE INN OF THE RED-CRAWFISH

They walked, and walked, and walked, until at last, towards evening, they arrived dead tired at the Inn of The Red-Crawfish.

"Let us stop here, a little," said the Fox, "that we may have something to eat and rest ourselves for an hour or two. We will start again at midnight, so as to arrive at the Field of Miracles by dawn to-morrow morning."

Having gone into the inn they all three sat down to table, but none of them had any appetite.

The Cat, who was suffering from indigestion and feeling seriously indisposed, could only eat thirty-five mullet with tomato sauce, and four portions of tripe with Parmesan cheese; and because she thought the tripe was not seasoned enough, she asked three times for the butter and grated cheese!

The Fox would also willingly have picked a little, but as his doctor had ordered him a strict diet, he was forced to content himself simply with a hare dressed with a sweet and sour sauce, and garnished lightly with fat chickens and early pullets. After the hare he sent for a made dish of partridges, rabbits, frogs, lizards, and other delicacies; he could not touch anything else. He had such a disgust for food, he said, that he could put nothing to his lips.

The one who ate the least was Pinocchio. He asked for some walnuts and a hunch of bread, and left everything on his plate. The poor boy, whose thoughts were continually fixed on the Field of Miracles, had got in anticipation an indigestion of gold pieces.

When they had supped the Fox said to the host:

"Give us two good rooms, one for Mr. Pinocchio, and the other for me and my companion. We will snatch a little sleep before we leave. Remember, however, that at midnight we wish to be called to continue our journey."

"Yes, gentlemen," answered the host, and he winked at the Fox and the Cat as much as to say: "I know what you are up to. We understand one another!"

No sooner had Pinocchio got into bed than he fell asleep at once and began to dream. And he dreamt that he was in the middle of a field, and the field was filled with shrubs covered with clusters of gold pieces, and as they swung in the wind they went zin, zin, zin, almost as if they would say: "Let who will come and take us." But when Pinocchio was at the most interesting moment, that is, just as he was stretching out his hand to pick handfuls of those beautiful gold pieces and put them in his pockets, he was suddenly wakened by three violent blows on the door of his room.

It was the host who had come to tell him that midnight had struck.

"Are my companions ready?" asked the puppet.

"Ready! Why, they left two hours ago."

"Why were they in such a hurry?"

"Because the Cat had received a message to say that her eldest kitten was ill with chilblains on his feet, and was in danger of death."

"Did they pay for supper?"

"What are you thinking of? They are too highly educated to dream of offering such an insult to a gentleman like you."

"What a pity! It is an insult that would have given me

so much pleasure!" said Pinocchio, scratching his head. He then asked:

"And where did my good friends say they would wait for me?"

"At the Field of Miracles, to-morrow morning at daybreak."

Pinocchio paid a gold piece for his supper and that of his companions and then he left.

Outside the inn it was so pitch dark that he had almost to grope his way, for it was impossible to see a hand's breadth in front of him. In the adjacent country not a leaf moved. Only some night-birds flying across the road from one hedge to the other brushed Pinocchio's nose with their wings as they passed, which caused him so much terror that springing back, he shouted: "Who goes there?" and the echo in the surrounding hills repeated in the distance: "Who goes there? Who goes there? Who goes there?" . . .

VIII

THE PUPPET FALLS AMONG ASSASSINS

He turned to look, and saw in the gloom two evil-looking black figures completely enveloped in charcoal sacks. They were running after him on tiptoe, and making great leaps like two phantoms.

"Here they are in reality!" he said to himself, and not knowing where to hide his gold pieces he put them in his mouth precisely under his tongue.

Then he tried to escape. But he had not gone a step when he felt himself seized by the arm, and heard two sepulchral voices saying to him:

"Your money or your life!"

Pinocchio, not being able to answer in words, owing to the money in his mouth, made a thousand low bows and a thousand pantomimes. He tried thus to make the two muffled figures, whose eyes were only visible through the holes in their sacks, understand that he was a poor puppet, and that he had not as much as a false penny in his pocket.

"Come now! Less nonsense and out with the money!" cried the two brigands threateningly.

And the puppet made a gesture with his hands to signify "I have got none."

"Deliver up your money or you are dead," said the tallest of the brigands.

"Dead!" repeated the other.

"And after we have killed you, we will also kill your father!"

"Also your father!"

"No, no, no, not my poor papa!" cried Pinocchio in a despairing tone; and as he said it, the gold pieces clinked in his mouth.

"Ah! You rascal! Then you have hidden your money under your tongue! Spit it out at once!"

But Pinocchio was obdurate.

And one of them seized the puppet by the end of his nose, and the other took him by the chin, and began to pull them brutally, the one up, and the other down, to constrain him to open his mouth, but it was all to no purpose. Pinocchio's mouth seemed to be nailed and riveted together.

Then the shortest assassin drew out an ugly knife and tried to force it between his lips like a lever or chisel. But Pinocchio as quick as lightning caught his hand with his teeth, and with one bite bit it clean off and spat it out. Imagine his astonishment when instead of a hand he perceived that he had spat a cat's paw on to the ground.

Encouraged by his first victory he used his nails to such purpose that he succeeded in liberating himself from his assailants, and jumping the hedge by the roadside he began to fly across the country. The assassins ran after him like two dogs chasing a hare; and the one who had lost the paw ran on one leg and no one ever knew how he managed it.

After a race of some miles Pinocchio could do no more. Giving himself up for lost he climbed the stem of a very high pine-tree and seated himself in the topmost branches. The assassins attempted to climb after him, but when they had reached halfway up the stem they slid down again, and arrived on the ground with the skin grazed from their hands and knees.

But they were not to be beaten by so little; collecting a quantity of dry wood they piled it beneath the pine and set fire to it. In less time than it takes to tell the pine began to burn and flame like a candle blown by the wind. Pinocchio, seeing that the flames were mounting higher every instant, and not wishing to end his life like a roasted pigeon, made a stupendous leap from the top of the tree and started afresh across the fields and vineyards. The assassins followed him, and kept behind him without once giving in.

The day began to break and they were still pursuing him. Suddenly Pinocchio found his way barred by a wide, deep ditch full of dirty water the color of coffee. What was he to do? "One! two! three!" cried the puppet, and making a rush he sprang to the other side. The assassins also jumped, but not having measured the distance properly—splash, splash! . . . they fell into the very middle of the ditch. Pinocchio who heard the plunge and the splashing of water, shouted out, laughing and without stopping:

"A fine bath to you, gentlemen assassins."

He felt convinced that they were drowned, when, turning to look he perceived that, on the contrary, they were both running after him, still enveloped in their sacks with the water dripping from them as if they had been two hollow baskets. . . .

IX

THE FOX AND THE CAT

Pinocchio set out; and as soon as he was in the wood he began to run like a kid. But when he had reached a certain spot, almost in front of the Big Oak, he stopped because he thought that he heard people amongst the bushes. In fact, two persons came out on the road. Can you guess who they were? . . . His two traveling companions, the Fox and the Cat, with whom he had supped at the Inn of the Red-Craw-fish.

"Why here is our dear Pinocchio!" cried the Fox, kissing and embracing him. "How come you to be here?"

"How come you to be here?" repeated the Cat.

"It is a long story," answered the puppet, "which I will tell you when I have time. But do you know that the other night, when you left me alone at the inn, I met with assassins on the road."

"Assassins! . . . Oh, poor Pinocchio! And what did they want?"

"They wanted to rob me of my gold pieces."

"Villains!" said the Fox.

"Infamous villains!" repeated the Cat.

"But I ran away from them," continued the puppet, "and they followed me, and at last they overtook me and hung me to a branch of that oak-tree."

And Pinocchio pointed to the Big Oak, which was two steps from them.

"Is it possible to hear of anything more dreadful?" said the Fox. "In what a world we are condemned to live! Where can respectable people like us find a safe refuge?"

Whilst they were thus talking Pinocchio observed that the Cat was lame of her front right leg, for in fact she had lost her paw with all its claws. He therefore asked her:

"What have you done with your paw!"

The Cat tried to answer but became confused. Therefore the Fox said immediately:

"My friend is too modest, and that is why she doesn't speak. I will answer for her. I must tell you that an hour ago we met an old wolf on the road, almost fainting from want of food, who asked alms of us. Not having so much as a fish-bone to give to him, what did my friend, who has really the heart of a Cæsar, do? She bit off one of her forepaws, and threw it to that poor beast that he might appease his hunger."

And the Fox, in relating this, dried a tear.

Pinocchio was also touched, and approaching the Cat he whispered into her ear:

"If all cats resemble you, how fortunate the mice would be!"

"And now, what are you doing here?" asked the Fox of the puppet.

"I am waiting for my papa, whom I expect to arrive every moment."

"And your gold pieces?"

"I have got them in my pocket, all but one that I spent at the Inn of the Red-Crawfish."

"And to think that, instead of four pieces, by to-morrow they might become one or two thousand! Why do you not listen to my advice? why will you not go and bury them in the Field of Miracles?"

"To-day it is impossible, I will go another day."

"Another day it will be too late!" said the Fox.

"Why?"

"Because the field has been bought by a gentleman, and after to-morrow no one will be allowed to bury money there."

"How far off is the Field of Miracles?"

"Not two miles. Will you come with us? In half an hour you will be there. You can bury your money at once, and in a few minutes you will collect two thousand, and this evening you will return with your pockets full. Will you come with us?"

Pinocchio thought of the good Fairy, old Geppetto, and the warning of the Talking-cricket, and he hesitated a little before answering. He ended however, by doing as all boys do who have not a grain of sense and who have no heart—he ended by giving his head a little shake, and saying to the Fox and Cat:

"Let us go: I will come with you."

And they went.

After having walked half the day they reached a town that was called "Trap for Blockheads." As soon as Pinocchio entered this town, he saw that the streets were crowded with dogs who had lost their coats and who were yawning from hunger, shorn sheep trembling with cold, cocks without combs or crests who were begging for a grain of Indian corn, large butterflies who could no longer fly because they had sold their beautiful colored wings, peacocks who had no tails and were ashamed to be seen, and pheasants who went scratching about in a subdued fashion, mourning for their brilliant gold and silver feathers gone for ever.

In the midst of this crowd of beggars and shamefaced creatures, some lordly carriage passed from time to time containing a Fox, or a thieving Magpie, or some other ravenous bird of prey.

"And where is the Field of Miracles?" asked Pinocchio.

"It is here, not two steps from us."

They crossed the town, and having gone beyond the walls they came to a solitary field which to look at resembled all other fields.

"We are arrived," said the Fox to the puppet. "Now stoop down and dig with your hands a little hole in the ground and put your gold pieces into it."

Pinocchio obeyed. He dug a hole, put into it the four gold pieces that he had left, and then filled up the hole with a little earth.

"Now, then," said the Fox, "go to that canal close to us, fetch a can of water, and water the ground where you have sowed them."

Pinocchio went to the canal, and as he had no can he took off one of his old shoes and filling it with water he watered the ground over the hole.

He then asked:

"Is there anything else to be done?"

"Nothing else," answered the Fox. "We can now go away. You can return in about twenty minutes, and you will find a shrub already pushing through the ground, with its branches quite loaded with money."

The poor puppet, beside himself with joy, thanked the Fox and the Cat a thousand times, and promised them a beautiful present.

"We wish for no presents," answered the two rascals. "It is enough for us to have taught you the way to enrich yourself without undergoing hard work, and we are as happy as folk out for a holiday."

Thus saying they took leave of Pinocchio, and wishing him a good harvest went about their business.

X

PINOCCHIO IS ROBBED

The puppet returned to the town and began to count the minutes one by one; and when he thought it must be time he took the road leading to the Field of Miracles.

And as he walked along with hurried steps his heart beat fast, tic, tac, tic, tac, like a drawing-room clock when it is really going well. Meanwhile he was thinking to himself:

"And if instead of a thousand gold pieces, I was to find on the branches of the tree two thousand? . . . And instead of two thousand supposing I found five thousand? and instead of five thousand that I found a hundred thousand? Oh! what a fine gentleman I should then become! . . . I would have a beautiful palace, a thousand little wooden horses and a thousand stables to amuse myself with, a cellar full of currant-wine, and sweet syrups, and a library quite full of candies, tarts, plum-cakes, macaroons, and biscuits with cream."

Whilst he was building these castles in the air he had arrived in the neighborhood of the field, and he stopped to look if by chance he could perceive a tree with its branches laden with money; but he saw nothing. He advanced another hundred steps—nothing; he entered the field . . . he went right up to the little hole where he had buried his gold pieces—and nothing. He then became very thoughtful, and forgetting the rules of society and good manners he took his hands out of his pockets and gave his head a long scratch.

At that moment he heard an explosion of laughter close to him, and looking up he saw a large Parrot perched on a tree, who was preening the few feathers he had left.

"Why are you laughing?" asked Pinocchio in an angry voice.

"I am laughing because in preening my feathers I tickled myself under my wings."

The puppet did not answer, but went to the canal and, filling the same old shoe full of water, he proceeded to water the earth afresh that covered his gold pieces.

Whilst he was thus occupied another laugh, and still more impertinent than the first, rang out in the silence of that solitary place.

"Once for all," shouted Pinocchio in a rage, "may I know, you ill-educated Parrot, what are you laughing at?"

"I am laughing at those simpletons who believe in all the foolish things that are told them, and who allow themselves to be entrapped by those who are more cunning than they are."

"Are you perhaps speaking of me?"

"Yes, I am speaking of you, poor Pinocchio—of you who are simple enough to believe that money can be sown and gathered in fields in the same way as beans and gourds. I also believed it once, and to-day I am suffering for it. To-day—but it is too late—I have at last learnt that to put a few pennies honestly together it is necessary to know how to earn them, either by the work of our own hands or by the cleverness of our own brains."

"I don't understand you," said the puppet who was already trembling with fear.

"Have patience! I will explain myself better," rejoined the Parrot. "You must know, then, that whilst you were in the town the Fox and the Cat returned to the field; they took the buried money and then fled like the wind. And now he that catches them will be clever."

Pinocchio remained with his mouth open, and not choosing to believe the Parrot's words he began with his hands and nails to dig up the earth that he had watered. And he dug, and dug, and dug, and made such a deep hole that a rick of straw might have stood up in it; but the money was no longer there.

He rushed back to the town in a state of desperation, and went at once to the Courts of Justice to denounce the two knaves who had robbed him to the judge.

The judge was a big ape of the gorilla tribe—an old ape respectable for his age, his white beard, but especially for his gold spectacles without glasses that he always was obliged to wear, on account of an inflammation of the eyes that had tormented him for many years.

Pinocchio related in the presence of the judge all the particulars of the infamous fraud of which he had been the victim. He gave the names, the surnames, and other details, of the two rascals, and ended by demanding justice.

The judge listened with great benignity; took a lively interest in the story; and was much touched and moved; and when the puppet had nothing further to say he stretched out his hand and rang a bell.

At this summons two mastiffs immediately appeared dressed as gendarmes. The judge then, pointing to Pinocchio said to them:

"That poor devil has been robbed of four gold pieces; take him up, and put him immediately into prison."

The puppet was petrified on hearing this unexpected sentence, and tried to protest; but the gendarmes, to avoid losing time, stopped his mouth, and carried him off to the lockup.

And there he remained for four months—four long months—and he would have remained longer still if a fortunate chance had not released him. For I must tell you that the young Emperor who reigned over the town of "Trap for Blockheads," having won a splendid victory over his enemies, ordered great public rejoicings. There were illuminations, fire-works, horse races, and velocipede races, and as a further sign of triumph he commanded that the prisons should be opened and all prisoners liberated.

"If the others are to be let out of prison, I will go also," said Pinocchio to the jailor.

"No, not you," said the jailor, "because you do not belong to the fortunate class."

"I beg your pardon," replied Pinocchio, "I am also a criminal."

"In that case you are perfectly right," said the jailor; and taking off his hat and bowing to him respectfully he opened the prison door and let him escape.

JAPANESE STORIES

THE STORY OF THE MAN WHO DID NOT WISH TO DIE

ADAPTED BY YEI THEODORA OZAKI

LONG, long ago there lived a man called Sentaro. His surname meant "Millionaire," but although he was not so rich as all that, he was still very far removed from being poor. He had inherited a small fortune from his father and lived on this, spending his time carelessly, without any serious thoughts of work, till he was about thirty-two years of age.

One day, without any reason whatsoever, the thought of death and sickness came to him. The idea of falling ill or dying made him very wretched.

"I should like to live," he said to himself, "till I am five or six hundred years old at least, free from all sickness. The ordinary span of a man's life is very short."

He wondered whether it were possible, by living simply and frugally henceforth, to prolong his life as long as he wished.

He knew there were many stories in ancient history of emperors who had lived a thousand years, and there was a Princess of Yamato, who it was said, lived to the age of five hundred. This was the latest story of a very long life on record.

Sentaro had often heard the tale of the Chinese King named Shin-no-Shiko. He was one of the most able and powerful rulers in Chinese history. He built all the large palaces, and also the famous great wall of China. He had everything in the world he could wish for, but in spite of all his happiness, and the luxury and splendor of his court, the wisdom of his councilors and the glory of his reign, he was miserable because he knew that one day he must die and leave it all.

When Shin-no-Shiko went to bed at night, when he rose in the morning, as he went through his day, the thought of death was always with him. He could not get away from it. Ah—if only he could find the Elixir of Life, he would be happy.

The Emperor at last called a meeting of his courtiers and asked them all if they could not find for him the Elixir of Life of which he had so often read and heard.

One old courtier, Jofuku by name, said that far away across the seas there was a country called Horaizan, and that certain hermits lived there who possessed the secret of the Elixir of Life. Whoever drank of this wonderful draught lived forever.

The Emperor ordered Jofuku to set out for the land of Horaizan, to find the hermits, and to bring him back a phial of the magic elixir. He gave Jofuku one of his best junks, fitted it out for him, and loaded it with great quantities of treasures and precious stones for Jofuku to take as presents to the hermits.

Jofuku sailed for the land of Horaizan, but he never returned to the waiting Emperor; but ever since that time Mount Fuji has been said to be the fabled Horaizan and the home of hermits who had the secret of the elixir, and Jofuku has been worshipped as their patron god.

Now Sentaro determined to set out to find the hermits, and if he could, to become one, so that he might obtain the water of perpetual life. He remembered that as a child he had been told that not only did these hermits live on Mount Fuji, but that they were said to inhabit all the very high peaks.

So he left his old home to the care of his relatives, and started out on his quest. He traveled through all the mountainous regions of the land, climbing to the tops of the highest peaks, but never a hermit did he find.

At last, after wandering in an unknown region for many days, he met a hunter.

"Can you tell me," asked Sentaro, "where the hermits live who have the Elixir of Life?"

"No," said the hunter; "I can't tell you where such hermits live, but there is a notorious robber living in these parts. It is said that he is chief of a band of two hundred followers."

This odd answer irritated Sentaro very much, and he thought how foolish it was to waste more time in looking for the hermits in this way, so he decided to go at once to the shrine of Jofuku, who is worshipped as the patron god of the hermits in the South of Japan.

Sentaro reached the shrine and prayed for seven days, entreating Jofuku to show him the way to a hermit who could give him what he wanted so much to find.

At midnight of the seventh day, as Sentaro knelt in the temple, the door of the innermost shrine flew open, and Jofuku appeared in a luminous cloud, and calling to Sentaro to come nearer, spoke thus:

"Your desire is a very selfish one and cannot be easily granted. You think that you would like to become a hermit so as to find the Elixir of Life. Do you know how hard a hermit's life is? A hermit is only allowed to eat fruit and berries and the bark of pine trees; a hermit must cut himself off from the world so that his heart may become as pure as gold and free from every earthly desire. Gradually after following these strict rules, the hermit ceases to feel hunger or cold or heat, and his body becomes so light that he can ride on a crane or a carp, and can walk on water without getting his feet wet.

"You, Sentaro, are fond of good living and of every comfort. You are not even like an ordinary man, for you are exceptionally idle, and more sensitive to heat and cold than most people. You would never be able to go barefoot or to wear only one thin garment in the winter time! Do you think that you would ever have the patience or the endurance to live a hermit's life?

"In answer to your prayer, however, I will help you in another way. I will send you to the country of Perpetual Life, where death never comes—where the people live for ever!"

Saying this, Jofuku put into Sentaro's hand a little crane

made of paper, telling him to sit on its back and it would carry him there.

Sentaro obeyed wonderingly. The crane grew large enough for him to ride on it with comfort. It then spread its wings, rose high in the air, and flew away over the mountains right out to sea.

Sentaro was at first quite frightened; but by degrees he grew accustomed to the swift flight through the air. On and on they went for thousands of miles. The bird never stopped for rest or food, but as it was a paper bird it doubtless did not require any nourishment, and strange to say, neither did Sentaro.

After several days they reached an island. The crane flew some distance inland and then alighted.

As soon as Sentaro got down from the bird's back, the crane folded up of its own accord and flew into his pocket.

Now Sentaro began to look about him wonderingly, curious to see what the country of Perpetual Life was like. He walked first round about the country and then through the town. Everything was, of course, quite strange, and different from his own land. But both the land and the people seemed prosperous, so he decided that it would be good for him to stay there and took up lodgings at one of the hotels.

The proprietor was a kind man, and when Sentaro told him that he was a stranger and had come to live there, he promised to arrange everything that was necessary with the governor of the city concerning Sentaro's sojourn there. He even found a house for his guest, and in this way Sentaro obtained his great wish and became a resident in the country of Perpetual Life.

Within the memory of all the islanders no man had ever died there, and sickness was a thing unknown. Priests had come over from India and China and told them of a beautiful country called Paradise, where happiness and bliss and contentment fill all men's hearts, but its gates could only be reached by dying. This tradition was handed down for ages from generation to generation—but none knew exactly what death was except that it led to Paradise.

Quite unlike Sentaro and other ordinary people, instead of having a great dread of death, they all, both rich and poor, longed for it as something good and desirable. They were all tired of their long, long lives, and longed to go to the happy land of contentment called Paradise of which the priests had told them centuries ago.

All this Sentaro soon found out by talking to the islanders. He found himself, according to his ideas, in the land of *Topsy-turvydom.* Everything was upside down. He had wished to escape from dying. He had come to the land of Perpetual Life with great relief and joy, only to find that the inhabitants themselves, doomed never to die, would consider it bliss to find death.

What he had hitherto considered poison these people ate as good food, and all the things to which he had been accustomed as food they rejected. Whenever any merchants from other countries arrived, the rich people rushed to them eager to buy poisons. These they swallowed eagerly hoping for death to come so that they might go to Paradise.

But what were deadly poisons in other lands were without effect in this strange place, and people who swallowed them with the hope of dying, only found that in a short time they felt better in health instead of worse.

Vainly they tried to imagine what death could be like. The wealthy would have given all their money and all their goods if they could but shorten their lives to two or three hundred years even. Without any change, to live on forever, seemed to this people wearisome and sad.

In the drug-shops there was a drug which was in constant demand, because after using it for a hundred years, it was supposed to turn the hair slightly gray and to bring about disorders of the stomach.

Sentaro was astonished to find that the poisonous globe-fish was served up in restaurants as a delectable dish, and hawkers in the streets went about selling sauces made of Spanish flies. He never saw anyone ill after eating these horrible things, nor did he ever see anyone with as much as a cold.

Sentaro was delighted. He said to himself that he would

never grow tired of living, and that he considered it profane to wish for death. He was the only happy man on the island. For his part he wished to live thousands of years and to enjoy life. He set himself up in business, and for the present never even dreamed of going back to his native land.

As years went by, however, things did not go as smoothly as at first. He had heavy losses in business, and several times some affairs went wrong with his neighbors. This caused him great annoyance.

Time passed like the flight of an arrow for him, for he was busy from morning till night. Three hundred years went by in this monotonous way, and then at last he began to grow tired of life in this country, and he longed to see his own land and his old home. However long he lived here, life would always be the same, so was it not foolish and wearisome to stay on here for ever?

Sentaro, in his wish to escape from the country of Perpetual Life, recollected Jofuku, who had helped him before when he was wishing to escape from death—and he prayed to the saint to bring him back to his own land again.

No sooner did he pray than the paper crane popped out of his pocket. Sentaro was amazed to see that it had remained undamaged after all these years. Once more the bird grew and grew till it was large enough for him to mount it. As he did so, the bird spread its wings and flew swiftly out across the sea in the direction of Japan.

Such was the wilfulness of the man's nature that he looked back and regretted all he had left behind. He tried to stop the bird in vain. The crane held on its way for thousands of miles across the ocean.

Then a storm came on, and the wonderful paper crane got damp, crumpled up, and fell into the sea. Sentaro fell with it. Very much frightened at the thought of being drowned, he cried out loudly to Jofuku to save him. He looked round, but there was no ship in sight. He swallowed a quantity of sea-water, which only increased his miserable plight. While he was thus struggling to keep himself afloat, he saw a monstrous shark swimming towards him. As it came nearer it opened its huge mouth ready to devour him. Sentaro was all but paralyzed with fear now that he felt his end so near, and screamed out as loudly as ever he could to Jofuku to come and rescue him.

Lo, and behold, Sentaro was awakened by his own screams, to find that during his long prayer he had fallen asleep before the shrine, and that all his extraordinary and frightful adventures had been only a wild dream. He was in a cold perspiration with fright, and utterly bewildered.

Suddenly a bright light came towards him, and in the light stood a messenger. The messenger held a book in his hand and spoke to Sentaro:

"I am sent to you by Jofuku, who in answer to your prayer, has permitted you in a dream to see the land of Perpetual Life. But you grew weary of living there, and begged to be allowed to return to your native land so that you might die. Jofuku, so that he might try you, allowed you to drop into the sea, and then sent a shark to swallow you up. Your desire for death was not real, for even at that moment you cried out loudly and shouted for help.

"It is also vain for you to wish to become a hermit, or to find the Elixir of Life. These things are not for such as you—your life is not austere enough. It is best for you to go back to your paternal home, and to live a good and industrious life. Never neglect to keep the anniversaries of your ancestors, and make it your duty to provide for your children's future. Thus will you live to a good old age and be happy, but give up the vain desire to escape death, for no man can do that, and by this time you have surely found out that even when selfish desires are granted they do not bring happiness.

"In this book I give you there are many precepts good for you to know—if you study them, you will be guided in the way I have pointed out to you."

The angel disappeared as soon as he had finished speaking, and Sentaro took the lesson to heart. With the book in his hand he returned to his old home, and giving up all his old vain wishes, tried to live a good and useful life and to observe the lessons taught him in the book, and he and his house prospered henceforth.

THE ACCOMPLISHED AND LUCKY TEAKETTLE

ADAPTED BY A. B. MITFORD

A LONG time ago, at a temple called Morinji, in the province of Jhôsiu, there was an old teakettle. One day, when the priest of the temple was about to hang it over the hearth to boil the water for his tea, to his amazement the kettle all of a sudden put forth the head and tail of a badger. What a wonderful kettle, to come out all over fur! The priest, thunderstruck, called in the novices of the temple to see the sight; and whilst they were stupidly staring, one suggesting one thing and another another, the kettle, jumping up into the air, began flying about the room. More astonished than ever, the priest and his pupils tried to pursue it; but no thief or cat was ever half so sharp as this wonderful badger-kettle. At last, however, they managed to knock it down and secure it; and, holding it in with their united efforts, they forced it into a box, intending to carry it off and throw it away in some distant place, so that they might be no more plagued by the goblin. For this day their troubles were over; but, as luck would have it, the tinker who was in the habit of working for the temple called in, and the priest suddenly bethought him that it was a pity to throw the kettle away for nothing, and that he might as well get a trifle for it, no matter how small. So he brought out the kettle, which had resumed its former shape and had got rid of its head and tail, and showed it to the tinker. When the tinker saw the kettle, he offered twenty copper coins for it, and the priest was only too glad to close the bargain and be rid of his troublesome piece of furniture. But the tinker trudged off home with his pack and his new purchase. That night, as he lay asleep, he heard a strange noise near his pillow; so he peered out from under the bedclothes, and there he saw the kettle that he had bought in the temple covered with fur, and walking about on four legs. The tinker started up in a fright to see what it could all mean, when all of a sudden the kettle resumed its former shape. This happened over and over again, until at last the tinker showed the teakettle to a friend of his, who said: "This is certainly an accomplished and lucky teakettle. You should take it about as a show, with songs and accompaniments of musical instruments, and make it dance and walk on the tight rope."

The tinker, thinking this good advice, made arrangements with a showman, and set up an exhibition. The noise of the kettle's performances soon spread abroad, until even the Princes of the land sent to order the tinker to come to them; and he grew rich beyond all his expectations. Even the Princesses, too, and the great ladies of the court, took great delight in the dancing kettle, so that no sooner had it shown its tricks in one place than it was time for them to keep some other engagement. At last the tinker grew so rich that he took the kettle back to the temple, where it was laid up as a precious treasure, and worshiped as a saint.

☙ ☙ ☙

THE TONGUE-CUT SPARROW

ONCE upon a time a cross old woman laid some starch in a basin, intending to put it in the clothes in her wash-tub; but a Sparrow that a woman, her neighbor, kept as a pet, ate it up. Seeing this, the cross old woman seized the Sparrow and, saying "You hateful thing!" cut its tongue and let it go.

When the neighbor woman heard that her pet Sparrow had got its tongue cut for its offense, she was greatly grieved, and set out with her husband over mountains and plains to find where it had gone, crying, "Where does the tongue-cut Sparrow stay? Where does the tongue-cut Sparrow stay?"

At last they found its home. When the Sparrow saw that its old master and mistress had come to see it, it rejoiced, and brought them into its house and thanked them for their kindness in old times. It spread a table for them, and loaded it with rice wine and fish till there was no more room, and made its wife and children and grandchildren all serve the table.

At last, throwing away its drinking-cup, it danced a jig called the Sparrow's dance, and thus they spent the day. When it began to grow dark, and there was talk of going home, the Sparrow brought out two wicker baskets and said, "Will you take the heavy one, or shall I give you the light one?" The old people replied, "We are old, so give us the light one; it will be easier to carry it." The Sparrow then gave them the light basket, and they returned with it to their home. "Let us open and see what is in it," they said. And when they had opened it and looked, they found gold and silver and jewels and rolls of silk. They never expected anything like this. The more they took out the more they found inside. The supply was inexhaustible, so that the house at once became rich and prosperous. When the cross old woman who had cut the Sparrow's tongue saw this, she was filled with envy, and went and asked her neighbor where the Sparrow lived and all about the way. "I will go, too," she said, and at once set out on her search.

Again the Sparrow brought out two wicker baskets, and asked as before, "Will you take the heavy one, or shall I give you the light one?"

Thinking the treasure would be great in proportion to the weight of the basket, the old woman replied, "Let me have the heavy one."

Receiving this, she started home with it on her back, the sparrows laughing at her as she went. It was as heavy as a stone, and hard to carry, but at last she got back with it to her house. Then, when she took off the lid and looked in, a whole troop of frightful creatures came bouncing out from the inside, and at once they caught her up and flew away with her.

☘ ☘ ☘

BATTLE OF THE MONKEY AND THE CRAB

A MONKEY and a Crab once met when going round a mountain.

The Monkey had picked up a persimmon-seed, and the

Crab had a piece of toasted rice-cake. The Monkey, seeing this, and wishing to get something that could be turned to good account at once, said, "Pray, exchange that rice-cake for this persimmon-seed." The Crab, without a word, gave up his cake, and took the persimmon-seed and planted it. At once it sprung up, and soon became a tree so high one had to look far up to see it. The tree was full of persimmons, but the Crab had no means of climbing it, so he asked the Monkey to scramble up and get the fruit for him. The Monkey got up on a limb of the tree and began to eat the persimmons. The unripe ones he threw at the Crab, but all the ripe and good ones he put in his pouch. The Crab under the tree thus got his shell badly bruised, and only by good luck escaped into his hole, where he lay distressed with pain, and not able to get up. Now, when the relatives and household of the Crab heard how matters stood, they were surprised and angry, and declared war, and attacked the Monkey, who, leading forth a numerous following, bade defiance to the other party. The crabs, finding themselves unable to meet and cope with this force, became still more exasperated and enraged, and retreated into their hole and held a council of war. Then came a rice-mortar, a pestle, a bee, and an egg, and together they devised a deep-laid plot to be avenged.

First, they requested that peace be made with the crabs; and thus they induced the king of the monkeys to enter their hole unattended, and seated him on the hearth. The Monkey, not suspecting any plot, took the *hibashi*, or poker, to stir up the slumbering fire, when bang! went the egg, which was lying hidden in the ashes, and burned the Monkey's arm. Surprised and alarmed, he plunged his arm into the pickle-tub in the kitchen to relieve the pain of the burn. Then the bee which was hidden near the tub stung him sharply in his face, already wet with tears. Without waiting to brush off the bee, and howling bitterly, he rushed for the back door; but just then some seaweed entangled his legs and made him slip. Then down came the pestle, tumbling on him from a shelf, and the mortar, too, came rolling down on him from the roof of the porch and broke his back, and so weakened him that he was unable to rise up. Then out came the crabs in a crowd, and brandishing on high their pinchers they pinched the Monkey so sorely that he begged them for forgiveness and promised never to repeat his meanness and treachery.

❧ ❧ ❧

MOMOTARO, OR LITTLE PEACHLING

A LONG long time ago there lived an old man and an old woman. One day the old man went to the mountains to cut grass; and the old woman went to the river to wash clothes. While she was washing a great thing came tumbling and splashing down the stream. When the old woman saw it she was very glad, and pulled it to her with a piece of bamboo that lay near by. When she took it up and looked at it she saw that it was a very large peach. She then quickly finished her washing and returned home intending to give the peach to her old man to eat.

When she cut the peach in two, out came a child from the large kernel. Seeing this the old couple rejoiced, and named the child Momotaro, or Little Peachling, because he came out of a peach. As both the old people took good care of him, he grew and became strong and enterprising. So the old couple had their expectations raised, and bestowed still more care on his education.

Momotaro finding that he excelled everybody in strength, determined to cross over to the island of the devils, take their riches, and come back. He at once consulted with the old man and the old woman about the matter, and got them to make him some dumplings. These he put in his pouch. Besides this he made every kind of preparation for his journey to the island of the devils and set out.

Then first a dog came to the side of the way and said, "Momotaro! What have you there hanging at your belt?" He replied, "I have some of the very best Japanese millet dumplings." "Give me one and I will go with you," said the dog. So Momotaro took a dumpling out of his pouch and gave it to the dog. Then a monkey came and got one the same way. A pheasant also came flying and said, "Give me a dumpling too, and I will go along with you." So all three went along with him. In no time they arrived at the island of the devils, and at once broke through the front gate; Momotaro first; then his three followers. Here they met a great multitude of the devils' retainers who showed fight, but they pressed still inwards, and at last encountered the chief of the devils, called Akandoji. Then came the tug of war. Akandoji hit at Momotaro with an iron club, but Momotaro was ready for him, and dodged him adroitly. At last they grappled each other, and without difficulty Momotaro just crushed down Akandoji and tied him with a rope so tightly that he could not even move. All this was done in a fair fight.

After this Akandoji the chief of the devils said he would surrender all his riches. "Out with your riches then," said Momotaro laughing. Having collected and ranged in order a great pile of precious things, Momotaro took them, and set out for his home, rejoicing, as he marched bravely back, that, with the help of his three companions, to whom he attributed all his success, he had been able so easily to accomplish his end.

Great was the joy of the old man and the old woman when Momotaro came back. He feasted everybody bountifully, told many stories of his adventure, displayed his riches, and at last became a leading man, a man of influence, very rich and honorable; a man to be very much congratulated indeed!!

❧ ❧ ❧

URASCHIMA TARO AND THE TURTLE

URASCHIMA Taro, which means in Japanese "Son of the Island," was the only and dearly beloved son of an old fisherman and his wife.

He was a fine, strong youth, who could manage a boat

more cleverly than any one else on the neighboring coast. He often ventured so far out to sea that neighbors warned his parents that he would sometime go too far and never return.

His parents knew, however, that he understood his boat and the sea very well, and they were never much concerned about him. Even when he failed to come back as soon as he was expected, they awaited his return without anxiety. They loved him better than their own lives, and were proud that he was braver and stronger than their neighbors' sons.

Early one morning, Uraschima Taro went to haul in his nets, which had been set the night before. In one of them, among some fishes, he found a small turtle. This he placed in the boat, by itself, where it would safely keep, until he could take it home. To his amazement, the turtle begged for its life in most pitiful tones. "Of what use am I to you?" it asked. "I am too small to eat, and so young that it will take me a long time to grow. Have mercy and put me back into the sea, for I do not want to die." Uraschima Taro had a very kind heart and could not bear to see anything that was small and helpless suffer; so he did as the turtle asked him.

Several years after this, when Uraschima Taro was one day far out at sea, a terrible whirlwind struck his boat and shattered it. He was a good swimmer, and managed for a long time to make progress toward the land; but as he was so far from shore in the rough sea, his strength at last gave out and he felt himself sinking. Just as he had given up hope, and thought that he would never see his dear parents again, he heard his name called and saw a large turtle swimming toward him.

"Climb on my back," shouted the turtle, "and I will carry you to land." When Uraschima Taro was safely sitting on the turtle's back it continued: "I am the turtle whose life you saved when you found me, little and helpless, in your net, and I am glad of this opportunity to show that I am not ungrateful."

Before they reached the shore, the turtle asked Uraschima Taro how he would like to be shown some of the wonderful beauties hidden under the sea. The young fisherman replied that the experience would please him. In a moment they were shooting down through the green water. He clung to the turtle's back, who carried him many, many fathoms below. After three nights they reached the bottom of the sea, and came to a wonderful palace of gold and crystal. Coral and pearls and precious stones dazzled his eyes; but inside, the palace was more beautiful still, and blazing fish scales lighted it.

"This," said the turtle, "is the palace of the sea-god. I am a waiting-maid to his lovely daughter, the Princess."

The turtle went to announce the arrival of Uraschima Taro to the Princess, and soon returning, led him to her presence. She was so beautiful that when she asked him to remain in the palace he gladly consented.

"Do not leave me, and you shall always be as handsome as you are now, and old age cannot come to you," she said.

So it happened that Uraschima Taro lived in the marvelous palace at the bottom of the sea with the daughter of the sea-god. He was so happy that the time passed by unheeded. How long he dwelt there he could not have told. But one day he thought of his parents; then he remembered that they must be troubled by his absence. The thought of them kept coming to him continually, and the longing to see them grew so strong that at last he told the Princess he must go to visit them. She begged him not to leave her and wept bitterly.

"If you go, I shall never see you again," she sobbed.

But he told her that he must see his father and mother once again; then he would return to the palace in the sea, to be with her always. When she found that she could not persuade him to remain, she gave him a small gold box, which, she told him, he must on no account open.

"If you heed my words," said she, "you may come back to me. When you are ready, the turtle will be there to bring you; but if you forget what I have told you, I shall never see you again."

Uraschima Taro fondly assured her that nothing in the world should keep him from her, and bade her farewell. Mounting the turtle's back, he soon left the palace far below. For three days and three nights they swam, and then the turtle left him on the familiar sands near his old home.

A PHEASANT ALSO CAME FLYING AND SAID: "GIVE ME A DUMPLING, TOO, AND I WILL GO ALONG WITH YOU."

He eagerly ran to the village and looked about for some of his comrades. All of the faces were strange, and even the houses seemed different. The children, playing in the street where he had lived, he had never seen before. Stopping in front of his own house, he regarded it with a sinking heart. There was the sound of music from a window above, and a strange woman opened the door to him. She could tell him nothing of his parents, and had never heard their names. Every one whom he questioned looked at him curiously. At last he wandered from the village and came to the burying ground. Searching about among the graves, he soon found himself beside a stone bearing the dear names he sought. The date showed him that his father and mother had died soon after he left them; and then he discovered that he had been away from his home three hundred years. Bowed with sorrow, he went back to the city. At each step he hoped to wake and find it all a dream, but the people and streets were real.

He thought of the Princess, and remembered the gold box she had given to him. It might be that he was under some cruel enchantment, and that this box contained the charm to break the spell. He eagerly raised the cover, and a purple vapor escaped and left the box empty. To his alarm, he noticed that the hand that held it had shriveled and grown suddenly old. Trembling with horror, he ran to a stream of water which ran down from the mountain, and saw reflected in its waters the face of a mummy.

He crawled fearfully back to the village, and no one recognized him as the strong youth who had entered it a few hours before. Nearly exhausted, he finally reached the shore, where he sat wearily on a rock and cried to the turtle. But he called to it in vain; the turtle never came, and soon his quavering voice was hushed in death.

Before he died, the people of the village gathered about him and listened to his strange story. Long afterward they told their children of the young man who, for the love of his parents, left a marvelous palace in the sea, and a Princess more beautiful than the day.

EAST INDIAN STORIES

THE SON OF SEVEN QUEENS

ADAPTED BY JOSEPH JACOBS

Once upon a time there lived a King who had seven Queens, but no children. This was a great grief to him, especially when he remembered that on his death there would be no heir to inherit the kingdom.

Now it happened one day that a poor old fakir came to the King and said, "Your prayers are heard, your desire shall be accomplished, and one of your seven Queens shall bear a son."

The King's delight at this promise knew no bounds, and he gave orders for appropriate festivities to be prepared against the coming event throughout the length and breadth of the land.

Meanwhile the seven Queens lived luxuriously in a splendid palace, attended by hundreds of female slaves, and fed to their hearts' content on sweetmeats and confectionery.

Now the King was very fond of hunting, and one day, before he started, the seven Queens sent him a message saying, "May it please our dearest lord not to hunt toward the north to-day, for we have dreamed bad dreams, and fear lest evil should befall you."

The King, to allay their anxiety, promised regard for their wishes, and set out toward the south; but as luck would have it, although he hunted diligently, he found no game. Nor had he more success to the east or west, so that, being a keen sportsman, and determined not to go home empty-handed, he forgot all about his promise and turned to the north. Here also he was at first unsuccessful, but just as he had made up his mind to give up for that day, a white hind with golden horns and silver hoofs flashed past him into a thicket. So quickly did it pass that he scarcely saw it; nevertheless, a burning desire to capture and possess the beautiful strange creature filled his breast. He instantly ordered his attendants to form a ring round the thicket, and so encircle the hind; then, gradually narrowing the circle, he pressed forward till he could distinctly see the white hind panting in the midst. Nearer and nearer he advanced, till just as he thought to lay hold of the beautiful strange creature, it gave one mighty bound, leaped clean over the King's head, and fled toward the mountains. Forgetful of all else, the King, setting spurs to his horse, followed at full speed. On, on he galloped, leaving his retinue far behind, keeping the white hind in view, never drawing bridle until, finding himself in a narrow ravine with no outlet, he reined in his steed. Before him stood a miserable hovel, into which, being tired after his long, unsuccessful chase, he entered to ask for a drink of water. An old woman, seated in the hut at a spinning-wheel, answered his request by calling to her daughter, and immediately from an inner room came a maiden so lovely and charming, so white-skinned and golden-haired, that the King was transfixed by astonishment at seeing so beautiful a sight in the wretched hovel.

She held the vessel of water to the King's lips, and as he drank he looked into her eyes, and then it became clear to him that the girl was no other than the white hind with the golden horns and silver feet he had chased so far.

Her beauty bewitched him, so he fell on his knees, begging her to return with him as his bride; but she only laughed, saying seven Queens were quite enough even for a King to manage. However, when he would take no refusal, but implored her to have pity on him, promising her everything she could desire, she replied, "Give me the eyes of your seven Queens, and then perhaps I may believe you mean what you say."

The King was so carried away by the glamor of the white hind's magical beauty that he went home at once, had the eyes of his seven Queens taken out, and, after throwing the poor blind creatures into a noisome dungeon whence they could not escape, set off once more for the hovel in the ravine, bearing with him his horrible offering. But the white hind only laughed cruelly when she saw the fourteen eyes, and threading them as a necklace, flung it round her mother's neck, saying, "Wear that, little mother, as a keepsake, while I am away in the King's palace."

Then she went back with the bewitched Monarch, as his bride, and he gave her the seven Queens' rich clothes and jewels to wear, the seven Queens' palace to live in, and the seven Queens' slaves to wait upon her; so that she really had everything even a witch could desire.

Now, very soon after the seven wretched hapless Queens had their eyes torn out, and were cast into prison, a baby was born to the youngest of the Queens. It was a handsome boy, but the other Queens were very jealous that the youngest among them should be so fortunate. But though at first they disliked the handsome little boy, he soon proved so useful to them, that ere long they all looked on him as their son. Almost as soon as he could walk about he began scraping at the mud wall of their dungeon, and in an incredibly short space of time had made a hole big enough for him to crawl through. Through this he disappeared, returning in an hour or so laden with sweetmeats, which he divided equally among the seven blind Queens.

As he grew older he enlarged the hole, and slipped out two or three times every day to play with the little nobles in the town. No one knew who the tiny boy was, but everybody liked him, and he was so full of funny tricks and antics, so merry and bright, that he was sure to be rewarded by some girdle-cakes, a handful of parched grain, or some sweetmeats. All these things he brought home to his seven mothers, as he loved to call the seven blind Queens, who by his help lived on in their dungeon when all the world thought they had starved to death ages before.

At last, when he was quite a big lad, he one day took his bow and arrow, and went out to seek for game. Coming by chance past the palace where the white hind lived in wicked splendor and magnificence, he saw some pigeons fluttering round the white marble turrets, and, taking good aim, shot one dead. It came tumbling past the very window where the white Queen was sitting; she rose to see what was the matter, and looked out. At the first glance of the handsome young lad standing there bow in hand, she knew by witchcraft that it was the King's son.

She nearly died of envy and spite, determining to destroy the lad without delay; therefore, sending a servant to bring him to her presence, she asked him if he would sell her the pigeon he had just shot.

"No," replied the sturdy lad, "the pigeon is for my seven blind mothers, who live in the noisome dungeon, and who would die if I did not bring them food."

"Poor souls!" cried the cunning white witch. "Would you not like to bring them their eyes again? Give me the pigeon, my dear, and I faithfully promise to show you where to find them."

Hearing this, the lad was delighted beyond measure, and gave up the pigeon at once. Whereupon the white Queen told him to seek her mother without delay, and ask for the eyes which she wore as a necklace.

"She will not fail to give them," said the cruel Queen, "if you show her this token on which I have written what I want done."

So saying, she gave the lad a piece of broken potsherd, with these words inscribed on it, "Kill the bearer at once, and sprinkle his blood like water!"

Now, as the son of seven Queens could not read, he took the fatal message cheerfully, and set off to find the white Queen's mother.

While he was journeying he passed through a town where every one of the inhabitants looked so sad that he could not help asking what was the matter. They told him it was because the King's only daughter refused to marry; therefore when her father died there would he no heir to the throne. They greatly feared she must be out of her mind, for though every good-looking young man in the kingdom had been shown to her, she declared she would only marry one who was the son of seven mothers, and who had ever heard of such a thing? The King, in despair, had ordered every man who entered the city gates to be led before the Princess; so, much to the lad's impatience, for he was in an immense hurry to find his mothers' eyes, he was dragged into the presence-chamber.

No sooner did the Princess catch sight of him than she blushed, and, turning to the King, said, "Dear father, this is my choice!"

Never were such rejoicings as these few words produced. The inhabitants nearly went wild with joy, but the son of seven Queens said he would not marry the Princess unless they first let him recover his mothers' eyes. When the beautiful bride heard his story, she asked to see the potsherd, for she was very learned and clever. Seeing the treacherous words, she said nothing, but taking another similar-shaped bit of potsherd, she wrote on it these words, "Take care of this lad, giving him all he desires," and returned it to the son of seven Queens, who, none the wiser, set off on his quest.

Ere long he arrived at the hovel in the ravine where the white witch's mother, a hideous old creature, grumbled dreadfully on reading the message, especially when the lad asked for the necklace of eyes. Nevertheless she took it off and gave it him, saying, "There are only thirteen of 'em now, for I lost one last week."

The lad, however, was only too glad to get any at all, so he hurried home as fast as he could to his seven mothers, and gave two eyes apiece to the six elder Queens; but to the youngest he gave one, saying, "Dearest little mother!—I will be your other eye always!"

After this he set off to marry the Princess, as he had promised, but when passing by the white Queen's palace he saw some pigeons on the roof. Drawing his bow, he shot one, and it came fluttering past the window. The white hind looked out, and lo! there was the King's son alive and well.

She cried with hatred and disgust, but sending for the lad, asked him how he had returned so soon, and when she heard how he had brought home the thirteen eyes, and given them to the seven blind Queens, she could hardly restrain her rage. Nevertheless she pretended to be charmed with his success, and told him that if he would give her this pigeon also, she would reward him with the Jogi's wonderful cow, whose milk flows all day long, and makes a pond as big as a kingdom. The lad, nothing loth, gave her the pigeon; whereupon, as before, she bade him go and ask her mother for the cow, and gave him a potsherd where on was written, "Kill this lad without fail, and sprinkle his blood like water!"

But on the way the son of seven Queens looked in on the Princess, just to tell her how he came to be delayed, and she, after reading the message on the potsherd, gave him another in its stead; so that when the lad reached the old hag's hut and asked her for the Jogi's cow, she could not refuse, but told the boy how to find it; and bidding him of all things not to be afraid of the eighteen thousand demons who kept watch and ward over the treasure, told him to be off before she became too angry at her daughter's foolishness in thus giving away so many good things.

Then the lad bravely did as he had been told. He journeyed on and on till he came to a milk-white pond, guarded by the eighteen thousand demons. They were really frightful to behold, but, plucking up courage, he whistled a tune as he walked through them, looking neither to the right nor the left. By and by he came upon the Jogi's cow, tall, white, and beautiful, while the Jogi himself, who was king of all the demons, sat milking her day and night, and the milk streamed from her udder, filling the milk-white tank.

The Jogi, seeing the lad, called out fiercely, "What do you want here?"

Then the lad answered, according to the old hag's bidding, "I want your skin, for King Indra is making a new kettle-drum, and says your skin is nice and tough."

Upon this the Jogi began to shiver and shake (for no Jinn or Jogi dares disobey King Indra's command), and, falling at the lad's feet, cried, "If you will spare me I will give you anything I possess, even my beautiful white cow!"

To this the son of seven Queens, after a little pretended hesitation, agreed, saying that after all it would not be difficult to find a nice tough skin like the Jogi's elsewhere; so driving the wonderful cow before him, he set off homeward.

The seven Queens were delighted to possess so marvelous an animal, and though they toiled from morning till night making curds and whey, besides selling milk to the confectioners, they could not use half the cow gave, and became richer and richer day by day.

Seeing them so comfortably off, the son of seven Queens started with a light heart to marry the Princess; but when passing the white hind's palace he could not resist sending a bolt at some pigeons that were cooing on the parapet. One fell dead just beneath the window where the white Queen was sitting. Looking out, she saw the lad, hale and hearty, standing before her, and grew whiter than ever with rage and spite.

She sent for him to ask how he had returned so soon, and when she heard how kindly her mother had received him, she very nearly had a fit. However, she dissembled her feelings as well as she could, and, smiling sweetly, said she was glad to have been able to fulfil her promise, and that if he would give her this third pigeon, she would do yet more for him than she had done before, by giving him the millionfold rice, which ripens in one night.

The lad was of course delighted at the very idea, and, giving up the pigeon, set off on his quest, armed as before with a potsherd, on which was written, "Do not fail this time. Kill the lad, and sprinkle his blood like water!"

But when he looked in on his Princess, just to prevent her becoming anxious about him, she asked to see the potsherd as usual, and substituted another, on which was written, "Yet again give this lad all he requires, for his blood shall be as your blood!"

Now when the old hag saw this, and heard how the lad wanted the millionfold rice which ripens in a single night, she fell into the most furious rage, but being terribly afraid of her daughter, she controlled herself, and bade the boy go and find the field guarded by eighteen millions of demons, warning him on no account to look back after having plucked the tallest spike of rice, which grew in the center.

So the son of seven Queens set off, and soon came to the field where, guarded by eighteen millions of demons, the millionfold rice grew. He walked on bravely, looking neither to the right nor left, till he reached the center and plucked the tallest ear, but as he turned homeward a thousand sweet voices rose behind him, crying in tenderest accents, "Pluck me too! oh, please pluck me too!" He looked back, and lo! there was nothing left of him but a little heap of ashes!

Now as time passed by and the lad did not return, the old hag grew uneasy, remembering the message "His blood shall be as your blood"; so she set off to see what had happened.

Soon she came to the heap of ashes, and knowing by her arts what it was, she took a little water, and kneading the ashes into a paste, formed it into the likeness of a man; then, putting a drop of blood from her little finger into its mouth, she blew on it, and instantly the son of seven Queens started up as well as ever.

"Don't you disobey orders again!" grumbled the old hag, "or next time I'll leave you alone. Now be off, before I repent of my kindness!"

So the son of seven Queens returned joyfully to his seven mothers, who, by the aid of the millionfold rice, soon became the richest people in the kingdom. Then they celebrated their son's marriage to the clever Princess with all imaginable pomp; but the bride was so clever, she would not rest until she had made known her husband to his father, and punished the wicked white witch. So she made her husband build a palace exactly like the one in which the seven Queens had lived, and in which the white witch now dwelt in splendor. Then, when all was prepared, she bade her husband give a grand feast to the King. Now the King had heard much of the mysterious son of seven queens, and his marvelous wealth, so he gladly accepted the invitation; but what was his astonishment when on entering the palace he found it was a facsimile of his own in every particular! And when his host, richly attired, led him straight to the private hall, where on royal thrones sat the seven Queens, dressed as he had last seen them, he was speechless with surprise, until the Princess, coming forward, threw herself at his feet and told him the whole story. Then the King awoke from his enchantment, and his anger rose against the wicked white hind who had bewitched him so long, until he could not contain himself. So she was put to death, and her grave plowed over, and after that the seven Queens returned to their own splendid palace, and everybody lived happily.

☙ ☙ ☙

WHO KILLED THE OTTER'S BABIES

ADAPTED BY WALTER SKEAT

THE Otter said to the Mouse-deer, "Friend Mouse-deer, will you be so good as to take charge of the children till I come back? I am going down to the river to catch fish, and when I come back, I'll share the catch with you." The Mouse-deer replied, "Very well! go along, and I'll look after the children." So the Otter went down to the river to catch fish.

(Here the story of What the Otter Did stops and the story of What Happened when the Woodpecker Sounded the War-gong commences.) The Mouse-deer was Chief Dancer of the War-dance, and as he danced he trod on the Otter's babies and crushed them flat. Presently the Otter returned home, bringing a string of fish with him. On arriving he saw that his children had been killed, and exclaimed, "How comes it, Friend Mouse-deer, that my babies have died?" The Mouse-deer replied: "The Woodpecker came and sounded the war-gong, and I, being Chief War-Dancer, danced; and, forgetting about your children, I trod upon them and crushed them flat."

On hearing this the Otter went and made complaint unto King Solomon, prostrating himself and saying: "Your Majesty's most humble slave craves pardon for presuming to address your Majesty, but Friend Mouse-deer has murdered your slave's children, and your slave desires to learn whether he is guilty or not according to the Law of the Land." King Solomon replied, saying, "If the Mouse-deer hath done this thing wittingly, assuredly he is guilty of death." Then he summoned the Mouse-deer before him.

And when the Mouse-deer came into the presence of the King, the King inquired of the Otter, "What is your charge against him?" The Otter replied, "Your slave accuses him of the murder of your slave's children; your slave would hear the Law of the Land." Then the King said unto the Mouse-deer, "Was it your doing that the Otter's children were killed?" The Mouse-deer replied, "Assuredly it was, but I crave pardon for doing so." "How was it, then," said the King, "that you came to kill them?" The Mouse-deer replied, "Your slave came to kill them because the Woodpecker appeared and sounded the War-gong. Your slave, as your Majesty is aware, is Chief Dancer of the War-dance; therefore your slave danced, and, forgetting about the Otter's children, your slave trod upon them and crushed them flat." Here the King sent for the Woodpecker also, and the Woodpecker came before him. "Was it you, Woodpecker," said the King, "who sounded the war-gong?" "Assuredly it was," said the Woodpecker,—"forasmuch as your slave saw the Great Lizard wearing his sword." The King replied, "If that is the case, there is no fault to be found in the Woodpecker" (for the Woodpecker was Chief Beater of the War-gong). Then the King commanded the Great Lizard to be summoned, and when he arrived, the King inquired, "Was it you, Lizard, wearing your sword?" The Great Lizard replied, "Assuredly it was, your Majesty." "And why were you wearing your sword?" The Great Lizard replied, "Your slave wore it forasmuch as your slave saw that the Tortoise had donned his coat of mail." So the Tortoise was summoned likewise. "Why did you, Tortoise, don your coat of mail?" The Tortoise replied, "Your slave donned it forasmuch as your slave saw the King-crab trailing his three-edged pike." Then the King-crab was sent for. "Why were you, King-crab, trailing your three-edged pike?" "Because your slave saw that the Crayfish had shouldered his lance." Then the King sent for the Crayfish, and said, "Was it you, Crayfish, who was shouldering your lance?" And the Crayfish replied, "Assuredly it was, your Majesty." "And why did you shoulder it?" "Because your slave saw the Otter coming down to devour your slave's own children." "Oh," said King Solomon, "if that is the case, you, Otter are the guilty party, and your complaint of your children's death cannot be sustained against the Mouse-deer by the Law of the Land."

❧ ❧ ❧

THE ALLIGATOR AND THE JACKAL

ADAPTED BY M. FRERE

A HUNGRY Jackal once went down to the riverside in search of little crabs, bits of fish, and whatever else he could find for his dinner. Now it chanced that in this river there lived a great big Alligator, who, being also very hungry, would have been extremely glad to eat the Jackal.

The Jackal ran up and down, here and there, but for a long time could find nothing to eat. At last, close to where the Alligator was lying among some tall bulrushes under the clear, shallow water, he saw a little crab sidling along as fast as his legs could carry him. The Jackal was so hungry that when he saw this he poked his paw into the water to try to catch the crab, when snap! the old Alligator caught hold of him. "Oh, dear!" thought the Jackal to himself, "what can I do? This great, big Alligator has caught my paw in his mouth, and in another minute he will drag me down by it under the water and kill me. My only chance is to make him think he has made a mistake." So he called out in a cheerful voice: "Clever Alligator, clever Alligator, to catch hold of a bulrush root instead of my paw! I hope you find it very tender." The Alligator, who was so buried among the bulrushes that he could hardly see, thought, on hearing this: "Dear me, how tiresome! I fancied I had caught hold of the Jackal's paw; but there he is, calling out in a cheerful voice. I suppose I must have seized a bulrush root instead, as he says," and he let the Jackal go.

The Jackal ran away as fast as he could, crying, "O wise Alligator, wise Alligator! So you let me go again!"

Then the Alligator was very much vexed, but the Jackal had run away too far to be caught. Next day the Jackal returned to the riverside to get his dinner as before; but because he was very much afraid of the Alligator he called out: "Whenever I go to look for my dinner, I see the nice little crabs peeping up through the mud; then I catch them and eat them. I wish I could see one now."

The Alligator, who was buried in the mud at the bottom of the river, heard every word. So he popped the little point of his snout above it, thinking: "If I do but just show the tip of my nose, the Jackal will take me for a crab and put in his paw to catch me, and as soon as ever he does I'll gobble him up."

But no sooner did the Jackal see the little tip of the Alligator's nose than he called out, "Aha, my friend! there you are. No dinner for me in this part of the river, then, I think." And so saying, he ran farther on and fished for his dinner a long way from that place. The Alligator was very angry at missing his prey a second time, and determined not to let him escape again.

So on the following day, when his little tormentor returned to the waterside, the Alligator hid himself close to the bank, in order to catch him if he could. Now the Jackal was rather afraid of going near the river, for he thought, "Perhaps the Alligator will catch me to-day." But yet, being hungry, he did not wish to go without his dinner; so to make all as safe as he could, he cried: "Where are all the little crabs gone? There is not one here and I am so hungry; and generally, even when they are under water, one can see them going bubble, bubble, bubble, and all the little bubbles go pop! pop! pop!" On hearing this the Alligator, who was buried in the mud under the river bank, thought: "I will pretend to be a little crab." And he began to blow, "Puff, puff, puff! Bubble, bubble, bubble!" and all the great bubbles rushed to the surface of the river and burst there, and the waters eddied round and round like a whirlpool; and there was such a commotion when the huge monster began to blow bubbles in this way that the Jackal saw very well who must be there, and he ran away as fast as he could, saying, "Thank you, kind Alligator, thank you; thank you! Indeed, I would not have come here had I known you were so close."

This enraged the Alligator extremely; it made him quite cross to think of being so often deceived by a little Jackal, and he said to himself, "I will be taken in no more. Next time I will be very cunning." So for a long time he waited and waited for the Jackal to return to the riverside; but the Jackal did not come, for he had thought to himself: "If matters go on in this way, I shall some day be caught and eaten by the wicked old Alligator. I had better content myself with living on wild figs," and he went no more near the river, but stayed in the jungles and ate wild figs, and roots which he dug up with his paws.

When the Alligator found this out, he determined to try and catch the Jackal on land; so, going under the largest of the wild fig-trees, where the ground was covered with the fallen fruit, he collected a quantity of it together, and, burying himself under the great heap, waited for the Jackal to appear. But no sooner did the cunning little animal see this great heap of wild figs all collected together than he thought, "That looks very like my friend the Alligator." And to discover if it were so or not, he called out: "The juicy little wild figs I love to eat always tumble down from the tree, and roll here and there as the wind drives them; but this great heap of figs is quite still; these cannot be good figs; I will not eat any of them." "Ho, ho!" thought the Alligator, "is that all? How suspicious this Jackal is! I will make the figs roll about a little, then, and when he sees that, he will doubtless come and eat them."

So the great beast shook himself, and all the heap of little figs went roll, roll, roll—some a mile this way, some a mile that, farther than they had ever rolled before or than the most blustering wind could have driven them.

Seeing this, the Jackal scampered away, saying: "I am so much obliged to you, Alligator, for letting me know you are there, for indeed I should hardly have guessed it. You were so buried under that heap of figs." The Alligator, hearing this, was so angry that he ran after the Jackal, but the latter ran very, very fast away, too quickly to be caught.

Then the Alligator said to himself: "I will not allow that little wretch to make fun of me another time and then run away out of reach; I will show him that I can be more cunning than he fancies." And early the next morning he crawled as fast as he could to the Jackal's den (which was a hole in the side of a hill) and crept into it, and hid himself, waiting for the Jackal, who was out, to return home. But when the Jackal got near the place, he looked about him and thought: "Dear me! the ground looks as if some heavy creature had been walking over it, and here are great clods of earth knocked down from each side of the door of my den, as if a very big animal had been trying to squeeze himself through it. I certainly will not go inside until I know that all is safe there." So he called out: "Little house, pretty house, my sweet little house, why do you not give an answer when I call? If I come, and all is safe and right, you always call out to me. Is anything wrong, that you do not speak?"

Then the Alligator, who was inside, thought, "If that is the case I had better call out, that he may fancy all is right in his house." And in as gentle a voice as he could, he said, "Sweet little Jackal."

At hearing these words the Jackal felt quite frightened, and thought to himself: "So the dreadful old Alligator is there. I must try to kill him if I can, for if I do not he will certainly catch and kill me some day." He therefore answered: "Thank you, my dear little house. I like to hear your pretty voice. I am coming in in a minute, but first I must collect firewood to cook my dinner." And he ran as fast as he could, and dragged all the dry branches and bits of stick he could find close up to the mouth of the den. Meantime, the Alligator inside kept as quiet as a mouse, but he could not help laughing a little to himself as he thought: "So I have deceived this tiresome little Jackal at last. In a few minutes he will run in here, and then won't I snap him up!"

When the Jackal had gathered together all the sticks he could find and put them round the mouth of his den, he set them on fire and pushed them as far into it as possible. There was such a quantity of them that they soon blazed up into a great fire, and the smoke and flames filled the den and smothered the wicked old Alligator and burned him to death, while the little Jackal ran up and down outside dancing for joy and singing:

"How do you like my house, my friend? Is it nice and warm? Ding-dong! ding-dong! The Alligator is dying! ding-dong, ding-dong! He will trouble me no more. I have defeated my enemy! Ring-a-ting! ding-a-ting! ding-ding-dong!"

❧ ❧ ❧

THE FARMER AND THE MONEY-LENDER

THERE was once a Farmer who suffered much at the hands of a Money-lender. Good harvests or bad the Farmer was always poor, the Money-lender rich. At the last, when he hadn't a farthing left, the Farmer went to the Money-lender's house and said, "You can't squeeze water from a stone, and, as you have nothing to get by me now, you might tell me the secret of becoming rich."

"My friend," returned the Money-lender piously, "riches come from Ram—ask *him*."

"Thank you, I will!" replied the simple Farmer; so he prepared three girdle-cakes to last him on the journey, and set out to find Ram.

First he met a Brahman, and to him he gave a cake, asking him to point out the road to Ram; but the Brahman only took the cake, and went on his way without a word. Next the Farmer met a yogi, or devotee, and to him he gave a cake, without receiving any help in return. At last he came upon a poor man sitting under a tree, and finding out he was hungry the kindly Farmer gave him his last cake, and, sitting down to rest beside him, entered into conversation.

"And where are you going?" asked the poor man, at length.

"Oh, I have a long journey before me, for I am going to

find Ram!" replied the Farmer. "I don't suppose you could tell me which way to go?"

"Perhaps I can," said the poor man, smiling, "for *I* am Ram! What do you want of me?"

Then the Farmer told the whole story, and Ram, taking pity on him, gave him a conch-shell, and showed him how to blow it in a particular way, saying: "Remember! whatever you wish for, you have only to blow the conch that way, and your wish will be fulfilled. Only, have a care of that Money-lender, for even magic is not proof against his wiles!"

The Farmer went back to his village rejoicing. In fact, the Money-lender noticed his high spirits at once, and said to himself, "Some good fortune must have befallen the stupid fellow, to make him hold his head so jauntily." Therefore he went over to the simple Farmer's house, and congratulated him on his good fortune in such cunning words, pretending to have heard all about it, that before long the Farmer found himself telling the whole story—all except the secret of blowing the conch, for, with all his simplicity, the Farmer was not quite such a fool as to tell that.

Nevertheless, the Money-lender determined to have the conch by hook or by crook, and, as he was villain enough not to stick at trifles, he waited for a favorable opportunity and stole the conch.

But, after nearly bursting himself with blowing the conch in every conceivable way, he was obliged to give up the secret as a bad job. However, being determined to succeed, he went back to the Farmer, and said coolly: "Look here! I've got your conch, but I can't use it; you haven't got it, so it's clear you can't use it either. Business is at a standstill unless we make a bargain. Now, I promise to give you back your conch, and never to interfere with your using it, on one condition, which is this—whatever you get from it, I am to get double."

"Never!" cried the Farmer; "that would be the old business all over again!"

"Not at all!" replied the wily Money-lender; "you will have your share! Now, don't be a dog in the manger, for, if *you* get all you want, what can it matter to you if *I* am rich or poor?"

At last, though it went sorely against the grain to be of any benefit to a Money-lender, the Farmer was forced to yield, and from that time, no matter what he gained by the power of the conch, the Money-lender gained double. And the knowledge that this was so, preyed upon the Farmer's mind day and night, so that he had no satisfaction out of anything.

At last there came a very dry season—so dry that the Farmer's crops withered for want of rain. Then he blew his conch, and wished for a well to water them, and lo! there was the well, *but the Money-lender had two*!—two beautiful new wells! This was too much for any Farmer to stand; and our friend brooded over it, and brooded over it, till at last a bright idea came into his head. He seized the conch, blew it loudly, and cried out, "Oh, Ram! I wish to be blind of one eye!" And so he was, in a twinkling, but the Money-lender, of course, was blind of both, and in trying to steer his way between the two new wells he fell into one, and was drowned.

Now, this true story shows that a Farmer once got the better of a Money-lender—but only by losing one of his eyes.

☙ ☙ ☙

TIT FOR TAT

ADAPTED BY M. FRERE

THERE once lived a Camel and a Jackal who were great friends. One day the Jackal said to the Camel, "I know that there is a fine field of sugarcane on the other side of the river. If you will take me across, I'll show you the place. This plan will suit me as well as you. You will enjoy eating the sugarcane, and I am sure to find many crabs' bones and bits of fish by the riverside, on which to make a good dinner."

The Camel consented, and swam across the river, taking the Jackal, who could not swim, on his back. When they reached the other side, the Camel went to eating the sugarcane, and the Jackal ran up and down the river bank, devouring all the crabs, bits of fish, and bones he could find.

But being a much smaller animal, he had made an excellent meal before the Camel had eaten more than two or three mouthfuls; and no sooner had he finished his dinner than he ran round and round the sugarcane field, yelping and howling with all his might.

The villagers heard him, and thought, "There is a jackal among the sugarcanes; he will be scratching holes in the ground and spoiling the roots of the plants." And they all went down to the place to drive him away. But when they got there they found to their surprise not only a Jackal, but a Camel who was eating the sugarcanes! This made them very angry, and they caught the poor Camel and drove him from the field and beat him and beat him until he was nearly dead.

When they had gone, the Jackal said to the Camel, "We had better go home." And the Camel said, "Very well; then jump upon my back, as you did before."

So the Jackal jumped upon the Camel's back, and the Camel began to recross the river. When they had got well into the water, the Camel said: "This is a pretty way in which you have treated me, friend Jackal. No sooner had you finished your own dinner than you must go yelping about the place loud enough to arouse the whole village, and bring all the villagers down to beat me black and blue, and turn me out of the field before I had eaten two mouthfuls! What in the world did you make such a noise for?"

"I don't know," said the Jackal. "It is a custom I have. I always like to sing a little after dinner."

The Camel waded on through the river. The water reached up to his knees—then above them—up, up, up, higher and higher, until he was obliged to swim. Then turning to the Jackal, he said, "I feel very anxious to roll." "Oh, pray don't; why do you wish to do so?" asked the Jackal. "I don't know," answered the Camel. "It is a custom I have. I always like to have a little roll after dinner." So saying, he rolled over in the water, shaking the Jackal off as he did so. And the Jackal was drowned, but the Camel swam safely ashore.

SINGH RAJAH AND THE CUNNING LITTLE JACKALS

ADAPTED BY M. FRERE

ONCE upon a time, in a great jungle, there lived a great lion. He was rajah of all the country round, and every day he used to leave his den, in the deepest shadow of the rocks, and roar with a loud, angry voice; and when he roared, the other animals in the jungle, who were all his subjects, got very much frightened and ran here and there; and Singh Rajah would pounce upon them and kill them, and gobble them up for his dinner.

This went on for a long, long time until, at last, there were no living creatures left in the jungle but two little jackals—a Rajah Jackal and a Ranee Jackal—husband and wife.

A very hard time of it the poor little jackals had, running this way and that to escape the terrible Singh Rajah; and every day the little Ranee Jackal would say to her husband: "I am afraid he will catch us to-day; do you hear how he is roaring? Oh, dear! oh, dear!" And he would answer her: "Never fear; I will take care of you. Let us run on a mile or two. Come; come quick, quick, quick!" And they would both run away as fast as they could.

After some time spent in this way, they found, however, one fine day, that the lion was so close upon them that they could not escape. Then the little Ranee Jackal said: "Husband, husband, I feel much frightened. The Singh Rajah is so angry he will certainly kill us at once. What can we do?" But he answered: "Cheer up; we can save ourselves yet. Come, and I'll show you how we may manage it."

So what did these cunning little jackals do but they went to the great lion's den; and, when he saw them coming, he began to roar and shake his mane, and he said: "You little wretches, come and be eaten at once! I have had no dinner for three whole days, and all that time I have been running over hill and dale to find you. Ro-a-ar! Ro-a-ar! Come and be eaten, I say!" and he lashed his tail and gnashed his teeth, and looked very terrible indeed. Then the Jackal Rajah, creeping quite close up to him, said: "Oh, great Singh Rajah, we all know you are our master, and we would have come at your bidding long ago; but, indeed, sir, there is a much bigger rajah even than you in this jungle, and he tried to catch hold of us and eat us up, and frightened us so much that we were obliged to run away."

"What do you mean?" growled Singh Rajah. "There is no king in this jungle but me!" "Ah, sire," answered the jackal, "in truth one would think so, for you are very dreadful. Your very voice is death. But it is as we say, for we, with our own eyes, have seen one with whom you could not compete—whose equal you can no more be than we are yours—whose face is as flaming fire, his step as thunder, and his power supreme." "It is impossible!" interrupted the old lion; "but show me this rajah of whom you speak so much, that I may destroy him instantly!"

Then the little jackals ran on before him until they reached a great well, and, pointing down to his own reflection in the water, they said, "See, sire, there lives the terrible king of whom we spoke." When Singh Rajah looked down the well he became very angry, for he thought he saw another lion there. He roared and shook his great mane, and the shadow lion shook his and looked terribly defiant. At last, beside himself with rage at the violence of his opponent, Singh Rajah sprang down to kill him at once, but no other lion was there—only the treacherous reflection—and the sides of the well were so steep that he could not get out again to punish the two jackals, who peeped over the top. After struggling for some time in the deep water, he sank to rise no more. And the little jackals threw stones down upon him from above, and danced round and round the well, singing: "Ao! Ao! Ao! Ao! The king of the forest is dead, is dead! We have killed the great lion who would have killed us! Ao! Ao! Ao! Ao! Ring-a-ting—ding-a-ting! Ring-a-ting—ding-a-ting! Ao! Ao! Ao!"

AMERICAN INDIAN STORIES

THE WHITE STONE CANOE

ADAPTED BY H. R. SCHOOLCRAFT

THERE was once a very beautiful Indian maiden, who died suddenly on the day she was to have been married to a handsome young warrior. He was also brave, but his heart was not proof against this loss. From the hour she was buried, there was no more joy or peace for him.

He went often to visit the spot where the women had buried her, and sat musing there, when, it was thought by some of his friends, he would have done better to try to amuse himself in the chase, or by diverting his thoughts in the warpath. But war and hunting had both lost their charms for him. His heart was already dead within him. He pushed aside both his war-club and his bow and arrows.

He had heard the old people say, that there was a path that led to the land of souls, and he determined to follow it. He accordingly set out, one morning, after having completed his preparations for the journey. At first he hardly knew which way to go. He was only guided by the tradition that he must go south. For a while he could see no change in the face of the country. Forests, and hills, and valleys, and streams had the same looks which they wore in his native place.

There was snow on the ground when he set out, and it was sometimes seen to be piled and matted on the thick trees and bushes. At length it began to diminish, and finally disappeared. The forest assumed a more cheerful appearance, the leaves put forth their buds, and before he was aware of the completeness of the change, he found himself surrounded by spring.

He had left behind him the land of snow and ice. The air

became mild, the dark clouds of winter had rolled away from the sky; a pure field of blue was above him, and as he went he saw flowers beside his path, and heard the songs of birds. By these signs he knew that he was going the right way, for they agreed with the traditions of his tribe. At length he spied a path. It led him through a grove, then up a long and elevated ridge, on the very top of which he came to a lodge. At the door stood an old man, with white hair, whose eyes, though deeply sunk, had a fiery brilliancy. He had a long robe of skins thrown loosely around his shoulders, and a staff in his hands.

The young Chippewayan began to tell his story; but the venerable chief arrested him before he had proceeded to speak ten words. "I have expected you," he replied, "and had just risen to bid you welcome to my abode. She whom you seek passed here but a few days since, and being fatigued with her journey, rested herself here. Enter my lodge and be seated, and I will then satisfy your inquiries, and give you directions for your journey from this point." Having done this, they both issued forth to the lodge door.

"You see yonder gulf," said he, "and the wide-stretching blue plains beyond. It is the land of souls. You stand upon its borders, and my lodge is the gate of entrance. But you can not take your body along. Leave it here with your bow and arrows, your bundle, and your dog. You will find them safe on your return." So saying, he re-entered the lodge, and the freed traveler bounded forward as if his feet had suddenly been endowed with the power of wings.

But all things retained their natural colors and shapes. The woods and leaves, and streams and lakes, were only more bright and comely than he had ever witnessed. Animals bounded across his path, with a freedom and a confidence which seemed to tell him there was no blood shed here. Birds of beautiful plumage inhabited the groves, and sported in the waters. There was but one thing in which he saw a very unusual effect. He noticed that his passage was not stopped by trees or other objects. He appeared to walk directly through them. They were, in fact, but the souls or shadows of material trees. He became sensible that he was in a land of shadows.

When he had traveled half a day's journey, through a country which was continually becoming more attractive, he came to the banks of a broad lake, in the center of which was a large and beautiful island. He found a canoe of shining white stone, tied to the shore. He was now sure that he had taken the right path, for the aged man had told him this. There were also shining paddles. He immediately entered the canoe, and took the paddles in his hands, when, to his joy and surprise, on turning round he beheld the object of his search in another canoe, exactly its counterpart in everything. She had exactly imitated his motions, and they were side by side.

They at once pushed out from shore and began to cross the lake. Its waves seemed to be rising, and at a distance looked ready to swallow them up; but just as they entered the whitened edge of them they seemed to melt away, as if they were but the images of waves. But no sooner was one wreath of foam passed, than another, more threatening still, arose.

Thus they were in perpetual fear; and what added to it, was the *clearness of the water*, through which they could see heaps of beings who had perished before, and whose bones lay strewed on the bottom of the lake. The Master of Life had, however, decreed to let them pass, for the actions of neither of them had been bad. But they saw many others struggling and sinking in the waves. Old and young of all ages and ranks, were there: some passed and some sank. It was only the little children whose canoes seemed to meet no waves.

At length every difficulty was gone, as in a moment, and they both leaped out on the happy island. They felt that the very air was food. It strengthened and nourished them. They wandered together over the blissful fields, where every thing was formed to please the eye and the ear. There were no tempests—there was no ice, no chilly winds—no one shivered for the want of warm clothes: no one suffered hunger—no one mourned for the dead. They saw no graves. They heard of no wars. There was no hunting of animals; for the air itself was their food. Gladly would the young warrior have remained there forever, but he was obliged to go back for his body. He did not see the Master of Life, but he heard his voice in a soft breeze.

"Go back," said this voice, "to the land from whence you came. Your time has not yet come. The duties for which I made you, and which you are to perform, are not yet finished. Return to your people, and accomplish the duties of a good man. You will be the ruler of your tribe for many days. The rules you must observe will be told you by my messenger, who keeps the gate. When he surrenders back your body, he will tell you what to do. Listen to him and you shall afterward rejoin the spirit, which you must now leave behind. She is accepted and will be ever here, as young and as happy as she was when I first called her from the land of snows." When this voice ceased, the narrator awoke. It was all the fabric of a dream, and he was still in the bitter land of snows, and hunger, and tears.

THE MAIDEN WHO LOVED A FISH

THERE was once among the Marshpees, a small tribe who have their hunting-grounds on the shores of the Great Lake, near the Cape of Storms, a woman whose name was Awashanks. She was rather silly and very idle. For days together she would sit doing nothing. Then she was so ugly and ill-shaped that not one of the youths of the village would have aught to say to her by way of courtship or marriage. She squinted very much; her face was long and thin, her nose excessively large and humped, her teeth crooked and projecting, her chin almost as sharp as the bill of a loon, and her ears as large as those of a deer. Altogether she was a very odd and strangely formed woman, and wherever she went she never failed to excite much laughter and derision among those who thought that ugliness and deformity were fit subjects for ridicule.

Though so very ugly, there was one faculty she possessed

in a more remarkable degree than any woman of the tribe. It was that of singing. Nothing, unless such could be found in the land of spirits, could equal the sweetness of her voice or the beauty of her songs. Her favorite place of resort was a small hill, a little removed from the river of her people, and there, seated beneath the shady trees, she would while away the hours of summer with her charming songs. So beautiful and melodious were the things she uttered that, by the time she had sung a single sentence, the branches above her head would be filled with the birds that came thither to listen, the thickets around her would be crowded with beasts, and the waters rolling beside her would be alive with fishes, all attracted by the sweet sounds. From the minnow to the porpoise, from the wren to the eagle, from the snail to the lobster, from the mouse to the mole—all hastened to the spot to listen to the charming songs of the hideous Marshpee maiden.

Among the fishes which repaired every night to the vicinity of the Little Hillock, which was the chosen resting-place of the ugly songstress, was the great chief of the trouts, a tribe of fish inhabiting the river near by. The chief was of a far greater size than the people of his nation usually are, being as long as a man and quite as broad.

Of all the creatures which came to listen to the singing of Awashanks none appeared to enjoy it so highly as the chief of the trouts. As his bulk prevented him from approaching so near as he wished, he, from time to time, in his eagerness to enjoy the music to the best advantage, ran his nose into the ground, and thus worked his way a considerable distance into the land. Nightly he continued his exertions to approach the source of the delightful sounds he heard, till at length he had plowed out a wide and handsome channel, and so effected his passage from the river to the hill, a distance extending an arrow's-flight. Thither he repaired every night at the commencement of darkness, sure to meet the maiden who had become so necessary to his happiness. Soon he began to speak of the pleasure he enjoyed, and to fill the ears of Awashanks with fond protestations of his love and affection. Instead of singing to him, she now began to listen to his voice. It was something so new and strange to her to hear the tones of love and courtship, a thing so unusual to be told she was beautiful, that it is not wonderful her head was turned by the new incident, and that she began to think the voice of her lover the sweetest she had ever heard. One thing marred their happiness. This was that the trout could not live upon land, nor the maiden in the water. This state of things gave them much sorrow.

They had met one evening at the usual place, and were discoursing together, lamenting that two who loved each other so, should be doomed always to live apart, when a man appeared close to Awashanks. He asked the lovers why they seemed to be so sad.

The chief of the trouts told the stranger the cause of their sorrow.

"Be not grieved nor hopeless," said the stranger, when the chief had finished. "The impediments can be removed. I am the spirit who presides over fishes, and though I cannot make a man or woman of a fish, I can make them into fish. Under my power Awashanks shall become a beautiful trout.

With that he bade the girl follow him into the river. When they had waded in some little depth he took up some water in his hand and poured it on her head, muttering some words, of which none but himself knew the meaning. Immediately a change took place in her. Her body took the form of a fish, and in a few moments she was a complete trout. Having accomplished this transformation the spirit gave her to the chief of the trouts, and the pair glided off into the deep and quiet waters. She did not, however, forget the land of her birth. Every season, on the same night as that upon which her disappearance from her tribe had been wrought, there were to be seen two trouts of enormous size playing in the water off the shore. They continued their visits till the pale-faces came to the country, when, deeming themselves to be in danger from a people who paid no reverence to the spirits of the land, they bade it adieu forever.

THE STAR WIFE

IN the days when the buffalo raced and thundered over the earth and the stars danced and sang in the sky, a brave young hunter lived on the bank of Battle River. He was fond of the red flowers and the blue sky; and when the rest of the Indians went out to hunt in waistcloths of skin he put on his fringed leggings all heavy with blue beads, and painted red rings and stripes on his face, till he was as gay as the earth and the sky himself. High-feather was his name, and he always wore a red swan's feather on his head.

One day, when High-feather was out with his bow and arrows, he came on a little beaten trail that he had never seen before, and he followed it—but he found that it went round and round and brought him back to where he had started. It came from nowhere, and it went to nowhere.

"What sort of animal has made this?" he said. And he lay down in the middle of the ring to think, looking up into the blue sky.

While he lay thinking, he saw a little speck up above him in the sky, and thought it was an eagle. But the speck grew bigger, and sank down and down, till he saw it was a great basket coming down out of the sky. He jumped up and ran back to a little hollow and lay down to hide in a patch of tall red flowers. Then he peeped out and saw the basket come down to the earth and rest on the grass in the middle of the ring. Twelve beautiful maidens were leaning over the edge of the basket. They were not Indian maidens, for their faces were pink and white, and their long hair was bright red-brown like a fox's fur, and their clothes were sky-blue and floating light as cobwebs.

The maidens jumped out of the basket and began to dance round and round the ring-trail, one behind the other, drumming with their fingers on little drums of eagle-skin, and singing such beautiful songs as High-feather had never heard.

Then High-feather jumped up and ran towards the ring, crying out, "Let me dance and sing with you!"

The maidens were frightened, and ran to the basket and jumped in, and the basket flew up into the sky, and grew smaller till at last he could not see it at all.

The young man went home to his wigwam, and his mother roasted buffalo meat for his dinner; but he could not eat, and he could not think of anything but the twelve beautiful maidens. His mother begged him to tell her what the matter was; and at last he told her, and said he would never be happy till he brought one of the maidens home to be his wife.

"Those must be the Star-people," said his mother, who was a great magician—the prairie was full of magic in those days, before the white man came and the buffalo went. "You had better take an Indian girl for your wife. Don't think any more of the Star-maidens, or you will have much trouble."

"I care little how much trouble I have, so long as I get a Star-maiden for my wife," he said; "and I am going to get one, if I have to wait till the world ends."

"If you must, you must," said his mother.

So next morning she sewed a bit of gopher's fur on to his feather; and he ate a good breakfast of buffalo meat and tramped away over the prairie to the dancing ring. As soon as he came into the ring he turned into a gopher; but there were no gophers' holes there for him to hide in, so he had to lie in the grass and wait.

Presently he saw a speck up in the sky, and the speck grew larger and larger till it became a basket, and the basket came down and down till it rested on the earth in the middle of the ring.

The eldest maiden put her head over the edge and looked all around, north and east and south and west.

"There is no man here," she said. So they all jumped out to have their dance. But before they came to the beaten ring the youngest maiden spied the gopher, and called out to her sisters to look at it.

"Away! away!" cried the eldest maiden. "No gopher would dare to come on our dancing ground. It is a conjuror in disguise!"

So she took her youngest sister by the arm and pulled her away to the basket, and they all jumped in and the basket went sailing up into the sky before High-feather could get out of his gopher skin or say a word.

The young man went home very miserable; but when his mother heard what had happened she said: "It is a hard thing you want to do; but if you must, you must. To-night I will make some fresh magic, and you can try again to-morrow."

Next morning High-feather asked for his breakfast; but his mother said, "You must not have any buffalo meat, or it will spoil the magic. You must not eat anything but the wild strawberries you find on the prairie as you go."

Then she sewed a little bit of a mouse's whisker on to his red feather; and he tramped away across the prairie, picking wild strawberries and eating them as he went, till he came to the dancing ring. As soon as he was inside the ring he turned into a little mouse, and made friends with the family of mice that lived in a hole under the grass; and the mother mouse promised to help him all she could.

They had not waited long when the basket came dropping down out of the sky. The eldest sister put her head over the edge, and looked all around, north and west and south and east and down on the ground.

"There is no man here," she said, "and I do not see any gopher; but you must be very careful."

So they all got out of the basket, and began to dance round the ring, drumming and singing as they went. But when they came near the mouse's nest the eldest sister held up her hand, and they stopped dancing and held their breath. Then she tapped on the ground and listened.

"It does not sound so hollow as it did," she said, "The mice have a visitor."

And she tapped again, and called out, "Come and show yourselves, you little traitors, or we will dig you up!"

But the mother mouse had made another door to her nest, just outside the ring, working very fast with all her toes; and while the maidens were looking for her inside the ring she came out at the other door with all her children and scampered away across the prairie.

The maidens turned round and ran after them; all but

the youngest sister, who did not want any one to be killed; and High-feather came out of the hole and turned himself into what he was, and caught her by the arm.

"Come home and marry me," he said, "and dance with the Indian maidens; and I will hunt for you, and my mother will cook for you, and you will be much happier than up in the sky."

Her sisters came rushing round her, and begged her to go back home to the sky with them; but she looked into the young man's eyes, and said she would go with him wherever he went. So the other maidens went weeping and wailing up into the sky, and High-feather took his Star-wife home to his tent on the bank of the Battle River.

High-feather's mother was glad to see them both; but she whispered in his ear: "You must never let her out of your sight if you want to keep her; you must take her with you everywhere you go."

And he did so. He took her with him every time he went hunting, and he made her a bow and arrows, but she would never use them; she would pick wild strawberries and gooseberries and raspberries as they went along, but she would never kill anything; and she would never eat anything that any one else had killed. She only ate berries and crushed corn.

One day, while the young man's wife was embroidering feather stars on a dancing-cloth, and his mother was gossiping in a tent at the end of the village, a little yellow bird flew in and perched on High-feather's shoulder, and whispered in his ear:

"There is a great flock of wild red swans just over on Loon Lake. If you come quickly and quietly you can catch them before they fly away; but do not tell your wife, for red swans cannot bear the sight of a woman, and they can tell if one comes within a mile of them."

High-feather had never seen or heard of a red swan before; all the red feathers he wore he had had to paint. He looked at his wife, and as she was sewing busily and looking down at her star embroidering he thought he could slip away and get back before she knew he had gone. But as soon as he was out of sight the little yellow bird flew in and perched on her shoulder, and sang her such a beautiful song about her sisters in the sky that she forgot everything else and slipped out and ran like the wind, and got to the dancing ring just as her sisters came down in their basket. Then they all gathered round her, and begged her to go home with them.

But she only said, "High-feather is a brave man, and he is very good to me, and I will never leave him."

When they saw they could not make her leave her husband, the eldest sister said: "If you must stay, you must. But just come up for an hour, to let your father see you, because he has been mourning for you ever since you went away."

The Star-wife did not wish to go, but she wanted to see her father once more, so she got into the basket and it sailed away up into the sky. Her father was very glad to see her, and she was very glad to see him, and they talked and they talked till the blue sky was getting gray. Then she remembered that she ought to have gone home long before.

"Now I must go back to my husband," she said.

"That you shall never do!" said her father.

And he shut her up in a white cloud and said she should stay there till she promised never to go back to the prairie. She begged to be let out, but it was no use.

Then she began to weep; and she wept so much that the cloud began to weep too, and it was weeping itself quite away. So her father saw she would go down to the earth in rain if he kept her in the cloud any longer, and he let her out.

"What must I do for you," he said, "to make you stay with us here and be happy?"

"I will not stay here," she said, "unless my husband comes and lives here too."

"I will send for him at once," said her father. So he sent the basket down empty, and it rested in the middle of the dancing ring.

Now when High-feather reached Loon Lake he found it covered with red swans. He shot two with one arrow, and then all the rest flew away. He picked up the two swans and hurried back to his tent, and there lay the dancing-cloth with the feather stars on it half finished, but no wife could he see.

He called her, but she did not answer. He rushed out, with the two red swans still slung round his neck and hanging down his back, and ran to the dancing ring, but nobody was there.

"I will wait till she comes back," he said to himself, "if I have to wait till the world ends." So he threw himself down on the grass and lay looking up at the stars till he went to sleep.

Early in the morning he heard a rustling on the grass, and when he opened his eyes he saw the great basket close beside him. He jumped up, with the two red swans still slung round his neck, and climbed into the basket. There was nobody there; and when he began to climb out again he found that the basket was half way up to the sky. It went up and up, and at last it came into the Star-country, where his wife was waiting for him. Her father gave them a beautiful blue tent to live in, and High-feather was happy enough for a while; but he soon grew tired of the cloud-berries that the Star-people ate, and he longed to tramp over the solid green prairie, so he asked his wife's father to let him take her back to the earth.

"No," said the Star-man, "because then I should never see her again. If you stay with us you will soon forget the dull old earth."

The young man said nothing; but he put on the wings of one of the red swans, and he put the other red swan's wings on his wife, and they leapt over the edge of the Star-country and flew down through the air to the prairie, and came to the tent where High-feather's mother was mourning for them; and there was a great feast in the village because they had come back safe and sound. The Star-wife finished embroidering her dancing-cloth that day; and whenever the Indians danced she danced with them. She never went back to the Star-maidens' dancing ring; but she still lived on berries and corn, because she would never kill anything,—except one thing, and that was the little yellow bird. It flew into the tent one day when High-feather had his back turned, and began to whisper into the Star-wife's ear; but it never came to trouble her again.

ARABIAN STORIES

THE STORY OF CALIPH STORK

CALIPH CHARID, of Bagdad, was reclining on his divan one pleasant afternoon, smoking his long pipe and sipping coffee from a handsome dish which a slave was holding for him, when his Grand Vizier, Mansor, entered and told him of a peddler in the court below whose wares might interest him. The Caliph, being in an affable state of mind, summoned the peddler, who, delighted with the opportunity, displayed all the treasures of his pack. There were pearls, rings, silks, and many other rich things. The Caliph selected something for himself, a handsome present for the Vizier, and another for the Vizier's wife.

Just as the peddler was putting the things back into his box, the Caliph noticed a small drawer and asked what it contained.

"Only something of no value, which I picked up in a street of Mecca," the peddler replied. He thereupon opened the drawer and showed the Caliph a small box, containing a black powder and a scroll written in characters which neither the Caliph nor his Grand Vizier could make out. The Caliph immediately decided that he wanted this strange scroll, and the peddler was persuaded to part with it for a trifle. Then the Vizier was asked to find some one to decipher its meaning.

Near the mosque lived a man called Selim, who was so learned that he knew every language in the world. When the Vizier brought him to interpret the scroll, the Caliph said to him:

"They tell me that you are a scholar and can read all languages. If you can decipher what is written here, I shall know that it is true, and will give you a robe of honor; but if you fail, I shall have you punished with many strokes, because you are falsely named."

Selim prostrated himself at the feet of the Caliph, and then took the scroll. He had not looked at it long when he exclaimed:

"My lord and master, I hope to die if this is not Latin."

"Well, if so, let us hear what it says," the Caliph impatiently answered. Selim at once began:

"Let him who finds this box praise Allah. If he snuffs the powder it contains, at the same time pronouncing the word 'Matabor,' he will be transformed into any creature that he desires, and will understand the language of all animals. When he wishes to return to his own form, let him bow to the east three times, repeating the word 'Matabor.' But remember if, while he is bird or beast, he should laugh, the magic word would be forgotten, and the enchantment would be on him forever."

The Caliph was delighted with the knowledge of Selim. He made him a splendid present, and told him to keep the secret. When he had dismissed the learned man, he turned to the Grand Vizier, and expressed a wish to try the powder.

"Come to-morrow morning early," said he, "and we will go together to the country and learn what the animals are talking about."

The Vizier came as he was ordered, and they left the palace without attendants. Beyond the town was a large pond where some handsome storks were often seen, and to this place they presently came. A grave and stately stork was hunting for frogs, while another flew about and kept him company.

"Most gracious lord," said the Vizier, "what think you of these dignified long legs, and how would you like to know their chatter?"

The Caliph replied that the stork had always interested him, and he would very much like a more intimate acquaintance. Taking the box from his girdle, he helped himself to a pinch of snuff and offered it to the Vizier, who followed his example.

Together they cried "Matabor," and instantly their beards disappeared, and feathers covered their bodies; their necks stretched out long and slender, and their legs shriveled into red and shapeless sticks. The Caliph lifted up his foot to stroke his beard in astonishment, but found a long bill in its place.

"By the beard of the Prophet, since I have not one of my own to swear by, but we are a pretty pair of birds, Mansor!"

"If I may say so, your Highness, you are equally handsome as a stork as when you were a Caliph," replied the Vizier. "I see our two relations are conversing over there; shall we join them?"

When they came near to where the storks were smoothing their feathers and touching bills in the most friendly manner, this was the conversation they overheard, "Will you have some of my frog's legs for breakfast, Dame Yellowlegs?" "No, thank you; I am obliged to practise a dance for my father's guests, and cannot eat." Thereupon Dame Yellowlegs stepped out, and began to pose most gracefully. The Caliph and the Vizier watched her, until she stood on one foot and spread her wings; then they both, at the same time, burst into such peals of laughter that the two storks flew away.

Suddenly, however, the Vizier ceased his mirth, and commenced bowing to the east. The Caliph recovered himself and did the same, but neither could think of the magic word.

"Mansor, just recall that unholy word, and I will become Caliph once more, and you my Grand Vizier. I have had enough of being a bird for one day."

"Most gracious lord, that dancing stork has undone us, for, since laughing at her antics, I cannot remember the word that will restore us to human shape."

So at last, in despair, the two unhappy birds wandered through the meadows. They appeased their hunger with fruits, for they could not bring themselves to eat frogs and lizards. As they dared not return to Bagdad and tell the people their chagrin, they flew over the city, and had the satisfaction of seeing signs of mourning and confusion. In a few days, however, while sitting on the roof of a house, they saw a splendid procession coming up the street, and the people welcoming the new ruler. "Hail! Hail Mirza, ruler of Bagdad!" they shouted.

The procession came nearer. At the head of it the Caliph

saw a man dressed in scarlet and gold, riding a handsome horse. He at once recognized the new ruler as the son of his worst enemy.

"Behold," said he, "the explanation of our enchantment! This is the son of Kaschnur, the magician, who is my great enemy, who seeks revenge. Let us not lose hope, but fly to the sacred grave of the Prophet and pray to be released from the spell."

They at once spread their wings and soared away toward Medina, but not being accustomed to such long flights, they soon became fatigued and descended to a ruin which stood in a valley below. The two enchanted birds decided to remain there for the night; then wandered through the deserted rooms and corridors, which gave of evidence of former splendor. Suddenly the Vizier stopped and remarked that if it were not ridiculous for a stork to be afraid of ghosts, he would feel decidedly nervous. The Caliph listened, and heard a low moaning and sobbing, which seemed to come from a room down the passage. He started to rush toward it, but the Vizier held him fast by a wing. He had retained the brave heart that he had possessed when a Caliph, however, and freeing himself from the Vizier's bill, he hurried to the room whence came the pitiful sounds. The moon shone through a barred window and showed him a screech owl sitting on the floor of the ruined chamber, lamenting in a hoarse voice. The Vizier had cautiously stolen up beside the Caliph; and at sight of the two storks, the screech owl uttered a cry of pleasure. To their astonishment it addressed them in Arabic, in the following words:

"I have abandoned myself to despair, but I believe my deliverance is near, for it was prophesied in my youth that a stork would bring me good fortune."

The Caliph, thus appealed to, arched his neck most gracefully and replied:

"Alas! Screech Owl, I fear we are unable to aid you, as you will understand when you have heard our miserable story."

He then related how the magician, Kaschnur, had changed them into storks and made his own son ruler of Bagdad. The screech owl became very much excited and exclaimed:

"How strange that misfortune should have come to us through the same man. I am Tusa, the daughter of the King of the Indies. The magician, Kaschnur, came one day to my father, to ask my hand in marriage for his son Mirza. My father ordered him thrown down stairs, and in revenge he managed to have me given a powder which changed me into this hideous shape. He then conveyed me to this lonely castle, and swore I should remain here until some one asked me to be his wife, and so freed me from the enchantment."

At the conclusion of her story, the screech owl wept anew and would not be consoled. Suddenly, however, she wiped her eyes on her wing and said:

"I have an idea that may lead to our deliverance. Once every month the magician, Kaschnur, and his companions meet in a large hall at this castle, where they feast and relate their evil deeds. We will listen outside the door, and perhaps you may hear the forgotten word. Then, when you have resumed human form, one of you can ask to marry me, that I too may be freed from this wretched enchantment; and the prophecy that a stork would bring me happiness would be fulfilled."

The Caliph and the Vizier withdrew and consulted over the situation. "It is unfortunate," said the Caliph, "but if we are to meet again, I think you will have to ask the screech owl to marry you."

"Not so, your Highness, I already have a wife, and would rather remain a stork forever than take another; besides, I am an old man, while you are young and unmarried, and much better suited to a beautiful Princess."

"That is it," said the Caliph. "How do I know that she will not prove to be some old fright?" As the Vizier was firm, the Caliph at last said he would take the chances and do as the screech owl required.

That very night it so happened that the magicians met at the ruined castle. The screech owl led the two storks through difficult passages till they came to a hole in the wall, through which they could plainly see all that transpired in the lighted hall. Handsomely carved pillars adorned the room, and a table was spread with many dishes. About the table sat eight men, among whom was their enemy, the magician. He entertained the company with many stories, and at last came to his latest—that of turning the Caliph and Vizier into storks—in relating which he pronounced the magic word. The storks did not wait to hear more, but ran to the door of the castle. The screech owl followed as fast as she could, and when the Caliph saw her he exclaimed:

"To prove my gratitude, O our deliverer! I beg you to take me for your husband."

Then the two storks faced the rising sun, and bowed their long necks three times. "Matabor!" they solemnly cried, together; and in an instant they were no longer storks, but stood before each other in their natural forms. In their joy they fell on each other's necks and forgot all about the screech owl, until they heard a sweet voice beside them, and turning beheld a beautiful Princess. When the Caliph recovered from his astonishment he said that he was now, indeed, enchanted and hoped to remain so always.

They then started at once for the gate of Bagdad; and when they arrived, the people were overjoyed, for they had believed their ruler dead. The magician was taken to the ruined castle and hanged, and his son was given the choice of the black powder or death. Choosing the powder, he was changed into a stork, and was kept in the palace gardens.

Caliph Charid and the Princess were married; and when their children grew old enough, the Caliph often amused them with imitations of the Grand Vizier when he was a stork,—while Mansor sat smiling and pulling his long beard.

❧ ❧ ❧

PERSEVERE AND PROSPER

ADAPTED BY A. R. MONTALBA

"HE that seeketh, shall find, and to him that knocketh shall be opened," says an old Arab proverb.

"I will try that," said a youth one day. To carry out his

intention he journeyed to Bagdad, where he presented himself before the Vizier.

"Lord!" said he, "for many years I have lived a quiet and solitary life, the monotony of which wearies me. I have never permitted myself earnestly to will any thing. But as my teacher daily repeated to me, 'He that seeketh shall find, and to him that knocketh shall be opened,' so have I now come to the resolution with might and heart to will, and the resolution of my will is nothing less than to have the Caliph's daughter for my wife."

The Vizier thought the poor man was mad, and told him to call again some other time.

Perseveringly he daily returned, and never felt disconcerted at the same often repeated answer. One day, the Caliph called on the Vizier, as the youth was repeating his statement.

Full of astonishment the Caliph listened to the strange demand, and being in no humor for having the poor youth's head taken off, but on the contrary, being rather inclined for pleasantry, his Mightiness condescendingly said: "For the great, the wise, or the brave, to request a Princess for wife, is a moderate demand; but what are your claims? To be the possessor of my daughter you must distinguish yourself by one of these attributes, or else by some great undertaking. Ages ago a carbuncle of inestimable value was lost in the Tigris; he who finds it shall have the hand of my daughter."

The youth, satisfied with the promise of the Caliph, went to the shores of the Tigris. With a small vessel he went every morning to the river, scooping out the water and throwing it on the land; and after having for hours thus employed himself, he knelt down and prayed. The fishes became at last uneasy at his perseverance; and being fearful that, in the course of time, he might exhaust the waters, they assembled in great council.

"What is the purpose of this man?" demanded the monarch of the fishes.

"The possession of the carbuncle that lies buried in the bottom of the Tigris," was the reply.

"I advise you, then," said the aged monarch, "to give it up to him; for if he has the steady will, and has positively resolved to find it, he will work until he has drained the last drop of water from the Tigris, rather than deviate a hair's breadth from his purpose."

The fishes, out of fear, threw the carbuncle into the vessel of the youth; and the latter, as a reward, received the daughter of the Caliph for his wife."

"He who earnestly wills, can do much!"

CHINESE STORIES

THE MOST FRUGAL OF MEN

A MAN who was considered the most frugal of all the dwellers in a certain kingdom heard of another man who was the most frugal in the whole world. He said to his son thereupon: "We, indeed, live upon little, but if we were more frugal still, we might live upon nothing at all. It will be well worth while for us to get instructions in economy from the Most Frugal of Men." The son agreed, and the two decided that the son should go and inquire whether the master in economic science would take pupils. An exchange of presents being a necessary preliminary to closer intercourse, the father told the son to take the smallest of coins, one farthing, and to buy a sheet of paper of the cheapest sort. The boy, by bargaining, got two sheets of paper for the farthing. The father put away one sheet, cut the other sheet in halves, and on one half drew a picture of a pig's head. This he put into a large covered basket, as if it were the thing which it represented—the usual gift sent in token of great respect. The son took the basket, and after a long journey reached the abode of the most frugal man in the world.

The master of the house was absent, but his son received the traveler, learned his errand, and accepted the offering. Having taken from the basket the picture of the pig's head, he said courteously to his visitor: "I am sorry that we have nothing in the house that is worthy to take the place of the pig's head in your basket. I will, however, signify our friendly reception of it by putting in four oranges for you to take home with you."

Thereupon the young man, without having any oranges at hand, made the motions necessary for putting the fruit into the basket. The son of the most frugal man in the kingdom then took the basket and went to his father to tell of thrift surpassing his own.

When the most frugal man in the world returned home, his son told him that a visitor had been there, having come from a great distance to take lessons in economy. The father inquired what offering he brought as an introduction, and the son showed the small outline of the pig's head on thin brown paper. The father looked at it, and then asked his son what he had sent as a return present. The son told him he had merely made the motions necessary for transferring four oranges, and showed how he had clasped the imaginary fruit and deposited it in the visitor's basket. The father immediately flew into a terrible rage and boxed the boy's ears, exclaiming: "You extravagant wretch! With your fingers thus far apart you appeared to give him large oranges. Why didn't you measure out small ones?"

☙ ☙ ☙

THE MOON-CAKE

A LITTLE boy had a cake that a big boy coveted. Designing to get the cake without making the little boy cry so loud as to attract his mother's attention, the big boy remarked that the cake would be prettier if it were more like the moon. The little boy thought that a cake like the moon must be desirable, and on being assured by the big boy that he had made many such, he handed over his cake for manipulation. The big boy took out a mouthful, leaving a crescent with jagged edge. The little boy was not pleased by the change, and began to whimper; whereupon the big boy pacified him by saying that he would make the cake into a half-moon. So he nibbled off the horns of the crescent, and gnawed the edge smooth; but when the half-moon was made, the little boy perceived that there was hardly any cake left, and he again began to snivel. The big boy again diverted him by telling him that, if he did not like so small a moon, he should have one that was just the size of the real orb. He then took the cake, and explained that, just before the new moon is seen, the old moon disappears. Then he swallowed the rest of the cake and ran off, leaving the little boy waiting for the new moon.

☙ ☙ ☙

THE LADLE THAT FELL FROM THE MOON

ONCE there was an old woman who lived on what she got by wile from her relatives and neighbors. Her husband's brother lived alone with his only son, in a house near hers, and when the son brought home a wife the old woman went to call on the bride. During the call she inquired of the bride whether she had not, since her arrival in the house, heard a scratching at night among the boxes containing her wedding outfit. The bride said she had not. A few days later the old woman came again, and during the visit the bride remarked that, before the matter was mentioned, she had heard no scratching among her boxes, but that since that time she had listened for it, and had heard it every night. The old woman advised her to look carefully after her clothing, saying that there were evidently many mice in the house, and that she would be likely at any time to find her best garments nibbled into shreds. The old woman knew there was no cat in the house, but she inquired whether there was one, and on hearing that there was not, she offered to lend the young woman her own black-and-white cat, saying that it would soon extirpate all the mice. The bride accepted the loan, and the old woman brought the cat, and left it in the bride's apartment. After a few hours the cat disappeared, and the bride, supposing it to have gone home, made no search for it. It did, indeed, go home, and the old woman secretly disposed of it; but several days later she came to the young woman and said that, when she lent the cat, her house had been free from mice, but that, as soon as the cat was gone, the mice came and multiplied so fast that now everything was overrun by them, and she would be obliged to take the cat home again. The young woman told her that the cat went away the same day that it came, and she had supposed it had gone home. The old woman said it had not, and that nothing could compensate her for the loss of it, for she had reared it herself; that there was never before seen such a cat for catching mice; that a cat, spotted as that one was, was seldom found; and that it was of the rare breed which gave rise to the common saying:

"A coal-black cat, with snowy loins,
Is worth its weight in silver coins."

and that the weight of her cat was two hundred ounces.

The young woman was greatly surprised by this estimate of the value of the lost cat, and went to her father-in-law and related all that had occurred. The father-in-law, knowing the character of the old woman, could neither eat nor sleep, so harassed was he by the expectation that she would worry his daughter-in-law till the two hundred ounces of silver should be paid. The young woman, being a new-comer, thought but lightly of the matter, till the old woman came again and again to make mention of the cat. When it became apparent that she must defend herself, the young woman asked her father-in-law if he had ever lent anything to the old woman; and when he said he could not remember having lent anything, she begged him to think carefully, and see if he could not recall the loan of a tool, a dish, or a fagot. He finally recollected that he had lent to her an old wooden ladle, but he said it originally cost but a few farthings, and was certainly not worth speaking about.

The next time the old woman came to dun for the amount due for her cat, the young woman asked her to return the borrowed ladle. The old woman said that the ladle was old and valueless; that she had allowed the children to play with it, and that they had dropped it in the dirt, where it had lain until she had picked it up and used it for kindlings. The bride responded: "You expect to enrich yourself and your family by means of your cat. I and my family also want money.

Since you cannot give back the ladle, we will both go before the magistrate and present our cases. If your cat is adjudged to be worth more than my ladle I will pay you the excess; and if my ladle be worth more than your cat, then you must pay me." Being sure that the cat would, by any judge, be considered of greater value than the ladle, the old woman agreed to the proposition, and the two went before the magistrate. The young woman courteously gave precedence to the elder, and allowed her to make the accusation. The old woman set forth her case, and claimed two hundred ounces of silver as a compensation for the loss of the cat. When she had concluded her statement, the judge called on the young woman for her defense. She said she could not disprove the statement, but that the claim was offset by a ladle that had been borrowed by the plaintiff. There was a common saying:

"In the moon overhead, at its full, you can see
The trunk, branch and leaf of a cinnamon tree."

A branch from this tree had one night been blown down before her father-in-law's door, and he had had a ladle made from the wood. Whatever the ladle was put into never diminished by use. Whether wine, oil, rice, or money, the bulk remained the same if no ladle beside this one were used in dipping it. A foreign inn-keeper, hearing of this ladle, came and offered her father-in-law three thousand ounces of silver for it, but the offer was refused. And this ladle was the one that the plaintiff had borrowed and destroyed.

The magistrate, on hearing this defense, understood that the cat had been a pretext for extortion, and decided that the two claims offset each other, so that no payment was due from either one.

❧ ❧ ❧

THE YOUNG HEAD OF THE FAMILY

THERE was once a family consisting of a father, his three sons, and his two daughters-in-law. The two daughters-in-law, wives of the two elder sons, had but recently been brought into the house, and were both from one village a few miles away. Having no mother-in-law living, they were obliged to appeal to their father-in-law whenever they wished to visit their former homes, and as they were lonesome and homesick they perpetually bothered the old man by asking leave of absence.

Vexed by these constant petitions, he set himself to invent a method of putting an end to them, and at last gave them leave in this wise: "You are always begging me to allow you to go and visit your mothers, and thinking that I am very hard-hearted because I do not let you go. Now you may go, but only upon condition that when you come back you will each bring me something I want. The one shall bring me some fire wrapped in paper, and the other some wind in a paper. Unless you promise to bring me these, you are never to ask me to let you go home; and if you go, and fail to get these for me, you are never to come back."

The old man did not suppose that these conditions would be accepted, but the girls were young and thoughtless, and in their anxiety to get away did not consider the impossibility of obtaining the articles required. So they made ready with speed, and in great glee started off on foot to visit their mothers. After they had walked a long distance, chatting about what they should do and whom they should see in their native village, the high heel of one of them slipped from under her foot, and she fell down. Owing to this mishap both stopped to adjust the misplaced footgear, and while doing this the conditions under which alone they could return to their husbands came to mind, and they began to cry.

While they sat there crying by the roadside a young girl came riding along from the fields on a water buffalo. She stopped and asked them what was the matter, and whether she could help them. They told her she could do them no good; but she persisted in offering her sympathy and inviting their confidence, till they told their story, and then she at once said that if they would go home with her she would show them a way out or their trouble. Their case seemed so hopeless to themselves, and the child was so sure of her own power to help them, that they finally accompanied her to her father's house, where she showed them how to comply with their father-in-law's demand.

For the first a paper lantern only would be needed. When lighted it would be a fire, and its paper surface would compass the blaze, so that it would truly be "some fire wrapped in paper." For the second a paper fan would suffice. When flapped, wind would issue from it, and the "wind wrapped in paper" could thus be carried to the old man.

The two young women thanked the wise child, and went on their way rejoicing. After a pleasant visit to their old homes, they took a lantern and a fan, and returned to their father-in-law's house. As soon as he saw them he began to vent his anger at their light regard for his commands, but they assured him that they had perfectly obeyed him, and showed him that what they had brought fulfilled the conditions prescribed. Much astonished, he inquired how it was that they had suddenly become so astute, and they told him the story of their journey, and of the little girl who had so opportunely come to their relief. He inquired whether the little girl was already betrothed, and, finding that she was not, engaged a go-between to see if he could get her for a wife for his youngest son.

Having succeeded in securing the girl as a daughter-in-law, he brought her home, and told all the rest of the family that as there was no mother in the house, and as this girl had shown herself to be possessed of extraordinary wisdom, she should be the head of the household.

The wedding festivities being over, the sons of the old man made ready to return to their usual occupations on the farm; but, according to their father's order, they came to the young bride for instructions. She told them that they were never to go to or from the fields empty-handed. When they went they must carry fertilizers of some sort for the land, and when they returned they must bring bundles of sticks for fuel. They obeyed, and soon had the land in fine condition, and so much fuel gathered that none need be bought. When there were no more sticks, roots, or weeds to bring, she told them to bring stones instead; and they soon accumulated an immense pile of stones, which were heaped in a yard near their house.

One day an expert in the discovery of precious stones came along, and saw in this pile a block of jade of great value. In order to get possession of this stone at a small cost, he undertook to buy the whole heap, pretending that he wished to use it in building. The little head of the family asked an exorbitant price for them, and, as he could not induce her to take less, he promised to pay her the sum she asked, and to come two days later to bring the money and to remove the stones. That night the girl thought about the reason for the buyer's being willing to pay so large a sum for the stones, and concluded that the heap must contain a gem. The next morning she sent her father-in-law to invite the buyer to supper, and she instructed the men of her family in regard to his entertainment. The best of wine was to be provided, and the father-in-law was to induce him to talk of precious stones, and to cajole him into telling in what way they were to be distinguished from other stones.

The head of the family, listening behind a curtain, heard how the valuable stone in her heap could be discovered. She hastened to find and remove it from the pile; and, when her guest had recovered from the effect of the banquet, he saw that the value had departed from his purchase. He went to negotiate again with the seller, and she conducted the conference with such skill that she obtained the price originally agreed upon for the heap of stones, and a large sum besides for the one in her possession.

The family, having become wealthy, built an ancestral hall of fine design and elaborate workmanship, and put the words "No Sorrow" as an inscription over the entrance. Soon after, a mandarin passed that way, and, noticing this remarkable inscription, had his sedan-chair set down, that he might inquire who were the people that professed to have no sorrow. He sent for the head of the family, was much surprised on seeing so young a woman thus appear, and remarked: "Yours is a singular family. I have never before seen one without sorrow, nor one with so young a head. I will fine you for your impudence. Go and weave me a piece of cloth as long as this road."

"Very well," responded the little woman; "so soon as your Excellency shall have found the two ends of the road, and informed me as to the number of feet in its length, I will at once begin the weaving."

Finding himself at fault, the mandarin added, "And I also fine you as much oil as there is water in the sea."

"Certainly," responded the woman; "as soon as you shall have measured the sea, and sent me correct information as to the number of gallons, I will at once begin to press out the oil from my beans."

"Indeed," said the mandarin, "since you are so sharp, perhaps you can penetrate my thoughts. If you can, I will fine you no more. I hold this pet quail in my hand; now tell me whether I mean to squeeze it to death, or to let it fly in the air."

"Well," said the woman, "I am an obscure commoner, and you are a famed magistrate; if you are no more knowing than I, you have no right to fine me at all. Now I stand with one foot on one side my threshold and the other foot on the other side; tell me whether I mean to go in or come out. If you cannot guess my riddle, you should not require me to guess yours."

Being unable to guess her intention the mandarin took his departure, and the family lived long in opulence and good repute under its chosen head.

☘ ☘ ☘

A DREADFUL BOAR

A POOR old woman who lived with her one little granddaughter in a wood was out gathering sticks for fuel, and found a green stalk of sugar-cane, which she added to her bundle. She presently met an elf in the form of a wild Boar, that asked her for the cane, but she declined giving it to him, saying that, at her age, to stoop and to rise again was to earn what she picked up, and that she was going to take the cane home, and let her little granddaughter suck its sap. The Boar, angry at her refusal, said that he would, during the coming night, eat her granddaughter instead of the cane, and went off into the wood.

When the old woman reached her cabin she sat down by the door and wailed, for she knew she had no means of defending herself against the Boar. While she sat crying, a vender of needles came along and asked her what was the matter. She told him, and he said that all he could do for her was to give her a box of needles. This he did, and went on his way. The old woman stuck the needles thickly over the lower half of her door, on its outer side, and then she went on crying. Just then a man came along with a basket of crabs, heard her lamentations, and stopped to inquire what ailed her. She told him, and he said he knew no help for her, but he would do the best he could for her by giving her half his crabs. The old woman put the crabs in her water-jar, behind her door, and again sat down and cried. A farmer soon came along from the fields, leading his ox, and he also asked the cause of her distress and heard her sad story. He said he was sorry he could not think of any way of preventing the evil she expected, but that he would leave his ox to stay all night with her, as it might be a sort of company for her in her loneliness. She led the ox into her cabin, tied it to the head of her bedstead, gave it some straw, and then cried again.

A courier, returning on horseback from a neighboring town, next passed her door, and dismounted to inquire what troubled her. Having heard her tale, he said he would leave his horse to stay with her, and make the ox more contented. So she tied the horse to the foot of her bed, and, thinking how surely evil was coming upon her with the night, she burst out crying anew. A boy just then came along with a snapping-turtle that he had caught, and stopped to ask what had happened to her. On learning the cause of her weeping, he said it was of no use to contend against sprites, but that he would give her his snapping-turtle as a proof of his sympathy. She took the turtle, tied it in front of her bedstead, and continued to cry.

Some men who were carrying mill-stones then came along, inquired into her trouble, and expressed their compassion by giving her a mill-stone, which they rolled into her back yard. A little later a man arrived carrying hoes and pickax, and asked her why she was crying so hard. She told him her grief, and he said he would gladly help her if he could, but he was only a well-digger, and could do nothing for her other than to dig her a well. She pointed out a place in the middle of her back yard, and he went to work and quickly dug a well.

On his departure the old woman cried again, until a paper-seller came and inquired what was the matter. When she had told him, he gave her a large sheet of white paper, as a token of pity, and she laid it smoothly over the mouth of the well.

Nightfall came; the old woman shut and barred her door, put her granddaughter snugly on the wall-side of the bed, and then lay down beside her, to await the foe.

At midnight the Boar came, and threw himself against the door to break it in. The needles wounded him sorely, so that when he had gained an entrance he was heated and thirsty, and went to the water-jar to drink. When he thrust in his snout the crabs attacked him, clung to his bristles and pinched his ears, till he rolled over and over to disencumber himself. Then in a rage he approached the front of the bed, but the snapping-turtle nipped his tail, and made him retreat under the feet of the horse, who kicked him over to the ox, who tossed him back to the horse; and thus beset he was glad to escape to the back yard to take a rest, and to consider the situation. Seeing a clean paper spread on the ground, he went to lie upon it, and fell into the well. The old woman heard the fall, rushed out, rolled the mill-stone down on him, and crushed him.

RUSSIAN STORIES

KING KOJATA

KING KOJATA ruled over a mighty kingdom, and was beloved by his subjects; but because he had no heir to his crown, both he and the Queen lamented. Once, while traveling through his territories, he came to a well that was filled to the brim with clear cold water; and being very thirsty, he stopped to drink. On the top of the water floated a golden vessel, which the King attempted to seize; but just as his hand touched it, away it floated to the other side of the well. He went around to where the vessel rested and tried again, with the same result. Every time the King touched the basin it glided from his grasp. At last, losing patience, he gave up trying to seize the vessel, and bending over the well, he began to drink. His long beard had fallen into the water, and when he had slaked his thirst and attempted to rise, he found himself held fast by it. After vainly pulling and jerking for some time, he looked down into the water and saw a hideous face grinning at him. Its eyes were green and shining, its teeth showed from ear to ear, and it held him by the beard with two bony claws. In horror, the king tried to extricate himself, but a terrible voice came from the depths of the well:

"You cannot get away, King Kojata, so do not make me pull your beard too hard. There is something at the palace of which you do not know; promise to give it to me, and I will release you."

The King did not know of anything that could have arrived at the palace during his absence worth the discomfort he was experiencing; so he very readily gave his promise, and was freed. When he had shaken the water from his beard, he looked in the well for the ugly monster which had held him captive, but he was nowhere to be seen. Summoning his attendants, he at once set out for home, where he arrived in a few days. The people along the way hailed him with delight; and when he reached the palace, the Queen led him to the royal chamber and showed him a beautiful son that had been born during his absence. His joy was so great that he forgot all else; but after a time he recalled with horror his compact with the monster of the well, and the meaning was all plain to him. The thought of what he had promised haunted him day and night, and the fear that something would happen to his little son tortured him. But as days and months passed, and the little Prince grew more beautiful all the time, the King at last forgot his fears and became happy once more.

Years went by without anything happening to disturb his peace of mind, and the Prince grew to be a beautiful youth, who was the joy and pride of the King and Queen. One day he went with the hunters to the forest, and while pursuing a wild boar, became separated from them. He got farther and farther away from his companions, and at last found himself alone in a dark part of the wood where he never before had been. Not knowing in which direction his path lay, he called again and again to the hunters. At last a hoarse voice answered him, and from the hollow trunk of a lime-tree appeared a hideous man with green eyes and terrible teeth.

"I've waited for you a long time, Prince Milan," said he.

"Who on earth may you be?" asked the Prince.

"Your father will tell you who I am. Just give my greetings to his Majesty, and tell him that I am ready to claim the debt he owes me."

The green-eyed man then disappeared into the hollow tree from which he came; and when the Prince reached home, he related his experience to his father. The King turned white, and cried:

"At last, it has come!" Then he explained to the Prince what had occurred at the well, and added, "Now my happiness is at an end, for you, my son, will be taken from me."

The Prince told the King not to despair, for though he might go away, he was certain to return to him. His father provided him with a handsome horse with golden stirrups, and the Queen gave him a cross to wear about his neck. When he had said farewell to his unhappy parents, he mounted his horse and rode for two days without stopping.

On the third day he came to a lake on whose smooth surface thirty ducks were swimming, while spread about upon the grass were thirty white garments. The Prince dismounted, and taking up one of the garments, seated himself behind a bush and waited to see what would happen. The ducks dived under the water and disported themselves for a time, then came ashore and putting on the little white garments, they became beautiful maidens, and disappeared. But there was one little duck that remained on the lake and swam about in the most distracted manner, uttering piteous cries. The Prince came from behind the bush and the little duck begged him to give back her garment. He had no sooner done so than before him stood the loveliest maiden he had ever seen.

"Thank you, Prince Milan, for restoring my garment," said she. "My name is Hyacinthia, and I am one of the thirty daughters of a King of the Underworld, to whose castle I will lead you, for he has waited long for you. Approach him on your knees and do not fear him, for I will be there to help you, whatever happens."

She tapped her little foot on the ground, which opened; and they were immediately transported to the palace of her father in the Underworld, which was carved from a single carbuncle. When his eyes became accustomed to the radiant light, the Prince saw the magician of the lime-tree sitting on a dazzling throne. His green eyes looked out from under a golden crown, and his hideous claws clutched the air with rage when he saw the Prince. Remembering what the maiden had told him, Prince Milan walked boldly up to the throne and knelt at the feet of the magician, who cursed in a voice that shook the Underworld. As the youth was not at all frightened, the magician at last stopped swearing. Laughing at his courage, he welcomed him to his palace, and showed him to a beautiful chamber which he was to occupy. On the following day he sent for him and said:

"You are very brave, Prince Milan, but you must pay the penalty for keeping me waiting so long for you. To-night build me a palace of gold and marble, with windows of crystal, and about it the most beautiful gardens in the world, or to-morrow I shall cut off your head."

The Prince went back to his chamber and sadly awaited his doom. That evening a small bee flew in through his window, and as soon as it entered the room it became Hyacinthia. "Why are you sad, Prince Milan?" she asked. He told her of her father's impossible command and added, "Naturally, I am not happy at the thought of losing my head."

"Do not be distressed about that," said she, "but trust to me." In the morning he looked out of the window and saw a wonderful marble palace, with a roof of gold.

When the magician beheld it, he exclaimed, "You have accomplished a great wonder, but I cannot let you off so easily. To-morrow I will place my thirty daughters in a row, and if you cannot tell me which one is the youngest, you will lose your head."

The Prince, however, was not cast down at this, for he thought he would have no trouble in recognizing Hyacinthia. That evening the little bee entered the room and told him that this task was quite as difficult as the first, because the sisters were all exactly alike. "But you will know me," said she, "by a little fly which you will discover on my cheek."

The next day the magician summoned him to his presence, and showed him the thirty daughters standing in a row. The Prince passed before them twice, without daring to choose; but he saw the little fly on the pink cheek of one of the maidens.

"This is Hyacinthia!" exclaimed he. The magician was greatly astonished; but not yet satisfied, he required of the Prince still another task.

"If, before this candle burns to the bottom," said he, "you make me a pair of boots reaching to my knees, I will let you go; but if you fail, you will lose your head."

"Then we must fly, for I love you dearly," said Hyacinthia, when the Prince had told her of this new task. She breathed on the window-pane, and straightway it was covered with frost;

then, leading Prince Milan from the chamber, she locked the door, and they fled through the passage by which they had entered the Underworld. Beside the smooth lake his horse was still grazing, and mounting it, they were borne swiftly away.

When the magician sent for the Prince to come to him, the frozen breath replied to the messengers, and so delayed the discovery of his escape. At last the magician lost patience and ordered the door burst open. The frozen breath mocked at him, and he hastened in pursuit of the fugitives.

"I hear the sound of horses' feet behind us," said Hyacinthia. The Prince dismounted, and putting his ear to the ground, answered, "Yes, they are near." Hyacinthia thereupon changed herself into a river, and the Prince became a bridge, and his horse a blackbird. Their pursuers, no longer finding their footprints, were obliged to return to the magician, who cursed them, and again sent them forth.

"I hear the sound of horses' feet behind us," again said Hyacinthia. The Prince put his ear to the earth and said, "Yes, they are nearly upon us." Thereupon Hyacinthia changed herself, the Prince and the horse, all into a dense forest in which many paths crossed, so that the followers were bewildered; and they again returned to the magician.

"I hear horses' feet behind us," said Hyacinthia a third time; and this time it was the magician himself. Hyacinthia took the little cross from the neck of the Prince, and changed herself into a church, the Prince into a monk, and the horse into the belfry; so that when the magician came up he lost all trace of them, and was obliged to return to the Underworld in great chagrin.

When he had departed, the Prince and Hyacinthia mounted the horse and rode till they came to a beautiful town.

"We must not enter," said she, "for we may not come out again." But the Prince would not take her advice, and insisted upon passing through the gates.

"Then," sadly replied the maiden, "when the King and Queen of the town come out to meet you, do not kiss the little child which they will lead by the hand, or you will forget me and never come back. As for me, I will become a milestone and wait for you here."

It was all as Hyacinthia had said. The King and Queen came out to greet him, and when the lovely little child ran up to him for a caress, he kissed its pretty face and forgot Hyacinthia.

The first and second day went by; and when the third day came, Hyacinthia wept, and became a little blue flower growing by the roadside. An old man came along, and digging up the flower carried it home with him and planted it in his garden. He watered and tended it carefully, and one day the little flower became a beautiful maiden.

"Why did you not leave me to die by the roadside?" she asked, and told the old man her story.

"To-morrow is Prince Milan's wedding day," said the old man.

Hyacinthia at once dried her tears, and presented herself at the palace, dressed like a peasant. She went to the cook and asked to be allowed to make the wedding cake. The cook was so struck with her beauty that he could not refuse the request. When the guests were all seated about the table, Prince Milan was called upon to cut the cake. As soon as he had done so, out flew two beautiful doves, which circled about his head.

"Dear mate," cried one of the doves, "do not leave me as Prince Milan left Hyacinthia."

The Prince, who suddenly recollected all he had forgotten, ran from the room and at the door found Hyacinthia and his horse awaiting him. They mounted and rode swiftly away to the kingdom of King Kojata, where the King and Queen received them with tears of joy, and they all lived in happiness to the end of their days.

❧ ❧ ❧

THE STORY OF KING FROST

A SHREWISH peasant woman had a daughter on whom she lavished everything she could get, and a stepdaughter whom she neglected and ill treated. In the mother's eyes the daughter had no faults, while the stepdaughter was always blamed, and, try as she might, the poor girl never could please. So unhappy was she made that her eyes were often red from weeping. The sight of her tear-stained face only angered the stepmother the more, and caused her to say to the girl's father:

"Send her away, old man. My eyes are tired of the sight of her, and my ears of the sound of her voice. Send her out of the house."

The father begged to have his daughter remain, but the shrew was determined to be rid of her, and gave him no peace. At last, when he could gainsay her no longer, he placed his daughter in a sledge and drove her to the open fields. Here he left her, with nothing to shield her from the bitter cold. Kissing her good-by, he drove away, not daring to look back at her.

Left alone by her father, the girl wandered across the bleak fields to the edge of the forest, where she sat down under a fir-tree and wept. A crackling sound caused her to look up, and she saw King Frost springing from one tree to another. When he reached the fir-tree he jumped down beside her with a bound. Snapping his fingers in her lovely face, he asked:

"Do you know who I am? I will tell you. I am King Frost."

"Hail to you, great King!" smiled the maiden. "Have you come for me?"

"Are you warm, fair maiden?" he asked in answer.

"Yes, quite warm, King Frost," the maiden replied, although she was shivering.

King Frost bent over her and snapped his fingers about her, until the air seemed full of needles. Again he asked, "Are you still warm, dear maiden?"

Her lips could scarcely move to utter the words, "Quite warm, King Frost."

He snapped his teeth and cracked his fingers, till all the air was filled with stinging things. His eyes glistened and for the last time he asked, "Are you warm, now, beautiful maiden? Are you still warm, my dear?"

She was now scarcely able to speak, but managed to gasp, "Still warm, King Frost."

The gentle girl's patience and uncomplaining endurance

caused King Frost to take pity on her suffering. He arrayed her in a robe, embroidered in silver and gold, and decked her with sparkling diamonds. She glittered and shone, and was dazzling to behold. Then placing her in his sleigh, he wrapped her in furs; and six white horses bore them swiftly away.

The stepmother, at home, was baking pancakes for the girl's funeral feast. "Go in the field," she said to her husband, "and bring your daughter's body home, so we can bury her." The old man rose to obey, when the little dog barked:

"Your daughter shall not die;
Her's cold and stiff shall lie."

The woman kicked the dog, then tried to coax it with a pancake, telling it to say:

"Her daughter shall have gold;
His be frozen stiff and cold."

When the little dog had swallowed the pancake, he barked:

"His daughter shall be wed;
Her's shall be frozen dead."

The woman beat the dog, then coaxed it with more pancakes; but the blows could not terrify it nor food persuade. It barked always the same. Suddenly the door opened, and a huge chest was thrust into the room, followed by the radiant stepdaughter, in a dress that dazzled them with its beauty.

As soon as the stepmother recovered from her astonishment, she ordered her husband to yoke the horses to the sledge, and take her own daughter to the field. "Take care you leave her in the same place," the old woman cautioned. The father left the girl as he was bidden, and returned to his home.

She was not long alone when King Frost came by.

"Are you warm, maiden?" he asked.

"You must be a fool not to see that my hands and feet are nearly frozen," she angrily replied.

The King danced in front of her, and cracked his fingers.

"Are you warm, maiden?" he asked her, over and over. She cried with rage, and called him rude names, until he froze the words on her lips, and she was dead.

The mother waited for her daughter's return until she became impatient; then she told her husband to take the sledge and go for her. "But don't lose the chest," she added.

The dog under the table, barked:

"Your daughter frozen cold,
Will never need a chest of gold."

The old woman was scolding the dog for telling lies, when the door opened. Rushing out to welcome her daughter and her treasures, she clasped the frozen body in her arms; and the chill of it killed her.

TALES FOR TINY TOTS

TELL US A TALE

BY EDWARD SHIRLEY

"TELL us a tale, dear mother—
  A fairy tale, do, please,
Take baby brother on your lap,
  We'll sit beside your knees,
We will not speak, we will not stir,
  Until the tale is told;
And we'll be, oh! so comfy,
  And just as good as gold."

"What shall it be, my children?
  Aladdin and his Lamp?
Or shall I tell the story
  Of Puss in Boots—the scamp?
Or would you like to hear the tale
  Of Blue Beard, fierce and grim?
Or Jack who climbed the great beanstalk?—
  I think you're fond of him.

"Or shall I tell you, children,
  About Red Riding Hood?
Or what befell those little Babes
  Who wandered in the Wood?
Or how sweet Cinderella went
  So gaily to the ball?"
"Yes, yes!" we cried, and clapped our hands;
  "We want to hear them all!"

LITTLE RED HEN

LITTLE Red Hen found a grain of wheat.

"Who will plant this?" she asked.

"Not I," said the cat.

"Not I," said the goose.

"Not I," said the rat.

"Then I will," said Little Red Hen.

So she buried the wheat in the ground. After a while it grew up yellow and ripe.

"The wheat is ripe now," said Little Red Hen. "Who will cut and thresh it?"

"Not I," said the cat.

"Not I," said the goose.

"Not I," said the rat.

"Then I will," said Little Red Hen.

So she cut it with her bill and threshed it with her wings.

Then she asked, "Who will take this wheat to the mill?"

"Not I," said the cat.

"Not I," said the goose.

"Not I," said the rat.

"Then I will," said Little Red Hen.

So she took the wheat to the mill, where it was ground. Then she carried the flour home.

"Who will make me some bread with this flour?" she asked.

"Not I," said the cat.

"Not I," said the goose.

"Not I," said the rat.

"Then I will," said Little Red Hen.

So she made and baked the bread.

Then she said, "Now we shall see who will eat this bread."

"We will," said cat, goose, and rat.

"I am quite sure you would," said Little Red Hen, "if you could get it."

Then she called her chicks, and they ate up all the bread. There was none left at all for the cat, or the goose, or the rat.

IN SEARCH OF A BABY

BY F. TAPSELL

"PLEASE, I'm lost." These words, and a thump! thump! on the door were what Mrs. Stone heard as she sat at supper in her tiny house in the wood.

She went to open the door, and there she saw a dear little girl about three years old.

"Please, I'm lost," again came the words, and two fat little fists went up to a pair of big blue eyes.

"Come in, little girl, and tell me all about it," said the woman. "Maybe I can help you to find your way."

The child let herself be led into the room; then all at once the two tiny fists came down from the two blue eyes, and she gave a quick look at the table.

"Are you having supper?" she said. "May I have supper too? I am ever so hungry."

"Yes, dear; of course you shall have some," was the reply. "See, you shall sit on this chair by my side. Now what will you have?"

"I think I would like some bread and butter with sugar on it—brown sugar, you know;" and soon the little girl was as happy as could be.

"What is your name, dear?" asked Mrs. Stone, when supper was over and the little girl had begun to think once more about how she was to find her way home.

"Meg," was the reply.

"But your other name, for you must have two names."

"No, my name is just Meg, of course; I don't have any other name," she said, a look of wonder in the big blue eyes.

"Do you know where you live?"

"Yes; I lives in the nursery. Didn't you know that?"

She was so sure that it did not seem any good to say any more about it. So Mrs. Stone only asked, "Where were you going when you came to my house?"

"To find a baby," was the reply. "Rob said that if I went

to a house in the wood they would give me one. Have you got a baby to give me?"

"No, dear; I am afraid I have not. But why do you want a baby? I am sure you have lots of dolls."

"Yes, of course I have; but then you see dolls are not alive. I want a real baby to play with.

"Enid won't play with me much now, for she says I am too small, and Rob is at school all the time."

"Why, who is that?" said a voice, and a man came in with a bag of tools.

Then the two little fists again went up to the blue eyes, for the little maid was shy of this great big man.

"Well, wife, so you have a friend, I see," he said. "Who is the little lass?"

"I don't know," said his wife. "It seems she was lost, and came here to ask her way. She says she came to find a baby."

"Come here, little one, and don't be afraid," said the man. "There never was a child yet who would not come to me," and as he spoke he drew her on to his knee. "Now, then, tell me all about it."

After one glance at the man's kind face Meg nestled up to him and began,—

"Nurse was so busy she could not be in the room with me.

"So I put on my hat and came to look for a baby; but I got lost on the way. At last I came to the wood and saw this house. She could not give me a baby as Rob said she would, but she gave me some tea, and bread and butter with sugar on it. We only have that on Sunday at home. Is this Sunday?"

"No, little miss," said the man. "But I expect you had it just for a treat, as you had got lost."

But just then steps were heard on the path, and there was a sharp knock at the door.

The latch was lifted, and a voice said,—

"Have you seen a little girl in a white frock pass this way?"

"Why, that must be Nurse," cried Meg.

In spite of being cross at Meg's having run away, Nurse had to laugh; then she bent down and said, "But what made you run away like this, Miss Meg?"

"Rob told me that if I came to the house in the wood I should find a real live baby; but he was wrong, for she," with a smile at Mrs. Stone, "is very nice, but she has not got a baby to give me."

"Of course not, child; but do you know that I have some news for you?"

"What is it? Do tell me?" cried the little girl.

"While you were away in the wood to look for a baby we have found a baby at home. You have a new baby brother. Come home with me now and you shall see him."

"A new little brother," said Meg, her eyes wide open with wonder. "He must have known I had gone out to look for one. So now I have got two new friends and a baby too. Come along, quick."

"Good-bye," she said to her new friends. "Thank you ever so much for being so kind, and for the supper.

"I am coming to have supper with you again soon, and then I will bring the new baby with me. You will give me and baby bread and butter with sugar on it, won't you?" and Meg trotted off as happy as a little queen.

☙ ☙ ☙

JOCK AND I AND THE OTHERS

FIRST of all, I must tell you you who I am.

My name is PE-NEL-O-PE, but Jock always calls me Pen. I am eight years old; Jock is half-past six.

We live with mother and father and Rover and Tibby in a house not very far from a large city.

Mother is the nicest person I know in all the world.

Father is a very big man. He always has lots of money in his pocket. He goes to business in a train every day.

We have a real farm, quite near to our house, where they keep cows, chickens, pigs, horses, and geese. Jock and I often go to see them all.

One day in summer we went to see the farmer. I had my blue dress on, so that the cows would not be angry when they saw me.

We met the farmer near the stable. "Come," he said; "I have something to show you to-day."

"What is it?" we said both at the same time.

"Come and see," was all that he would say.

Then he took us into the stable where he keeps Nobby, the big brown horse, who likes sugar.

Now Nobby was not there, but in the straw were seven little puppy dogs—oh, so sweet and cuddly!

Jock danced round and round the farmer. "May we have one?" he said.

"Ask mother," said the farmer, and off we ran at once.

Mother was at the garden gate.

We ran up to her. Jock was first, but it was nearly a dead heat. Mother opened the gate and said,—

"Well, what have you seen to-day?"

"O mother," said Jock, out of breath.

"O mother *dear*," I said, out of breath also.

"Farmer has such lovely puppies," we both said at once. "May we have one to keep?"

By this time we both had our arms round mother's waist, and she was laughing.

"Yes, we can," I said, for I *knew*.

"If *father* says yes," said mother. "You must ask him when he comes home."

So we went to the station to meet him. Jock took his bag, and I took his paper parcel to carry it home for him.

On the way home I asked him if he liked dogs, and he said, "Of course."

Then Jock said, "*Little* dogs?"

"Oh, yes."

"*Puppy* dogs?"

"One at a time is all right."

"One puppy dog with brown spots on white?" Jock went on.

"Where is it?" asked father, and his eyes were laughing; you could not see his mouth for his beard.

Then we told him, and he said "Yes," just at the garden gate. So that was how we got Rover.

* * * * * *

Rover was very soft and downy when he first came to us. But he soon grew to be a big dog.

Jock and I taught him many tricks; and he can beg very nicely, if we let him get on the couch in the dining-room.

We put sugar on his nose, and he waits until we count One, Two, THREE.

Then he throws the sugar into the air and catches it.

☙ ☙ ☙

DOLLY DIMPLE

BY F. TAPSELL

"OH dear, I am so lonely, and it is so dark! I do want my dear Dolly Dimple. I think I will go and fetch her." And little four-year-old Babs got out of bed and felt her way to the door.

The door was just a wee crack open. As she peeped in, Babs saw that there was a light in the room, and the sight which met her eyes almost made her cry out.

On the floor stood Dolly Dimple in her very best frock, and Mr. Jollyman was asking her to dance with him.

Teddy Bear was at work on the big drum, and the clown was turning the organ to make music for the dolls to dance to.

The tin soldiers, on the backs of cows, pigs, and sheep from the Noah's Ark were having a sham fight.

The dolls from the dolls' house were going for a ride in the big horse and cart.

"It is too bad of them to go and have a good time like this when I am in bed," thought Babs, "and I am going to take Dolly Dimple away with me all the same."

But when she tried to pick up the doll and carry her off, Mr. Jollyman flew at her in a fury.

He began to kick her bare legs till Babs thought she would have no shins left at all; but she would not run away.

"I want Dolly Dimple," she said. "She is my doll, and you have no right to try to keep her away from me."

"She is yours in the day, but not at night," was the reply. "How do you think we toys could live if we had no life but the one we endure at your hands? It is in the night that we live and have our good times, for we know you are safe in bed then."

"I don't care what you say; I will have her," cried Babs, very angry now.

She tried once more to get hold of Dolly Dimple; but before she could do so, Mr. Jollyman turned to the soldiers, and said the one word, "Charge."

There was a great noise and a rush, and right down upon the little girl came camels, horses, lions, tigers, sheep, and pigs.

But just as she thought her last hour was come, she heard the word "Halt," and then the sound of Dolly Dimple saying, "No, don't kill her. She is very good to me most of the time."

The rest of the dolls had begun to dance once more, but Dolly Dimple came up to the little girl and took hold of her arm.

"I am queen here in the night," she said. "I will not hurt you, as you have been good to me, and I know you love me. If you like, I will come and stay with you till you go to sleep. Pick me up."

So Babs picked up the doll, and took it back to bed with her, and hugged it in her arms.

☘ ☘ ☘

THE TALE OF PETER RABBIT

BY BEATRIX POTTER

ONCE upon a time there were four little Rabbits, and their names were—Flopsy, Mopsy, Cotton-Tail, and Peter. They lived with their Mother in a sandbank, underneath the root of a very big fir-tree.

"Now, my dears," said old Mrs. Rabbit one morning, "you may go into the fields or down the lane, but don't go into Mr. McGregor's garden: your Father had an accident there; he was put in a pie by Mrs. McGregor."

"Now run along, and don't get into mischief. I am going out."

Then old Mrs. Rabbit took a basket and her umbrella and went through the wood to the baker's. She bought a loaf of brown bread and five currant buns.

Flopsy, Mopsy, and Cotton-tail, who were good little bunnies, went down the lane to gather blackberries.

But Peter, who was very naughty, ran straight away to Mr. McGregor's garden, and squeezed under the gate!

First he ate some lettuces and some French beans, and then he ate some radishes; and then, feeling rather sick, he went to look for some parsley.

But round the end of a cucumber frame, whom should he meet but Mr. McGregor!

Mr. McGregor was on his hands and knees planting out young cabbages, but he jumped up and ran after Peter, waving a rake and calling out, "Stop, thief!"

Peter was most dreadfully frightened; he rushed all over the garden, for he had forgotten the way back to the gate. He lost one of his shoes among the cabbages, and the other shoe amongst the potatoes.

After losing them, he ran on four legs and went faster, so that I think he might have got away altogether if he had not unfortunately run into a gooseberry net, and got caught by the large buttons on his jacket. It was a blue jacket with brass buttons, quite new.

Peter gave himself up for lost, and shed big tears; but his sobs were overheard by some friendly sparrows, who flew to him in great excitement, and implored him to exert himself.

Mr. McGregor came up with a sieve, which he intended to pop upon the top of Peter, but Peter wriggled out just in time, leaving his jacket behind him; and rushed into the tool-shed, and jumped into a can. It would have been a beautiful thing to hide in, if it had not had so much water in it.

Mr. McGregor was quite sure that Peter was somewhere in the tool-shed, perhaps hidden underneath a flower-pot. He began to turn them over carefully, looking under each.

Presently Peter sneezed—"Kerty-schoo!" Mr. McGregor was after him in no time, and tried to put his foot upon Peter, who jumped out of a window, upsetting three plants. The window was too small for Mr. McGregor, and he was tired of running after Peter. He went back to his work.

Peter sat down to rest; he was out of breath and trembling with fright, and he had not the least idea which way to go. Also he was very damp with sitting in that can.

After a time he began to wander about, going lippity-lippity—not very fast, and looking all around.

He found a door in a wall; but it was locked, and there was no room for a fat little rabbit to squeeze underneath.

An old mouse was running in and out over the stone door-step, carrying peas and beans to her family in the wood. Peter asked her the way to the gate, but she had such a large pea in her mouth that she could not answer. She only shook her head at him. Peter began to cry.

Then he tried to find his way straight across the garden, but he became more and more puzzled. Presently, he came to a pond where Mr. McGregor filled his water-cans. A white cat was staring at some goldfish; she sat very, very still, but now and then the tip of her tail twitched as if it were alive. Peter thought it best to go away without speaking to her; he had heard about cats from his cousin, little Benjamin Bunny.

He went back toward the tool-shed, but suddenly, quite close to him, he heard the noise of a hoe—scr-r-ritch, scratch, scratch, scratch. Peter scuttered underneath the bushes. But, presently, as nothing happened, he came out, and climbed upon a wheelbarrow, and peeped over. The first thing he saw was Mr. McGregor hoeing onions. His back was turned toward Peter, and beyond him was the gate!

Peter got down very quietly off the wheelbarrow, and started running as fast as he could go, along a straight walk behind some black-currant bushes.

Mr. McGregor caught sight of him at the corner, but

Peter did not care. He slipped underneath the gate, and was safe at last in the wood outside the garden.

Mr. McGregor hung up the little jacket and the shoes for a scarecrow to frighten the blackbirds.

Peter never stopped running or looked behind him till he got home to the big fir-tree.

He was so tired that he flopped down upon the nice soft sand on the floor of the rabbit-hole, and shut his eyes.

His mother was busy cooking; she wondered what he had done with his clothes. It was the second little jacket and pair of shoes that Peter had lost in a fortnight!

I am sorry to say that Peter was not very well during the evening.

His mother put him to bed, and made some camomile tea; and she gave a dose of it to Peter!

"One table-spoonful to be taken at bed-time."

But Flopsy, Mopsy, and Cotton-tail had bread and milk and blackberries for supper.

☙ ☙ ☙

THE MILLER, HIS SON, AND THEIR ASS

ONCE upon a time there was a miller who lived in a little house beside his mill. All day long he worked hard, but at night he went home to his wife and his little boy.

One day this miller made up his mind that he would take his ass to the fair and sell it. So he and his boy said farewell to the dame and started off. They had not gone far when they met a number of girls coming from the town.

"Look!" said one of them. "Did you ever see such stupid fellows? They are walking when one of them might be riding."

When the miller heard this he bade the boy get up on the ass, while he tramped along merrily by its side. Soon they came to a number of old men standing by the side of the road talking together.

"Look at that," said one of them. "Look at that young

rascal riding, while his poor father has to walk. Get down, you idle fellow, and let your father ride."

Upon this the son got down from the ass, and the miller took his place. They had not gone very far when they met two women coming home from market.

"You lazy old man!" they cried at once. "How dare you ride when your poor little boy is walking and can hardly keep pace with you?"

Then the miller, who was a good-natured man, took his son up behind him, and in this way they went to the town.

"My good fellow," said a townsman whom they met, "is that ass your own?"

"Yes," replied the miller.

"I should not have thought so, by the way you load him," said the man. "Why, you two are better able to carry the beast than he is to carry you."

"Well," said the miller, "we can but try."

So he and his son got down, and tied the legs of the ass together. Then they slung him on a pole, and carried him on their shoulders. It was such a funny sight that the people laughed and jeered at them.

The poor ass was very uncomfortable, and tried hard to get off the pole. At last, as they were passing over a bridge, he pulled his legs out of the rope and tumbled to the ground. He was so frightened that he jumped off the bridge into the river and was drowned.

Do you know what this story teaches you?

If you try to please everybody, you will please nobody.

☙ ☙ ☙

THE VISIT TO SANTA CLAUS LAND

JACK and Margaret were growing more excited each day, because Christmas was so near. They talked of nothing but Santa Claus.

"Don't you wish you could *see* him?" they said over and over.

One night, just before Christmas, Mother tucked them in bed and left them to go to sleep. But Jack wiggled, Margaret wriggled. At last they both sat up in bed.

"Jack," Margaret whispered, "are you asleep?"

"No," said Jack, "I can't go to sleep. Margaret, don't you wish you could see Santa Claus? What's that?"

They both listened, and they heard a little *tap, tap* on the window. They looked, and there, right in the window, they saw a funny little Brownie.

"What's that I heard you say? You want to see Santa Claus? Well, I am one of his Brownies. I am on my way back to Santa Claus Land. I'll take you with me if you want to go."

Jack and Margaret scrambled from their beds.

"Come on, show us the way!" they cried in great excitement.

"No, indeed," said the Brownie. "No one must know the way to Santa Claus Land. Kindly wait a moment."

Then the Brownie took something soft and thick and dark, and tied it around Jack's eyes. Next he took something soft and thick and dark, and tied it around Margaret's eyes.

"How many fingers before you?" he asked.

Both of them shook their heads. They could not see a wink.

"Very well, now we're off," said the Brownie.

He took Jack's hand on one side, and Margaret's on the other. It seemed as if they flew through the window. They went on swiftly for a little while, then the Brownie whirled them round and round until they were dizzy, and off they went again. The children could not tell whether they were going north, south, east, or west. After a time they stopped.

"Here we are," said the Brownie.

He uncovered their eyes, and the children saw that they were standing before a big, thick gate.

The Brownie knocked and the gate was swung open. They went through it, right into Santa Claus's garden.

It was a very queer garden. There were rows and rows of Christmas trees, all glittering with balls and cobwebby tinsel, and instead of flower beds there were beds of every kind of toy in the world. Margaret at once ran over to a bed of dolls.

"Let's see if any of them are ripe," said the Brownie.

"Ripe?" said Margaret in great surprise.

"Why, of course," said the Brownie. "Now if this one is ripe it will shut its eyes."

The Brownie picked a little doll from the bed and laid it in Margaret's arms. Its eyes went half shut, and then stuck.

"No, it's not ripe yet," said the Brownie. "Try this one."

He picked another one, and this one shut its eyes just as if it had gone to sleep.

"We'll take that one," he said, and he dropped it into a big sack he was carrying.

"Now this one cries, if it's ripe," he said as he picked a lovely infant doll. The Brownie gave it a squeeze, and the doll made a funny squeaking noise.

"Not quite ripe," he said, and he put it back into the bed. He tried several others, and he picked a good many. Some of them cried, some said "Mamma" and "Papa," and some danced when they were wound up.

"Oh, do come over here, Margaret!" Jack called.

Margaret ran over to another bed and there were drums—big drums, little drums, and middle sized drums; yellow drums, blue drums, green drums, red drums.

"Can we gather some of these?" said Jack to the Brownie.

"Why, of course. Let's see if this one is ripe."

The Brownie took up a little red drum, and gave it a thump with a drum stick. But it made such a queer sound that Jack and Margaret both laughed out loud. The little red drum was put back into the bed, and the Brownie tried another big one. It went *Boom! Boom! Boom! Boom! Boom!* and Jack and Margaret marched all along the bed, keeping step to it.

When they had finished picking drums, they went over to a bed filled with horns. That was the most fun of all. Some of them made very queer noises, and on some the Brownie played jolly little tunes.

The next bed they came to was filled with toys which could be wound up. There were trains, automobiles, dancing dolls, climbing monkeys, hopping birds, funny wobbling ducks, and every kind of toy you could think of. The children stayed at this bed for a long time.

At last Margaret said: "But where is Santa Claus? We wanted to see him."

"Oh, to be sure," said the Brownie. "Come along," and he led them down a long, winding walk, to the edge of the garden. Then he pointed to a hill in the distance.

"Do you see that large white house? There is where he lives."

The children stared at it. It was so white that it seemed to shine in the distance.

"Walk right across here," said the Brownie, "then up the hill to Santa Claus's house."

"Oh, must we walk across there?" said Margaret. She stared down at the deep dark chasm between the garden and the hill; across it was stretched a narrow plank.

"Walk carefully," said the Brownie, "and mind you don't look down; for if you do, I'm afraid you won't see Santa Claus to-night."

"We'll be very careful," said Jack. "Come along, Margaret," and he took his little sister's hand and they started across the plank.

They had almost reached the middle of it when Jack looked down.

"Oh!" he said, and gave Margaret a pull.

She looked down too, and cried "Oh, Oh!" and down, down, down they went.

Suddenly they landed with a thump. They sat up and rubbed their eyes. There they were right in their own beds at home. Mother opened the door.

"Are you awake, children?" she said.

"Oh, Mother, we haven't been asleep. We've been to Santa Claus Land, and we nearly saw Santa Claus!"

Then they told her all about it, and Mother just smiled.

THE GREEDY BROWNIE

THERE was once a little Brownie who lived in a hollow tree stump. He had been busy all the day playing pranks. His pranks had taken him far away from home to the house of a very important laird. Into the laird's cup of wine he had dropped some sour berries which he had picked on his way. He also put thistles into his boots, so that when the laird had drawn them on he had screamed out with pain.

The Brownie had been away all the day, so that when at last he turned to go back to his home he felt really very tired. On his way back to the wood he passed by a cozy-looking farmhouse. The door of the dairy was open. The Brownie thought this would be a very nice cool place in which to rest for a few moments. So he slipped into the dairy, and curled himself up underneath the bench to have a nice little doze.

He was so weary that once he had fallen asleep he never woke up again until it was quite dark, when he was disturbed by two lassies who had come into the dairy.

One was carrying a candle in her hand, and by its light the pair espied a big bowl of cream on the shelf. The naughty girls thought that they would drink it for supper. They could only find one spoon on the shelf, so they decided they would each have a spoonful in turn. Lassie Jean took the bowl and carried it to a bench in the corner, and Lassie Meg followed it with the candle. No sooner had the two girls settled themselves than the Brownie, who was now wide awake, and who was himself feeling that some supper might not be out of place, crept up behind them and blew out the candle.

The lassies at first were very much concerned at being in the dark; nevertheless they determined they would drink the cream, all the same.

Lassie Jean filled the spoon with the rich delicacy. She was about to raise it to her lips when the naughty Brownie poked his head over her shoulder, and lapped it out of the spoon before it had reached her mouth. Lassie Meg, believing that Lassie Jean had already swallowed some cream while she had had none, stretched out her hand to take away the spoon from her friend. Lassie Jean was not willing to give it up, since she said she had not yet tasted any cream. Lassie Meg was unwilling to believe her, for she declared she had heard her lapping the cream.

Without waiting for Lassie Jean to explain, she snatched the spoon out of her friend's hand. She filled it with cream from the bowl, and was about to raise it to her lips when the Brownie jumped from behind Lassie Jean, and settling himself behind Lassie Meg's shoulders, poked forward his head, and again lapped up the cream from out of the spoon.

Lassie Jean in her turn snatched back the spoon from Lassie Meg. Thus they went on, for every time one or the other raised the spoonful of cream to her lips it was lapped up by the Brownie. This continued until the bowl was emptied. The Brownie was full of cream, but the poor lassies had not so much as tasted one drop, although each believed the other had drunk it all.

The lassies were still quarreling when the door of the dairy was opened, and the farmer's wife entered, carrying a lighted candle in her hand. The moment that she did so the Brownie hopped under the bench and the lassies started up guiltily.

The farmer's wife caught sight of the empty basin. She was very angry with them indeed. When they tried hastily to explain, each blaming the other, the farmer's wife would not listen, but only grew the more angry. She told them that, since they had supped so well, they should have none of the scones and eggs which she had prepared for the evening meal in the kitchen.

When the farmer's wife had entered she had left the door open, so while she was busily scolding the lassies the Brownie slipped out from under the bench and made his escape. As he ran chuckling down the road, he could still hear her angry voice drowning the attempted explanations of the bewildered lassies. When the little fellow curled himself up some time later in the tree trunk he was still laughing.

THE FAIRIES' PASSAGE

BY JAMES CLARENCE MANGAN

TAP, tap, tap, rap! "Get up, gaffer Ferryman,"
"Eh! Who is there?" The clock strikes three.
"Get up, do, gaffer! You are the very man
We have been long, long, longing to see."
The ferryman rises, growling and grumbling,
And goes fum-fumbling, and stumbling, and tumbling
Over the wares on his way to the door.
But he sees no more
Than he saw before;
Till a voice is heard: "O Ferryman dear!
Here we are waiting, all of us, here.
We are a wee, wee colony, we;
Some two hundred in all, or three,
Ferry us over the river Lee,
Ere dawn of day,
And we will pay
The most we may
In our own wee way!"

"Who are you? Whence came you?
What place are you going to?"
"Oh, we have dwelt over-long in this land;
The people get cross, and are growing so knowing, too!
Nothing at all but they now understand.
We are daily vanishing under the thunder
Of some huge engine or iron wonder;
That iron, ah! it has entered our souls."
"Your souls? O gholes,
You queer little drolls,
Do you mean. . . .?" "Good gaffer, do aid us with speed,
For our time, like our stature, is short indeed!
And a very long way we have to go;
Eight or ten thousand miles or so,
Hither and thither, and to and fro,

With our pots and pans
And little gold cans;
But our light caravans
Run swifter than man's."

"Well, well, you may come," said the ferryman affably;
"Patrick, turn out, and get ready the barge."
Then again to the little folk; "Tho' you seem laughably
Small, I don't mind, if your coppers be large."
Oh, dear, what a rushing, what pushing, what crushing
(The watermen making vain efforts at hushing
The hubbub the while), there followed these words.
What clapping of boards,
What strapping of cords,
What stowing away of children and wives,
And platters and mugs, and spoons and knives,
Till all had safely got into the boat,
And the ferryman, clad in his tip-top coat,
And his wee little fairies were safely afloat!
Then ding, ding, ding,
And kling, kling, kling,
How the coppers did ring
In the tin pitcherling.

Off, then, went the boat, at first very pleasantly,
Smoothly, and so forth; but after a while
It swayed and it sagged this and that way, and presently
Chest after chest, and pile after pile,
Of the little folks' goods began tossing and rolling,
And pitching like fun, beyond fairy controlling.
O Mab! if the hubbub were great before,
It was now some two or three million times more.
Crash! went the wee crocks and the clocks; and the locks
Of each little wee box were stove in by hard knocks;
And then there were oaths, and prayers, and cries:
"Take care"—"See there"—"O, dear, my eyes!"
"I am killed!"—"I am drowned!"—with groans and sighs,
Till to land they drew.

"Yeo-ho! Pull to
Tiller-rope thro' and thro'!"
And all's right anew.
"Now, jump upon shore, ye queer little oddities.
(Eh, what is this? . . . where are they, at all?
Where are they, and where are their tiny commodities?
Well, as I live" . . .) He looks blank as a wall,
Poor ferryman! Round him and round him he gazes,
But only gets deeplier lost in the mazes
Of utter bewilderment. All, all are gone,
And he stands alone,
Like a statue of stone,
In a doldrum of wonder. He turns to steer,
And a tinkling laugh salutes his ear,
With other odd sounds: "Ha, ha, ha, ha!
Fol lol! zidzizzle! quee quee! bah! bah!
Fizzigig-giggidy! pshee! sha sha!"
"O ye thieves, ye thieves, ye rascally thieves!"
The good man cries. He turns to his pitcher,
And there, alas, to his horror perceives
That the little folk's mode of making him richer
Has been to pay him with withered leaves!

❧ ❧ ❧

THE WORLD

"THE world is wet," said the little frog;
"What isn't water is mostly bog."
"Oh, not at all!" said the little fly;
"It's full of spiders, and very dry!"
"The world is dark," said the moth polite,
"With ruddy windows and bows of light."
"My poor young friend, you have much to learn:
The world is green," said the swaying fern.
"O listen to me," sang the little lark:
"It's wet and dry, and it's green and dark.
To think that's all would be very wrong;
It's arched with blue, and it's filled with song."

FANCIFUL STORIES

WHITE MAGIC

BLIND folks see the fairies,
Oh, better far than we,
Who miss the shining of their wings
Because our eyes are filled with things
We do not wish to see.
They need not seek enchantment
From solemn printed books,
For all about them as they go
The fairies flutter to and fro
With smiling friendly looks.

Deaf folk hear the fairies,
However soft their song;
'Tis we who lose the honey sound
Amid the clamor all around
That beats the whole day long.
But they with gentle faces
Sit quietly apart;
What room have they for sorrowing
While fairy minstrels sit and sing
Close to each listening heart?

—From London *Punch*.

THE BROWNIES

BY JULIANA HORATIA EWING

I

"CHILDREN are a burden," said the tailor, as he sat on his bench stitching away.

"Children are a blessing," said the kind lady in the window.

It was the tailor's mother who spoke. She was a very old woman and nearly helpless. All day she sat in a large armchair knitting rugs.

"What have my two lads ever done to help me?" continued the tailor, sadly. "They do nothing but play. If I send Tommy on an errand, he loiters. If I ask him to work, he does it so unwillingly that I would rather do it myself. Since their mother died I have indeed had a hard time."

At this moment the two boys came in, their arms full of moss which they dropped on the floor.

"Is there any supper, grandmother?" asked Tommy.

"No, my child, only some bread for breakfast to-morrow."

"Oh, grandmother, we are so hungry!" and the boy's eyes filled with tears.

"What can I do for you, my poor children?" said the good woman.

"Tell us a story, please, so that we can forget we are hungry. Tell us about the brownie that used to live in your grandfather's house. What was he like?"

"Like a little man, they say."

"What did he do?"

"He came early in the morning before any one in the house was awake, and lighted the fire and swept the room and set out the breakfast. He never would be seen and was off before they could catch him. But they often heard him laughing and playing about the house."

"Did they give him any wages, grandmother?"

"No, my dear, he did the work for love. They always set

a pan of clear water for him, and now and then a bowl of bread and milk."

"Oh, grandmother, where did he go?"

"The Old Owl in the woods knows; I do not. When I was young many people used to go to see the Old Owl at moonrise, and ask her what they wanted to know."

"How I wish a brownie would come and live with us!" cried Tommy.

"So do I," said Johnny.

"Will you let us set out a pan of water for the brownie, father?" asked Tommy.

"You may set out what you like, my lad, but you must go to bed now."

The boys brought out a pan of water. Then they climbed the ladder to the loft over the kitchen.

Johnny was soon in the land of dreams, but Tommy lay awake thinking how he could find a brownie and get him to live in the house. "There is an owl that lives in the grove," he thought. "It may be the Old Owl herself. When the moon rises, I'll go and find her."

II

The moon rose like gold and went up in the heavens like silver. Tommy opened his eyes and ran to the window. "The moon has risen," said he, "and it is time for me to go." Downstairs he crept softly and out into the still night.

"Hoot! hoot!" cried a voice from the grove near the house.

"That's the Old Owl," thought Tommy. He ran to a big tree and looked up. There he saw the Old Owl, sitting on a branch and staring at him with yellow eyes.

"Oh, dear!" said Tommy, for he did not like the Owl very well.

"Come up here! Come up here!" she cried.

Tommy climbed the tree and sat face to face with her on the big branch.

"Now, what do you want?" said the Owl.

"Please," said Tommy, "I want to know where to find the brownies, and how to get one to come and live with us."

"Oo-hoo! oo-hoo!" said the Owl. "That's it, is it? I know of three brownies."

"Hurrah!" said Tommy. "Where do they live?"

"In your house," said the Owl.

"In our house! Whereabouts? Why don't they work?" cried Tommy.

"One of them is too little," said the Owl.

"But why don't the other two do something?" said Tommy. "Nobody does any work at our house except father."

"They are idle, they are idle," said the Old Owl.

"Then we don't want them," said Tommy. "What is the use of having brownies in the house if they do nothing to help us?"

"Perhaps they don't know what to do."

"I wish you would tell me where to find them," said Tommy. "I could tell them what to do."

"Could you, could you? Oo-hoo! oo-hoo!" and Tommy could not tell whether the Owl was hooting or laughing.

"Of course I could. They might get up early in the morning and sweep the house, and light the fire, and spread the table before my father comes downstairs."

"So they might!" said the Owl. "Well, I can tell you where to find one of the brownies, and he can tell you where to find his brother. Go to the north side of the pond, where the moon is shining on the water, turn yourself around three times, while you say this charm:

'Twist me and turn me and show me the elf—
I looked in the water and saw—'

Then look in the water, and think of a word which rhymes with 'elf' and makes the charm complete."

Tommy knew the place very well. He ran to the north side of the pond, and turning himself around three times, he repeated the charm. Then he looked in and saw—himself.

"Why, there's no one but myself. I can't think of the right word. What can it be? I'll go back and ask the Old Owl," thought Tommy. And back he went. There sat the Owl as before.

"Oo-hoo," said she, as Tommy climbed up. "Did you find out the word?"

"No," said Tommy, "I could find no word that rhymes with 'elf' except 'myself.'"

"Well, that is the word! Now, do you know where your brother is?"

"In bed in the loft," said Tommy.

"Then all your questions are answered. Good night;" and the Old Owl began to shake her feathers.

"Don't go yet," said Tommy, humbly; "I don't understand you. I am not a brownie, am I?"

"Yes, you are, and a very idle one, too," said the Old Owl. "All children are brownies."

"But are there really any brownies except children?" inquired Tommy, in a dismal tone.

"No, there are not. Now listen to me, Tommy. Little people can do only little things. When they are idle and mischievous, they are called boggarts, and they are a burden to the house they live in. When they are thoughtful and useful, they are brownies, and are a blessing to every one."

"I'll be a brownie," said Tommy. "I won't be a boggart. Now I'll go home and tell Johnny."

"I'll take you home," said the Owl, and in a moment Tommy found himself in bed, with Johnny sleeping by his side.

"How quickly we came," said Tommy to himself. "But is it morning? That is very strange! I thought the moon was shining. Come, Johnny, get up, I have a story to tell you."

III

While his brother was rubbing his eyes Tommy told him of his visit to the Old Owl in the grove.

"Is that all true?" asked Johnny.

"It is all just as I tell you, and if we don't want to be boggarts, we must get up and go to work."

"I won't be a boggart," said Johnny, and so the two brownies crept softly down the ladder into the kitchen. "I will light the fire," said Tommy. "And you, Johnny, can dig some potatoes to roast for breakfast." They swept the room and laid the table. Just as they were putting the potatoes in a dish they heard footsteps.

"There's father," said Tommy; "we must run."

The poor tailor came wearily down the stairs. Morning after morning he had found an untidy room and an empty table. But now when he entered the kitchen, he looked around in great surprise. He put his hand out to the fire to see if it was really warm. He touched the potatoes and looked at the neat room. Then he shouted, "Mother, mother! boys, boys, the brownie has come!"

There was great excitement in the small house, but the boys said nothing. All day the tailor talked about the brownie. "I have often heard of Little People," he said, "but this is wonderful. To come and do the work for a pan of cold water! Who would have believed it?"

The boys said nothing until they were both in bed. Then Tommy said: "The Old Owl was right, and we must stick to the work if we don't want to be boggarts. But I don't like to have father thinking that we are still idle. I wish he knew that we are the brownies."

"So do I," said Johnny.

Day after day went by and still the boys rose early, and each day they found more and more to do. The brownies were the joy of the tailor's life.

One day a message came for the tailor to go to a farmhouse several miles away. The farmer gave him an order for a suit of clothes, and paid him at once. Full of joy at his good fortune, he hurried home. As he came near the house, he saw that the garden had been weeded. "It's that brownie!" he said; "and I shall make a suit of clothes for him."

"If you make clothes for the brownie, he will leave the house," said the grandmother.

"Not if the clothes are a good fit, mother. I shall measure them by Tommy, for they say the brownies are about his size."

At last a fine new suit with brass buttons was finished and laid out for the brownie.

"Don't the clothes look fine?" said Tommy, when he came down in the morning; "I'll try them on."

The tailor rose earlier than usual that day, for he wished to catch a glimpse of the brownies. He went softly downstairs. There was Johnny sweeping the floor, and Tommy trying on the new suit.

"What does this mean?" shouted the father.

"It's the brownies," said the boys.

"This is no joke," cried the tailor, angrily. "Where are the real brownies, I say?"

"We are the only brownies, father," said Tommy.

"I can't understand this. Who has been sweeping the kitchen lately, I should like to know?"

"We have," said the boys.

"Who gets breakfast and puts things in order?"

"We do! we do!" they shouted.

"But when do you do it?"

"Early in the morning before you come down."

"But if you do the work, where is the brownie?"

"Here," cried the boys; "we are the brownies, and we are sorry that we were boggarts so long."

The father was delighted to find how helpful his boys had become. The grandmother, however, could hardly believe that a real brownie had not been in the house. But as she sat in her chair day after day watching the boys at their work, she often repeated her favorite saying, "Children are a blessing."

☙ ☙ ☙

THE STORY OF PETER PAN

ONCE upon a time there were three children named Wendy, John, and Michael, who lived with their father and mother in London. One evening the father and mother were invited to a party, and the mother, after lighting the dim lamp in the nursery and kissing them good-night, went away. That evening a little boy climbed in through the window, whose name was Peter Pan. He was a curious little fellow, very conceited, very forgetful, and yet very lovable. The most remarkable thing about him was that he never grew up. There came flitting in through the window with him his fairy, whose name was Tinker Bell. Peter Pan woke all the children up, and after he had sprinkled fairy dust on their shoulders, he took them away to the Neverland, where he lived with a family of lost boys. Tinker Bell was jealous of the little girl Wendy, and she hurried ahead of Peter Pan and persuaded the boys that Wendy was a bird who might do them harm, and so one of the boys shot her with his bow and arrow.

When Peter Pan came and found Wendy lying lifeless upon the ground in the woods he was very angry, but he was also very quick-witted. So he told the boys that if they would build a house around Wendy he was sure that she would be better. So they hurried to collect everything they had out of which they could make a house. Though she was not yet strong enough to talk, they thought perhaps she might sing the kind of house she would like to have, so Wendy sang softly this little verse:

"I wish I had a pretty house,
The littlest ever seen,
With funny little red walls
And roof of mossy green."

When the house was done Peter Pan took John's hat for the chimney, and the little house was so pleased to have such a capital chimney that smoke at once began to come out through the hat. All that night Peter Pan walked up and down in front of Wendy's house, to watch over her and keep her from danger while she slept.

All these children lived in an underground cave, and the next day, when Wendy got well, they all went down into the cave and Wendy agreed to be their mother and Peter their father. They had many good times together. They also had some exciting adventures with the red-skins and with a pirate named Captain Hook and his crew. After a time the red-skins became their friends, and Peter rescued his family from the pirates' ship.

One day Wendy and her brothers realized that they had been away so long that perhaps their mother had forgotten them and shut the window of the nursery so that they could not get back. They decided to hurry home. When they reached home Peter Pan was before them, and he closed the window so that they could not get back. But when he heard the children's mother singing such a sad song inside, his heart was made tender and he opened the window and the children crept back safely into their mother's arms. Wendy's mother invited Peter Pan to stay and be her child, but Peter was so afraid that he would have to go to school and grow up and be a man that he went back to his home in fairy-land.

Wendy promised to go once a year and stay a few days with Peter Pan and clean house and mend his clothes. Let us picture them in the little house that was built for Wendy, which the fairies had put up in the branches of a pine-tree. The birds are singing in their nests and in the branches, and far below the clouds you can see the land and the sea. Wendy is sewing for Peter and Peter Pan is playing his pipes while she works. When night comes the woods are full of flashing lights like little stars, because the fairies are flitting around the house where Peter and Wendy live, and are singing to them as they go to sleep.

In a few days Wendy will go back to John and Michael to tell them what a good time she had on her visit in the little house in the woods.

SIR LARK AND KING SUN

BY GEORGE MACDONALD

"GOOD morrow, my lord!" in the sky alone,
Sang the lark as the sun ascended his throne.
"Shine on me, my lord; I only am come,
Of all your servants, to welcome you home.
I have flown right up, a whole hour, I swear,
To catch the first shine of your golden hair."

"Must I thank you then," said the king, "Sir Lark,
For flying so high and hating the dark?
You ask a full cup for half a thirst:
Half was love of me, and half love to be first.
There's many a bird makes no such haste,
But waits till I come: that's as much to my taste."

And King Sun hid his head in a turban of cloud,
And Sir Lark stopped singing, quite vexed and cowed;
But he flew up higher, and thought, "Anon
The wrath of the king will be over and gone;
And his crown, shining out of its cloudy fold,
Will change my brown feathers to a glory of gold."

So he flew—with the strength of a lark he flew;
But, as he rose, the cloud rose too;
And not one gleam of the golden hair
Came through the depths of the misty air;
Till, weary with flying, with sighing sore,
The strong sun-seeker could do no more.

His wings had had no chrism of gold;
And his feathers felt withered and worn and old;
He faltered, and sank, and dropped like a stone.
And there on his nest, where he left her, alone
Sat his little wife on her little eggs,
Keeping them warm with wings and legs.

Did I say alone? Ah, no such thing!
Full in her face was shining the king.
"Welcome, Sir Lark! You look tired," said he;
"*Up* is not always the best way to me.
While you have been singing so high and away,
I've been shining to your little wife all day."

He had set his crown all about the nest,
And out of the midst shone her little brown breast;
And so glorious was she in russet gold,
That for wonder and awe Sir Lark grew cold.
He popped his head under her wing, and lay
As still as a stone, till King Sun was away.

THE IMPS IN THE HEAVENLY MEADOW

BY KATE E. BUNCE (after RUDOLF BAUNBACH)

TO Heaven's Meadows, bright with flowers and sunshine,
The little children go,
When they have had enough of life's sad dreaming,
And leave the earth below.

But as they had not time to learn their lessons
Before they went away,
There is a school, where all the angel children
Must work four hours a day.

With golden pencils upon silver tablets,
They copy fairy tales,
And learn to keep their halos bright and shining,
And sing, and play their scales.

And twice a week they glide with merry laughter
All down the Milky Way,
And homeward in the evening wander softly
Upon a sunset ray.

But Sunday is the day they love and long for,
  Then all the children go
And play from morn till night within a meadow
  Where flowers in thousands grow.

The meadow is not green, but blue and golden
  The flowers like dewdrops bright;
When it is night, they burn and glow and glisten—
  Men call them stars of light.

Through Heaven's gate they all must pass to find it,
  Where Peter with the key
Keeps watch and warns the little angels kindly
  How good they all must be.

They must not fly about or run too quickly,
  Nor go too far away,
And when upon his golden key he calls them,
  Then they must all obey.

One day it was so very hot in Heaven
  That good St. Peter slept,
And when the little angel children saw it,
  Away they quickly crept.

Ah! then they ran and flew about with laughter,
  And fluttered far and wide,
So far they wandered that of Heaven's meadow
  They reached the other side.

They came to where the strong, tall, wooden paling
  Shuts all that place away,
Where idle, careless, mischief-loving, naughty,
  The Imps of Darkness stray.

And there the angels stopped, devoutly wishing
  Some opening there might be,
So that they might each one in turn peep through it,
  And see what they could see.

But not a chink or hole, for all their seeking,
No gleam of light pierced through,
So with their little wings outspread and eager,
Right to the top they flew.

And looking down they saw with awe and wonder,
Imps all as black as soot;
Each had two horns and each a tail to play with,
And hoof, instead of foot.

They heard the rustle of the angel feathers,
They felt the cool sweet air,
And, lifting up their little coal-black faces,
They saw Heaven's children there.

Then with one voice they cried: "Oh! angel Children,
You look so good and fair,
We pray you, let us come up into Heaven
And play a little there.

"We will not tweak nor pull your shining feathers,
But be so very good;
We will not try and steal your little halos,
But all do as we should."

Then quick they flew away for Jacob's ladder,
(Peter was still asleep),
And placed it safely, where from Heaven to Imp-land
The way was dark and steep.

Then every little imp, with shouts and laughter,
Helped by an angel's hand,
Scrambled right over the great wooden paling,
And stood in Heaven's land.

They all, with air sedate and pious faces,
Discreetly walked around,
Their tails like trains upon their arms upholding,
And eyes upon the ground.

The little angels fluttered round in rapture,
  And showed the lovely flowers,
And bade them listen to the thrilling voices
  Of birds in Heaven's bowers.

And gently led them by the crystal streamlets,
  Bade them on dewdrops feast,
And showed them where the silver moon was rising
  To light them from the east.

Alas! when all the little demons saw her,
  The moon, so large and round,
They all began to roar, and growl, and gibber,
  And leap from off the ground;

And mocked the great white moon with ugly faces,
  Turned somersaults in air,
And when the angels prayed them cease, in terror,
  They vowed they did not care.

They trampled down the grass in Heaven's Meadow,
  They tore the flowers about,
And flung them on the earth beyond the paling,
  With gibe, and jeer, and shout.

They chased the birds that sang among the tree-tops
  And hushed their music sweet,
They pulled the little angels' tender feathers
  And trod upon their feet.

Then to the good St. Peter cried the angels
  To help them in their pain,
And if he would but this one time forgive them,
  They would be good again.

Then rose St. Peter from his peaceful dreaming—
  An angry saint was he—
He wrung his hands and clasped his head in horror,
  And seized his golden key.

Then blew a mighty blast in wrath upon it;
  Back all the angels flew,
And wide he threw the door of heaven open,
  And thrust the children through.

And then he called two great and powerful angels,
  The strongest of the race,
To chase the little demons out of Heaven,
  And clear the holy place.

They gathered up the little imps in armfuls,
  Bore them with mighty stride,
And flung them over the strong wooden paling
  Down on the other side.

And though they fought and lashed their tails and whimpered,
  And kicked with might and main,
To Heaven's Meadow, bright with sun and flowers
  They never came again.

For two long months the little angel-children
  Were not allowed to play
Before the door of Heaven in the meadow,
  But stayed in all the day.

And when again they sought the Heavenly Meadow
  Each child with humble mind
Must lay aside its little shining halo,
  And leave its wings behind.

But all the flowers that on that day of sorrow,
  Flung out and scattered were,
Took root and bloom again in earth's green meadows,
  As daisies white and fair.

THE BIRTHDAY HONORS OF THE FAIRY QUEEN *

BY HAPGOOD MOORE

ONCE upon a time there lived in green Erin a little girl by the name of Nora. Her home was a small thatched cottage of stone beside the brae at the foot of a mountain, in the midst of a woodland so deep that in the summer time when the trees were full the sun got its rays inside but a few hours of the day and you could see of the star-dust that covers the fields of the sky no piece larger than the palm of your hand.

It was a famous meeting-place for the fairies, this haunt at the foot of the mountain by the stream, for the Little Folk from the heather above used nightly to foregather in the meadow with the Little Folk from the woodland below, and there they danced the long night through among the shamrocks. But although Nora had heard about the fairies from her grandmother, who sat all day tending the peat fire, and something more about them from her mother when of an evening after supper she had time to speak to Nora of herself when she was a girl, yet Nora had never in all her life set eyes upon one of these feasters of the forest. For the fairies, mind you, come only to two kinds of folk, to those who believe in them and to those who need them. Now Nora believed in the fairies all right, all right, but she had never been in need of them until now, at this time that I'm telling ye of.

Now this same Nora was one of these lasses that is a wee bit gloomery. And ye don't know what this same gloomery is? Well, she was at times hindered by a rainy mornin' disposition. So it was plain enough to the fairies that she was in some need of them.

One day Nora went into the deep of the wildwood a few steps below her mother's cottage to a trysting-place where she often resorted when she had the time from her daily duties.

* First published in *John Martin's Book.* Reprinted by special permission.

She had been unusually heckled that morning, as all of us are at times, by being obliged to do many things for the which she had little liking. The spot was a favorite one of Nora's.

There was a shelter of rocks above, almost like a cave or roof, and below there was a tiny stream of water that ran out of a spring in the back of the hill and sang its way down the slope to the brae below. In this pool Nora nearly always laid some field flowers, because they kept fresher there than anywhere else. From the low seat that Nora had made out of a stone in the back of her shelter she looked out into a sunny place in the woods, around which stood, as if they were pillars of a woodland palace, six gray beeches.

Now upon this sunny afternoon that I am speaking of, hardly had Nora reclined upon her bench, feeling a bit drowsy no doubt with the heat, yet not quite sleepy you know, listening to a robin singing with the voice of Eden, when she heard a light tapping on the wall of the largest beech, the one that was nearest to the place where she was lying. At first when she heard this sound she thought that it was the robin redbreast that she had noticed hopping up and down in the open place in the sunlight, and yet she knew well that robins do not drum upon the bark of trees like woodpeckers. So she jumped lightly up and ran to the tree, and at once she was aware that the tapping was from inside the tree. And between the taps that were no louder than those of a branch against a window-pane she distinctly heard a very tiny voice.

"How tiny was the voice, Michael aroon?"

You are asking me how tiny was the voice? Let me see if I can tell you. You have heard the sound of the rivulet when it falls upon the mossy stones in the pasture by the barway? Well, it was about as loud as the echo of that if you should walk thirty paces away and then listen. So Nora had to put her ear up close against the breast of the beech-tree and even then the voice sounded no louder than the sound of a beech-leaf when it falls from a branch into the moss-bed. But she could hear what that voice was saying, and it was these words: "Nora, my darling, turn the key and let me out." Nora looked around in amazement, but sure enough, there on the breast of the beech, about the height of her heart, was a small key of the color of the bark, that she had never noticed before, though she had hugged that beech-tree every morning of her life. So Nora turned the key at once, and out stepped——"

"A fairy, Michael?"

Yes, better than a fairy, a dryad, that is a fairy of the tree. For a fairy of a tree is as much higher in rank than a fairy of the meadow as a duchess is than a goose-girl. She was about the size of the robin redbreast, and she was dressed all in green, except a lovely cloak of red that, when it was folded about her, made her look very much indeed like the redbreast himself, and she was no bit bigger than the robin either.

"Nora Mavourneen," said the dryad, " I have been noticing that you seem a bit sad-hearted of late, and for no reason either that anybody knows, so if you don't mind I will take you with me for a walk this afternoon through fairyland, and we will see if we cannot do something to restore your good spirits again."

At these words Nora danced for joy, and you would never have been able to guess that she had ever known a downhearted moment. So the dryad clapped her tiny hands three times, and out of the open door into the beech-tree stepped a little gnome who came and bowed low before them, holding in his hands a silver salver on which lay a little pellet.

"How little was the pellet, uncle?"

"Well, what would you say if I told you that it was as small as a humming bird's egg? Oh, you think it was smaller than that? Well, how about the seed of a coriander? No? Then I will tell you the truth. It was as small as the gnat that gets into your eye, that feels as big as a rat."

So Nora took the pellet from the platter and thanked the gnome kindly and she ate it down, and no sooner had she swallowed it than she was no bigger than the dryad herself.

So the dryad took her by the hand and they walked gaily into the beech-tree door, and the door shut behind them.

They went down and down a lot of winding stairs that were lighted only by small windows in the bark of the tree that Nora had never noticed before and could never find afterward. It was very cool and pleasant, for they could hear the sap go singing on its way from the roots up to the branches and leaves and when a summer shower went by they could hear the rain-drops as they went singing down the trunk outside to the roots. After they had reached the foot of the stairs they walked for a long way through a cool corridor. It was not quite dark, for Little People stood at every turn who seemed to be doing what fireflies do on summer nights in the grass, and each one whistling to himself as he held his softly shaded lantern aloft. Down the side passages Nora could see thousands of tiny miners at work. And what do you think they are doing?

"Digging for gold and diamonds."

They were tending the woodland plants that hang their golden blossoms in the pathways and carrying up the dewdrops that sparkle like diamonds from their leaves in the daybreak. And it was pleasant to see them work, for they were all singing.

By and by Nora and the dryad came to a place where there was a brighter light ahead, and as they drew nearer Nora could see that they had come to the bank of the pond that is below Nora's cottage, only that they were under the surface, looking up through a light so soft that it cast no shadows. And now the dryad took Nora's hand and she found herself in a little boat, no bigger than a leaf, sailing across the pond but still beneath its surface. And here she saw on every hand, working amid the mire and the mirk, such jolly little divers, who were feeding the fish and tending the pond lily roots, and, like all the others, singing at their tasks.

Now you will know of course that they were on their way to the home of the fairy queen. And it was but a short while before they were there. I need not tell you, children, how lovely is her palace, with its golden floor and silver walls and its hangings of the colors of the rainbow. Nor need I say how beautiful is her majesty herself, with wings like the most splendid butterfly and a gown like the morning and a face like the sunshine.

It seems that Nora had come upon the queen's birthday, and she was just giving the birthday honors. So Nora and the dryad stood in the background and watched the scene. Around the throne stood gallant fairy gentlemen clad like beetles and dragon flies for splendor and ladies whose long gowns hung like the light on the waterfall of Loughmareen. But to the amazement of Nora, those who came forward to receive the honors were for the most part dressed like workmen and many of them were bent with hard labor. As each advanced and made obeisance, the royal herald read the exploit for which the rank of knighthood was about to be conferred. For one he read: "To our faithful servant who covered the lilies of Moira from the attack of the Frost King"; and to another: "To the gallant yeoman who watered the grain field of Kilvellin"; and to still another: "To him who dug the trench by the roadside and kept safe the highway to Throselwait Fair." And as each came forward the trumpets pealed in triumph, and after a gold star had been pinned upon the new knight's breast the gentlemen and ladies of the court greeted them with hearty reverence. And Nora looked in the smiling face of the dryad, but said nothing.

Then Nora herself, in a breathless moment of fear, was presented to the queen, and the queen kissed her daintily just above her lips on both sides. And suddenly Nora found herself back on her stony bench by the spring with the branches of the beech-tree waving silently before her.

"Oh, mothereen and grandmotherkin," she cried as soon as she got home, and she ran home all the way—"let me tell you about the wonderful visit I have been making out in the wildwood." And after she had told her story, mothereen said, "I think Nora has been dreaming," but grandmotherkin said, "No, daughter, I think our little acushla has had her eyes opened the day." Then Nora in triumph showed the two dimples where the fairy queen had kissed her. And do you know, my darlings, I cannot but think that she told the truth after all, for ever after, if one kissed Nora upon those two dimples or even touched them or even looked at them, she would break into the sweetest smile, and she never was gloomerin' or lowerin' any more.

LIST OF BEST BOOKS OF FAIRY TALES AND CHILDREN'S POEMS

ANDERSEN, HANS CHRISTIAN . . . *Fairy Tales*
ANDERSEN, HANS CHRISTIAN . . . *Wonder Stories*
ASBJÖRNSEN, P. C. . *Fairy Tales from the Far North*
BALLARD, SUSAN . . *Fairy Tales from Far Japan*
BARING–GOULD, S. . . . . . *The Crock of Gold*
BRENTANO, CLEMENS . . . . . *New Fairy Tales*
BREWER, DAVID H. . . . *Adventures in Fairyland*
BROWNE, F. . . . . *The Wonderful Chair*
BUNCE, JOHN THACKERY
Fairy Tales: Their Origin and Meaning
CARMEN SYLVA . . . . *A Real Queen's Fairy Tales*
CARROLL, LEWIS . . . . . *Alice in Wonderland*
CARROLL, LEWIS . . . . *Through the Looking Glass*
CHISHOLM, LOUEY . . . . . *The Golden Staircase*
COATES, H. T. . . . *Children's Book of Poetry*
CROKER, T. CROFTON *Fairy Legends and Traditions of Ireland*
CURTIN, JEREMIAH *Tales of the Fairies and of the Ghost World*
EWING, J. H. . . . . *The Brownies*
FRERE, M. . *Old Deccan Days, or Hindoo Fairy Legends*
GRIMM, THE BROTHERS . . . . . *Fairy Tales*
HARRISON, MRS. BURTON . *The Old Fashioned Fairy Book*
HERFORD, OLIVER . . *Child's Primer of Natural History*
HAUFF, WILLIAM . . . . *Fairy Tales*
HIGGINSON, THOMAS W.
Tales of the Enchanted Islands of the Atlantic
HORWITZ, CARRIE NORRIS . . . . . *Fairy Lore*
INGELOW, JEAN . . . . *Fairy Stories*
JACOBS, JOSEPH . . . . *Celtic Fairy Tales (2 vols.)*

Jacobs, Joseph . . . *English Fairy Tales* (2 *vols.*)
Jacobs, Joseph . . . . . *Indian Fairy Tales*
Jerrold, W. . . . . *The Reign of King Oberon*
Keightley, T. . . . . . . *Fairy Mythology*
Kennedy, H. A. . . . *The New World Fairy Book*
Kupper, Grace H. . . . . *Stories of Long Ago*
Laboulaye, E. . . . . *Fairy Tales*
Lang, Andrew . . . . . . *Nursery Rhyme Book*
Lang, Andrew . . . . . . *The Arabian Nights*
Lang, Andrew . . . . . *The Green Fairy Book*
Lang, Andrew . . . . . *The Red Fairy Book*
Lang, Andrew . . . . . *The Yellow Fairy Book*
Lang, Andrew . . . . . . *The Princess Nobody*
Lear, Edward . . . . *Nonsense Books*
Lockwood, Ingersoll
Baron Trump's Marvelous Underground Journey
Mullney, Ione . . . *Fairy Tales from Afar*
Mulock, Dinah M. . . . *Adventures of a Brownie*
Mulock, Dinah M. . . . *The Little Lame Prince*
Munkittrick, J. . . . . . *The Moon Prince*
Mother Goose . . . . . . *Nursery Rhymes*
Naake, J. T. . . . . . . *Slavonic Fairy Tales*
Nichols, Ida Preston
Princess Girlikin and other Fairy Tales
Ozaki, Yei Theodora . . . *The Japanese Story Book*
Paulding, James Kirke *A Christmas Gift from Fairyland*
Pyle, Howard . . . . . *The Wonder Clock*
Rhys, Ernest . . . . *Fairy Gold*
Rolfe, W. F. . . . *Fairy Tales in Prose and Verse*
Stockton, F. R. . . . . . *The Floating Prince*
Stevenson, Robert Louis . . *Child's Garden of Verses*
Stoddard, R. H. . . . . *Adventures in Fairyland*
Wahlenberg, Anna . . . . . *Swedish Fairy Tales*
Waterhouse, A. J. . . . . *Children's Poems*
Wiggin, Kate Douglas, and Nora Archibald Smith
Tales of Laughter
Wiggin, Kate Douglas, and Nora Archibald Smith
Magic Casements